Expecting the Sheikh's Baby
by Kristi Gold

'First I must warn you, I've already removed all my clothing. And I've built a fire for our enjoyment.'

The image of Ash lying naked before the hearth jumped into Karen's brain. A slow, uneven breath escaped her lips. 'That sounds…' *Heavenly.* 'Interesting.'

'Oh, I am certain it will be. More interesting than either you or I could imagine. Have I been successful in encouraging you to leave early?'

He'd encouraged Karen to fantasise about making love with him. The conception should be her only concern, but she couldn't help considering the pleasure Ash was offering. So what if she actually let go enough to enjoy the process? After all, she was a woman and he was a man—a virile, seductive, enticing man. Her libido was restless and he was offering to appease it.

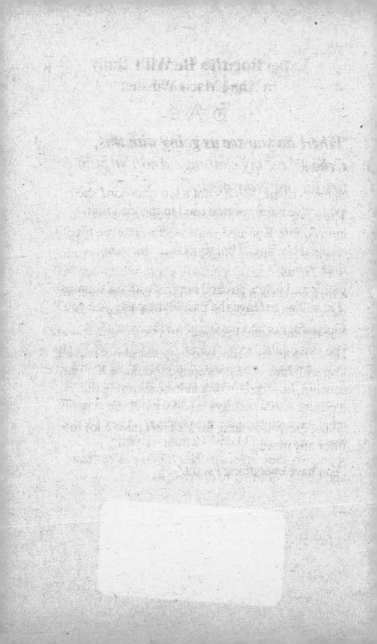

Born To Be Wild
by Anne Marie Winston

୬ ❀ ଓ

'Where do you see us going with this, Celia?'

She was silent. 'That's not a fair question,' she said. 'I've barely gotten used to the idea that you're back again.'

'It hasn't been any longer for me,' he pointed out, 'and I'm used to it.' He took her face between his palms and gently stroked her lips with his thumbs. 'I'm willing to leave the past in the past. Are you?'

She hesitated and his hands dropped away. 'Or are you still punishing me for all those years ago?' His voice was rough, frustrated, impatient. 'I'm not looking for an affair for a few weeks while I'm in town, so if that's all this is going to be, tell me now.'

'What are you looking for? I don't have a lot to offer any more.'

'You have everything I want.'

Available in September 2004 from Silhouette Desire

Expecting the Sheikh's Baby
by Kristi Gold
(Dynasties: The Barones)
and
Born To Be Wild
by Anne Marie Winston
(Dynasties: The Barones)

Taming the Outlaw
by Cindy Gerard
and
Tangled Sheets, Tangled Lies
by Julie Hogan

The Cowboy Claims His Lady
by Meagan McKinney
(Montana)
and
Sleeping With Beauty
by Laura Wright

Expecting the Sheikh's Baby
KRISTI GOLD

Born To Be Wild
ANNE MARIE WINSTON

SILHOUETTE®
Desire™

*First published in Great Britain 2004
Silhouette Books, Eton House, 18-24 Paradise Road,
Richmond, Surrey TW9 1SR*

The publisher acknowledges the copyright holders of the
individual works as follows:

Expecting the Sheikh's Baby © Harlequin Books S.A. 2003
Born To Be Wild © Harlequin Books S.A. 2003

*Special thanks and acknowledgement are given to
Kristi Gold and Anne Marie Winston for their contribution to the
Dynasties: The Barones series.*

ISBN 0 373 04995 1

51-0904

*Printed and bound in Spain
by Litografia Rosés S.A., Barcelona*

SILHOUETTE®

Desire™

are proud to introduce

DYNASTIES:
THE DANFORTHS

Meet the Danforths—a family of prominence...
tested by scandal, sustained by passion!

Coming Soon!
Twelve thrilling stories in six 2-in-1 volumes:

EXPECTING THE SHEIKH'S BABY
by
Kristi Gold

KRISTI GOLD

has always believed that love has remarkable healing powers and feels very fortunate to be able to weave stories of romance and commitment. As a bestselling author, she's learned that although accolades are wonderful, the most cherished rewards come from the most unexpected places, namely from personal stories shared by readers. Kristi resides on a farm in Central Texas, USA with her husband and three children, along with various animals. She loves to hear from readers and can be contacted at KGOLDAUTHOR@aol.com or PO Box 11292, Robinson, TX 76716, USA.

Acknowledgements

Special thanks to former Bostonite and honorary Texan Sandy Blair for her incredible information and wonderful insight.

Prologue

The man could be her father, but that was impossible.

Her father was dead.

Karen Rawlins touched her trembling fingertips to the photograph of Paul Barone included in the Boston newspaper along with a story covering the Barone family's latest reunion. The article also reported the tale of the unsolved mystery from years ago surrounding the abduction of Paul's twin brother, Luke, serving as confirmation of what Karen had recently learned from the yellowed pages of her grandmother's diary—her loving grandparents had lived a lie for over half a century.

Karen sat in the only home she had known, deep in the heart of Montana, while too many unanswered questions haunted her as keenly as her memories. Had her father known about the journal Karen had found among her grandmother's belongings? Had he learned of the deception before his untimely death? Had he known that he had been born to a wealthy Massachusetts family only to be kidnapped by the woman he had always considered his mother, and that his name was not Timothy Rawlins but Luke Barone?

Karen tossed the newspaper aside knowing she would never have all the answers she craved. Everyone who could fill in the blanks was gone. Her grandparents had died only months apart two years before in peaceful slumber, and her parents had been killed in a devastating car crash a year ago.

Dealing with the overwhelming loss and this new insight into her family tree might have been easier if Karen hadn't ended her engagement to Carl. But that had been a blessing. She preferred to live her life alone as long as she could live her life as she wanted. That had not been Carl's intent. Carl's intent had involved control. He'd wanted a wife who would hang her life on his whims, not a woman with dreams and opinions and career goals. She refused to mourn that ending.

Karen wrapped her hands around a mug of coffee, trying to absorb some warmth, though the July weather outside was warm and wonderful. Still she felt chilled to the marrow, even in the comfortable kitchen that smelled of cinnamon and radiated kindness, an ideal depiction of home and hearth. She also felt utterly alone.

Needless to say, it had not been a banner year for Karen Rawlins. It then occurred to her that she had no reason to stay in Silver Valley. The single-stoplight town had nothing to offer but bittersweet recollections and the realization that much of what she'd believed about her family, her legacy, was false—except for the fact that her parents and grandparents had loved her without reservation.

Perhaps Boston held more opportunities. Exciting opportunities. A place to regroup and grow. Karen decided then and there to seek out the Barones, to tell Paul what details she knew about his missing brother with the hope that the family would welcome her with open arms and open minds. She would find a good job and maybe one day establish her own interior design business. She would make a good life for herself. A new life. And in order to fill the empty space in her soul, Karen would attempt to have a child, someone to love her without conditions.

No, it had not been a banner year for Karen Rawlins, but it could be—would be—from this point forward. She would simply have to make it happen, and she would achieve all of her goals without the interference of a man.

One

Oh, heck, not him again.

From behind the marble counter of the Barone family's famed Baronessa Gelateria, Karen Rawlins knocked her elbow on the edge of the cash register and stifled a yelp that would surely drown out the rendition of "Santa Lucia" filtering from the overhead speakers. She also bit back a litany of mild curses directed at the lone man seated in the corner booth next to the windows. A man who stood out like a searchlight among the Barone family Italian ice-cream shop's simple, traditional decor.

Karen prided herself on having a designer's eye and this particular male was designed to perfection. His exotic good looks presented the perfect portrait of the consummate dark, mysterious stranger.

But Sheikh Ashraf Saalem was no stranger to Karen. She'd met him last month during the welcoming party given in her honor by the Barones. Yes, he had been somewhat charming, maybe even slightly charismatic—okay, more than slightly—but much too confident for Karen's comfort. As far as she was concerned, overt confidence denoted control. She didn't care for controlling men, even if they could give a woman the shakes with only a sultry look, and he'd given her plenty of those the last time she'd been in his company. She also hadn't been able to forget what else he had given her that night.

A kiss.

An earth-tilting, knock-me-over, make-me-tremble kiss. A kiss she hadn't been able to ignore.

But she had to ignore it, ignore him, especially now. Ignore his occasional glances, his eyes as dark as Baronessa's popular espresso. Not an easy task even though he had exchanged his traditional Arabian clothing for professional corporate attire—a beige silk suit and a turtleneck pullover as black as his silky thick hair. He looked like any businessman taking a break from the fast-paced corporate world of finance, yet he still exuded an authoritative aura. But he wasn't just any man, a fact that had become all too apparent from the moment Karen had met him—and kissed him.

After one more furtive glance, Karen went back to straightening the sundae bowls lined up beneath the counter. She had a job to do, a nice job working in the gelateria alongside her wonderful cousin, Maria. Almost a month ago, she'd been lovingly welcomed by her new family, had accepted the assistant manager position and in turn gained a whole slew of relatives as well as a nice apartment that had once belonged to her other cousin Gina. Now that her life was back on track, she certainly didn't have the time or desire to be distracted by a man, even if he happened to be a charismatic prince.

As if her will had left the building without her, Karen

stole another quick glance. How could she possibly over-look his presence since the shop was practically deserted? No surprise the place was empty considering the post-lunch hour and that the earlier September deluge had now ended. Those who had taken refuge from the elements had made their way back into the Boston streets to re-sume their midafternoon activities.

Everyone except the sheikh. He was the only patron aside from another couple sequestered in the opposing corner booth, holding hands and talking in whispers while their gelato turned to fruity soup. What a waste of good ice cream, Karen thought. What a display of ridic-ulous sentimentality.

Karen mentally scolded herself for her cynical attitude. Who could say this particular couple wouldn't find for-ever happiness? Just because she had decided she wouldn't drape her dreams on a life partner didn't mean others couldn't find that proverbial soul mate.

"I see you have a visitor."

Karen's gaze snapped from the love duo to Maria's subtle smile and mischievous wide brown eyes. "Why didn't you tell me he'd come in?" She honestly hadn't meant to sound so irritable, but watching the young cou-ple moon over each other had prompted Karen's less-than-jovial mood. So had Ashraf ibn-Saalem's surprise appearance.

"You were down in the basement when he arrived," Maria said. "And I didn't realize you would be so inter-ested."

"I'm not." Karen slapped a rag across a counter that didn't need cleaning, working it over with a vengeance. "As far as I'm concerned, he's just another customer having his coffee."

Maria moved to Karen's side and sent a not-so-discreet

glance in the sheikh's direction. "My guess is he didn't come in here to escape the rain or to have coffee or gelato." She leaned closer to Karen and said in a whisper, "Considering the look he keeps giving you, I do believe he could be here for a different kind of dessert, if you know what I mean."

Karen knew exactly what Maria had meant, and she wasn't about to be the sheikh's sweet, now or ever. Turning her back to the dining room, she leaned against the counter and shot a quick glance over her shoulder. "He's not giving me any kind of look. He's reading the newspaper."

"He's pretending to read the paper, but he's much more intrigued by you."

Karen pushed up the sleeves on her white blouse and checked her watch, more out of nervousness than real interest in the time, although she did have an impending appointment. A very important appointment. "Doesn't he have a job?"

"Oh, yes. He's very successful, or so Daniel tells me. Some sort of independent financial consultant. He travels all over the world."

Daniel, another cousin, was the son of Karen's father's twin brother, Paul, and the reason why the sheikh had attended the welcome party. "That sounds fairly suspect to me."

Maria propped her elbows on the counter and rested her cheeks on her palms. "Job or no job, he's wealthy. And royalty." She suddenly came to attention. "And he's heading this way."

Karen froze, as if adhered to the counter at her back by the icy apprehension traveling up and down her spine.

"May we help you, Sheikh Saalem?"

Staring straight ahead, Karen heard the creak of the

counter stool yet still couldn't force herself to turn around.

"It would help me greatly if you would call me Ash. In America, I prefer to dispose of the title, at least among friends. And I do consider the Barones to be my friends."

"Of course," Maria said. "Any friend of Daniel's is certainly a friend of ours. Right, Karen?"

Karen flinched at the sudden jab of Maria's elbow in her side. Realizing she had no room to run, she finally turned to face the sheikh. "Yes. Friends. Of course."

As far as grins went, Karen would qualify Ash Saalem's as awe-inspiring. Why did he have to be so annoyingly gorgeous?

"You're looking well today, Ms. Rawlins," he said in a voice as smooth and liquid as quicksilver.

He kept his eyes fixed on hers and Karen wanted to look away but decided to stand her ground. "Thank you."

"Are you enjoying your work here, Karen?"

Karen couldn't believe he had the audacity to call her by her first name. She couldn't believe her pulse had the nerve to quicken over hearing him say it. Of course, he'd been bold enough to kiss her that night, so why not dispense with all formality? "As a matter of fact, I love working here. Very much." She forced an overly sweet smile, yet her lips felt stiff with the effort. "Speaking of work, can I get you anything else?"

He leaned forward, bringing with him a trace of rich cologne and blatant self-assurance. "What do you have in mind?"

Oh, no you don't. Karen was in no mood for playing the innuendo game. "Maybe some gelato. It's very refreshing. Helps to cool one off." Ice cream was the only thing she planned to offer him today, or any day for that matter.

"What if I asked for some of your time? Perhaps dinner once you are through with your duties?"

"I really don't think—"

"Miss, I need some service over here."

Karen glanced at the end of the counter where a middle-aged businessman sporting a cheap suit and an edgy expression waited impatiently. She visually searched the area for Maria, who had conveniently disappeared.

"Excuse me," Karen said to the sheikh and headed to the customer. She took a pencil from the pocket of her apron along with the order pad. "What can I get for you, sir?"

The man's expression was pickle-sour. "A cup of coffee."

"Espresso, cappuccino or maybe—"

"Plain coffee, black, to go."

"Certainly. I've just started a fresh pot to brewing."

He released a gruff sigh. "I'm in a hurry."

So was Karen. In a hurry to get out of there before she did something inane like actually agree to Ash's offer of dinner. "It should only be a few more minutes."

"You have yet to answer my question, Karen."

Karen glanced at Ash then gave the grumpy guy her best smile. "Excuse me just a moment." She sidestepped until she was again in front of the sheikh, feeling as if she were caught in a verbal volley. "I don't have time for dinner. I have somewhere I have to be after work."

"Somewhere important?"

More than he realized. "You could say that."

"Then this is somewhere that I would not be welcome?"

Karen decided he would probably be more than welcome at the fertility clinic, at least to provide a donation. Who in their right mind would turn him down? Of course, she would. Not that she intended to reveal what she was about to do. "It's an appointment. A doctor's appointment."

Concern called out from his dark eyes. "Are you ill?"

"Just a routine exam." Not exactly a lie. "I'm fine."

His frown dissolved into a stop-and-drop grin. "I would attest to that without the benefit of an examination, although I would not mind further investigation."

"Is that coffee ready yet?" the sour man barked.

Karen welcomed the interruption on one level. On the other hand, she felt trapped between two persistent men intent on shredding her last nerve. She afforded the stranger a polite smile. "One more minute and the coffee should be done."

He slapped his palm on the counter. "I don't have another minute, so if you'll quit talking to your boyfriend and get me my coffee, then I can get out of here. Some of us have jobs to do."

Karen clenched her teeth and spoke through them. "I understand, sir, but the coffee's not quite done yet. Could I get you a glass of water while you're waiting?" Would you like to wear it? she wanted to say and would have except she'd been told the customer was always right. Even the fussy ones.

"I don't want any damned water. I want my coffee."

Ash had seemed unaffected by the jerk until that moment when a dangerous look came across his face. He took off his jacket, systematically laid it across the stool next to him and pushed up the sleeves of his shirt. Karen froze from fear that the sheikh was about to engage in fisticuffs with the irritable stranger. Instead, he walked around the counter, picked up a paper to-go cup, filled it with the last of the remaining lukewarm coffee from the previous pot, then turned and slid it in front of the man.

"This is in exchange for your absence," he said in a low, menacing voice. "I realize there is no sign on the door indicating this establishment does not serve jack-asses, but rest assured, that will be remedied after your departure."

The man scowled. "You arrogant son of a—"

"My arrogance should not concern you. If you fail to leave the premises in thirty seconds, however, you should concern yourself with what I might do to encourage your departure."

The man stormed out the door sans coffee, sending Karen and Ash an acid look through the window.

When Karen could finally speak, she turned and stood toe-to-toe with the prince. She would estimate him to be not more than six feet tall, but in the small space that separated them, he seemed as massive as the ancient oak in the backyard of her former Montana home. "Was that really necessary?"

"I refuse to tolerate insolence, particularly when a woman is the target of disrespect."

Oh, good grief. "I really didn't need to be rescued."

His expression remained solemn. "My apologies. I tend to forget chivalry has lost its appeal in America."

Karen felt somewhat remorseful since she realized he'd had honorable intentions. She also felt somewhat tense when he continued to survey her with his extreme dark eyes. The least she could do was thank him. "I appreciate your good intentions."

His features softened into a look that could only be described as patently provocative. "You could show your gratitude by having dinner with me tonight."

"I told you I don't have the time." She didn't have the guts.

Maria suddenly appeared and eyed them both standing behind the counter, face-to-face. "Karen, did you hire the sheikh while I was downstairs?"

Karen reached under the counter and snatched up her car keys. "He was helping out with a rowdy customer."

"How nice of you, Ash," Maria said. "Wasn't it nice of him, Karen?"

Karen's stubborn gaze came to rest on Ashraf Saalem once more. Certain aspects of him were very nice. Nice and sexy. But she wouldn't describe his eyes as nice. More like lethal in a most sensual sense.

She unhooked her gaze from the sheikh and addressed Maria. "Is Mimi here yet? I really need to go swoon." Stupid, stupid mouth. "I mean I need to go soon. To my appointment."

Maria grinned and flipped her hand toward the front door. "Go ahead. I can handle it until she gets here. We still have some slack time before the evening crush."

Karen felt the pull of an inadvisable crush on an overbearing, arrogant, exotic prince. Stupid, stupid libido.

Keys in hand, she headed toward the door before Ash had another chance to knock her resistance out from under her.

"I will be in touch, Karen."

Karen gripped the door handle, intending to exit, but halted at the sound of his enticing voice. She only hesitated for a moment before rushing to her car and speeding off before she was tempted to go back and accept his offer. Before she gave in to those magnetic eyes and that seriously sinful voice. Before she forgot that she had no desire to become involved with any man, especially a man who considered himself her protector.

Thank heavens she had managed a quick getaway.

* * *

Ashraf Saalem had no intention of letting Karen Rawlins get away. From the moment he'd laid eyes on her at the welcome soiree, from the instant he had spontaneously kissed her, he had wanted her. He still wanted her and he intended to have her, even if forced to practice the utmost in patience.

Ash was not known for his patience. He would never have gained his own fortune had it not been for persistence. He would have never left the security of his family's business and come to America had he been willing to endure his father's demands.

"Oh, darn."

Maria Barone's mild oath brought Ash's attention to her. "A problem?"

She held up a black leather handbag. "Karen was in such a rush that she left her purse."

Ash saw Karen's carelessness as an opportunity to utilize a bit more strategy to convince her to see him again, this time alone. "I will be most happy to return it to her."

"Now?"

"Yes. I would think she might need it since I assume it contains her driver's license and any means she would have to pay for services."

Maria looked hesitant, wary. "You have a point. But I'm not sure she'll be too thrilled if I tell you where she's going."

"She mentioned a doctor's appointment."

"She did?"

Maria need not know that the revelation had come after some coercion on his part. "Do you know the whereabouts of the doctor's office?"

A slight-of-frame, gray-haired woman breezed up to

Maria and offered, "She asked me directions to Industrial Drive at Blakenship yesterday, the two hundred block, so I'm guessing that's the location."

Maria gave the waitress a scolding look. "Mimi, Karen might not like you passing on that information."

The woman rolled her eyes. "She has to have her purse, doesn't she? Besides, I don't think he's going to pilfer her credit cards."

"I guess you're right," Maria said.

Ash held out his hand to Maria and she finally relinquished the bag to him. "You may trust that I will find Ms. Rawlins and deliver it safely."

"Good luck," Maria said.

Ash wasn't one to rely on luck, but he would use his powers of persuasion. He gave the two women a polite nod. "I'm certain I will be back soon."

The lady named Mimi favored him with a smile. "I'm sure you will since Karen works here. That missy is a looker, all right."

Without responding, Ash left the building, unable to hold back his own smile over his good fortune. He had something Karen Rawlins needed, and she had something he wanted. Quite simply he wanted her. At least this was a beginning.

On that thought, Ash strode to the silver Rolls-Royce Corniche parked at the curb, slipped into the seat and drove away, his impatience escalating as he wove through heavy downtown traffic. After what seemed an interminable amount of time, he turned off onto the side street Maria had mentioned and approached a redbrick building that appeared to be a clinic.

Ash pulled into the parking lot and when he noticed the sign that read Milam Fertility Center, he assumed he'd come to the wrong place. Then, near the entrance, he caught sight of a blue compact car that resembled the one he'd seen Karen drive away in at Baronessa's.

He took the first available space several rows away, grabbed her purse and left the car to take his place by the hood where he could still view her vehicle. Presuming she had already entered, he decided to wait until she came out even if it took several hours. He had many questions to ask Karen, the most important being why she had chosen a clinic that catered to those intending a pregnancy. Then the sedan's door opened and Karen stepped from the car.

Ash saw his chance and strode across the parking lot, finding her bent halfway in, halfway out of the car. He paused a moment to study the bow of her hips and the pleasing shape of her legs extending from the skirt she wore as she conducted a search for, most likely, the handbag.

"Are you looking for this?"

She barely avoided bumping her head as she spun around to face him. "What are you doing here?" Her voice held a note of shock, as did her expression.

He dangled the purse before her. "I have come to return this to you."

She snatched it from his hand. "Thank you. I didn't realize I'd left it."

Obviously. "Now it is your turn to answer a question." He sent a direct look at the nearby sign. "What are you doing here?"

She worked the bag's strap round and round her slender fingers. "I told you I have—"

"An appointment, I know. But what business would you have at this establishment? Are you applying for employment?"

She looked almost alarmed. "Of course not." After

closing the door with a thrust of her bottom, she leaned back against it, looking quite annoyed. "You shouldn't concern yourself with why I'm here."

Her guardedness frustrated Ash though he had no call to interrogate her. But he had to know why she was here. "I would greatly like to understand your purpose for being at this particular place."

"You don't need to understand. This is my business, not yours."

"It is my business if you are involved with someone with whom you plan to have a child, if that is your reason for being here."

"Why is that your business?"

"Because I would cease to insist that you see me socially. I would not want to intrude on another man's territory."

Her gold-green eyes turned to feminine fire. "For your information, Sheikh Saalem, I am no man's territory. In this day and time, a woman doesn't need a man to have a baby, at least not all of a man." By the discomfort in Karen's expression, Ash discerned that she regretted the revelation.

He streaked a hand over his jaw, not quite certain what to make of Karen's disclosure. "Then you plan to have a child on your own?"

She tipped up her chin in defiance. "Yes, I do. Artificial insemination."

That did not set well with Ash. He understood the need for the procedure in some instances, but not in this case. "Do you mean insemination with some stranger's sperm?"

A blush spread across her cheeks. "I don't care to discuss sperm with a sheikh."

"But you would consider having a child by a man you know nothing about?"

"Yes, and that's my prerogative. I'm thirty-one and I'm not getting any younger. It's the right time in my life to do this."

Ash pondered her words, her purpose. Yes, he definitely had something Karen needed. Services he no doubt would be willing to give her, with great pleasure. And she had something else he wanted as well. The ability to have a child, the means for him to settle into a permanent relationship with a woman whom he found both intelligent and alluring. He had waited many years to find that particular someone since his father had thwarted his first attempt.

"Perhaps I could assist you in the matter," he said.

Her eyes went wide. "You mean you're willing to make a donation for me to use?"

"I have no desire to share my affections with a plastic receptacle. I prefer making a child the way nature intended for a man and woman to procreate."

Karen shook her head. "No way. I'm not going to allow…well, allow…*that*."

Ash moved closer and brushed a lock of wavy brown hair from her shoulder. He suspected Karen enjoyed a challenge, much like him, and if he had to use that device, then so be it. "Are you afraid?"

The willful look she gave him verified his assumption. "Of course I'm not afraid. Why would I be?"

He braced a hand on the car and leaned forward. "Perhaps you fear what you might feel if you allowed me to make love to you. What we might experience together."

He heard a slight catch in her breath, the only sign she had been affected by his words. "It wouldn't be a good idea, that's all."

"It is an exceptional idea. For some time now I've considered having a family of my own. This would benefit us both."

Her sigh brimmed with impatience. "I only want a baby, not a relationship."

"A baby who would not know his father? I believe that if you search your soul, you would not want this for your child, considering what you have recently learned about your father's kidnapping."

Karen studied the toe of her functional black canvas shoes, avoiding his gaze. "I don't have a choice. I want a baby more than anything."

With a fingertip, Ash nudged her chin up until she looked at him. He saw only indecision in her eyes, not total refusal. Enough to propel him forward in his planning. "I am offering you a choice. I am willing to father your child."

She eyed him with suspicion. "And exactly what would you expect in return?"

He had given his heart to a woman once, and only once. He had no more left to give in that respect. But he could give Karen the baby she desired and a comfortable home, a secure future. "I want to have you as my wife."

She frowned. "That's nuts. We don't know each other."

"What better way to become acquainted?"

"I don't want to get married. I almost made that mistake not long ago." Again she looked chagrined, as if she had revealed too much.

Ash had no call to be envious of another man who'd had Karen's affections in the past, yet surprisingly he was. No matter. If given the chance, he would attempt to make her forget any former liaison, especially one that appeared to have caused her pain. He could personally relate to that concept.

In order to do that, he must convince her that marriage would be favorable for them both, even if it meant proposing terms that were anything but amenable. "Perhaps we should have an agreement. If you decide not to continue the marriage, you are under no obligation to uphold the arrangement. You would be free to leave after the birth of our child."

"You mean divorce?"

The word sounded harsh in Ash's ears. It went against everything he believed. "Yes."

She worked her bottom lip between her teeth several times before saying, "I take it you would want to stay involved with the baby after the agreement ends."

He would do everything in his power to make certain that there would be no need to discuss custody of their child. He would do everything humanly possible to prevent their marriage from ending. "Of course. Would you not want that?"

"I suppose that would be best."

Ash sensed impending victory. "Then we are agreed?"

"No." She straightened and slipped the purse's strap over one thin shoulder. "I need to keep my appointment. Weigh all my options until I've reached a decision."

Ash pushed away from the sedan and gestured toward the building's entrance, not quite ready to concede defeat. "Go inside with my blessing, Karen. And while you are there, think of me." He slipped his arms around her waist. "Think of us. Consider what I am offering you, a father your child will know. The means to create life through an act that will give us both pleasure."

He pulled her closer and kissed her—a kiss meant to

persuade, to tantalize, to keep him foremost in her mind. Her lips were firm against his, but with only slight coaxing, Karen finally opened to him and he took supreme advantage, slipping his tongue inside the soft, sweet heat of her mouth, but only once. A brief glimpse of how it could be between them.

With great effort, Ash stepped away from her, withdrew a business card from his pocket and pressed into her palm with an added stroke of his thumb over her wrist. "Here are the numbers where I can be reached when you make your decision. Decide wisely."

Karen remained as still as a pillar as Ash walked away. Hopefully good judgment would reign and she would see the logic in his offer and agree to his proposal. If not right away, then he would simply have to try harder to persuade her.

Two

The man knew no shame.

Karen couldn't believe that Ash Saalem had kissed her in a wide-open parking lot that afternoon. She couldn't believe that he'd offered to father her child. She couldn't believe that she was actually considering his proposition.

After pouring a glass of Chianti, Karen strolled into the living room and slumped onto the sofa in hopes of clearing her mind. She loved the fourth-floor brownstone apartment generously provided by the Barones. Gina had decorated the place beautifully with Italian silk sofas, an antique writing table, Turkish rugs. But the elegant furnishings and accoutrements wouldn't fair well with an active toddler.

She was getting way ahead of herself. First she had to conceive, *then* she could decide on the living arrangements. At present the conception should be her top priority. That and Ash's offer, not his masterful mouth. She needed to get the kiss off her mind so she could think clearly, not a measly mission by any means. Neither was deciding the best option for having a baby.

She sipped the wine and thought about the day's events. During her appointment at the clinic, she had been instructed on what the procedure entailed and the possible cost, emotionally and physically, if she wasn't successfully inseminated after several attempts. She had sorted through some sample profiles of prospective donors, most too good to be true. She had watched several couples in the waiting room looking anxious and hopeful—and in love.

Maybe Ash was right. Did she really want to bring a baby into the world not knowing its heritage, considering she'd grown up not knowing the truth about hers? Could she really trust that the sperm donors were being completely honest? After all, she had recently learned that much of what she'd believed about her family lineage had been skewed by dishonesty.

Feeling emotionally drained, Karen set her wineglass on a coaster on the end table and stretched out on the sofa on her back. She'd eaten a light supper of pasta and vegetables but hadn't tasted much of anything. Too much to think about, too little time. If she decided to go through with the insemination, she needed to make the arrangements in less than three days since that would be right before the most fertile time during her cycle. The same held true if she decided to accept the sheikh's arrangement.

Just thinking about making love with Ash brought about a round of chills mixed with a flash-fire heat. She couldn't deny that the idea held some appeal. She also couldn't deny that his kiss had left its mark on her libido. Both kisses.

The doorbell buzzed, sending Karen off the sofa in a rush. She experienced a prickly surge of panic thinking Ash might have decided to pay her a visit expecting an answer she wasn't quite ready to give. It would be just like him to show up, unannounced, and come upon her wearing a threadbare gray sweatshirt and equally ragged black leggings. She would send him on his way—as long as he kept his mouth to himself.

As she looked through the peephole and saw Maria at her threshold, Karen was relieved and maybe just a teeny bit disappointed that Ash hadn't come by to convince her with more kisses. Absolutely ridiculous.

Karen opened the door to her cousin and smiled. "Hey, you. What brings you to the top floor this time of night?"

"Just wanted to visit," Maria said, her shoulders slumped as if she carried the obligations of the universe.

Karen was immediately concerned, considering Maria had looked incredibly tired of late. The gelateria required long hours and hard work, especially for Maria, its manager. A lot of responsibility for a young woman, yet Maria, even at the tender age of twenty-three, handled it remarkably well. Or so Karen had believed until tonight.

"Come on in," Karen said and gestured toward the sofa. "Take a load off. I was having a glass of wine. Join me."

Maria dropped onto the sofa and tipped her head back. "No wine for me."

"Maybe something else, then? I could fix us some tea."

"No thanks."

"Are you okay? You look exhausted." And she sounded depressed.

She shrugged. "I took the stairs from my apartment

instead of the elevator. I'm a little winded, but otherwise I'm fine.''

Maria always climbed the two flights to visit Karen on the fourth floor and she'd never even broken a minor sweat. Something was seriously wrong, and Karen aimed to get to the bottom of Maria's distress.

Karen sat on the wing chair facing the sofa. ''Okay, so what's up?''

Maria managed a faint smile. ''You go first. I want to hear about your baby-making appointment.''

''Not that much to tell, really. I had an interview, discussed financial terms, then I got a sneak preview of perspective sperm donors.''

''That must have been interesting.''

Not as interesting as Ash's suggestion. Karen wasn't sure she needed to burden Maria with her dilemma, but she had no one else to turn to. Maria had become a good friend to Karen, a confidante, and she always seemed so wise.

''I have another offer on the table,'' Karen began. ''In terms of a father for my child.''

Maria instantly perked up. ''Really? That wouldn't happen to have come from a handsome Arabian prince, would it?''

She eyed Maria suspiciously. ''Did he tell you?''

''I promise he didn't tell me anything. I only knew that he was bent on returning your purse to you.''

''So that's how he knew where to find me.''

''I'm sorry, Karen.'' Maria looked more than a tad contrite. ''Actually, Mimi gave him the directions and I gave him the purse. He's very persuasive.''

''No kidding,'' Karen muttered.

''He's also absolutely head over heels for you.''

''Good heavens, Maria. I barely know the man.'' But

if the sheikh had his way, that would be remedied shortly on a very intimate level.

"Exactly what did his offer entail?" Maria asked.

"He's willing to father my child. The natural way."

Laying a hand on her chest, Maria said, "Oh, my. That could be great fun."

Exactly Karen's current thought, and her quandary. "Fun, yes. Wise, I doubt it."

"And he was serious?"

"Very serious. But he won't do it unless we're married. He did say that we could make it a conditional marriage and if I decide to end it, I can after the baby's born."

"Are you going to do it?"

Was she? The terms of the arrangement didn't seem as absurd once she'd voiced them to Maria. "I don't know. Part of me thinks that I would be a total fool to do it. Another part of me…well, that part—"

"Thinks you'd be a fool not to know the father considering the blank spaces in your own family. Not to mention, the sheikh probably has incredible genes and making a baby with him would be an out-of-this-world experience."

Karen couldn't hold back her smile. "Yes, that's basically what that part of me is saying. The feminine part." She turned serious again. "But he's got that whole macho thing going. That was very apparent when he took it upon himself to come to my rescue today at the shop. I could have handled that guy myself."

"He was only concerned for your welfare."

"I understand that, to a point. But he's too in control and I couldn't tolerate living with someone who tries to keep a tight rein on me all the time."

Maria shifted on the couch, looking unquestionably

uncomfortable. "That could be a problem only if you're not clear on what you expect from him. Who knows? It might even lead to a permanent relationship."

"Not likely. We're from two entirely different worlds."

Maria murmured, "Stranger things have happened." She pushed her dark, shoulder-length hair back with one hand. "Regardless, every child should know both its mother and father if at all possible. Family is everything."

Karen understood that all too well having recently lost the only family she'd ever known. And she also surmised that something was terribly wrong with Maria considering the hint of sadness in her voice. Feeling totally selfish, she said, "Your turn now, cousin dear. Tell me what's bothering you."

A steady stream of tears rolled down Maria's face, catching Karen off guard, inciting her concern. "Maria, what's wrong?"

"It's a long, painful story, Karen."

Karen moved from the chair and seated herself beside Maria on the sofa. "I have all night. Please tell me what's going on. I'm really worried about you."

Maria lifted her plain white blouse and rested a hand on her abdomen. "This is what's going on."

Karen noticed a prominent belly bulge beneath the waistband of Maria's black slacks. Realization suddenly dawned and it had nothing to do with her cousin putting on a few extra pounds from sneaking too much gelato. "Are you—"

"Pregnant? Yes. And no one knows. No one can know. At least no one except you."

More confused than ever, Karen let a few moments of

silence pass between them while she allowed the shock to subside. "Who is he?"

Maria sighed. "Someone I've been secretly seeing since January."

"Secretly? Is he married, Maria?"

"Worse. He's a Conti."

Shock came calling again as Karen tried to assimilate the information. Her cousin had just told her that she was pregnant by a man who belonged to a family that had been sworn enemies of the Barones for decades. Both families—the Contis and the Barones—seemed determined to hang on to old recriminations. No wonder Maria didn't want anyone to know.

"His name is Steven," Maria continued. "He's beautiful and caring and I'm totally in love with him."

"He sounds wonderful, Maria. Other than the family thing, what's the problem?"

"The family thing is the problem. With so much going on of late—the gelato sabotage that happened right before you came, the warehouse fire—everything's in an uproar because some of the family think the Contis are behind it. They would never accept our relationship. It would only tear us and the families farther apart if they found out about us."

"Maybe your relationship and this baby will help settle the rift."

"I can't imagine that happening, at least not now. In fact, I'm not even up to dealing with it. I want to get away for a while, somewhere out of town. Think things through. And that's what I intend to do, right away, since I'm already starting to show."

"How far along are you?" Karen asked.

"Four months."

Another surprise to Karen. But come to think of it,

Maria had started wearing her blouse over her slacks, something Karen hadn't given much thought until now. "If I can do something, just name it."

"I'll need you to handle the shop in my absence."

"Of course." Karen would do anything for Maria considering what Maria had done for her—made her feel welcome and wanted, as if she were a sister, not a long-lost cousin. "Does Steven know about your plans to leave?"

"He doesn't even know about the baby."

Stunned, Karen asked, "Why not?"

"It wouldn't be fair to lay this on him now. Not until I decide what I'm going to do."

"You're not considering giving up the baby, are you?"

Maria looked mortified. "No! I love this baby and even if it doesn't work out between Steven and me, I'll at least have a part of him with me always."

"Do you really have so little hope that you and Steven can make this work?"

"I want to hope, Karen. Really, I do, but I'm afraid the relationship is doomed. We have too many obstacles to overcome."

Karen's heart went out to Maria. Hopefully a little time away would clear her mind. "Where do you plan to go?"

"That's why I'm here. Do you still own your old house in Montana?"

"I've recently sold it to a friend of the family."

"Then I guess that's out."

Karen thought a moment and considered another option. The perfect place for a sabbatical. "I have two dear friends in Silver Valley, the Calderones. They have a wonderful ranch and I'm sure they would love to have you as a guest for as long as you'd like."

Maria's expression brightened. "Do you really think so?"

"I'm almost positive but I'll give them a call in the morning and run it past them."

Maria grasped Karen's hand. "You're a lifesaver, Karen. I'm so happy to have you in the family."

"I'm happy to be in the family." And Karen was. Only a few months before she had felt totally alone. Now she had her understanding cousin to lean on as well as other new friends. She also had…Ash? The sneaky sheikh once again had wriggled his way into her psyche.

Coming to her feet, Maria stretched with her hands on the small of her back. "Lately every muscle in my body protests if I stand or sit too long."

Karen rose. "You need to try and get some rest."

"I haven't been able to sleep well."

Karen doubted she would sleep all that well tonight either with so much weighing on her mind. "Take a hot bath and relax. Works for me. I'll let you know what the Calderones say, but you can probably consider it a done deal."

Maria gave Karen a quick, heartfelt hug. "Thanks for making the arrangements. I owe you one."

"Just come back soon. I'm going to miss you."

"I'll miss you, too. But you have to promise me that no matter what, you can't tell Steven anything. Or the family. I don't want anyone to know why I've left."

"Won't everyone be worried about you?"

"I'll leave the family a note explaining I need some time away. Steven, too. And now that that's settled, what are you going to do about Ash's offer?"

"I have no idea. I have a lot to consider."

Maria walked to the door then faced Karen. "No matter what you decide, you know I'll support you. But I do hope you give the proposal some serious consideration. It would be so wonderful for your baby to have a relationship with its father.''

Karen's heart ached for Maria who hadn't been able to openly share her joy with the father of her child or her family. Recalling the missing links to her own family chain, Karen could no longer deny the importance of having both parents actively involved. She also couldn't deny that Sheikh Ashraf Saalem would probably be a prime candidate for producing top-notch offspring. And she definitely couldn't deny that he would be the prime candidate for providing the utmost in pleasure, either. Annoyingly, that thought excited her.

Too much to think about, too little time.

''I've always known you to be a man of few words, Ash, but today you're quieter than usual.''

Ash looked up from his half-eaten room service fare to find Daniel Barone scrutinizing him with unconcealed curiosity. ''I have much on my mind at present.'' So much that food had lost all appeal.

''This mood of yours doesn't have anything to do with my investments, does it?''

His current state had nothing to do with monetary measures and everything to do with one particular woman. ''I asked you here today solely for the sake of camaraderie, not business.''

''Good. I was beginning to assume you were about to tell me I'm destined for poverty, the reason why we're eating in privacy instead of a restaurant.''

Ash had asked Daniel to join him for lunch in his penthouse suite to make certain he was accessible should Karen call. To this point, it had yet to happen. The later the hour, the more concerned Ash had become that perhaps Karen had decided to utilize the fertility clinic. For all he knew, she could be there now, becoming impregnated by some stranger.

"As always, your investments are thriving," Ash assured his friend. "You will continue to be a very wealthy man."

Pushing back from the dining table, Daniel tossed his napkin aside, looking pleased. "That's great to know even though I have everything a man could need with my new wife."

Ash felt a little twinge of envy over his friend's good fortune in finding a suitable mate. "Then I can presume your honeymoon went well?"

Daniel presented a roguish grin. "Oh, yeah. Very well. But it's far from over. Just ask Phoebe. For such a quiet lady, she's certainly full of surprises."

Ash predicted that the not-so-quiet Karen could be full of pleasant surprises as well. If only he would be afforded the opportunity to find out. "I'm happy that you are pleased with your choice."

"And to think I tried to fix you and Phoebe up at Karen's party," Daniel said. "Good thing you didn't hit it off."

A very good thing, Ash decided, not that Phoebe wasn't an attractive woman. But that night Karen had garnered his complete attention. Admittedly, he had wanted her in a very elemental way. He still wanted her. Yet with each passing moment he saw his opportunity to have her dwindling.

"I am still surprised that you've married, considering your former habits," Ash said.

Daniel frowned. "If you're referring to previous women, you're a fine one to talk. You've had more than your share."

"True, but I have met someone who could possibly put that to an end."

"Someone special?"

"Your cousin Karen."

Daniel slapped his palm on the table, effectively rattling the silverware. "You know, Phoebe swore this was going to happen but I never thought it would go beyond the night you met. Karen didn't seem too happy when you kissed her in the reception line."

"It was a simple show of welcome."

"It was a simple come-on, if you ask me. So how long have you and Karen been an item?"

"I'm not certain I understand your meaning."

"How long have you been seeing each other?"

Ash was unsure how to respond. "We've been negotiating."

"Negotiating? That's a weird term for dating."

"Actually, we have gone beyond the dating phase."

Daniel released a wry chuckle. "I have to hand it to you, Ash. You work fast."

"I've asked her to be my wife."

"Make that from zero to sixty in a matter of seconds. When did this all come about?"

"I've intended to marry for some time now. Karen is the perfect prospect."

"Yeah, Karen's a nice woman. Not too shabby in the looks department, either."

"I beg your pardon?"

"She's very attractive."

"I would have to agree with you in that respect."

"So when's the wedding?"

As far as Ash was concerned, today would not be soon enough. "Unfortunately she has yet to give me her answer. I'm not certain that she sees the mutual benefits that marriage will bring.''

Daniel scowled. ''Well, hell, Ash, if that's the way you proposed, it's not surprising she hasn't bothered to answer you.''

''It's a bit more complex than a simple proposal. Karen and I have both expressed our desire to have a child. We've discussed having one together. I have insisted that we marry for the sake of that child.''

''Then this doesn't have anything to do with love?''

Ash didn't expect Daniel to fully understand. Why would he when he was so obviously in love with his wife? ''I am very fond of Karen, and I have every intention of making a comfortable life for her and our child in a secure, permanent relationship.''

''You make it sound like a retirement fund.'' Daniel shook his head. ''I'm not sure how well this is going to work, putting the cart before the horse.''

When Ash showed his confusion with a frown, Daniel added, ''Having the marriage and a baby before you have a commitment that involves two people who care about each other.''

''I'm a realist, Daniel. At times it is necessary to accept that the choices we make should be based on what is best for all concerned, not on emotions.''

''So you're saying that all you expect is a continuing fondness for Karen?''

''I expect nothing beyond what I know to be true, that we will marry in order to produce a child. I can't deny that I find Karen to be a very desirable, passionate woman. I plan to enjoy those aspects.''

Daniel's expression reflected concern. ''When the passion fades, I hope that something more exists. Otherwise, you might be in for a tough life together.''

Ash gave Daniel's words some consideration, and though he found wisdom in them, he couldn't allow himself to become entangled in emotions, especially if Karen decided that she wanted to dissolve the marriage after the birth of their child despite his efforts to dissuade her. Before he could concern himself with that, she must first agree to be his wife.

"And one more thing, Ash," Daniel said. "The Barones take family very seriously. Karen has only been a member for a short time but she's been completely accepted."

"I understand." And he did. Ash realized all too well the strength of family ties, or in his case, chains.

Daniel's expression went stern. "And just so you know, you might be a good friend, but if you do anything to hurt her, you will have to answer not only to the rest of the family but to me as well."

He had no intention of hurting Karen. He had no intention of allowing her to cause him pain, either. "You can rest assured that I will take very good care of her."

"Speaking of family," Daniel said, "what is yours going to think about you marrying an American?"

Ash saw no reason to tell them immediately. Perhaps later, after the birth of their child. Or perhaps he would call his father following the marriage ceremony if only to inform him that he had not been able to interfere this time.

Ash had waited thirty-six years for the moment when he could prove that the king of Zhamyr no longer had control over his son's life. "I no longer concern myself with my family's approval. And I have no obligations as heir since that duty falls on my eldest brother."

The phone rang and Daniel immediately rose in response. "I'll get it. I told Phoebe to call when she's ready for me to come home."

Ash couldn't hold back a cynical smile brought about by more envy. "I see she has you shackled."

Daniel turned with his hand on the phone. "We haven't tried shackles yet, but you never know." He answered with a brief hello, said, "Send her up," then dropped the receiver onto its cradle.

"I take it your wife has decided to personally escort you home," Ash said.

"It's not my wife who's on her way up here."

"Then who?"

"The woman you intend to make your wife."

Three

———

With every solitary ping of the elevator climbing to the top floor of the New Regents Hotel, Karen's heart beat double-time in her chest.

She was the lone occupant in the car with the exception of a starched and polished attendant who stood in the corner wearing a blue-tailored suit and a poker-faced expression. More than likely, he thought her to be one of the catering staff since she was dressed for work in a black skirt and tailored white blouse. Of course, she was about to meet with a prince who could very well expect her to cater to his every whim. But not if she could help it. She only had one goal in mind—a father for her child. And to conduct her own little interview to make sure that the sheikh fit the father bill.

Karen felt totally out of her element when the doors opened with quiet efficiency to a hallway covered in rich red carpet. She doubted it had been rolled out for her, simple Karen Rawlins from Nowhere, Montana.

The attendant stepped out and kept his hand on the door to prevent its closure. With his free hand, he indicated the entrance at the end of the corridor. "Sheikh Saalem's penthouse, madam."

She hoped he'd meant madam in a polite sense and didn't mistakenly believe she was there to service the sheikh. Surely not. Now if he knew she was wearing skimpy zebra-striped underwear—her one secret indulgence—she could understand where he might make that assumption. But unless he had X-ray vision, he had no way of knowing that.

The man cleared his throat and made a flicking motion on his chin. Did he expect a tip? Karen considered supplying a verbal one—lose the toupee.

Just when Karen reached into her bag for a few bucks, he said, "Mustard, miss."

Only then did Karen realize she was sporting the remnants of a sandwich she had consumed in record time during her drive to the hotel. Embarrassed, she used the oval mirror across the hall to remove the yellow chin smudge with a napkin she'd stuffed in her purse. While she was at it, she secured the clip holding her hair in a loose upsweep then checked her lipstick. Luckily it was still there, and so was the attendant. From the mirror's reflection, she noticed that he was ogling her. Ogling her legs, to be more accurate.

She rolled her eyes to the ornate ceiling, turned and forced a smile. "Thank you. That will be all."

He gave her a brusque nod, backed into the elevator and closed the doors. How nice that he'd immediately left with little effort on her part, Karen thought. Dismissed with nothing more than a simple command.

Standing before the double doors to the sheikh's suite, clutching her basic black bag to her chest, Karen acknowledged she could get used to saying ''That will be all'' like some demanding debutante, especially if it encouraged others to do her bidding.

She seriously doubted it would work on Ash Saalem. She also doubted she would be able to get any words out once she faced his high-voltage sensuality, live and in person. But last night, after weighing Maria's advice, she'd decided to go through with the arrangement—if Ash satisfactorily answered her questions.

Yes, I will marry you and have your baby. That will be all.

Slipping the strap of her purse over her shoulder, Karen pressed the buzzer and sucked in a deep breath, expecting to be met by Ash. She certainly didn't expect to be greeted by her cousin Daniel.

''What are you doing here?'' she asked in a remarkably calm tone despite her surprise.

Daniel stepped into the hall and gave her a wily grin. ''Visiting with a friend. What are you doing here? Business or pleasure?''

Karen had no idea what Daniel had learned from Ash and frankly, she wasn't sure she wanted to know. From the moment she'd met him, Daniel had stepped into the role of the big brother Karen had never had. A big brother who delighted in teasing her. She refused to provide fodder for the ridicule mill. ''I'm here on business.'' Not exactly a fib.

Daniel rubbed his jaw and his grin deepened. ''Is Ash going to check out your portfolio?''

''Something like that.'' As much as she cherished Daniel, she wanted him to leave. She was anxious enough without his prodding. ''Tell Phoebe I said hi, will you?''

"Sure." Daniel leaned forward, lowered his voice and said, "Don't forget the Do Not Disturb sign."

That will be all. "It's business, Daniel."

"If you say so." Daniel departed, taking his skeptical grin with him, leaving Karen alone with the sheikh who now stood at the door looking calm and composed, and subtly sinful in his casual tan polo shirt and black slacks.

"Come in," he said with a sweeping gesture.

Karen passed by Ash while maintaining enough distance between them to prevent inadvertently touching him. The pleasant scent emanating from him teased her senses, a one-of-a-kind fragrance that smelled a lot like incense, exotic but not overbearing. It reminded her of the patchouli oil Sunrise Bowers, Silver Valley's lone hippie and video store manager, had bathed in. It had that certain kind of distinctiveness, and Karen imagined it bore some equally unique name. Arabian Nights, Desert Sunset, Sex in the Sand.

Good grief.

To avoid looking at Ash, Karen turned her attention to the suite's opulent living area. A row of French doors opening onto a verandah revealed the downtown Boston skyline and the still overcast skies.

To her right, she noted a cherry wood dining table littered with lunch remains, to her left a sitting area with tan leather-covered sofas and chairs surrounding a small redbrick fireplace. And straight ahead, an open door revealed a king-size bed covered in a gold brocade spread. Quite different from the particle-board furniture, thin bath towels and faulty A/C she'd encountered in the motels where she had stayed on previous trips. Very nice decor indeed. Especially the bedroom and she definitely needed to stop looking at that.

The front door closed behind Karen, startling her. She

spun around and blurted, "Nice place. Do you come here often?"

What was she thinking? She sounded like some barfly executing a bad pick-up line, not a smart, sophisticated woman bent on a mission. But Ash had a knack for making her totally tongue-tied and thought-challenged.

Ash took a couple of steps toward her. "I reside here at the moment."

"Where do you normally live?"

"Wherever my business happens to take me. I have no permanent residence."

As if he were some sort of superpowered pulley, Karen moved toward him. She took her purse from her shoulder and hugged it again, as if it provided her some protection from his magnetism. "Really? That seems odd, not having a place to call home."

"I'm hoping to settle in Boston."

He shortened the space between them with another stride, bringing them almost as close as they'd been the previous day behind Baronessa's counter. Karen had no real desire to move back though she probably should.

"Why are you here, Karen?"

"I want to ask you a few questions."

Ash gestured toward the sofa. "Would you like to be seated first?"

Sitting seemed like an extremely good idea. "Sure."

Karen claimed the end of the couch, expecting Ash to take the club chair across from her. Instead, he dropped onto the opposite end of the sofa and crossed one leg over the other, his arm draped on the back of the couch. He looked so at ease it almost angered Karen. So did her reaction to his nearness, the sudden images of him taking her down for the count on the nice plush woven rug at their feet.

At least her hormones wouldn't fail her when it came time to make a baby with him. She swallowed hard.

"You may speak first," Ash said.

Darn tootin', she would. She pointed at him. "That's it. That's exactly what I want to talk to you about."

"I'm not clear on your meaning."

"I think you should know upfront that for the past thirty-one years I've been inclined to express myself openly without anyone's permission."

He had the absolute gall to grin. "I find that to be one of your more intriguing qualities. But then I find everything about your mouth quite intriguing."

Karen's face went brush-fire hot. Back to the point. "My point is that I'm quite capable of taking care of myself and my needs in all respects."

"I have found that certain needs are better taken care of by others."

"Such as?" Boy, had she fallen right into that one.

His grin disappeared, replaced by a sultry, seductive expression. "Intimate needs."

Karen had no problem picturing Ash taking care of those needs. "I guess you could be right in that respect."

"Could be?"

"When it comes to conception. And that brings me to some important health issues. Do you have any known illness, disease, a family history of any diseases, mental illness?"

"I am in perfect health."

Karen would have to agree with that, or so it appeared. Very healthy indeedy. But those were only superficial aspects. "When was your last physical?"

"Two months ago with a prominent physician in New York. But if you are still concerned, I would be glad to allow you to examine my medical records, or anything else you might choose to examine.''

''That won't be necessary.'' Loads of fun, but not necessary.

She searched her brain to try and remember exactly what the forms at the fertility clinic contained. Only one other question came to mind. ''Do you have any hobbies?'' Like that really mattered in the grand scheme of things.

''I like to ski, which is how I met your cousin Daniel. In the Pyrenees. I also enjoy the Alps.''

''And your education?''

''I studied in France.''

''Then you speak French?''

''Yes. I am quite proficient in several tongues.''

She knew all about his proficient tongue, more than she'd ever bargained for. ''Now, if we should happen to be successful in becoming pregnant—''

''We will be successful. My father has five sons and three daughters. Several of my brothers have that many offspring and so do my sisters. We, too, will have no trouble in that regard.''

Karen only wanted one baby, not a brood. ''I certainly hope you're right about your fertility. That it won't take more than one time for me to become pregnant.''

''I admire your optimism, Karen, but I would think it best if we make more than one attempt.''

She wasn't sure she'd survive more than one time, especially if he did justice to her overstimulated imagination. ''Only if it's necessary. And after we achieve conception, I would prefer a platonic relationship.'' She figured he could very well rescind his offer after that little bomb.

"Then you do not wish me touch you after you become pregnant?"

"I think that's best."

Ash's stern expression said he believed otherwise. "I will agree not to touch you."

That was easy. Too easy. "Good."

"Unless you ask it of me."

Karen didn't plan on asking him any such thing. "I would really want to do it soon." Oh, cripes. "The wedding ceremony, I mean."

"Why the hurry?"

Karen felt a bout of stammering coming on so she drew in a deep breath and sat on her hands. When she became tense, she tended to flail them around. "The, uh, fertilization…" That sounded like a request for lawn service. "The attempt at conception needs to happen in the next four days at the latest. I'm sure we can use the courthouse." *Foot, get thee out of my mouth!* "I mean use the courthouse for the wedding, not the conception."

Ash looked as though he greatly enjoyed her floundering. "I agree that it might be inappropriate to make love on the courthouse lawn, although I admit it might be interesting to find a secluded place behind a hedge."

Vivid images filtered into Karen's brain like a clear cable channel that showed after-hours movies with titles that included words like "confessions" and "diaries." Visions of making love with Ash on the lawn, against the wall, in an exquisite king-size bed. Making a baby, she corrected. Love wasn't going to enter into it. Ever.

"If I do consent, will you make the arrangements or should I?" she asked.

His grin reappeared. "You wish me to find a hedge?"

He was obviously determined to keep her off balance, and quite possibly off her feet and in his bed after they were married. She refused to let that happen. "I'm referring to the *wedding* arrangements."

"I will handle all arrangements."

"Then I take it you wouldn't have a problem with having the wedding in the next four days?"

"I would gladly rearrange my schedule to accommodate you."

Not exactly what Karen had envisioned when she'd considered getting married, a quick service in a judge's chambers. But those were old, worn-out dreams that didn't matter any longer. Reality did. Practicality did. "I would want everything in writing."

His expression turned from seductive to solemn. "Do you not trust me?"

She didn't trust herself around him. "I think it's wise."

"I will have the papers drawn up."

"And that would include the clause about parting after the baby's born?"

Ash again looked more than a little miffed. "Yes, I would include that clause in the terms."

"Good." Karen quickly came to her feet. "I think that covers everything."

Ash rose to stand before her. "Then you have decided?"

"I have, and my answer is okay." There it was, and not so very painful after all.

Ash slipped his hands in his pockets as if he needed a means to control them. Unfortunately, Karen had no pockets in her skirt, not that she was going to touch him. Not that she wanted to touch him. Okay, maybe she did just a little.

"Are you saying we are agreed?" he asked with a hint of disbelief in his voice.

"Yes."

Ash's expression looked victorious. "I am pleased you see the advantages to our union."

She could think of one really nice advantage—the conception. "There is one more thing. When you make the arrangements, will you see if you can set it up around lunchtime?"

"That will be satisfactory. We could spend the rest of the afternoon meeting our objectives."

Coming from anyone else, that would have sounded like a dull, business proposition to Karen. Coming from Ash, it sounded like an invitation to sin. "I'm on the schedule to work evenings at the gelateria."

"You would not consider taking the day off?"

She thought about Maria and her impending departure. After making the call that morning to the Calderones who were thrilled to open their home to Maria, everything but the date and time had been set. Karen saw the wedding as the perfect opportunity for Maria to escape. Maria could serve as Karen's attendant then sneak away. A perfect plan.

But if Maria left that particular day, then Karen would have to work that evening, unless someone would be willing to pull a double shift. She had time to plan that later. Right now she needed to get back to her job before people started wondering where she was. Wouldn't they be shocked to know?

"Karen, is something troubling you?"

Karen brought her focus back to Ash who was studying her thoughtfully. "I'm just thinking about work. I'll see what I can do about taking the day off."

"Very good. I see no need to postpone the honeymoon."

Honeymoon? Well, she supposed that was what it was

in a sense. "I better get back to Baronessa now. I'm already late." She was already imagining their lovemaking in great detail, not a good idea at all.

Karen had almost made it to the door and merciful escape until Ash called her back. "Yes?"

"Perhaps we should seal our bargain with a kiss."

At least he'd asked her permission this time. "Do you really think that's necessary?" There went the flying hands. She clasped them tightly before her.

"I believe it would be favorable to familiarize ourselves with each other before we are in bed together. If my kisses continue to make you nervous then it will be much worse when I make love to you."

Karen's traitorous eyes targeted the bedroom at his back. "Your kisses don't make me nervous." Her shaky voice betrayed her.

"Then you should have no objections now."

When he moved closer, Karen's mouth started flapping along with her hands. "Let's keep it simple, shall we? I mean, this is more or less a business arrangement and—"

Ash caught both her hands and held them against his sturdy chest. "You are still nervous, Karen."

"I am not!" What a fish tale.

He took her hands, turned them over and kissed each palm. "You need not be anxious around me. I promise I will treat you with great care."

"I'm not breakable." At the moment she felt like delicate crystal, poised to shatter the moment he laid his mouth on hers.

He leaned forward, a thin thread away from her lips that began to twitch and tremble. "Nevertheless, I promise I will be very gentle with my hands." He leaned closer. "And with my mouth."

His deep, tempting voice threatened to make Karen

sway. She stiffened her frame, determined not to faint. "As long as you get the job done," she said with as much challenge as she could muster.

"I most certainly plan to get the job done, and quite sufficiently," he said, his voice barely above a whisper.

A long stretch of silence passed as Ash stared into Karen's eyes. She prepared for the fallout from his kiss, but the kiss didn't come. And then something incomprehensible happened to Karen. She kissed him first. Thoroughly, without the slightest hesitation.

She met his open mouth with an eagerness she didn't invite, at least not consciously. Met his tongue with a few strokes of her own. Met the last of her resistance when he tugged her fully against him at the expense of her resolve.

That will be all….That will be all….That will be—

Suddenly her back was against the door and Ash was leaning into her and she was mentally scolding her legs not to wrap around his waist. His hands came to rest on her hips and hers were at the dip of his strong spine threatening to move lower to explore his regal rearend.

His mouth was gentle yet firm against hers while his tongue made silky forays between her parted lips. His fingertips traveled in feather strokes over her bottom, up her waist, then his thumbs grazed the sides of her breasts in a maddening, circular motion.

When Ash pressed against her, Karen was well aware the sheikh had a secret weapon below the fabric of his slacks. If she didn't stop this insanity immediately, she might get to experience its potency right here, right now, on the floor near the door without ceremony. Without the *wedding* ceremony.

That will definitely be all….

But it wasn't Karen who broke the kiss. Ash did. Yet

he kept his arms securely around her as he said, "I believe that was much more effective than a handshake." Then he stepped back and surveyed her from scalp to shoes.

Karen could only imagine what she looked like at that moment, probably glassy-eyed and red-lipped without the benefit of lipstick because she doubted she had any left on her lips. Several strands of her unruly hair rained down into her face, a few in her eyes. Regardless, she had no trouble seeing Ash standing there with his hands back in his pockets and the sultry smile back on his face.

Karen finger-combed her hair away, straightened her blouse and picked up her purse that had somehow landed on the floor. "I need to go now. Thank you. I look forward to hearing from you." Such cold, dry departing words considering that hot, wet kiss.

His smile could stop a speeding missile. "I certainly look forward to when we next meet, hopefully before we make our appearance at the altar."

Karen felt like a wooden marionette with hinges instead of joints. "We probably shouldn't see each other until the wedding."

"Are you concerned that we might not be able to stop with only a kiss?"

Exactly. "I'm going to be busy."

He nodded. "As you wish, Karen. I will keep myself busy as well until our wedding day, though I have no doubt I'll be thinking of you often. Of us. Together."

Karen needed to get out of there and fast. She reached behind her for the door handle. "Call me when you have the arrangements set."

"You may depend on it."

Karen jerked open the door and closed it behind her without giving the sheikh a second glance. But she knew deep down that in the next few days she would definitely be giving him, giving the wedding, giving his heady kisses more than a second thought.

"You may kiss your bride."

After all of Karen's anxious moments the past three days, the sleepless nights, the endless soul-searching and whirlwind planning, it had all come down to this moment. Even though they had signed a prenuptial arrangement outlining the terms of the marriage only a few hours ago, she still questioned the wisdom of agreeing to the proposal. But it was much too late to turn back now.

Karen looked from the nice lady judge to Sheikh Ashraf ibn-Saalem, her husband. *Oh, my.*

She half expected to find I've-got-you-now in Ash's expression. Instead, she saw a glimmer of hesitation in his dark eyes, her own questions reflected in his gaze as if maybe he, too, wondered if they had done the right thing.

Karen waited with nervous anticipation to seal the deal while her cousins Daniel and Maria looked on. Yet Ash only brushed her lips with an innocent kiss and gave her hand a reassuring squeeze, the same hand that now sported a gold band encrusted with multi-colored stones including several diamonds. Ash had told her it once belonged to his mother, the queen of Zhamyr. And now it was on Karen's finger, a woman who was very far removed from royalty.

Ash, on the other hand, didn't have a ring. Karen had considered buying him one until he'd allowed as how he didn't care for rings. No big deal, Karen decided. Real marriages required rings, not those with the sole goal of producing a child. If it had been more, she would have insisted Ash wear some kind of wedding band. After all, he was her husband and she would definitely want women to know that the sheikh was off the market *if* the marriage were real.

Daniel moved forward, slapped Ash on the back and said, "Welcome to the family."

Ash shook Daniel's hand. "I am most happy to be related to you if only by marriage."

Maria offered Karen the bouquet of roses that Ash had presented to Karen before the wedding. "You make a lovely bride, cousin."

Karen took the flowers and gave Maria a sympathetic look. "And you will, too, some day."

"I hope so." Maria glanced at Daniel and Ash, who were still conversing. "I need to go," she said in a hushed voice.

"Sure." Karen turned to Ash. "I'll be in the ladies' room for a few moments." At least she could be assured he wouldn't follow her and Maria in there. Or at least she thought he wouldn't. But just in case he had other ideas, she told him, "We can meet out front in a few moments."

Ash sent her a sly grin. "On the courthouse lawn?"

The rogue. The sexy, self-assured rogue. "On the steps. Standing on the steps."

Ash bowed. "As you wish, my lovely wife."

Wife. Karen wasn't sure she would ever get used to being his wife. But she was his wife, if only temporarily, and she might as well get used to it. Get used to that and the fact that tonight they would be together in every way.

As Karen followed Maria down the hallway, she shivered with anticipation when she considered making love with Ash. When she considered she might like it.

Thankfully the restroom was deserted, allowing Karen and Maria a few moments alone before Maria departed for Montana. "Do you have the train tickets?" Karen asked.

Maria patted her purse. "Right here. The train leaves at 3:00 p.m. and I should arrive in Silver Valley day after tomorrow by bus. I called Louis and he said he'd be glad to pick me up. He was so nice, and I can't thank you enough."

"Give Louis and Magdalene my love." Karen hugged Maria. "Take care, okay?"

Maria swiped at her face now moist with tears. "I will. I'll call you when I get there."

"You do that, and stop crying." Karen sniffed. "You're going to make me blubber all over my wedding dress." A simple white satin sheath that she'd purchased the day after she'd said yes to the sheikh—the day after she'd decided to change her life and her future by marrying a man she barely knew.

"You take care, too," Maria said. "And, Karen, keep your options open, as well as your heart. You never know what might come of this union."

"Hopefully, a baby." And nothing more. "You do the same, okay?"

"I'll try," Maria assured her.

And so would Karen. She would try to keep an open mind. But an open heart? That seemed somewhat dangerous. As dangerous as the pleasant thought of spending hours in Ash's arms. Her husband.

Oh, wow.

Four

"**I** can't believe you're actually working on your wedding day, missy."

From behind the counter, Karen regarded Mimi Fazano, a five-foot, sixty-something, dynamo waitress with short-cropped gray hair who had as much earthy charm as the old-time atmosphere of the gelateria. "It was a simple courthouse ceremony. Not that big of a deal, really. Just something to make everything official." To Karen, the whole concept of being married to Ash still didn't seem official. Maybe tonight. Maybe after she was in Ash's bed, in his arms, making love with him. Procreating, she reminded herself. Making a baby, not actually making love.

Mimi shoved the cash register drawer closed with one bony hip. "You should be enjoying your honeymoon. Why, my Johnny, God rest his soul, took me to Florida after our wedding. Of course, we had to stay with his mother. Such a mama's boy, my Johnny. But I loved him dearly for over forty years.''

Karen smiled through a sudden bout of melancholy. She had so wanted to hold out for love before she married. Instead, she had entered into a daddy deal with a prince. ''It happened so quickly that we didn't have time to plan a trip.''

Mimi narrowed her brown eyes. ''You don't happen to have a little peanut in the shell? A bun in the oven? Not that I would ever pass judgment. Johnny, may he sleep with the angels, never got me pregnant. But we certainly had a fine time trying all those years.''

''No, no baby on board.'' Not yet. Maybe tonight. Maybe when she and Ash took to his bed, her with a bad case of raging hormones and him with a serious case of seductiveness. She certainly didn't need to think about that during her shift or she'd be in danger of anointing customers with gelato.

Mimi eyed her with skepticism. ''Regardless of your reasons for hurrying this wedding, you should be celebrating right now. It's not every day a woman gets married. Unless you're my poker partner, Carol Ann, who's on her fifth husband now. Or maybe it's her sixth. I've lost count. But in your case, since this is your first experience with matrimony, you should be with that young man of yours. And here you are, hard at work.''

Karen glanced around the sparsely occupied dining room. ''I'm not really doing that much at the moment.''

Mimi cackled. ''You could be if you went home to your new husband. If he's like most men, he's waiting anxiously for a nighttime ride with his bride.''

Ashraf Saalem wasn't like most men Karen had known, and that in itself was a little frightening at times. She couldn't always read him and she had to confess his air of mystery did draw her on some level. The thought of him waiting at the hotel suite for her—waiting to make love to her—caused her pulse to trip several times. If he was still speaking to her. He had been none too pleased when she'd nixed a trip out of town and hadn't arranged to take the remainder of the day off.

But with Maria now on her way to Montana, the shop would be short-staffed and Karen had promised to look after things in Maria's absence. "Mimi, you and I both know that it's going to be hectic tonight."

"That's why I've called that Veronica with the platinum hair, the one who's just a few eggs short of a carton. All that bleach must've destroyed a few brain cells. But the men certainly like her."

Karen had learned early on that Mimi thought anyone under the age of sixty qualified as a girl. "True, Veronica is a little slow. For that reason, and since Maria won't be here, I need to stay at least for a while. I promise I'll leave at eight when the mayhem dies down." By then she should be ready to join Ash. She'd be a little less nervous. After finishing the cup of cappuccino she now clutched in her hand, she should probably lay off the caffeine just to be on the safe side.

Mimi frowned. "Speaking of Maria, I'm wondering what's going on with that girl. It's not like her to take off at all much less on the day of her cousin's wedding."

"Something unexpected came up." Karen hoped Mimi dropped it for now. Eventually she would have to inform the staff that Maria wouldn't be back for a while, after she knew for certain that her cousin was settled in Montana.

"I think what's been ailing our Maria has something to do with a man," Mimi announced in her trademark crusty voice.

Karen fumbled with her cup of cappuccino, nearly spilling its contents on her white blouse. The phone rang, giving her a welcome interruption. "Baronessa," she answered with a fake smile in her voice.

"I am beginning to wonder if I will ever have my wife here with me."

Karen set the cup on the counter and white-knuckled the phone as her palms began to perspire, along with the rest of her. "Um, it's going to be at least another few hours."

Ash's rough sigh filtered through the line. "That is a long time for a man to wait on his wedding day."

"I'm sorry but it's going to get pretty uncontrollable here now that the evening crowd is beginning to arrive."

"I would suggest that once you arrive here it could become a bit uncontrollable as well. In a very pleasant way."

She didn't want to react to the innuendo, but Karen couldn't prevent the stream of heat mixed with chills flowing through her. At least he didn't seem angry. At least he was speaking to her, loud and clear. "I'll be there as soon as I can get away."

"I hope you arrive soon. The champagne is now chilling but I fear the ice is melting as we speak."

So was Karen in response to his deep, husky voice. "I'm not sure I should have any champagne. It makes me kind of crazy."

"I would have no objection to you being a bit crazy. I must admit that I'm feeling somewhat that way at the moment, imagining divesting you of your clothing."

Karen glanced over her shoulder at Mimi who pretended not to listen. "Will that be all?"

"First I must warn you, I've already removed all of my clothing. And I've built a fire for our enjoyment."

The image of Ash lying naked before the hearth jumped into Karen's brain like a practiced pole-vaulter. A slow, uneven breath escaped her lips. "That sounds…" *Heavenly*. "Interesting."

"Oh, I am certain it will be. More interesting than either you or I could imagine. Have I been successful in encouraging you to leave early?"

He'd encouraged Karen to fantasize about making love with him. The conception should be her only concern, but she couldn't help considering the pleasure Ash was offering. So what if she actually let go enough to enjoy the process? After all, she was a woman and he was a man—a virile, seductive, enticing man. Her libido was restless and he was offering to appease it.

Tonight, and only tonight, she would allow herself the freedom to give up a little control to gain a little satisfaction and hopefully a child. Tonight, and only tonight, she would give herself completely to the sheikh, at least from a physical standpoint. Emotionally, she would have to remain strong.

"Karen, shall I tell you what else I have imagined?"

Once more she glanced at Mimi who was grinning like mad. Karen propped a hand on the freezer case housing the gelati then immediately pulled back. If she didn't, she was in grave danger of melting every last vat of the ice cream. "That's really not ne—"

"I am greatly curious to know how your bare skin will feel to my hands. How you will taste. All of you. How you will feel surrounding me when I bring you to—"

"I've got to go now."

Karen slammed down the phone and turned at the sound of Mimi's grainy laugh.

"My, my, missy. Either that phone's on fire or you've

suddenly decided you're in a big hurry to get out of here.''

The only fire present at the moment had landed on Karen's face. Blushing, she said, ''Well, Ash probably has dinner waiting on me.'' A feast of the senses. ''I guess I really hate to disappoint him, so—''

Mimi waved a hand in dismissal. ''Get out of here. We'll handle it fine, as I'm sure you'll handle your husband fine.''

Another round of rough laughter followed Karen all the way out Baronessa's door.

All the way home, Karen gave her ovaries a pep talk. If they chose to cooperate, then she could happily get the job done tonight. If they didn't, then she would have to continue to make love with Ash a little longer.

Now why was that not such a terrible prospect? Karen knew why. During the phone call he'd had her worked up and woozy with only a few well-chosen words said in a voice that could persuade a saint to sin. Of course, he could be all talk and no action. And someone could show up on her doorstep next January and hand her a million bucks, too.

Karen arrived at the hotel in a remarkably short time considering the commuter traffic and her inability to focus on driving. In the elevator, she was grateful that the attendant kept his eyes to himself. She was strung so tight that she might have to slug him if he even looked at her crossways.

Once outside the penthouse door, Karen hesitated. What if Ash hadn't been kidding? What if he did greet her naked as the day he was born? Surely not. But if he happened to be without clothing, she would keep her eyes averted and try not to fall out in the foyer.

Drawing in a broken breath, she started to knock then remembered that Ash had given her a card key. She rummaged around in her purse—the pesky culprit that had brought her to this moment. And it couldn't even accommodate her enough to cough up the key.

When Karen finally found it, she slipped the card into the lock with trembling fingers and opened the door to find the suite starkly silent and completely dark except for the warm glow of firelight radiating from the small hearth in the sitting area.

Karen visually searched the room, her gaze coming to rest on the plush chair facing the door, a chair containing her new husband. Her naked new husband.

Obviously he was a man of his word, Karen decided. A man with a body that could melt a midwinter Montana snowfall.

Her eyes immediately homed in on his bare chest revealing smooth bronzed skin stretched tight over his pecs, the territory interrupted only by a fine smattering of dark hair that spanned the space between his collarbones. Below that, a ribbon of masculine hair traveled to his navel. Below that…

Karen didn't dare look any farther but that was exactly what she did while trying to breathe with some semblance of normality. He sat with his legs stretched out before him, crossed at the ankles, a champagne flute balanced in one hand and an expression that told her he was somewhat amused over her inability to tear her eyes away. He seemed as comfortable with his nudity as Karen was uncomfortable with it.

Karen wasn't altogether uncomfortable; she was fascinated. Fascinated by the sensual image he presented. Fascinated that he was already fully aroused. Normally she was a butt connoisseur but considering Ash's ample attributes, she had no doubt that he could handle the conception quite well. But could she?

Tossing her overnight bag onto the adjacent sofa, Karen headed toward the bathroom muttering, "I need a shower." She needed a tank of oxygen.

As she passed him, Ash caught her wrist. "I will have the champagne poured for you on your return."

She didn't look at him for fear she might forgo the shower. "Good. And do you mind putting something on?"

"Music?"

"Clothes."

"If that is what you wish. I'll have on my robe when you rejoin me."

"Good."

"And I look forward to having you remove it."

So did Karen. "I'll be back in a few minutes."

In the bedroom, Karen closed the door and collapsed her boneless body against it. She hugged her arms to her chest to stop the shivers, but it didn't work. She wasn't sure her legs would work, either, but she had to move. She had to bathe and prepare for the conception. Prepare for whatever Ash had planned for her tonight. As if she could really prepare for that.

Ash could not imagine what was taking Karen so long in the bath. He supposed it was possible that she was anxious. Perhaps he had inadvertently shocked her with his nudity, though he had given her fair warning. Perhaps he should remember that they were unfamiliar with each other. He would take care of that soon, if she ever returned.

In reality, he was experiencing some unease despite the fact that seeing Karen come through his door, even fully clothed, had served to fuel his desire for her. Created a need so strong that the force of it had taken him aback.

Ash paced the length of the room while he considered the reasons behind his own disquiet. Normally, he had no qualms whatsoever when it came to making love. He had learned at a relatively young age to pleasure a woman and take his own pleasure from the act. He had been groomed by the best, a beautiful woman five years his senior who had been uninhibited and an excellent teacher. He had always thought fondly of her, and through the years, he had practiced what she had so skillfully taught him.

Tonight his concern centered on only one woman—his wife. He worried he might not be able to break down Karen's resistance so she would allow herself to take without hesitation what he offered. He worried that perhaps she would only view the consummation as a means to an end, that she would see him as being no better than a stallion providing breeding services. He longed to have her know him as a man, not as a prince. A man who very much wanted her, all of her, including her trust and her respect.

That was very important to him, and something he had not desired from a woman in many years. Fifteen years, to be exact. But he would not think about that tonight. He would turn all his energy to Karen and her needs. He would utilize every method he had learned and some he had discovered through experimentation, and there were many in his repertoire.

First, he would remember to maintain control, take his time, go slowly....

"Ash?"

He turned to find Karen dressed in a flowing, sheer

lace gown the color of a desert rose that revealed the shadowed curves of her body, her light brown hair framing her face in soft waves.

The vision of Karen standing there backlit by the fire, and the knowledge that she was his, at least for tonight, caused Ash to grow hard as slate beneath the robe he now wore, every muscle in his body growing taut from a need to take her right where she now stood.

But when he saw the hesitancy in her eyes, he remembered that he needed to pace himself, stay in control, rely on gentle persuasion and not the desperation for release that his body demanded. "Come with me," he said as he held out his hand to her.

She moved slowly toward him and took his hand. When he guided her to the sofa and pulled her down to his side, she frowned. "What's wrong with the bedroom?"

He poured her a glass of champagne from the bottle set in the silver bucket resting on the coffee table before them. "The bedroom will come later. Perhaps we should talk first."

He offered her the flute and noticed her hands trembled as she took it from him. Ash experienced a slight tremor as well, but it had nothing to do with stress. The faint outline of her nipples exposed through the gossamer lace covering her round breasts, the dark shading at the apex of her thighs, engaged him in the ultimate battle for control.

She stared at the champagne, rimming a slender finger round and round the edge of the glass. "What do you want to talk about?"

What I am going to do to you, with you. "Your day." He shifted slightly, keeping a comfortable distance between them in order to keep his desire temporarily at bay.

"Would you like something to eat? I can have room service deliver a tray."

"No. I grabbed a burger this afternoon."

"Are you sure you would not like something that will help you maintain your strength?"

"Why would I need any strength?"

"Because I intend to preoccupy you until the early hours of the morning."

Color rose high in her cheeks, a few shades lighter than the negligee. "Oh." She twirled a lock of hair around one slender finger, sparking Ash's imagination. "I'm okay. I had an order of fries, too."

Ash placed his champagne on the table and draped one arm casually along the back of the sofa. "You seem tired."

She took a sip of the wine then clutched the glass to her breasts. "I am. It was a long day."

Ash suddenly wished he were the champagne flute. "Yes, it was. A very long, hard day." Coming upon an idea that might make her more at ease, he took the glass from her and set it next to his. "Lie back."

"Ash—"

"I only want to help you relax."

With wariness calling out from eyes that appeared golden in the firelight, she stretched out with her head resting on the sofa's arm, her arms folded beneath her breasts. Ash brought her legs across his lap, taking care not to come near his burgeoning erection. The slightest bit of contact in that area would make him forget his vow of patience.

He began his ministrations with her feet, delicate feet with toenails painted the color of her red gown. He worked her instep, her heels, those delicate toes that he found very intriguing. When he moved his massage up to her calves, she tensed and he realized that he would have another battle on his hands to make her relax. Continued conversation might aid in his cause to distract her as he worked his way to his destination.

"Where was Maria off to in such a hurry today?" he asked.

Karen closed her eyes. "She had somewhere she had to be."

"Baronessa?"

"No."

He slipped his hand to the inside of Karen's knee and waited for her reaction. When she remained still, keeping her eyes closed, he continued his gentle stroking and the conversation. "I find it odd that she would leave knowing you were recently wed."

"She needed a vacation."

"Does this mean she will not be returning for a while?"

"I'm not sure how long she'll be gone."

"Where did she go?"

She sighed. "Montana. And her location has to remain a secret. You can't tell anyone, not even Daniel."

Ash found that to be surprising news, Maria traveling to the state where Karen once resided. He also found it odd that she obviously was in hiding. But that Karen trusted him enough to take him into her confidence pleased him. "I assure you I will tell no one. Yet I am wondering what business she has in Montana."

"No business. Just a break. That's all I'm at liberty to say at this time."

Ash thought of several ways he could make her talk yet he wasn't in the mood for more conversation. He slipped his fingertips to the inside of her thighs and Karen's eyes snapped open.

"Are you feeling more relaxed?" he asked as he continued caressing her leg with tempered movements.

"Not exactly."

"Tell me what I might do to assist you."

She released a slow, strained breath when he moved his fingertips up a fraction. "You're doing okay."

Okay? That did not set well with Ash. Determination drove him from the sofa and onto his knees beside her. Her lips, like her toes, were painted a deep crimson. Very tempting, but he wasn't ready to kiss her yet. At least not there.

"What are we doing now?" she asked, her voice as uneasy as her eyes.

"*You* are to remain where you are and enjoy." He lowered one thin strap and whisked his lips over her bare shoulder, then proceeded to do the same with the other strap. He could feel her heart thrumming where his chest pressed against her breasts and he knew that he was somewhat successful with his seduction.

"You are very beautiful," he murmured as he massaged her bare shoulders. "Are you relaxed yet?"

She hid a yawn behind her hand. "I'm definitely getting there. You're doing fine."

At least his efforts had been elevated from "okay" to "fine." He vowed to arrive at "wonderfully" soon. He pledged to give her the gratification she deserved, to prove to her that meeting her needs meant more than meeting his own. But not yet, not until he knew she was completely ready for him. Until he knew he had her full attention.

When Ash moved to the end of the sofa, Karen sent him a confused look. "Why did you stop?"

He pulled her up to his side, brought his arm around

her and nudged her head against his shoulder. "You should rest."

"Rest?"

He whisked a kiss across her forehead and stroked her hair. "You're tired from your day."

"I'm fine, really." She yawned again.

"Are you certain?"

"It's the champagne."

"You've had only a few sips."

"I told you it makes me crazy."

He leaned forward, slid the champagne glass from the table and held it to her lips. "You should have more then."

Smiling, she took another drink then ran her tongue over her lips, stirring Ash's body. "This is very good. French?"

He considered licking the moisture at the corner of her mouth but with great effort restrained himself. Unfortunately, one part of his body showed no sign of restraint. "Yes, it's French. The best."

"Of course. What else but the finest things for a prince?"

Ash had hoped that she would forget his status and see him only as her prospective lover. "Tonight I am simply a man. A man in the company of a beautiful woman who happens to be his wife."

"I never had any doubt about your manliness." She sent a pointed look at the obvious ridge beneath his robe.

"I will be more than happy to remove all your doubts and allow you to remove this robe to uncover the proof." She reached for the robe's sash and he stopped her with a hand on her wrist. "After you rest awhile."

"I'm honestly not that tired."

Nor was Ash, but he was determined. "Why the hurry?

Would you not prefer us to proceed at a leisurely pace? Or would you prefer hard and fast?''

"Yes. I mean no." She glanced away. "Leisurely is fine, I guess."

Ash smiled to himself as he offered her another sip of champagne that she gladly took. Obviously there was a side of Karen he had yet to uncover, a sensual facet that longed for wild, uninhibited lovemaking. He looked forward to accommodating her at some point in time. Tonight he chose to savor each moment.

After Ash set the glass aside and twined their fingers together, Karen studied their joined hands. "Very large," she murmured.

"Large?"

"Your hands. They're big. But then you're kind of big…all over."

"Does that concern you?"

"Not really."

"Good. Now lay your head back on my shoulder and close your eyes for a while."

"But what about the baby?"

As suspected, creating a child was still her principal plan. Ash's plan involved taking her attention off the conception and onto the process of achieving that goal. "We have all night to learn each other. Right now you need to relax. I prefer you awake and energized before we go any further."

She settled back against him. "Okay, if you insist." Her head snapped up again. "But I'm not going to sleep."

Yet it wasn't long before Karen's steady breathing echoed in the silent room and Ash realized she was indeed asleep. He had wanted her to relax, perhaps not quite that much, but as he'd said, there were still many hours left in the night.

If he had his way, they would come together every night for the rest of his days. But unless he could convince Karen to allow him to touch her after she conceived, to stay with him long after their child was born, these few moments might be all he ever had. He intended to make the most of them.

Time was on his side. For now.

Five

Karen had no concept of time or place, only that she was in a bed and she had no idea how she'd gotten there. Once she came fully awake, she glanced to her right at the green glow of the nearby clock that read half-past midnight. She looked to her left to see a figure stretched out beside her.

Ashraf Saalem. Her husband. Naked again.

The break in the heavy curtains allowed streamers of light coming from the Boston skyline to fall over him as he lay on his belly, his arms crossed above his head on the pillow, his face turned toward the window. Karen rolled to her side and studied the rise and fall of his strong back, the strength of his spine and the taut curve of his buttocks.

He was a magnificent man and he was hers for the taking. Or so she'd thought. She had wanted him to make love to her on the sofa, had almost begged him to continue, but her pride had prevented her from doing so. Yes, she had been tired, more than she'd realized. But not so exhausted that she wouldn't have gladly let him continue. Yet she had felt very secure curled up at his side, with his arm wrapped around her and her head against his shoulder. So relaxed that in only a matter of minutes, she had fallen asleep. And somehow he had carried her into the room without her notice. What else had he done?

Karen patted her chest and realized her gown was still intact. So was her need for him. Her need to create a child, she corrected. After all, that was why she was here, to make a baby.

On that thought, Karen reached out her hand to touch him then pulled back. For some reason she was afraid to rouse him, to unleash the power she inherently knew he possessed. A shudder ran through her, not from fear but from excitement, from the notion that this could be more than she could handle, making love with Ash.

As concerns whirled around in her head, Karen's hand moved to his back where she pressed a palm between his shoulder blades. His body temperature was volcanic, not surprising at all. Everything about him reminded her of fire, able to consume a woman's good sense in a matter of moments.

He didn't stir at all, even when she sent a fingertip down the track of his spine to the dip immediately below his waist. She couldn't stop there. Oh, no, not when faced with the tempting prospect of testing the firmness of his butt. She ran her palm over that masculine terrain, then on to the back of his hair-covered thighs, then back up again.

She felt like a child discovering clay for the first time, felt like a woman in dire need as she explored with abandon, tracing a fingertip lightly along the cleft, stopping right where his thighs came together. Karen squeezed her own thighs tightly against the onslaught of damp heat when she considered going farther in her journey.

She wanted him. Oh, how she wanted him. She wanted to know how it would feel to have him turn her into a mass of mindless feminine need.

Funny that Carl should enter her mind at that moment. She'd never wanted him with the same desperation. But then Carl's idea of lovemaking had entailed a once-a-week session whether needed or not. Afterward, Karen had always felt somewhat used, cheated, unsatisfied, and she hadn't known how to tell him. He hadn't asked, either.

Forcing her ex-fiancé from her mind, Karen turned her focus solely on her new husband. With a good deal of bravado, she inched closer to him and rested her lips against his back. Even if she didn't wake him, she would definitely enjoy her exploration.

"I see you're awake now."

Karen rolled away to find Ash had turned his face toward her. "So are you." Obviously, dummy.

A laugh rumbled low in his chest. "I have yet to sleep."

"But—" Karen couldn't think of one thing to say. He had known all along what she was doing. Maybe that should have embarrassed her, but for some reason it didn't. It gave her an odd sense of power.

"Are you feeling more refreshed?" he asked.

She was feeling hot and bothered. "Yes."

He worked his way to his side, facing her. "Refreshed enough to continue with our honeymoon?"

Oh, yeah. "If you're not too tired now."

He ran a slow finger down the cleft of her breasts. "I have never felt more animated in my life."

When he moved over her, Karen's breath caught in her chest. He reached for the bedside lamp and snapped it on, completely illuminating the room. "What are you doing?" she asked in a scratchy voice.

He hovered above her, his thick dark hair unkempt and incredibly sexy, his dark eyes roaming leisurely over her body. "I want to see you. All of you."

Karen could see all of him—almost. She could see the width of his sculpted chest, the flat plane of his belly, but she couldn't see anything below that. She could feel him, though. Could feel his "secret weapon" pressing against her hip and she wouldn't be a bit surprised if she spontaneously combusted at any given moment.

"Take off your gown," he said in a low, lusty voice.

"Don't you want to do it?"

"I would gladly do it, but I would prefer to watch you undress for me."

Karen didn't have one whit of will left to protest. When she started to slip her arms out of the straps, Ash commanded, "Stand by the bed."

Stand? She wasn't sure she could. "Why?"

"It would give me pleasure to watch the material fall away from your body. I believe you will enjoy it as well."

Karen wasn't so sure about that. She'd never undressed for a man before, not even Carl who preferred darkness. She had never really seen Carl naked in the light.

But if she did what Ash had requested, she would definitely be able to see every fabulous part of him and that drove her out of the bed.

She tossed back the covers from her lower body and slid off the mattress to stand on jelly legs. Ash remained on his side, his elbow bent and his jaw braced on his palm, his near-black eyes trained on her face.

Forcing her gaze to remain locked on his, Karen slipped her arms from the straps then tugged the bodice down, baring her breasts. A cool draft of air flowed over her and that, combined with the heat in Ash's eyes, caused her flesh to pebble.

Only then did she venture a glance below Ash's waist to garner his true reaction. A very observable reaction. And as she slowly slid the gown down, she experienced a heady sense of control as she watched him grow and swell right before her eyes. She paused when she had the fabric worked below her abdomen, hesitated to increase the tension. Not that Ash looked the least bit tense, at least not his face. Had it not been for his current state of arousal, it would seem that this was an everyday occurrence for him. Maybe it was.

Karen refused to ponder how many women he had asked to do this for him. She only considered that she was doing it for him now, and that he was, for all intents and purposes, her husband, even if not in the truest sense of the word.

She managed a smile as she shimmied the gown from her hips. It fell in a pool of lace at her feet and she stepped over it, bringing her closer to the bed.

Ash sat up, draped his legs over the side of the bed and perched on the edge to face her. While Karen stood there fighting chills and heat, he visually scanned her body.

"Do you approve?" she asked.

He brought his gaze back to her eyes. "Come closer and I will show you how much I approve."

She moved forward and came to a stop immediately before him. He parted his legs and pulled her between them. With a gentle fingertip, he traced a circular path around one breast then the other. "Very beautiful," he murmured.

When he flicked his tongue over one nipple, then the other, Karen swayed forward in offering. He suckled her and she felt the steady pull all the way to her womb and lower.

He kept his hands braced on her waist while she propped her hands on his shoulders to keep from toppling over. Then he took his mouth away. Karen wanted to groan from the loss of sensation, but not for long as he kneaded her bottom much the same as she had his. "You feel very good." He explored and fondled her buttocks, with each pass coming nearer to the point between her legs where she needed his attention the most.

He brought his hands around to her hips and stroked her pelvis all the while watching her. When he finally made it to the layer of curls, an almost pleading sound climbed up Karen's throat and came out of her mouth despite her attempts to stop it. Never had she been so close to begging someone to soothe the ache. Never had she been so close to coming apart.

"Do you wish me to touch you, Karen?"

"Yes," she said on a breathy sigh.

"Then I shall and you will watch."

And she did watch him, watched as he parted her flesh. Watched as he made maddening passes over and around her tender, aching center, first lightly, then more insistent, then lightly again, almost teasing her into total oblivion. "You are beautiful here, too," he said, his gaze leveled on the place he now touched.

Karen was lost in the eroticism of the moment as he caressed her with a proficiency she had only fantasized about until now. Her knees almost buckled, and had it not been for her grip on his shoulders, she might have fallen. But that didn't stop Ash's carnal assault on her senses or the threatening climax building and building in Karen.

Then he took his hands away. This time Karen groaned, or more like moaned. Was he determined to drive her insane? If he told her she needed to rest, she'd have to sock him.

"I'm not finished," he assured her. "I simply want to feel you when you reach your climax." He took her hands into his and tugged her forward. "Come to me now."

Karen straddled his thighs and, with his help, lowered herself onto him in slow increments. Before she could attempt to take all of him inside her, Ash stopped her with a solid grip on her waist. "Relax for a moment."

Relax? How could she relax? Not in this position. And why was he so intent on her relaxing? "I'm fine," she insisted.

"You will be better in a moment." Keeping one hand on her waist, he touched her with the other, stroked her without mercy until he brought her back to that place where nothing mattered but sheer sensation. The orgasm hit her in strong, mind-bending jolts.

This time Ash groaned and muttered something she didn't understand but it sounded almost desperate, followed by "Do with me what you will. You are in control now."

"My pleasure."

And it was. The ultimate pleasure. All thoughts of the purpose of this union left Karen's mind as she immersed herself in the moment. With Ash's hands planted firmly on her hips, she moved in a rhythm that began slowly before growing wild and reckless.

She kissed Ash with all the passion bubbling inside

her, tangled her tongue with his in frantic forays not unlike the love they now made. Karen was consumed by a power she couldn't comprehend when Ash broke the kiss and in a harsh voice said, *"Now."*

With that, he pushed her hips down until he was deeper inside her, deeper than Karen ever thought possible. His chest heaved against her breasts and his body tensed. She felt the pulse of his climax from the inside out, felt him shudder with the force of it.

Ash collapsed onto his back, bringing Karen down with him. He continued to tremble, or maybe she was trembling; Karen couldn't tell since they were so closely joined. His heart beat in an erratic rhythm against her cheek while hers fluttered in her chest.

They stayed that way for a time, silent, until Ash rolled her over and rose above her. She expected him to say something but instead he kissed her, a languid, gentle, honeyed kiss that contrasted with their uncontrolled lovemaking. A tender kiss that spoke to Karen on a level she didn't want to acknowledge.

Ash moved up onto the bed, taking her with him to share his pillow as they faced each other. He enfolded her in his strong arms, stroked her hair, made her feel protected and appreciated for the first time in a long time. Had she ever felt this way before? No, and that frightened her.

Ash spoke to her in whispers, concerned that he had been too forceful. She assured him he had been wonderful, and that made him smile, a smile as soft as his continuing kisses. A fissure of emotion opened in Karen's heart, one she had been so determined to keep closed. She told herself that it was only an illusion, that what she now felt for Ash was a product of incredible sex. Told her heart to stay strong, stay protected.

They remained that way for a long time, holding each other in the quiet aftermath, Karen savoring his arms surrounding her. Then he slipped one hair-roughened thigh between her legs and rubbed intimately against her. The dam broke again, the sensations came calling again, and Karen opened herself to him again. He entered her with a slow steady glide, caressed her with capable fingers until she was lost to everything, lost to him. Lost to a moment where she started to believe that this mysterious man who filled her body so completely could easily fill the void in her soul.

Ash collapsed heavily against her, but she didn't find the weight a burden at all. She reveled in it, reveled in the feel of him, the roughness of his jaw against her cheek, his warm, ragged breath playing over her neck where he had buried his face. Much sooner than she would have liked, he moved from atop her but kept his arm resting across her abdomen and his cheek against her cheek. When she heard the sound of his steady breathing and knew that he slept, only then did reality take hold.

She had given him everything tonight in hopes of creating a child and in turn, when she'd taken him inside her body, he'd threatened to enter her heart. She couldn't allow that to happen. She couldn't give up a good deal of her soul to another man for fear that he might want it all.

This one night with Ash would have to be enough. But deep down she worried it never would be.

Shortly before dawn, Ash walked onto the balcony with a cup of coffee and feelings he could not explain.

He had correctly assumed that making love with Karen would be a most pleasurable experience, and it had been that and more. But he had not bargained for the odd heaviness in his heart after they had made love, a heaviness that still existed. It went far beyond desire and called up a wariness from deep within his soul.

He did not fear many things. He had braved the steep slopes of mountains, conquered the vast, unpredictable spectrum of investing, disentangled himself from his father's hold and left the only home he had ever known to pursue his own path in the world. Falling in love with another woman—a woman who might leave him as well—was something he dare not encounter. He could not allow himself anything beyond warm feelings for her. He could not want more from her, or from himself.

His obligation to Karen should be based solely on creating a child and establishing a relationship built on mutual respect, not love. He had learned to shield himself against succumbing to those emotions, yet in one night Karen had exposed him in a way no other woman had in fifteen years. He would be damned if he gave into that weakness.

Granted, he did crave her passion, appreciated her strength and wanted her with every breath that he took. Even the cool Boston breeze did nothing to quell the heat when he considering rejoining her in bed to reach even greater heights. He had not even begun to show her all the ways a man and woman could take pleasure in each other. He preferred to reveal those aspects a little at a time. If she decided to allow him that honor in the coming months. The coming years.

"I'm leaving now."

Ash turned to see Karen standing in the doorway dressed in a white tailored shirt and black skirt, her hair pulled back into a plait. Unless he was mistaken, she looked ready to return to work, and that infuriated him.

Carefully he set his cup of espresso down on the patio

table and with effort kept a tight rein on his temper. ''Where are you off to so early in the morning?''

''Work. I have to open up since Maria won't be there.''

''People actually prefer ice cream for breakfast?''

''You'd be surprised but no, most come in for pastries and coffee. We have quite a few regular customers who show up every morning when we open at seven.''

Ash fisted his hands into the pockets of his robe. ''I assume you will be off earlier today due to your morning arrival?''

''Actually, I'm not sure. I need to see who's on the schedule. I'll probably have to stay until tonight.''

''And after that?''

She frowned. ''What do you mean?''

''Will you join me here?''

She threaded her bottom lip between her teeth. ''I guess I could, at least for another couple of nights. My fertile cycle won't be over until then.''

Ash took another step, anger steeping inside him. ''Then you have no intention of us living together as man and wife?''

''I don't know. I mean, I love my apartment and I can't imagine you would be happy living there.''

''I would be happy living wherever you might be.''

Her gaze wavered. ''Maybe we should discuss it later. If I don't leave now, I won't beat the traffic and I'll be late. I promised Maria I would look after things in her absence.''

She had promised Ash nothing beyond being the mother of his child and that thought angered him more. ''When Maria returns, it will not be necessary for you to remain employed.''

Her mouth opened then fell closed. "Ash, I intend to continue working at Baronessa. I love my job."

"And if you become pregnant?"

"I can work up until a few weeks before the baby's born."

"I have no say in the matter?"

"No, you don't. I enjoy my independence. I will not stay home and do nothing. If there is a baby, I'll consider my options then."

Ash was caught between fury and frustration. Desire and determination. The fire in Karen's eyes fueled an illogical need to sweep her up into his arms and take her back to bed to use every sensual tactic he knew to make her forget work, forget everything but him.

With a strength he didn't know he possessed, he simply said, "You may return to your job now. We will discuss this and our living arrangements later."

She sent him an acrimonious look. "Thank you so much for your permission, but in terms of my job there's really nothing more to discuss."

Changing strategy, he sent her a smile. "Could I perhaps persuade you into kissing me goodbye? Something that will carry me through the day until we are together tonight?"

She sighed. "Oh, all right. I guess one little goodbye peck would be okay, although I'm not feeling very affectionate toward you at the moment."

Something Ash was determined to remedy. He strode toward her and without the slightest pause, claimed her mouth with the force of his anger, his desire. And Karen responded as she had the day she'd agreed to his proposal, as she had last night, as if she were trying to prove exactly who was in control. Ash was beginning to wonder about that very thing.

Their mouths sealed together as if each breath they drew depended on the other. Karen's bag dropped to the cement floor and her arms came around his neck. Ash circled her waist, cupped her buttocks, pulled her against him to let her know that he could easily take this further, take her beyond the limits.

Karen didn't allow anything beyond the kiss and pulled away. She picked up the bag and sent him a playful smile. "Hold that thought until tonight."

He would rather hold her. "You would leave me now in such a predicament?"

Her gaze came to rest on his predicament. "Go take a cold shower."

"That, my dear wife, is a total fallacy. Cold water does not provide relief."

She shrugged. "Well, you probably need some time to rebuild your stamina after last night anyway."

"I would not wager on that, and neither should you."

She smoothed a slender hand over her blouse. "In the meantime, order some orange juice. It's supposed to aid in fertility. I'll see you later."

With that she was gone, leaving Ash with his discomfort and a strong determination.

They had much to learn about each other, and much to decide. He refused to consider living apart from her. After all, he was her husband. Of course, the penthouse had been anything but a real home to him, except last night when Karen had been in his bed, in his arms. But this hotel room was only temporary, as it had been with all the places he had occupied over the past few years. He considered moving to Karen's current residence. An apartment would not do if they had a child, which left only one option.

Fueled by his goal, Ash made his way back into the suite and picked up the phone. If good fortune chose to be gracious, the living arrangements would be decided today.

Six

"**Y**ou must come with me now."

Karen looked up from the booth where she'd been taking an order to find Ash standing beside her. He wore a black business suit, a white Arabian headdress covering his dark hair and an expression that said he meant business. "What are you doing here?"

"I am in need of your immediate assistance."

Was he expecting a nooner? "I can't just up and leave."

"Oh, yes you can, honey," said the lady with flaming red hair and equally red lips seated at the booth. "If a hunky stranger came in demanding my assistance, I'd leave in a minute."

Karen fought the little nip of pride. "He's not a stranger."

"I'm her husband," Ash said. "We were married yesterday."

The lady's eyes widened as she leveled her gaze on Karen. "And you're at work?"

Ash gave her a winning smile. "My point exactly. I've told her that we could be sunning ourselves on a private beach in the Mediterranean were she not so devoted to her job."

The redhead released a grating chuckle. "Hell, honey, if my order's holding you up, I'll get my own ice cream."

Feeling trapped, feeling like an idiot, Karen gritted her teeth and aimed her scowl on Ash. "Now you know, *dear*, I have to work in order to keep you in your designer clothes."

Ash seemed unaffected by the lie. "I would prefer you keep me out of my clothes."

The lady let go a round of strident laughter, drawing Mimi from across the room to the booth to ask, "Is there a problem over here?"

Ash extended his hand to Mimi. "I believe we have not officially met. I am Sheikh Ashraf Saalem, Karen's husband."

"Oh, yes, I remember you." Mimi shook Ash's hand and fairly blushed. "My, my, you are quite a specimen. My Johnny, God save his soul, was about as handsome as you, but not quite as tall. Are you here to see your wife?"

Ash slipped his arm around Karen's waist. "I need to steal her away for a time."

"By all means, take her," Mimi said.

Feeling totally outnumbered, Karen told Mimi, "I can't leave now, not during the lunch rush."

"Of course you can, missy. We've got plenty of people to cover for you. Now run along and take care of your husband. We can handle it without you."

Karen wanted to take care of Ash, all right. She wanted

to remove her apron and stuff it into his sexy mouth. Instead, she handed Mimi the pad and released a frustrated sigh. "Okay, but I'll be back soon."

The redhead laughed again. "Take your time, honey. Rome wasn't made in a day. Neither is good lovin'."

Karen untied her apron and tossed it underneath the counter. After grabbing her purse, she headed out the door muttering, "This better be good."

"I assure you it will be," Ash said from behind her.

Karen stopped in the middle of the sidewalk. She had no idea where they were going or if Ash had even come in a car, though she doubted he'd used public transportation.

Ash gestured toward a silver sedan parked at the curb. A Rolls-Royce. A convertible Rolls-Royce with the top down. Figures, Karen thought. Only the best.

Ash opened the door for her and she slipped inside to settle into the soft seat. Had she not been so put out over the interruption, she might have enjoyed the luxurious feel of the leather.

When Ash seated himself behind the wheel, she sent him a hard look. "Do you mind telling me where we're going? And it better not be back to the hotel for a quickie." Karen experienced an unwanted thrill thinking about that prospect. Darn his sexy sheikh self.

"I have something I want to show you," he said.

She rolled her eyes. "I've already seen it, Ash."

He turned on the ignition and the car purred to life and so did Karen when he smiled. "Although having you examine 'it' again is a pleasant thought, that is not my goal." He sent her a sultry glance. "At least not at the moment."

Now why was she so disappointed? "Then exactly what is your goal?"

He pulled into traffic before saying, "It's a surprise, one I think will please you."

Karen couldn't imagine what else he could possibly do to please her. He had done it all last night. "I don't necessarily like surprises."

"You will like this one."

Karen resigned herself to the fact that Ash wasn't going to give an inch, at least not at the moment, and sat back to enjoy the feel of the wind on her face, thankful she'd braided her hair that morning. If not, she would probably resemble Medusa before they reached their destination.

After leaving Boston proper, they traveled along a winding highway that skirted the shoreline in places, revealing a crescent beach covered in golden sand, the water beyond it a sage green. Karen could certainly appreciate the view considering she hadn't really experienced the sea's beauty before coming to Boston. But the stately historic houses to Karen's left that faced the ocean captured her attention the most.

She commented to Ash about their magnificence and he only smiled. Obviously he had no appreciation for the historical significance of the area.

Forty minutes later, Ash passed through the Marblehead area and drove up a winding hedge-lined drive leading to a house—a beige Colonial-style, two-story house surrounded by elm and birch trees with a stand of sugar maple set out near the edge of the property. She could envision the kaleidoscope of color when the foliage began to change with the season in a matter of weeks. Right now the verdant lawns were plush and pristine, the rows of hedges neatly manicured. Yet the cracked and peeling brown paint on the trim around the dormers told her the house hadn't faired as well. But the twelve-paned windows and the double chimneys captured Karen's imagination and prompted her fantasy of living in such an elegant home. "This place is unbelievable. But what are we doing here?"

Ash put the car in park and shut off the ignition. "You will soon see."

Before Karen could ask more questions, Ash rushed around to open the door for her. She left the car and inhaled the tangy scent of sea air coming from the harbor that served as a backdrop to the estate.

Karen followed Ash up the rock walkway and when he reached the heavy entry doors, she asked, "Who lives here?"

Ash fished a key from his pocket. "We will."

Stunned, Karen searched for some appropriate retort until she followed him inside to a breathtaking foyer that would make even the most stoic person take immediate notice. The ceilings had to be at least twenty feet high, and a wide staircase covered in a faded blue carpet climbed to the upper floors. Overcome with curiosity, she walked to the bottom of the stairs, crouched down and lifted a corner of the carpet. As she suspected, the rug hid the original flooring, most likely wide board pine that had been pegged with wood, not nails.

As usual, she slipped into designer mode and immediately saw the possibilities. The entry walls were in need of a good coat of paint and she figured the rest of the house's interior would as well. A nice, patterned wallpaper here and there would definitely restore its original charm and—

Wait a minute, Karen thought as she took a mental step back. Had she actually heard Ash correctly? Did this incredible place belong to him?

Karen straightened and turned to Ash who looked very

pleased at the moment. "I could've sworn you told me that you didn't own a home."

"I do as of this morning."

"Excuse me?"

"I purchased the house this morning."

"Just like that? You went out and got a loan—"

"I paid with cash."

Of course he had. "Let me get this straight. You got up, had your coffee, took a shower then went wandering up the Massachusetts coastline until you came upon this house?"

He leaned against the banister. "Actually, I spoke with Daniel this morning and when I told him what I intended to do, he suggested this place. It was built in the 1800s and used mainly as a summerhouse. Unfortunately its been tied up in an estate dispute for years, the reason for its current disrepair. I immediately saw its potential."

So did she, darn it. "It's very nice." A designer's dream kind of nice.

"The paperwork will not be finalized for a few days," Ash continued. "As far as I am concerned, it is now ours."

Ours? Marrying Ash was one thing. Having a baby with Ash was another. But owning a home with him? That sounded much more like a real marriage than Karen was prepared to deal with at the moment. "You just took it upon yourself to buy a house for us to live in without consulting me?"

"Had you not been so determined to work, I would have consulted you. Daniel told me of your background in interior design and I believed you would be happy to decorate it as you saw fit."

And he had seen fit to buy a house without her input. "It definitely needs work." Karen walked to the banister where Ash now stood and scratched the surface with a thumbnail. "Someone painted over the mahogany. They've covered the original flooring. This house should be restored to its original state."

"And I trust it will with your vision."

Karen turned back to Ash, trying desperately to ignore how much she would cherish making this house all that it could be. "It would take money. A lot of money and a lot of time."

"Money is not an issue, and neither is time. I'm certain there are craftsmen in Boston who would do the restoration justice. Daniel is now researching those for me."

Good old Daniel, Karen thought. She had a few things to say to him, too. But she really couldn't blame her cousin. As far as Daniel knew, Karen and Ash were living in wedded bliss, planning a future together. A house was simply the next step. A gorgeous house that could be made even better.

Karen could already imagine the details. Imagine what it would be like if she were given free rein. Even if Ash hadn't provided her the opportunity to stamp her seal of approval before he bought the place, at least she could maintain some control over what was done with it from this point forward. "I would want to oversee everything."

Ash smiled. "I had hoped you would. Shall we see the rest of the house?"

Oh, no. Until Karen got some things straight, she refused to fall completely in love with this place any more than she dared fall in love with him knowing that by doing so she could face certain emotional peril. "First, I want to know what's going to happen to this house after we're no longer together."

Ash's expression turned hard, unforgiving. "You mean after the *divorce?*"

She flinched over his sudden ire. "That's exactly what I mean."

His eyes narrowed and went almost black. "It would be yours. I have no use for a house if I have no family with which to share it."

Karen felt suddenly remorseful over her lack of consideration when she saw the hurt in Ash's eyes, heard it in his tone. He had provided a home, a beautiful home, for her and their child. The least she could do was thank him then worry about the rest later. "I'm sorry, Ash. Really, it's wonderful. I only wish you would have talked to me about it first."

"And how was I to do that when you were so intent on going to work?" He folded his arms across his chest, looking powerful and no less angry. "I believed this would solve our living arrangements. There are four bedrooms on the second floor, one we will set up for our child, and one I plan to use as my office. It will be up to you to decide what will be done with the others."

"We can discuss that later." Karen automatically held out her hand. Nothing more than a friendly action, she told herself, even though she'd recently discovered that touching Ash was just this side of heaven. "Can you show me the rest of the house now?"

He gestured toward the entry opening to another room but failed to take her hand. "After you."

Karen fought the knifelike pain that impaled her heart over his refusal to touch her. She couldn't really blame him. He was only being considerate and she had carelessly ruined the moment by bringing up the whole divorce issue. But she was too afraid to hope that their marriage could be permanent. Too afraid to believe that she wouldn't eventually drown in Ash's need to stay in control of his life, their decisions. She had to remain adamant even though every time she was near him her heart executed a little tumble and she found herself wishing that they had a marriage based on more than an agreement. But they didn't.

Karen followed Ash through the adjacent living room, bare except for a white brick fireplace in the corner, and into a small hallway where he opened the door to a room with twelve-foot ceilings and muted gray walls with contrasting white molding. A dusty teardrop chandelier hung above her and dull hardwood floors creaked beneath her feet.

Considering the size of the area, Karen assumed it to be a formal parlor or dining room, albeit a large one, until Ash announced, "This is the master suite."

Karen turned to Ash, her eyes wide. "A bedroom? It's huge."

He allowed a slight smile to surface. "Yes, and through there," he pointed toward an open door, "is the master bath. It has been updated with the addition of a shower and a new bath, both large enough for two."

The image of her and Ash sharing the shower, her and Ash reclining in the tub, her and Ash making love, filtered into her consciousness.

Why, oh, why, had she believed she could remain detached knowing how much she'd been drawn to him since that first time he'd kissed her? She had to remain emotionally detached even while occupying the same house, the same bed. Or the same tub.

"That sounds nice," Karen said. "What do you plan to do about furnishing this room?"

"That would be up to you. I have arranged for an open

account at the best furniture store in the city. You may choose anything you like.''

"Don't you want to have some say in it?''

"I trust your judgment, as long as the bed is comfortable and accommodating.''

Beds, Karen thought. More than one bed. More than one bedroom. Ash could have this one. He deserved to have this one. After all, he had paid for the house. She could take one of the others, stay there in her own bed. A lovely, lonely bed instead of sharing one with Ash. Yes, that would be best. That would be totally unappealing, but necessary if she wanted to remain emotionally grounded. She would have to broach that subject carefully so as not to anger him more.

Karen walked to the paned, double doors that opened to a wood plank porch surrounded by a low brick wall covered in clinging vines. The land sloped toward the harbor where various craft moved across the water. She could only imagine what a scene the panorama would present at sunrise and sundown. "This is very nice.''

"The wall allows for some privacy if you are seated.''

Karen suddenly realized Ash was standing behind her, very close considering his cologne and deep voice wafted around her like a fine, sensual mist. "Then I guess we could add a patio table, maybe some lounge chairs and have our morning coffee there without having to get dressed.''

"I suppose that people could do whatever they wish there without getting dressed.'' Ash's voice was low, deep, boldly seductive.

The words seemed to hang in the air along with a sudden spark of electric tension.

"You said the rest of the bedrooms are upstairs?'' Karen asked, annoyed by the tremor in her voice.

"Yes. This suite was added on at some point in time. It is totally segregated from the other living quarters. There is a small room across the corridor that would serve as a temporary nursery until our child is older."

"That's a good thing." Ash's close proximity was not, Karen decided. Ash's hands on her shoulders were not. Her reaction to his touch was not.

It took every ounce of Karen's fortitude to keep from turning around, turning into his arms and turning up the heat. Although right now, she felt as if she were about to go up in a blaze of glory despite the coolness of the room.

Before Karen could give everything over to a need for him that seemed determined to run a course she couldn't control, Ash dropped his hands and stepped away.

"Shall we see the upstairs now?" he asked.

Karen turned from the doors and met his dark gaze. She saw a glimpse of undeniable desire. The same desire she imagined was reflected in her own eyes.

"Yes, let's go upstairs," she said, sounding too harried, too uncomfortable. "I'd like to see the layout of the bedrooms. I'm sure I could find one that suits my needs."

"Does this one not suit your needs?"

"Oh, it's wonderful, but I think it should be yours."

"I would prefer we share this one."

Karen detected another hint of anger in his tone. "I'm not sure that's a good idea."

He reached out and traced a fingertip down the line of her jaw. She noticed a softness in his eyes she had never seen before. "I am only asking for a chance for us to get to know each other better, Karen. That is most important to me. That and making certain that you have all that you need while you're carrying our child. I ask that you please allow me that much. As per the terms of our arrangement, I will not touch you unless you ask it of me.''

Karen supposed she could allow him to share her bed temporarily, as long as he still agreed to forgo any real intimacy once she was pregnant. She couldn't allow him to take control of her life...or her heart. But as he continued to regard her with his dark, assessing eyes, one thing became all too clear.

Living with Ash might prove to be incredibly difficult—because falling for him could be all too easy.

The drive back into the city was spent in silence. Ash was still reeling from Karen's concern about what would become of the house if they parted ways. His concern centered on what would become of him. He refused to be shoved out of her life and their child's life should she attempt to discard him like yesterday's market report.

He would simply have to try harder to convince her that they should remain together. How he would do that, he had no idea. Or perhaps he did. One thing existed between them that could not be denied—desire. Fortunately that was one aspect he could use to his advantage. That and quite possibly his temporary absence from her life.

While Karen had been upstairs surveying the rooms, Ash had received a call from an overseas investor requesting his services. Though Ash would have preferred not to leave, he had been forced to agree to a planning meeting in Europe or lose the lucrative deal. On a positive note, distance might aid him in his cause with his reluctant wife. And he was probably a fool to think that Karen might miss his company.

When they pulled up at the curb several feet from Baronessa, he put up the convertible's top to allow more privacy and shifted in the seat to face Karen. "I need to speak to you about tonight," he said. "I'm afraid that I have been called away on business. I must leave immediately."

She looked somewhat displeased. "Today?"

"This evening."

"Then we won't be able to…" She flailed her hands about for a moment before clasping them in her lap. "You know."

"Make love? I am afraid not. This cannot wait."

"Neither can I. I mean…I only have a couple of fertile days left."

"If we have not yet achieved conception, our attempts will have to be postponed until next month." And he would be insane between now and that time if he could not touch her.

"You'll be gone a month?" The disappointment in her tone pleased Ash.

"I foresee no more than two weeks."

More silence ensued until she finally said, "What time does your plane leave?"

"At 6:00 p.m."

"I won't be off work until seven."

Ash reached across the console and patted her stocking-covered thigh, letting his hand linger there. "I suppose duty calls."

"Yes, I guess you're right."

She toyed with the top button of her blouse and the simple gesture made Ash's blood boil, his body come to life. He wanted her now. He wanted her to want him. Perhaps he could convince her to take the afternoon off, to take the opportunity to spend their last moments together engaged in some pleasurable activities. However, he would not try to convince her with words.

He drew a slow path from her knee to immediately beneath the hem of her skirt, wishing he had bought a sedan with a bench seat to give him better access. "It seems we are at cross-purposes due to our responsibilities."

She kept her eyes fixed on the dashboard. "Yes, we are."

He drew circles on her thigh with a slow fingertip. "It is a shame, not having the time or opportunity to spend our evening together."

"Yes. A real shame."

"Of course, I suppose we could consider returning to the hotel for an hour or so, but then I do have to pack."

"And I really need to get back to work."

He inched his hand higher. "Are you certain?"

She still refused to look at him. "No... Yes. I'm sure Mimi's wondering where I am."

With his free hand, he cupped her jaw and drew her face around to give her a kiss. She responded with an ardor that matched his own, with the soft play of her tongue against his leaving no doubt in Ash's mind that she wanted him, too.

After breaking the kiss, he said, "Come to the hotel with me."

Ash saw a trace of indecision in her eyes then a determined look that he did not care for. "I have to go to work now, and you have to get ready for your trip."

He stroked his thumb along the inside of her thigh. "Are you certain you would not like more memories to keep while I'm away? We would not have to return to the hotel."

Her shallow breathing told Ash she most certainly

might. "In a car in broad daylight, where anyone could see us?"

"Would anyone blame me for bringing my wife pleasure?"

She closed her legs tightly, trapping his hand, halting his upward progress. "We can't do it here. We'll be arrested. Besides, there's not enough room."

He bent his lips to her ear and whispered, "There are many ways to make love, Karen, regardless of the location. I am willing to show you."

She pulled his hand away and placed it in his lap. "I think we both need to remember the terms. We don't make love after I'm pregnant. Otherwise, it will only complicate things."

"Then we will not make love unless you make the request." Determination to break down her resistance, as she had so easily broken his, hurtled through Ash on the heels of his anger and his insatiable need for this woman. "And you will ask me, Karen. You most definitely will."

Karen hadn't asked Ash to make love to her. Of course, he'd been out of town for fifteen days, ten hours and twenty minutes, give or take a few. Even though she'd occupied her time with her work at Baronessa and supervising the house's remodeling, she still thought of him throughout the day and well into the night. Thought often of his kisses, his touch, his lovemaking—when she wasn't considering what to do about the sleeping arrangements when he returned.

As of two days ago, she had vacated the apartment after moving the few belongings she'd brought from Montana into the house. The workers had put the finishing touches on the master suite—an elegant rose-patterned paper on one wall of the bedroom, new Italian tile in the bath, newly restored hardwood floors—before starting renovations on the kitchen. The first go-round of furniture had been delivered yesterday, including the king-size four-poster bed, the only bed she had ordered so far. And just thinking about occupying it tonight, alone, magnified Karen's loneliness, a loneliness that had haunted her since Ash's departure. The same loneliness she had intimately known before she'd come to Boston.

Several times she had talked with Maria, thankful that her cousin sounded much less heavy-hearted, but even those conversations hadn't filled the empty space in Karen's soul. Neither had Ash's occasional calls, most made while she was at Baronessa. He hadn't said anything out of the ordinary, only basic inquiries about the house and her job, yet Karen was more aware of what he hadn't said—that he missed her.

All for the best, Karen told herself repeatedly. She already had too many confusing emotions running around in her head. She would be better off keeping the relationship with Ash on a platonic level—unless she wasn't pregnant. And in a matter of moments, she would find out.

Karen was only three days late but the test guaranteed that was enough time to see the results. While she readied for work, she made a point not to look at the white stick sitting on the jade-colored marble vanity before the allotted time had passed, even though the temptation was overwhelming.

Standing before the mirror, Karen braided her unruly hair as the seconds turned into minutes. She brushed her teeth, resisting another urge to sneak a peek. She applied her lipstick and sent a coral smudge down her chin at the sound of her watch's alarm, signaling the moment of truth had arrived.

After fumbling for the button to cut off the annoying shrill, Karen couldn't seem to force her feet to move. Funny, she had been so eager to end the suspense and now she was almost afraid—afraid of being disappointed. Maybe even a little afraid of the reality of bringing a child into the world with a man she found so very hard to resist. A man very in control of his world.

Karen swiped the lipstick smudge away from her chin with a tissue and only then did she approach the test. Her hand trembled as she reached out to take it, her pulse thrummed in her ears, her heart pummeled her chest.

She lifted the stick and studied the results for a split second, looked away, looked back, then looked away again. The answer to her question, to her dreams, finally registered.

Positive.

She was pregnant. Pregnant and stunned, happy and scared, crying in celebration of the miracle. And in the silence of the bathroom, in a deserted house, she had no one with whom to share the news. Not even the man who had made this possible, the father of her baby.

Karen supposed she could call Ash although she wasn't sure about his schedule, and she also wasn't sure this kind of news should be delivered by phone. He had told her he might be coming back to Boston tomorrow, but then he had told her he would only be gone for two weeks.

Maybe she should have waited until his return to take the test, but somehow Karen hadn't really expected it to be positive. Besides, the sooner she learned the results, the better. Now she could begin to prepare, make appointments, change her eating habits, lay off the caffeine. Now she could rest assured that her goal had been met, the conception completed and she had no reason to make love with Ash.

She might not have a reason, but that didn't make her want him any less.

Karen moved through her day at Baronessa in a euphoric haze, smiling often yet experiencing a bout of wistfulness when she waited on one family with two charming little girls. Her heart felt heavy as she witnessed the love and affection in the doting parents' expressions as they looked at each other, looked on patiently as the girls' exuberance came out in boisterous behavior over an outing that involved ice cream.

She found herself imagining what it would be like to have that closeness in her life, to have a man whose love for her was obvious even to an ordinary bystander. To have a child look at her with a different yet no less important love.

At least she would have her baby. At least she wouldn't be completely alone.

By the time Karen returned to the house that evening, her feet ached, her mind swam and she couldn't seem to shake the subtle yearning. After having a light supper in the form of a heart-healthy TV dinner, she took to the shower and stayed until the water turned cold, touching her belly every now and then as if that might make it real. But it still wasn't real to her. Maybe when she told Ash the news it might sink in. If she ever saw him again.

On her way out of the bathroom, Karen checked the test again, irrationally believing that the results had changed, only to find they remained the same. She was still pregnant, thrilled to be pregnant, and still lonely.

Karen retrieved her gown from the end of the bed but hesitated before slipping it on. Instead, she studied the two closets across the room, both seeming to sum up her relationship with Ash. Two people cohabitating in the same bedroom, two people from two different worlds practically living two separate lives.

She opened the door to the closet containing Ash's clothing that he'd had moved to the house after he took ownership. Several times she had surveyed his belongings but she'd never touched a thing. Tonight she gave into an urge she didn't understand and ran a hand along the row of suits and shirts. She came upon one hanger that held a long white linen robe with metallic gold trim interspersed with burgundy. An official-looking Arabian robe. She'd never seen him wear it, yet she could imagine it on Ash, imagine him looking regal and stately and incredibly handsome.

Like some lonely wife dressing in her absent husband's oxford shirt, Karen took the robe from its hanger, dropped the towel secured around her and slipped it on over her naked body. The fabric felt somewhat scratchy against her skin and it was much too long in the sleeve and hem. Still, she had no desire to remove the garment or to take away the lingering scent that was so unique to Ash. Wearing it made her feel closer to him somehow even though miles separated them, both physically and emotionally.

"Do you find my *djellabah* satisfactory?"

Caught. It was Karen's only thought when she heard the compelling voice coming from behind her.

She was still caught—caught between wanting to slink underneath the hanging clothes to hide out with the shoes, and needing to make sure she wasn't dreaming.

She chose the latter and turned to find Ash standing in the open bedroom door, looking dark and intense and beautiful. But he wasn't smiling. In fact, he looked almost angry. Then she noticed a box in his hand—the packaging for the pregnancy test she had so carelessly discarded atop the vanity instead of in the trash where it belonged.

Her gaze zipped from the box to his intense eyes full of questions. "I didn't know you'd come in."

"I am most definitely here and have been since early this afternoon."

"Where were you?"

"On the second floor in a room that I have set up as an office. The equipment was delivered today while you were at work."

She had prepared her dinner and taken a shower totally clueless. And he hadn't even bothered to make his presence known. "Did you not hear me come in?"

"I was aware of your arrival."

"And you didn't tell me?"

He raised the all but forgotten box. "Is there something you perhaps would like to tell me?"

Karen hugged her arms around her waist, suddenly chilled. "The rabbit kicked the bucket."

"The rabbit?"

She couldn't suppress her joy that came out in a smile. "I'm pregnant."

Karen waited for his reaction, waited for a grin, for a hug, for him to speak. He only stood there, silent and sullen.

"Aren't you going to say something?" Karen asked, unable to wait any longer to know what he was thinking.

"I'm pleased."

Pleased? He was simply pleased? Her smile disappeared. "Great. I'm thrilled. In fact, this is the most wonderful day of my life." Until he showed up with his lukewarm response to a life-altering occurrence.

For a moment he looked as though he might step forward, maybe even to hold her, something she desperately wanted at that moment. Instead, he said, ''I have some business to attend to. I'll be upstairs.''

He turned and walked away, leaving Karen alone wearing his robe and feeling as if she had just been dealt a severe blow to her heart. She told herself that his apathy was probably due to shock. Or maybe he was even a little afraid, same as her.

But Karen seriously doubted that anything would ever frighten Sheikh Ashraf ibn-Saalem.

Seven

Ash could not comprehend the fear that had almost consumed him over learning of Karen's pregnancy. He should be holding his wife, celebrating the impending birth of his child but instead he had escaped to the confines of his office.

Years ago he had learned that at certain times, detachment was required to remain focused. Tonight he could not begin to concentrate on work. He could only see Karen, the joy in her face when she'd announced the pregnancy. He could only consider how he had wanted to scoop her into his arms, kiss her into oblivion and take her to the bed in celebration.

Instead he had run from the worry that now that they had created a child, she might leave him much sooner despite the terms of their agreement. He had once been deserted by a woman whom he had loved with every thread of his being, only to face the sting of her betrayal when she had taken the money his own father had offered and left him without a glance.

Though he had survived, he had vowed to avoid repeating that mistake, pledged not to give in to those detrimental emotions, and for years he'd been successful. Until Karen.

What was it about her that had him doubting himself as a man? Regardless, he must consider his new wife. He must somehow convince her that what they had found together could lead to a solid future, if not a relationship formed by love. In order to do that, she deserved his utmost care and attention.

Ash shut down the computer and tossed aside the file folder to go in search of his bride. He found her in the master bedroom sitting on the edge of the mattress, a modest cotton nightgown covering her from neck to knees, a weathered and faded black book in her lap.

When she gazed up at him, Ash immediately noticed the tears. A strong surge of remorse, of protectiveness sent him forward, sent him to her side to wrap his arm around her delicate shoulder. "I am very sorry, Karen. You have obviously suffered from my disregard."

She swiped at her face with trembling fingers. "It's not only your reaction to the baby." She nodded toward the book. "It's this. My grandmother's journal. I was reading the part where she talks about bringing my father home after she stole him from the hospital, how she knew it was wrong."

Ash had heard the story from Daniel, had been told about the deaths of Karen's parents the year before, yet it had had little impact on him until now. "And she chose to keep a child that was not rightfully hers."

"Yes, but obviously she had a lot of guilt over that choice. That doesn't make it right, but I've forgiven her for it. I only wish I could have told her so before she died."

He brushed a lock of her hair away from her cheek, now dampened with tears. "You loved her greatly."

"With all of my heart."

"*Ílli faat maat,*" he said.

"What does that mean?"

"The past is dead. Let bygones be bygones." Such sage words coming from someone who had been unable to follow his own advice. He had never forgiven his father. Most likely he never would.

Karen drew in a ragged breath then released it slowly. "I had two wonderful grandparents and I couldn't have asked for a better mother or father. Now they're all gone and I can't even tell them about the baby."

Ash held her tighter, experiencing more regret over how he had treated her earlier. "I am here for you, Karen. I will be here for you and our child."

She gave him a pleading look. "Could you hold me for a little while?"

"I would most gladly do that."

When Karen tossed back the covers and beckoned him into the bed, Ash realized that he would soon undergo a definitive test of strength. He removed only his shirt and shoes, believing that to be the best in this circumstance. They settled into the bed, her back to his chest with his arms securely around her. He fought his body's demands, the urge to strip out of his slacks and briefs, the need to cup her breasts in his palms, to peel the gown from her body and set a course over her naked flesh with his hands and mouth. Yet he recognized that she needed only solace.

Her breathing soon sounded steady and her body relaxed against his. His desire was still present, and so were the emotions threatening to surface from a place he had successfully kept shielded for many, many years.

Assured she now slept, Ash lowered his hand to Karen's soft belly that held their unborn child. She had given him the promise of new life and the hope that his legacy would live on. She had given him more than he'd ever thought possible.

His resistance waned as the emotional armor began to dissolve and in that moment, Sheikh Ashraf ibn-Saalem who had strove to be bound to no one, indebted to no one, was in grave danger of giving his new wife a liberal share of his heart, only to risk that she, too, would leave him.

In order to prevent history from repeating itself, he would not pressure her for intimacy. He would provide only comfort for however long it took to convince her to trust him. He would have to be content knowing that she needed at least that much from him now. Perhaps one day she would need more.

Karen couldn't believe how good she had felt over the past week. Her energy level was better than she'd ever imagined it to be considering her doctor had told her that morning that she might feel sleepy at times. Truth be known, she'd had trouble sleeping even though she had spent her nights in the security of Ash's arms since his return, engaged in quiet conversation and nothing more.

She'd had the devil of a time convincing him to wear some kind of clothes to bed because he preferred to sleep in nothing at all, but he'd finally agreed to pajama bottoms although he'd refused to wear a shirt. And oddly enough, he'd seemed happy to only hold her. Many times she had almost given in to the urge to turn to him and ask him to make love to her, but she hadn't. In part her pride had prevented her from doing so, but her concerns over becoming too emotionally tied to him had kept her from acting on the impulse. Whatever the reasons, she had avoided any intimate contact, and she was frankly going nuts. Maybe she would be a total fool to invite his complete attention, to ask him to make love to her, but she was beginning not to care about the darned arrangement or the original terms. Especially tonight.

While she had been finishing up the dinner dishes, he'd joined her in the not-quite-renovated kitchen immediately following his shower, something that had become a part of their routine. But even with him dressed in a plain white T-shirt and a pair of equally plain pajama bottoms, her covered in a short navy silk robe and intentionally nothing else, the process seemed anything but routine.

Every innocent contact they'd made while completing the task had Karen's lively libido coming to attention. Every whiff of his shower-fresh scent made her want to climb all over him without reservation. Every word he uttered, be it about his work or hers, sounded like bedroom talk to her ears.

"How have you been feeling?" he asked as he dried the last remaining pan.

Like a wicked, wanton female. "I'm feeling really good. I did have a craving today."

He smiled. "And what would that be?"

"Don't laugh."

"I will try to refrain."

"Olives. Spanish olives. I was in the middle of the dining room at work and I wanted one. Actually, I wanted the whole jar."

Ash released a slight chuckle. "I would have to say that is an odd craving."

If he only knew what else she'd been craving, he might

not be so surprised by the olives. Karen wagged a suds-covered finger at him. "You said you wouldn't laugh."

"My apologies. I'm pleased to hear you've been well." His expression turned suddenly serious. "I am concerned that you are doing too much with your work at the gelateria and the renovations here."

She shrugged. "So far I have enough energy to handle it, so you don't have to worry."

"The new appliances should be arriving by the end of the week. At least this dishwashing will not be necessary. I also believe I should begin interviewing housekeepers."

Karen wanted to tell him that this activity wasn't so bad at all, especially since it provided the opportunity to spend more quality time with him at night, to know him better. She felt somewhat successful in that regard although he still retained a hint of mystery, enough to keep her guessing more often than not.

"I don't mind doing a few dishes," she said. "Besides, it's only the two of us. We really don't need a housekeeper."

"This is a large house, Karen. When the baby arrives, you'll not have much time to allow for upkeep."

She slipped the final dish into the drainer. "If you really think that's necessary, I suppose I wouldn't mind some help around here."

"I will begin the interview process as soon as possible."

She rested her damp hands on the edge of the sink. "I think I should be involved, too. I don't want just anybody coming into the house."

He raised a dark brow. "Do you not trust my judgment?"

"I'm not saying that. I'd just like to be a part of the

process.'' She grinned. ''Besides, what if I want to hire a houseboy?''

Ash looked as if he'd just swallowed something bitter. ''You would wish to have a man tending to the chores?''

''Sure. Why not? I mean, you're drying the dishes, aren't you? And you're handling it quite well, I might add.''

The sensual look he now gave her was downright deadly. ''I enjoy working with my hands, although I have never used them on dishes before now.''

Karen was more interested in having him use his hands on her. As if he'd read her mind, he tossed the dish towel aside, reached around her to put away the plate in a cabinet while bracing a palm on her hip and pressing his body into her back.

Karen bit her lip to keep from blurting out, I want you here and now, on the drop cloths covering the floor, on the island bar, up against the refrigerator, anything to keep the hormones happy. After all, that was exactly what this uncanny, uncontrollable desire for Ash's attention was all about. A raging case of pregnancy hormones. At least that sounded logical.

Ash closed the cabinet door above Karen's head while she pulled the stopper from the sink. She froze with her hands in the disappearing water when his palms came to rest on her shoulders. ''Exactly what services would you require of a houseboy?'' His tone held a touch of amusement.

She sent him a teasing grin over one shoulder. ''You know, mopping the floors, vacuuming and, of course, the occasional massage.''

He lightly kneaded the muscles at her nape. ''Do you not like my massages?''

She tipped her head forward to give him better access. "Oh, you do all right in that department."

"Only all right?"

"Okay, better than all right. Especially when you hit the right spot." As far as Karen was concerned, he wasn't anywhere near that spot. Not yet, but he would be if she had any say in the matter.

Ash moved his massage to her lower back. "Is this better?"

Without thought of the consequences, Karen pulled his hand around to her breast and leaned back against him. All that solid, strong, warm maleness effectively incited her cravings—the ones not involving food—as well as her determination to have what she knew he could give her. "I could use a little attention here."

He palmed her breasts, rubbing his thumbs across her nipples, effectively bringing every inch of her to attention. "Is this satisfactory?"

Oh, yes. "You're getting there."

"Where is it you wish me to be?" His warm breath fanned her neck, fueled the fire.

She guided his palm from her breast to immediately beneath her belly. "I need…"

"What is it you need, Karen?" His coarse whisper made her shiver, made her want.

She reached back and slid her fingertips through his damp hair. "I need you, Ash. I need to be with you in every way."

"What are you asking of me?"

He knew exactly what she was asking, but if he wanted to hear her say it, Karen could definitely do that. "I'm asking you to make love to me."

"Are you absolutely certain?"

"Yes."

He pulled her hair away from her shoulder and planted soft kisses along her neck. "Then perhaps we should retire to our bed."

The bed seemed somehow too intimate. If they made love here in the kitchen, Karen could convince herself it was only sex, not lovemaking. She could trick her head into thinking that she was driven only by basic, biological urges. Convincing her heart was another matter altogether.

She pressed against Ash, finding him already aroused. No real surprise there. "Forget about the bed. I don't want to wait."

"I would not want to harm you or our child."

She looked back at him. "My doctor said that making love is fine."

"You have seen a doctor?"

"Actually, this morning."

He clasped her shoulders, turned her around and studied her with fierce, dark eyes. "And you did not consider that I might wish to accompany you?"

Nothing like destroying the mood. "They had a last-minute cancellation so there really wasn't time to call you. I had to take it or wait another month. Besides, I knew you were busy and it was only the first of many."

He dropped his hands from her shoulders. "Exactly. It was the first. I should have been there. I would have made the time."

Karen had done everything for herself for so long, it hadn't occurred to her that something as simple as a doctor's appointment would mean so much to him. "Today was only a routine exam. Everything's fine. You can come with me next month. They might do a sonogram then and we'll have our first picture."

Ash strode from the kitchen and into the adjacent parlor without another word. Karen hurried to catch up to him, frustrated that he always seemed so determined to run away. She was determined not to let him this time. "Where are you going?"

"I am in need of some fresh air," he replied without slowing.

Once inside the bedroom, Ash threw open the French doors and walked onto the porch, stopping at the brick wall to stare at the harbor.

Karen came to his side while he stood white-knuckling the ledge as if he wanted to tear it apart with his bare hands. "So that's it, huh? I asked you to make love to me exactly as you said I would and now you're no longer interested?"

"Perhaps I'm not in the mood."

She let out a humorless laugh. "That's not what your mood indicator was telling me in the kitchen."

He kept his profile to her but she could still see his anger in the hard set of his jaw. "I cannot deny that I want you, but I also cannot deny that I am disappointed that you did not think to involve me today."

"I'm sorry, Ash." And she sincerely was. "I don't know what else I can say."

He sent her a brief glance before returning his attention to the glistening sea stretched out before them. "I would ask for your promise that you will consider me from this point forward when it comes to our child."

In any other instance, Karen might have argued he was being unreasonable. But right now she didn't want this night to end in bitter words and wounded feelings. She wanted to end it in his arms—a place where she could lose herself in a passion that defied common sense. "I promise. It won't happen again."

"Good."

Karen swallowed her pride and found it much easier going down than she'd expected. "Since that's settled, do you think maybe we could take up where we left off in the kitchen?"

Ash remained silent for a moment then pushed away from the wall. Karen's heart dropped to her bare feet when she assumed he was about to go back inside. Instead he came up behind her and folded his arms around her middle, pulling her back against him. "A remarkable view, do you not agree?"

Karen didn't care about the view. She didn't care about anything at the moment aside from making love with him. Although she felt secure and safe in his strong arms, she wanted more than security. She needed more than to be held. She was afraid to ask him again, afraid of his rejection.

She rested her arms loosely over his. "Yes, it's a nice view. Whoever built the house did a remarkable job with the layout."

"I've been told that the original owner was a sea captain," he said. "He was gone for months at a time while his wife waited for his return. I imagine she probably stood in this very spot, watching for his ship's arrival."

"A very romantic notion." Provided they cared about each other, Karen thought. How nice to consider that someone's love story had unfolded in the place where she and Ash now stood—two people whose future together was no more than a huge question mark beyond the present.

Ash slipped one hand immediately beneath the opening of her robe at her collarbone, keeping his other arm at her waist. "I can only imagine their reunion after spending such a lengthy time apart."

Karen could only imagine Ash's hand on her breast

again, but she decided to proceed with caution and allow him to take the lead, at least for now. "I'm sure the reunion must have been passionate. If neither one of them took lovers while they were separated."

"He would not be in need of another lover." He lowered his palm in small, tantalizing increments, until it came to rest immediately above her breast. "His wife would be all that he needed, and she would not be in need of another man."

"Then he must have been one incredible lover."

Finally Ash cupped her bare breast beneath the robe, causing Karen's breath to hitch hard in her chest. He thumbed her nipple slowly, gently. "Pleasing his wife would be of the utmost importance."

The conviction in Ash's tone caused Karen to shiver. "Do you think they made love in our bedroom?"

He rimmed the shell of her ear with his clever tongue. "Perhaps they never made it beyond this porch. Perhaps he lifted her skirts and undid his trousers and took her right here because he could not wait."

Karen felt the tug of the sash at her waist as well as the strong pull of desire. "I could understand his hurry." At the moment she wanted Ash to hurry but as usual he took his time, grazing his warm lips across her neck as he slowly opened her robe, allowing the cool ocean air to breeze over Karen's bare skin. The wisp of wind did nothing to alleviate the heat jetting through her entire body.

"I suppose had they chosen to make love here," he continued, "someone might have seen them."

"Maybe that's why they built this wall." Karen's voice sounded coarse with need as visions of Ash making love to her on the porch flickered in her hazy brain.

He planted his palm above her belly while he continued to fondle her breast with the other. "True, but the wall only offers so much privacy if one is standing. Any passing sailor would have seen what they were doing."

"Only if he had some high-powered binoculars, and I'm not sure they made those back then," Karen said, proud that she had come up with a solid argument at such a mindless time.

"But they most certainly have those now." He circled a fingertip around her navel, sending Karen's heart into a mad dash against her chest. "Perhaps someone is watching us."

She again nudged her bottom against Ash, hoping to encourage him, finding he didn't need any encouragement. "Are you saying we should continue this inside?"

"Only if you so desire."

She only desired him, longed for what he could give her. Here. Now. "Why should we? We're hidden enough. No sailor could tell what we're doing."

Ash skated his fingertips through the covering of curls between her legs. "He could most certainly tell."

Karen drew in another sharp breath as he made one slow pass over her flesh, then another, not quite hitting the mark. "How would he know?"

He began to ply her with gentle, breath-stealing strokes, this time directing his attention exactly where she needed it the most. "Even if he could not see what I'm doing, he would recognize it by your expression alone."

An almost guttural sound escaped Karen's lips as Ash worked his magic to appease the ache, as he continued to speak to her in a deep, hypnotic voice that caressed her as surely as his skilled hand. "He would know how I am touching you. He would envy me."

Ash effectively fed the firestorm in Karen with only a

few well-chosen words and well-placed caresses. When the wind picked up in intensity, so did Ash's stroking.

"Can you imagine what he is seeing in your face, Karen, knowing it's only moments before you give in?"

Karen closed her eyes, not yet wanting to let go of the pleasure. But she could do nothing, *nothing,* to stop it, when Ash whispered, "He would know, Karen. He would know the moment I made you—"

Karen rode surge after surge of a climax that hit her with a resounding fury. Her body trembled, her legs felt as if they might give way, but Ash was there, holding fast to her as she fought to recover her respiration. Ash brought her face back and dipped his head to kiss her, his tongue deftly advancing then withdrawing between her parted lips, reminding her that she still wanted more. She wanted it all.

She started to turn in his arms but he stopped her with a firm, "No," and an equally firm grasp on her shoulders.

He stepped back and Karen regarded him over one shoulder to find him twisting his shirt over his head. His beautiful, bare chest took on a copper glow as it reflected the last remnants of the sun. He snaked out of his pajama bottoms, revealing his complete arousal, and Karen was completely at his mercy.

He came back to her and nudged her legs apart with his palms. "Open for me, Karen."

She did as he asked without question yet she wasn't at all sure how this was going to work. He slipped her robe from her shoulders, bunched it between her and the wall and said, "Cross your arms on the ledge."

Again, she did as he asked and again she looked over her shoulder. "Ash, are you sure—"

"There are many ways to make love, Karen." She felt

the gentle nudge of his erection. "You only need to trust me."

Karen did trust him, trust that he would take good care of her, and she wasn't wrong to do so. He guided himself inside her then braced her hips with his palms, angling her away from the wall. Karen rested her forehead on her folded arms to absorb the sensations as Ash curled into her, filling her body completely, his chest so solid against her back, one arm folded around her middle, one hand drifting lower to touch her again. With her senses heightened to the surroundings, she was mildly aware of the sound of lazy waves lapping against the shore in the distance, Ash whispering lyrical words she didn't understand yet whose meaning became quite clear as he rocked against her, setting a calm cadence at first, then moving faster, deeper. So close, she thought as she moved in sync with Ash. So close, as if they were remarkably one body, completely in tune with each other.

All sounds gave way to Ash saying her name over and over as he continued to move inside her. After one long, deep thrust, Karen gave in to another floor-tilting release and Ash went taut against her with his own.

After a time, he pulled away, moved in front of her, leaned back against the wall and took her into his arms. She relished the feel of their damp, bare skin touching at every point, relished the strong beat of his heart against her cheek, the way he leisurely slid his fingertips up and down her spine. The way he took all her weight, a solid cushion against the wall that couldn't be too comfortable on his own back. Yet he continued to hold her as if that didn't matter, as if her comfort was all that mattered. As if *she* was all that mattered.

The sky had turned a mix of muted grays and pinks, and a few stars appeared on the horizon along with a sprinkling of lights around the harbor. The air had grown considerably colder, but Karen didn't care. As far as she was concerned, they could stay like this all night.

When Ash tensed, Karen glanced up to find he looked troubled. "What's wrong?"

He smoothed a hand through her hair. "I was much too rough in light of your condition."

She kissed his chin and gave him a reassuring smile. "I guarantee I bear no bruises."

"I should have been more considerate," he said. "I should be more careful with you."

"Ash, it's really okay. Junior is barely walnut-sized. When I get big and fat, then you might have to be more careful." She laughed from the joy of that thought. "Or maybe I'll have to be careful not to crush you."

Finally, he smiled. "Then I can assume we will enjoy more of these moments?"

How could she refuse? How could she give up what she'd found with him? She could take what he offered from a physical standpoint and simply remember to keep a firm grip on her emotions. At least she hoped she could. "If you're really, really good to me, I guess we can do this again. If not, I'm definitely hiring that houseboy. Or maybe even a sailor."

He lightly kissed her lips. "I plan to be very good to you. You will not require another man. But now you need to retire to bed."

Karen shrugged and grinned. "Fine by me. I have no objections to continuing this in the bedroom."

"You need to sleep."

Not that again. "I'm not at all sleepy. Besides, I need another bath with all this humidity, not to mention our recent activities."

His smile returned. "Are you registering a complaint about our activities?"

"Not at all. I just feel a little sticky."

He ran his hands along her bottom and tugged her fully against him. "You feel quite good, in my opinion. But a bath will most certainly help you relax. I will draw one for you."

Ash kissed her forehead, moved her aside then walked toward the bedroom with masculine grace, without hesitation, as always totally comfortable with his nudity. Karen, on the other hand, felt a little more inhibited now faced with the reality of the situation. She was standing naked on a deck at dusk. At least they didn't have any neighbors close by. Determined to remedy the situation, she grabbed her robe from where it had landed on the floor, slipped it on and bent to gather Ash's discarded clothes.

"Are you coming inside or do you wish to taunt the sailor some more?"

Karen straightened and saw Ash standing in the open doors to the bedroom, still naked, his arms folded across his broad chest. Another swift rush of heat spiraled through her, settling in intimate places that should be more than satisfied, but weren't, thanks to her husband standing there looking like some magazine centerfold.

She joined Ash inside the bedroom where she tossed his clothes onto the bed. "Do you want to take a bath with me?"

He looked mock-surprised. "What has become of my cautious wife?"

Gone from the premises. "Maybe she just can't get enough of her husband."

He stroked his whisker-shadowed jaw and grinned. "Ah. That could prove to be very interesting."

"I certainly hope so."

Karen took Ash's offered hand and followed him into the bathroom where he turned on the water in the tub. He removed her robe again, paused to kiss her again, before he helped her up the two steps and into the now-full bath. Instead of joining her, much to Karen's disappointment, he remained on the top step and told her, "I will see to your needs."

And he did, beginning with washing her hair, kneading her scalp with firm yet gentle strokes. He even managed to avoid getting too much water in her eyes while rinsing the shampoo away. After that, he squeezed a large dab of rose-scented shower gel in his palm and bathed her from forehead to toes, taking his time with his ministrations. Karen watched with growing interest and building desire as he lingered at her breasts then slipped his hand beneath the water to touch her again.

When Karen realized his intent, she said, "Ash, I've already... Twice, in fact."

"You will again."

"But I'm not sure I can again." She wasn't sure if she could take it if she could.

"Do not underestimate yourself, Karen." He caressed her with tempered, tender strokes. "Do not underestimate me."

Who could argue that? It was Karen's last thought when Ash began another sensual assault with his talented hands. He was so thorough with his touch, so smooth with his moves, slipping a finger inside her just as another orgasm claimed her with as much force as the others.

After the shock waves subsided, Karen stared at Ash in awe. She'd had three climaxes tonight. Three. Obviously she'd been saving them up, or maybe it was simply

Ash's skill. Ash, who looked mighty proud at the moment.

"Did I not tell you it would happen again?" he said.

His arrogance caused her to blurt out, "How do you know I wasn't faking it?"

"I would greatly question a man who could not discern pretend from reality."

Carl shoved his way into Karen's mind, not a welcome thought at all. "Believe me, those men do exist."

"In my opinion, that is total sacrilege, not knowing when you have pleased a woman or not." He bent his head and circled his tongue around one nipple, then the other.

Karen struggled to remain coherent. "Maybe some women are better at pretending."

He raised his head and frowned. "Trust me, I would know whether you were pretending."

Little did he know, she had been pretending—pretending that she didn't have feelings for him. And if she wasn't careful, Karen was afraid he would see right through that pretense. "Exactly how much experience have you had with other women?" Now why had she asked that at a time like this?

Ash nudged her legs farther apart with his palms, touched her again and darned if she wasn't excited again. "Whatever has happened in my past, in your past, does not matter," he said. "What happens between us does."

Karen couldn't take his absence in the tub any longer. She splashed water in his face, bringing about Ash's luminous grin. "You can either get in here with me now, or I'm getting out and we can initiate the new floor."

He looked down at the tile beneath his feet. "Far be it for me to argue since the floor would be less than comfortable."

Ash slid into the tub where they faced each other. After sinking into the water, he lifted Karen's leg over his thigh then slipped inside her.

She absorbed the taste and feel of his tongue as he kissed her, welcomed the absolute power of his body as he moved in perfect step with hers. Somehow he found an erogenous zone she didn't know she owned and she shattered again. He whispered her name as he reached his climax with a shudder and a sharp breath.

Karen felt weak, thoroughly satisfied and unequivocally lost. She wondered how this could feel so right. She wondered how she could even consider giving her heart to a man who was everything she'd been determined to avoid. A man who clung to his control as steadfastly as the Boston ivy clung to the trellis outside the window. How could she ever learn to accept that aspect of him when she had battled for her own independence time and again with Carl?

Carl was an overbearing guy-type who refused to see women as anything but a necessary commodity. Ash had an inherent tenderness beneath the steely facade. A tenderness he'd shown her at times, especially during lovemaking. But could she ever trust that he wouldn't try to keep her under his thumb?

Karen didn't want to think about that right now. She only wanted to lie in her husband's arms, cherish these wondrous moments.

After a time, she finally said, "That was exactly what I needed."

"Let us not forget your need for olives," Ash said with an endearing chuckle followed by another tender kiss. "I will buy you olives. I will buy you cases of olives, if that is what you desire. Whatever you wish from me, you only need ask."

Would she be wrong to one day ask him to love her? Would she be crazy to fall in love with him?

Crazy or not, it was only a matter of time, if it wasn't already too late.

Eight

"Are you Luke Barone's child?"

Karen pivoted on the sidewalk in front of Baronessa's entrance to find a black-clad elderly woman with thinning white hair and deep-set brown eyes glaring at her. She stood next to a dark blue sedan parked at the curb where a driver leaned back against the hood. Had it not been for that, Karen might have assumed the woman to be homeless.

"Luke was my father. I'm Karen Saalem. Who are you?"

The woman took a tentative step toward Karen. "It doesn't matter who I am, but one thing you must know. As a member of the Barone family, you, too, will be cursed."

Karen felt as if she'd been set down in the middle of some voodoo B movie. She might have been more wary if the woman hadn't been so frail and looked so harmless, except for her severe eyes. "Well, I don't really believe in curses so I guess I'll take my chances."

"You should believe," the crone warned. "You are no different from the rest. You'll be cursed to love a man who will never love you."

Karen had heard about all of the melodrama she could take. Through a false smile she said, "Have a nice day," then walked into the shop.

Daniel sat at the counter with a cup of coffee in hand, a smile to greet her. "Hey, if it's not the sheikh's wife."

Karen tossed her purse beneath the counter. "Actually, today it appears I'm a Barone and cursed."

Daniel inclined his head, looking confused. "Care to explain that?"

She nodded toward the window where the woman still stood. "Some strange lady stopped me outside and told me I'm cursed."

Daniel slipped from the barstool and peered out the windows. "What is she doing here?"

"I have no idea," Karen said. "I don't even know who she is."

Daniel reseated himself at the counter and took a long drink of coffee as if it were whiskey. "She's Lucia Conti and she's nothing but trouble."

Karen leaned on the counter. "You mean *that* Lucia Conti? The one who despises the entire Barone clan? Maria mentioned her to me when I first came to Boston but I guess I didn't realize she was still around."

"Yeah, she's still around. And she's been cursing the family since the thirties. The old Valentine's Day curse. Oddly enough, some strange things have happened on Valentine's Day, including your father's kidnapping."

Karen was too pragmatic to believe in curses and more

inclined to believe in coincidences. "Well, guess I'm officially a part of the family now."

She made the remark with a touch of humor but Karen couldn't disregard Lucia's words. Was she in love with a man who couldn't love her in return? Ash had never said he loved her last night, but then she hadn't told him either. Besides, curses were for fools. Love could be too, if one wasn't loved in return.

She turned her attention back to Daniel. "What are you doing here so early in the morning?"

"I have a couple of things I need to ask you."

Karen tied her apron around her waist and shoved a pencil behind her ear. "Shoot."

"The whole family is wondering about Maria. Since you two are so close, and since you were the last person to see her, I decided to ask if you know where she is."

Uh-oh. "She's taking a vacation."

Daniel appeared skeptical. "Without telling anyone? I find that kind of weird."

Karen wasn't sure how she should answer. She also wasn't sure why Daniel's voice had taken on a tinny quality, or why her vision had begun to blur and her limbs felt weighted. She was vaguely aware of Mimi standing behind her, of the door opening and someone coming inside, mildly cognizant of the fact that her legs felt like mush and in about two seconds they wouldn't be able to hold her as she began to wilt and fade like a week-old flower....

When Karen came to, she was on her back on the floor behind the counter, someone's coat propped under her neck. Daniel was crouched beside her and Mimi was hovering above her. "Call nine-one-one," Daniel said. "Then call her husband."

Karen gathered her strength and raised her head. "No!

I'm fine. It was just a dizzy spell. I haven't had any breakfast yet."

Mimi knelt and with Daniel's assistance helped Karen up into a sitting position. Karen was thankful that today she'd opted to wear slacks. Otherwise, her skirt would probably be around her neck about now.

"Are you sure you're okay?" Daniel asked with concern.

Karen still felt somewhat light-headed but much better than she had a few moments ago. "I'm okay." She glanced at Mimi. "Could you come with me into the restroom, Mimi? I need to splash some water on my face."

"No problem, missy. If you're sure you can walk."

"I won't know unless I try."

Mimi and Daniel helped her to her feet and she braced one hand on the counter. Once she was assured that everything was moderately okay, she took a baby step.

"I still think I should call a doctor," Daniel said.

"I'll call him in a little while. I'm sure I'll be fine as soon as I get something to eat."

With Mimi holding on to her arm and Daniel trailing behind them, Karen walked cautiously toward the restroom. At the door Daniel told her, "I'll be right outside if you need me."

"We'll be okay," Karen told him, hoping that were true. Should she faint again, Mimi was too small to catch her.

"Good thing I caught you," Mimi said as Karen stood over the sink, splashing water in her face.

She studied Mimi from the mirror's reflection. "You caught me?"

"Yes, right before you landed on the floor. So when is the baby due?"

Karen's pallor turned pink. "How did you know?"

Mimi patted Karen's back. "The fainting was my first clue but I guess you could say you have that glow about you."

After staring in the mirror at her disheveled hair and colorless lips, Karen decided she looked anything but glowing. "The baby's due in late May."

Mimi grinned. "Wonderful news! You know, I would've given my Johnny's favorite bowling ball to have a baby." Her sigh was wistful. "But we had each other."

Karen wiped her face with a towel, turned from the sink and leaned back against it. "You must have really loved each other."

"Very much." Mimi's mellow expression melted into a frown. "You, missy, need to take some time off. You're working too hard."

"But Maria would—"

"Rather walk across a blistering sidewalk barefoot than see something happen to you or your baby."

So would Karen. "I'll shorten my hours."

"I imagine your man will have something to say about that once he finds out about your spell."

Karen had no doubt he would, which was why she didn't intend to tell him. He would only worry and most likely insist that she quit her job. She wouldn't do that unless she was in danger of compromising the pregnancy. She would simply stay off her feet as much as possible, take several breaks and eat regular meals. "I'd prefer you not tell him."

Mimi clicked her tongue and shook her head. "Starting out your married life with secrets isn't a good thing at all."

True, Karen thought, but she was already keeping a

secret. A big secret. He had yet to know that she felt far more for him than only mere affection, despite the fact she didn't want to. "I'll think about what you're saying. In the meantime, let's get back to work. Veronica is probably rattled having to take care of the morning customers all by herself."

"She was that way the minute she walked in the door." Mimi drew Karen into a brief hug, taking both of them by surprise. "You be careful today. If you even begin to look the least bit shaky, I'm going to call your husband myself."

Karen had no doubt she would. "It's a deal. First I need to make a call to my doctor."

Mimi and Daniel stayed immediately outside the break room while Karen made the call to the doctor's office. She spoke with a nurse who assured Karen that it was, in fact, normal to have dizzy spells during pregnancy. She also told Karen that she would have the physician call her when he returned to see his afternoon patients.

After she hung up, Karen reentered the dining room and, at Mimi's insistence, took a seat by Daniel at the counter with a glass of milk and a cherry-filled pastry. While she nibbled on the roll, Daniel continued to stare at her.

She gave him a determined look. "I'm not going to fall off this stool, if that's what you're worried about."

He gave her his infamous grin. "You look like hell, Karen."

"Gee, thanks."

"Is your new husband wearing you out?"

She thought about the night before, their lovemaking. He was wearing her down, wearing her resistance down with every kiss, every touch. "Ash is fine, but I hope you won't tell him about this little incident."

"Don't you think he has a right to know? After all, he is your husband."

Yes, he was her husband, in name only—and a born protector who valued his control. Telling him that she'd fainted would only unearth that side of him. Things were going so well between them, she didn't dare upset the applecart. "Look, Daniel, if you must know, I'm pregnant. That's probably why I got a little dizzy. It's normal. I've promised Mimi I would take it easy."

He forked a hand through his brown hair and grinned. "I'll be damned. Congratulations. I'm not at all surprised Ash got you pregnant so quickly. He's pretty fast at everything he does."

Except for lovemaking, Karen thought. In that case, he was slow and easy in most instances. Again she recalled the night before on the porch, in the tub, the way he had loved every last inch of her so thoroughly. If she didn't quit thinking about that, she might faint again.

Karen concentrated on shredding the pastry to avoid Daniel's continued scrutiny. "How's Phoebe?"

"Phoebe is great. In fact, that's the other reason why I'm here. She wants us to have dinner together before we leave town again."

"I thought you just got back."

"We did, but we want to travel some, see the world. Phoebe likes a little adventure and I'm just the man to give it to her. Every day and every night."

No wonder Daniel and Ash were such good friends. They were both class-A rogues. After tossing aside the remnants of her pastry, Karen stood. She already felt much stronger.

"I hate to end our little visit, Daniel, but I have work to do."

"Okay," Daniel said as he stood beside her. "But promise me you'll take care of yourself, okay."

"Okay."

"And tell Ash about today. If you don't, I will."

Karen's mouth fell open. "You wouldn't dare."

Daniel took his jacket from the adjacent stool and slipped it on. "Yeah, I will. You're a Barone, and you're stubborn like the rest of us. You're also family and I don't want anything to happen to you because of an over-abundance of pride. Ash deserves a healthy, happy wife and child."

Karen recognized that there was a good deal of logic in her cousin's words, but she wasn't sure that informing Ash of today's events would help their situation. She also realized he deserved the truth. "Okay, I'll tell him."

"Great," Daniel said then headed out the door.

Karen decided that if she sugarcoated the situation, told Ash that she had been a little dizzy today, then she could get by without concerning him too much.

She would tell him tonight, when she returned home.

Ash waited in the den for Karen's return, nursing a quarter-full tumbler of scotch while attempting to maintain some semblance of calm. Considering what he had learned an hour before, it was all he could do not to down the entire bottle.

He had found out about Karen's troubles first through Daniel, who had extended a dinner invitation for the evening if "Karen was feeling up to it." Daniel had said no more other than Ash needed to ask his wife about something that had happened that morning. When he'd attempted to call Karen at Baronessa, Mimi had not been so discreet when she informed Ash that Karen had fainted. The waitress's assurances that no other episodes had occurred during the day had done nothing to quell Ash's concerns or his anger over Karen not bothering to call him immediately. Had he not learned that his bride was on her way, he would have gone to Baronessa's and insisted that she allow him to drive her home.

Ash had struggled with his own guilt over the possible role he had played in Karen's illness. Last night he had thought of nothing but his own desire to make love to her. She could very well have paid the price for his careless disregard of her condition.

From this point forward, he would implement the greatest of care, treat her in the way she deserved to be treated, even if that meant keeping his hands to himself until he was certain that lovemaking would not compromise Karen's health or their child's. A difficult prospect considering how much it had meant to have her ask him to make love to her, how much it had meant to hold her the way he had wanted since the day they had married, how much he'd begun to treasure each moment in her presence.

He battled his own wariness over the vulnerability she had begun to uncover within him. She was everything he desired in a woman, and everything he had feared when it came to matters of the heart. Yet when he heard the front door open, it took all his strength not to go to her and take her in his arms. Instead he forced himself to remain seated and struggled to keep his resolve intact.

Karen walked into the room and he immediately noticed the lack of color in her cheeks. "Hi, there." Her voice was as fragile as her smile.

Ash decided to maintain his composure and allow her the benefit of an explanation. "How was your day?"

She tossed her purse and keys onto the end table and collapsed onto the sofa. "Hectic."

"Nothing momentous occurred?"

She pulled her legs beneath her and rolled her neck on her shoulders. "Just the usual."

Ash took a long drink, leaned forward with his elbows braced on his knees and grasped the tumbler between his palms, his grip threatening to shatter the glass. "Fainting is a part of your normal routine?"

Karen straightened, her eyes wide with comprehension. "Did Daniel tell you?"

"No, not precisely. He did voice his concern over your health as well as his congratulations. Mimi, however, was quite frank."

She waved a hand in dismissal. "It was nothing. Only a dizzy spell."

Ash maintained a death grip on the glass while holding on to a thin thread of control. "I do not consider it to be nothing. You're doing too much. You're keeping insane hours at Baronessa then coming home to oversee the renovations. Your lack of sleep is also affecting your health as well as our child's."

"I've been getting plenty of sleep, with the exception of…" Her gaze wavered and a tinge of pink washed over her face. "Last night was an exception."

Last night was still fresh on Ash's mind, again feeding his guilt. "I am well aware that my behavior last evening could have contributed to your problems this morning."

She sighed. "Come on, Ash. We didn't engage in heavy calisthenics."

"We were careless. I was careless."

"You were very careful."

"Not on the porch."

"I told you, I'm not fragile. I also told Mimi that I needed to stay off my feet as much as possible. I can run the register while she and the staff wait on customers."

"And I told Mimi that you might not be returning to work for some time."

Karen bolted from the sofa. "You had no right to make that decision."

"What would you have me do? If you will not take care of yourself, then I most certainly will do it for you."

She clenched her hands at her sides. "I don't need a keeper."

Ash set his glass aside, rose and looked into her eyes. "Do you sincerely believe that your current schedule is benefiting our unborn child or you?"

She hesitated a moment before her anger appeared once more. "I wouldn't do anything, *anything,* to hurt this baby. It means everything to me!"

"Then you must stop and consider what is best." Ash decided that moderation in tone would be to his benefit. "You have much to do with the work on the house and the preparation for our child's arrival. Would it not be best to complete those tasks?"

"But Maria's gone and Mimi—"

"Assures me she can handle Baronessa. You can maintain communication by phone and supervise from here. I'm certain Maria would find that agreeable."

Karen lowered her eyes and rubbed a hand across her forehead. "I guess you're right. My doctor did mention that I might want to take it easy for a few days." Her gaze snapped back to his. "But after the restoration on the house is complete, I'll decide then whether to return to work."

"I respect your decision."

"And furthermore…" She frowned. "What did you say?"

"I said I respect your decision regarding your work.

However, I do hope that we can openly discuss your options when the time comes.''

A fleeting look of surprise passed over Karen's expression. ''Sure. I'm open to discussion. As long as you realize I can be pretty darned stubborn.''

''As I can be at times.''

A hint of a smile curled the corners of her full lips. ''Now why doesn't that surprise me?''

Right then Ash wanted nothing more than to hold her, yet he doubted the wisdom in that, doubted he would be satisfied with only an innocent embrace. Considering Karen's current problems, he would be wise to temper his need for her, even if it meant he would have to eventually sleep on the sofa. ''Daniel has invited us to join him and his new wife for dinner, if you are feeling well enough to do so.''

She tipped up her chin in determination. ''I'm feeling fine, thank you. I do need to take a quick bath first.''

He was immediately thrust back to their shared bath, their shared bodies. ''We are to meet them in an hour so you have time.''

''Good.''

Ash felt his control faltering with every remembrance of the night before. Felt his body stir to life. ''Do you need any assistance, should you become dizzy again?''

''I haven't been dizzy since this morning.'' Her smile was now in full bloom. ''And if you *help* me with my bath, we'll never be ready in an hour.''

With that she walked away, leaving Ash alone with the realization that in all of his years, he had never met anyone quite like Karen—a self-assured woman whose determination matched his own, whose sensuality and inner beauty drew him beyond desire. And in all of his years of learning, he had never been taught candid expression of his emotions. Yet there had been a time when he had given his all, bared his soul and left his heart open.

Perhaps it was time to face his fears and risk learning to feel again, for both his sake and his wife's. But if he chose that path, how would he deal with Karen's departure after their child's birth? If luck prevailed, he would never have to face that. He would simply have to try harder to convince Karen to stay, even if that meant opening old wounds.

Karen was determined to have a good time, not an easy feat when she watched Daniel and Phoebe from across the dinner table, watched the way Daniel softly stroked Phoebe's shoulder, occasionally touching her blond hair and hanging on her every word. Despite her jaded perspective, Karen found herself longing to have the same relationship, that same obvious, unconditional love. If only she could believe that that might happen with her husband.

At the moment she felt less than optimistic. Ash had his arm resting casually over her chair, but he'd failed to touch her. He'd barely spoken to her other than to ask her what she wished for dinner. At least he hadn't ordered for her, allowing her that much freedom. He hadn't scolded her, either, when she'd picked at her salmon and relinquished her plate to the waiter before finishing half the meal.

Logically, she understood Ash's concerns and she agreed that taking some time off would be good for her and the baby. But logic didn't come into play when her fears of being stripped of making her own decisions haunted her, or the fact that she was bordering on a love for him that seemed so completely unwise.

She regretted that she wanted him in her bed, wanted

him in her life despite the lack of wisdom in those wishes. Maybe the time would come when she'd be ready to make a commitment. And maybe he would tell her that she was wrong to expect more from him than his role as the father of her child. Was she willing to take that risk?

"Do you know about our cousin, Reese?"

Daniel's query interrupted Karen's musings, drawing her back into the conversation. She searched what remained of her brain. "Maria's brother?"

"Yeah," Daniel said. "One of Uncle Carlo's sons."

"I remember Maria mentioning him once. She said he's been gone for years."

"We saw him in Harwichport when we were on our honeymoon," Phoebe said. "No one in the family has seen him for a long time."

Daniel took a drink of wine. "You'd probably like him, Ash. He's used his trust fund to make a fortune as a day trader. Now he basically sails around the world in his schooner. I was surprised to see him back in the States."

"Considering the number of Barone cousins, I'm surprised I remembered his name," Karen said.

Phoebe laughed softly. "It's a large family. But the good thing is, you'll never be lacking in support."

Karen appreciated the support she'd received from both Daniel and Maria, yet at times she still felt alone. Or she had until Ash entered her life. "Why did Reese leave?"

"There was a scandal involving a woman," Daniel said. "A society deb who pinned her pregnancy on him. He refused to marry her even when Uncle Carlo and Aunt Moira insisted he do the right thing. As it turned out, the baby wasn't his after all. After that, he left and he hasn't been back. I think he felt somewhat betrayed by his parents' mistrust.''

"I can certainly understand how that might drive a son from his parents' home," Ash said.

Karen was more than curious about the conviction mixed with anger in Ash's tone, but before she could ask him to elaborate, Daniel said, "Enough about the family. Let's toast the soon-to-be new addition."

Phoebe and Daniel raised their glasses of wine while Ash and Karen hoisted their water goblets. Ash had turned down any alcoholic beverages in deference to her condition, something Karen very much appreciated.

When they touched their glasses together, Daniel said, "To Ash and Karen and their baby to be."

"I was thrilled when Daniel told me you're pregnant, Karen," Phoebe said.

Ash touched Karen's face with a reverence she'd never before experienced. "And I am happy my wife has honored me with a child."

"To new life," Phoebe said then gave her smile to Daniel. "And to love."

Overcome with emotion, Karen was unable to hold back the threat of tears. She excused herself from the table and said, "I'll be back in a minute. I need to freshen up."

Ash caught her hand and studied her with concern. "Are you not feeling well?"

"I'm okay. Really." But she wasn't.

Karen rushed away from the table, ran from all the love radiating from Daniel and Phoebe. And in many ways she was very much trying to escape her feelings for Sheikh Ashraf ibn-Saalem, but she feared she was already now, and forever, his captive.

Nine

After they arrived home, Karen went immediately into the bathroom to prepare for bed. Many times during the return drive, she'd sensed Ash had wanted to say something, yet he'd remained silent, almost brooding. She had no idea what had brought about his melancholy mood. She had no doubt what had provoked hers. Confusion, plain and simple. So much she needed to ask him, so many things she should tell him.

When she left the bathroom, she found Ash standing on the opposite side of the bed wearing only his pajama bottoms as well as a guarded expression. As Karen began to turn down the covers, he asked, "Would you prefer I sleep on the sofa?"

She paused with her hand on the sheet and stared at him. "Why would I want that?"

"I thought you might be more comfortable having the bed to yourself."

"It's a king-size bed, Ash. I barely know you're there." An out-and-out lie. She always knew when he was there, and when he wasn't.

"If you are certain."

She slipped beneath the sheet and patted the space next to her. "I'm sure."

After Ash settled in, Karen snapped off the light. The room went completely dark except for the muted light filtering in from the sheers covering the French doors. As he always did, Ash settled her against him with her back to his front, his arms wrapped securely around her. Silence pervaded and so did the questions whirling around in Karen's mind.

"Ash, are you awake?"

"Yes."

"Why do you think that two people as different as Phoebe and Daniel fall in love?"

"I suppose for some it's not a choice."

"Have you ever been in love?" When he didn't immediately answer, Karen added, "I'm sorry. It's really none of my bus—"

"Once."

The word echoed in the darkened bedroom. "Oh" was all Karen could think to say. She didn't want to push him but at least she now had hope that he was capable of loving someone.

"I was very young, and very foolish," he continued, surprisingly without Karen's prodding. "She was considered a commoner and my father disapproved. I had been willing to give up my title and inheritance for her, but instead she took the money that my father offered and walked away."

Karen could tell by his tone that the admission was costing him. "I'm sure that hurt quite a bit."

"I survived," he said. "I left my father's business immediately after that. We haven't spoken since."

"And how long ago was that?"

"Fifteen years."

Fifteen years? "What about your mother?"

"She died when I was in my teens."

It suddenly dawned on Karen that Ash had lived most of his adult life without his family. At least she'd had the good fortune to have hers around much longer. "Don't you ever think about making amends with your father?"

"No. His only concern is his wealth, his title. But I assure you that I will not treat our child with such disregard."

Karen trusted Ash would treat their child with great care. "I still think you should try to talk to him. I mean, regardless of what he's done, I'm sure he still loves you. After all, you're his son."

"He has no real concept of love. I, too, have come to realize that it is better not to put too much stock on those emotions. I have preferred to live my life through logic."

Karen's hope began to fade, replaced by her own need for self-protection. "I guess love isn't all it's cracked up to be. Who needs it, right?" She did.

At first Karen thought she'd only imagined the sudden change in Ash when his hold seemed to loosen around her. But when he unexpectedly rolled onto his back, away from her, she knew she wasn't imagining it at all.

"Did you love him?" he asked.

"My father?"

"Your ex-fiancé."

Karen thought she had at one time but obviously she'd been mistaken. She'd never entertained the same feelings for Carl that she now had for Ash. Feelings she had best put aside. "I think my relationship with him had as much to do with convenience as caring, although I did believe I cared for him at one time. We lived in a small town with few prospects and at the time I thought he was offering a good deal. But when I finally realized he wanted to own me, I backed out.''

''In what way did he try to own you?''

''I wanted to open my own design business and he preferred that I stay home and be a rancher's wife. I couldn't live with a man who ignored my dreams.''

Another stretch of silence suspended the conversation until Ash finally asked, ''What dreams do you have, Karen?''

At least he had bothered to ask. Carl never had. ''I want to have a happy, healthy child.'' *I want you to love me.* The thought vaulted into Karen's brain and only then did she realize how much she wanted his love. But if Ash had closed himself off to the possibility, chances were that wasn't going to happen.

''How about you?'' she asked, trying not to sound too dejected. ''What dreams do you have?''

''I prefer to think of them as goals, not dreams. Many I have already obtained in business. I hope to provide a stable home for our child, with two parents who work together to make certain that happens.''

The response was almost void of emotion, and Karen's hope died completely. He hadn't said he wanted more than a partnership. He hadn't even hinted at love.

Karen rested one arm over her eyes and tried to fight back the tears for the second time tonight. Then to her surprise, Ash picked up her hand resting at her side and twined his fingers with hers. He lifted it to his lips for a gentle kiss then said, ''May you have pleasant dreams tonight, Karen.''

She wouldn't, that much she knew, because the dream

of having a real marriage, something she had never thought to consider when he had entered her life, was starting to disappear.

"Are you Karen Saalem?"

For the second time in as many days, Karen again confronted a stranger only this time the stranger stood at her front door and happened to be a man. A tall, lean man, strikingly handsome with shocking blue eyes that contrasted with his dark hair. He wore a tailored navy suit and a stoic expression that said he meant business. Since Karen didn't recognize him, she automatically assumed he was there to see Ash. But Ash had left that morning for a few appointments, so the guy was out of luck. After Ash's declarations last night, Karen feared so was she.

"If you're looking for my husband, he's not available at the moment."

"I'm here to see you."

Karen frowned. "Okay. And you are?"

"Steven Conti."

Great. Just what Karen needed this morning—Maria's lover on her doorstep probably armed with questions she wasn't prepared to answer. She gave him a polite smile instead of offering her hand. He didn't look as if he was in the mood for pleasantries. "What can I do for you?"

He rubbed his neck with one palm and released a harsh, weary sigh. "I need to speak with you about Maria."

As she'd suspected. Karen considered telling him she was busy but decided there wasn't any use putting off the inevitable. Besides, he looked as if he could use a good listener, and that was all she intended to do—listen.

Karen stepped aside and gestured toward the foyer. "Come in." After leading him into the living room, she pulled the drop cloth from the sofa and said, "Have a seat."

"I don't want to sit," he said. "I want to know where Maria is."

She faced him and wrung her hands. "Maria is on vacation."

"I don't believe it. I suspect her family found out about our relationship and sent her away to prevent us from being together."

At least Karen could tell him this much. "That's not true, Steven. Maria left of her own accord."

"Then you know where she is."

She hated that she had to withhold the truth, considering his obvious distress. But her vow of secrecy to Maria took precedence over his problems. "I promise she's safe. She needed some time to think things through. That's all."

"I have to know where she is. I have to talk to her."

"I can't tell you that. I promised Maria I wouldn't."

He forked his fingers through his dark hair and pinned Karen with angry eyes. "What about me? Do you think it's fair that she left me only a note without any explanation other than she needed time away?"

The abject pain in his voice cut Karen's heart to the quick. "It doesn't matter what I think. I have to respect Maria's wishes."

"Whether you tell me or not, I'm going to find her, no matter how long it takes. But you could make it easier on me by telling me where she is now."

"I wish I could, but I can't."

Steven clasped Karen's arms and she saw up close and personal the extent of his anguish. "I'm asking you to please reconsider. I'm asking you to have some compassion."

"And I am asking you to unhand my wife."

Steven dropped his hands and they both turned to see Ash standing in the den's entrance, his arms folded across his chest. Dressed in a suit and the traditional *kaffiyeh*, he looked formally businesslike, except for the menacing glare aimed at both Karen and Steven.

Steven put up his hands, palms forward. "Look, I don't want to cause any trouble here. I have enough of my own." He pulled a card from his jacket pocket and handed it to Karen. "Call me if you change your mind."

Steven brushed past Ash on his way out of the room, muttering "Sorry" and leaving Karen alone to face Ash's anger, and her own.

When she heard the front door close, she turned that anger on Ash. "What was that all about?"

"I believe I should be asking that question. What is your relationship with that man?"

"It doesn't involve you."

He took a step forward. "I see a stranger with his hands on my wife and this does not involve me?"

Karen braced her hands on her hips. "Do you really think I'd let some stranger into the house?"

"If he's not a stranger, then who is he?"

She had no choice but to tell him. "Steven Conti, Maria's lover."

Ash didn't seem all that shocked by the revelation but he definitely seemed angry. "What did he want with you?"

"He wanted me to tell him Maria's location, which, of course, I couldn't because of my promise to Maria. So you can just calm down."

"How was I to know that he was not threatening you?"

Karen released a bark of a laugh. "If you hadn't been

so determined to jump to conclusions, you would have noticed that Steven is in a lot of pain. He's totally lost without Maria.''

Ash's features softened, but only slightly. ''I only know that I saw some strange man with his hands on my wife.''

''Well, now you know the truth.'' Karen tossed the card onto the end table and the drop cloth back over the sofa. ''I don't appreciate you storming in here like some superhero determined to come to my rescue.''

''When I came upon you, I could only consider that—'' He looked away. ''It does not matter.''

Karen experienced a sharp sense of awareness and a little nip of satisfaction. ''Were you jealous, Sheikh Saalem?''

His gaze zipped back to her. ''Jealousy is an imprudent emotion. My concern was with your safety.''

''I suppose you could be right. You didn't seem at all jealous the other night over the prospect that some sailor could be watching us make love.''

His eyes went dark as midnight. ''That was only fantasy, Karen. Had I known that some man had seen you naked, I would have been tempted to do him bodily harm.''

''Oh, really?'' She folded her arms and smiled. ''And you're not jealous? I suppose that would be beneath a strong, emotionless prince like yourself.''

He raked the *kaffiyeh* from his head and hurled it across the room. ''I reacted as a man, not as a prince.''

''A man who was concerned with his wife's safety, I know.'' Karen strolled to the club chair, sat and pulled her legs beneath her. ''Of course, any normal husband might be a little jealous considering that Steven Conti is a very attractive man. But since this marriage is in name only, I certainly understand why that wouldn't enter your mind."

Ash took a stalking step forward. "What do you want from me, Karen?"

"The truth."

"What truth?"

"That you wondered if maybe I had taken another lover, unlike the sea captain's devoted wife. That maybe you had some doubts that you haven't been giving me everything I need so I decided to turn to someone else."

He braced his hands on the chair's arms on either side of Karen. "Have you not found my attentions satisfactory?"

"You've been a very considerate lover."

"Considerate?" Ash leaned closer, only inches from her mouth. The tension hung thick between them, their eyes locked together and their bodies in close proximity. "Obviously I have failed if that is how you wish to describe our lovemaking. Perhaps I should endeavor to prove to you that I am capable of more than consideration."

Karen knew all too well that if she threw down the proverbial gauntlet, Ash would be more than willing to take it up. Maybe there wasn't much wisdom in that considering what he'd told her last night, but she couldn't deny that she still wanted him in a very elemental way, even if she couldn't have his love. "Go ahead, prove it."

He pushed away from the chair. "I would be glad to prove it if I were assured you were feeling up to it."

Karen glanced at his now distended fly. "Obviously you are quite *up* to it."

"My current condition does not take precedence over yours."

She sent him a challenging look. "I'm personally feeling quite well.'' She pulled the sweatshirt over her head and tossed it onto the floor, leaving her clad in a black lace bra and jeans. ''Do you care to find out for yourself how I'm feeling?''

Karen saw the indecision as well as the desire in his eyes, but he remained motionless. At least he hadn't run away.

After slowly lowering the zipper, she wriggled out of her jeans and dropped them on the floor to join her sweatshirt. She felt really, really wicked and very determined to get his attention through whatever means necessary. She decided she did have his attention when he visually followed the movement as she traced the lace band below her navel with a fingertip. ''Are you absolutely, positively sure you're not interested?''

Ash tore his jacket away and sent it sailing across the room, startling her. Karen wasn't surprised when he pulled her up into his arms, expecting him to carry her into the bedroom. She didn't expect him to seat her on the drop-cloth-covered sofa and yank her panties away. And she definitely wasn't prepared when he fell to his knees, parted her legs and began a sensual assault with his mouth.

With every pass of his soft, abrading tongue over her susceptible center, Karen felt as if she might fall into some carnal abyss, never to return. With every slide of his finger deep inside her, she came closer and closer to calling out from the sheer pleasure of it all. But she didn't dare stop him, nor could she halt the explosive climax that claimed her with steady waves of pure bliss.

Ash rose and stared down at her with eyes as intense as his intimate kiss. ''Was I *considerate* enough?''

Karen took a few moments to catch her breath. ''Oh, yes, very considerate.'' She came to her knees and tugged away his belt then lowered his zipper. "But it seems to me that you could use a little consideration, too."

After she freed him, Karen let go of her inhibitions and took him into her mouth. He molded her scalp with his large palms and let her explore his length with her lips, her tongue, but only for a short time before he framed her head in his hands and pulled her away.

"Enough."

She looked up at him with a grin. "Are you sure?"

"No." He joined her on the sofa in a rush and after kicking his slacks and briefs away he took her down onto the cushions and entered her with a deep thrust.

He kissed her thoroughly as he moved inside her in an erotic tempo. He fondled her breasts through the lace of her bra then suckled her through the fabric. It was as if they fed each other, consumed by a desire that knew no limits. As if the passion between them took on a life of its own and nothing could prevent it from taking control.

Ash braced his palms on either side of her and rose up on straightened arms, taking most of his weight from her. "Am I being considerate enough?"

"You're doing okay." But she wasn't at all okay. She ached for him, ached from a love that she hadn't welcomed at all. She tugged him back into her arms, against her sprinting heart, as the steady pace he had kept took an almost frantic turn.

Karen was vaguely aware of the sound of a truck's engine shutting down, the opening and closing of doors. Realization that the work crew had arrived only heightened the tension. "Hurry," she said in a harsh whisper.

He raised his head, his face showing the strain of his impending climax. "No."

"The workers are here and I unlocked the—"

Ash cut off her words with another electrifying kiss

and again Karen was lost, not caring who might find them, not caring about anything but Ash's powerful body and his remarkable stamina.

When she heard the back door open, Ash brought her legs around his waist, touched her again and she came completely apart. He buried his face in her neck and shuddered forcefully in her arms.

The sound of footsteps forced Karen back into reality. At least the louvered doors to the kitchen were closed, affording some privacy. She worked her way from beneath Ash, grabbed her jeans and sweatshirt from the floor but after a harried visual search couldn't find her underwear. Figuring some clothes were better than none, she yanked on her pants and shirt.

"Are you looking for these?"

Karen glanced up to find Ash dangling her black lace panties from one finger. She snatched them from his hand and stuffed them into her back pocket. "Get dressed," she hissed. "They're liable to come in here at any moment."

Ash looked over his shoulder toward the opening leading to the kitchen. "If they do not have the decency to knock, then my state of undress should not come as any surprise."

Karen almost smiled as she studied his state of undress, the now totally wrinkled tailored shirt covering him from the thighs up, his tie hanging askew, his dark, thick hair a total mess. He looked sexy as hell, but this was no time for Karen to stand and gawk at him.

She grabbed his pants and briefs from the floor and flung them at him. "Put these on. You might not be concerned with your reputation, but I have to work with these guys."

Ash complied, slowly rising from the sofa, taking his

sweet time putting his slacks back on. Karen adjusted her clothing, pulled a cloth band from her pocket and piled her hair into a ponytail.

Although they were now somewhat presentable, Karen assumed that if anyone happened to come into the room he would immediately know what had transpired only moments before by the guilt on her face.

Then the foolishness of what she had done bit into her. She'd given in to her own needs, his sensual lure, knowing what it would do to her emotionally. What it would continue to do to her if she kept allowing it to happen. She had to remember that this had nothing to do with love, at least on Ash's part. Had to remember that every time he made love to her, he staked a claim to another piece of her heart and soon there would be nothing left.

"This is not supposed to be this way between us," Karen muttered.

Ash paused from tucking his shirt into his waistband. "How is it supposed to be?"

"We said we were going to keep this relationship platonic."

"You said as much, Karen, not me. And what of the other night when you claimed we would share in more of these moments?"

"I've changed my mind." He had changed it when he'd told her he was incapable of loving again. "I shouldn't be asking you anymore."

He stepped forward and took her hands into his. "Yet you keep asking me. Am I wrong for answering you? Am I to be strong enough for us both?"

She had been wrong to start believing that maybe he was able to love her. Wrong to believe that more could exist between them beyond passion.

Karen pulled her hands from his. "You're right. It is

my fault. But our intimacy only complicates everything. It's important to me to stay in control of my life.''

"I have no intention of owning you, Karen, unlike your ex-fiancé. I only want to take care of you and our child.''

Again he'd failed to mention having any feelings for her. "I don't need to be protected." *I need your love.* "And this isn't just about my relationship with Carl. A few months ago my whole life was totally out of control. I can't let that happen again.''

"You continue to misjudge my motives. Everything I have done has been out of concern for your welfare.''

But not because of his love for her, Karen realized. "We need to remember that we both entered into this arrangement knowing it wouldn't be permanent.''

"So you believe,'' he murmured as he moved across the room, picked up his jacket and folded it over one arm. "Then perhaps we should begin acting as if that were the case. I cannot do that with you in my bed. I am not that strong.''

He turned and headed toward the exit, then faced her again, some unnamed emotion reflecting from his dark eyes. "I will arrange to have a bedroom suite delivered tomorrow. I will leave you with your celibacy. I will also expect you to leave me with mine.''

In other words, don't touch me, Karen thought. She felt as if she'd been pummeled about the head and heart even though she realized it would be best to keep her distance, physically and emotionally.

"Fine,'' she said with confidence, although she felt as if she were dying inside. "If you'd prefer to sleep in another room, I won't bother you.''

"I prefer that you—'' He looked away. "It does not

matter. You have already decided what will be.'' He spun
on his heels and walked away.

Karen laid her hand on her abdomen, the place that
sheltered her unborn child, trying to remember why she
had agreed to this arrangement in the first place. When
she and Ash parted ways, at least she would have her
baby. A baby that would bind them for years.

Had she made a mistake? No. Regardless of how desperately she hurt inside, she would never regret having
him in her life, having him as her baby's father. She
would probably always regret that she hadn't been strong
enough not to love him.

Later that evening, Karen climbed into bed, alone.
She'd spent most of the morning meeting with the con-
tractor and workers who were nearing completion on the
kitchen. Next they would move on to the nursery, as soon
as she selected the wall coverings from the samples she'd
obtained earlier in the week.

She wanted to include Ash in the process but since
their earlier encounter, he'd gone to his office and hadn't
come out except to grab a plate of food to take back
upstairs with him. Several times she'd stood outside his
office door, preparing to ask him if he'd like to be involved in the decorating decisions. But each time she'd
been poised to knock, pride made her pull away. He'd
said he didn't want to be bothered, and she needed to
respect that no matter how badly it hurt.

On the brink of a good cry, Karen decided she could
use something to distract her, a friendly voice. A friend.
Besides, she needed to tell Maria about Steven's surprise
visit. She also hadn't spoken to her cousin since she'd
called and told her about the baby several days ago and
her absence from work.

After snatching the phone from its cradle, Karen dialed the Calderones' number, hoping Maria might answer. She loved Louis and Magdalene, but both could talk the kernels off a corncob. Karen wasn't in the mood to answer any questions, and knowing the couple as she did, either one would sense something was terribly wrong, then she'd spend the evening playing twenty questions.

As luck would have it, Maria did answer on the second ring, "Calderone residence."

"So how are things in the great state of Montana?" She sounded falsely cheerful, even to her own ears.

"Karen! It's so great to hear your voice."

"Yours, too." Karen bit her lip to thwart a sob. "How are you feeling?"

"Pregnant," Maria said. "Lonely."

"I know the feeling."

"Uh-oh. You sound depressed."

"I'm a little blue."

"Want to talk about it?"

"That's partly why I'm calling, but first I wanted to tell you that Mimi has everything under control at Baronessa. I've been in touch with her by phone several times."

"As I told you before, Karen, I understand you need some time off. Mimi's been around a long time. She can handle things in our absence."

"I really appreciate that, Maria." Now for the hard part. "Second, I need to tell you something that involves your situation."

"The family knows where I am." Maria's voice held an edge of panic.

"Not the family. At least not that I'm aware of. But it could be only a matter of time before Steven does."

"How?"

"He paid me a visit, but I promise I told him nothing other than that you'd left by choice. He thought someone in the family found out about you two and shipped you off."

"Did he say anything else?"

"Only that he'd find you, no matter how long it takes."

Maria's dejected sigh filtered through the phone line. "I can't stop him if he tries. Maybe he'll give up before that happens."

"Are you sure you don't want him to find you?"

"I don't know what I want anymore. Don't get me wrong, the Calderones have been wonderful. I only thought that being here might help me sort things through but I'm still confused."

Karen could definitely relate. "I hope you get everything squared away soon. Steven is really hurting."

"I know. But I still have so much to consider."

"So do I. Obviously this confusion must be the result of a full moon or a family thing since I'm in the same boat."

"Then this mood of yours has to do with you and Ash."

"You could say that."

"You're in love with him, aren't you?"

Karen should be shocked by Maria's uncanny knack at reading her so well, but she wasn't. "Yes, like an idiot, I've totally fallen for him."

"That's wonderful, Karen." Maria sounded sincerely happy.

"No, it's not."

"Why?"

"Because he can never feel the same about me."

"He told you that?" Now Maria sounded shocked.

"Not in so many words, but he had a bad experience with another woman and he's decided he doesn't have any use for those emotions. Neither did I, until I met him."

"People do change, Karen."

"I'd love to believe that, but Ash is very set in his ways. And he's so infuriatingly protective where I'm concerned. You know how I feel about that."

"Yes, I know, and you need to stop and consider that maybe your history with Carl is coloring your judgment. Maybe Ash's feelings for you directly relate to him wanting to take care of you. You know how men can be. Voicing those feelings doesn't always come easily for them. My guess is that you're both too proud to come clean."

Could that be the case? Could Ash be fighting his feelings for her, too? That was almost unfathomable. "You could be right, but I'm too scared too hope."

"Love is a very scary business, Karen. Someone has to make the first move."

Meaning her, Karen decided. "I've really thought about telling him how I feel, but we had an argument this morning and he's angry with me. I basically told him that I didn't want any more intimacy between us. He hasn't spoken to me since."

"Oh, Karen. I know this is tough, but maybe you should choke down some of that Barone pride and let him know you've fallen in love with him. What's the worst thing that could happen?"

"He could reject me. I don't think I can take that."

"Are you sure he doesn't think you've rejected him?"

Karen had rejected Ash in many ways. Rejected his concern for her, rejected her feelings for him, or at least she'd tried—unsuccessfully. The tears began to roll down her cheeks in a steady stream, but she spoke around them with effort. "You're probably right, Maria. I just don't know what to do next."

"I'll tell you what you need to do. Go out tomorrow and buy a nice skimpy negligee and supplies for an intimate dinner for two, complete with candles. Make that meal, wear that gown, or nothing at all, then spill your guts."

Karen laughed through her tears. "Sounds like a plan. A good one."

"Of course it is. You have the opportunity to spend your life with the man you love. Some people never have that."

Feeling remorseful, Karen said, "I believe you could have that, too, Maria. With Steven."

"Don't worry about me. I only want you to make sure you don't squander the opportunity. As they say, nothing ventured, nothing gained."

That suddenly seemed to make perfect sense to Karen. She had taken a risk coming to Boston. If she hadn't, she would have missed out on knowing Maria and her new family. She would have missed out on a new life. She might never have the baby she'd always wanted, and she definitely never would have met Ash—a man who would definitely be worth the risk.

She would tell him everything tomorrow night, tell him that she loved him, tell him that she wanted to make the marriage work. And maybe, just maybe, she might find that he did have feelings for her, too. If not, then she would make an effort to convince him that life wasn't as worthwhile without having someone to love—and being loved in return.

Ten

After spending a restless night on the downstairs sofa, Ash awoke to find Karen gone. She had left without telling him where she was going, without leaving some kind of note as to when she might return. In an irrational, blind panic, he rushed into the bedroom, thankfully discovering that her belongings still remained. He called Baronessa but no one there had seen her or expected to see her. Last, he contacted the doctor's office to learn that she wasn't scheduled to come in for another month.

He then began to worry that she was searching for a new place to reside while he sat alone in his office, pondering how his pride and fear could have cost him the most important person in his life.

Yesterday he'd had the perfect opportunity to state his case. Instead, he had given in to a desire for Karen that knew no bounds. He had escaped before he had told her that a life without her would mean much less to him. But he'd also recalled their conversation two nights ago when she'd said she had no need for love, and then yesterday when she had told him she no longer wanted his attention.

Yet he wondered if perhaps she was afraid as well. He suspected she feared that he would try to control her life. In reality, she was very much in control of his. She commanded his every waking moment, his every thought, and now, though he had waged a battle against it, she had slipped past the barrier he had so carefully built around his emotions. He could no longer deny that he felt much more than fondness for Karen.

Ash refused to give up on their marriage. If she could not believe that he respected her individuality, her independence, everything she was as a woman, lover and friend, he would simply have to prove it.

He needed more time to think things through yet he did not have that luxury. He had a busy schedule beginning in less than an hour, two appointments involving important clients. What was more important, business or his wife?

His wife. A few months ago he would never have considered rearranging his agenda for anyone unless an absolute emergency had arisen. A few weeks ago, he had lived a desolate life, or so it now seemed. Now that he realized how very much he loved his wife.

As far as he was concerned, his current dilemma—finding some way to prove himself to Karen—definitely qualified as an emergency. He would cancel the appointments. He would find some means to demonstrate how much she meant to him, even if it took all day. Even if it took the rest of his life.

Even if he was forced to give Karen her freedom.

*   *   *

Karen returned from the market midafternoon with her arms full of groceries and her heart heavy with dread. She'd left early that morning before Ash had awakened, before she had to face him. She wasn't quite ready to do that yet.

After she slipped the roast into the oven, she went upstairs to make sure he wasn't home, although his car hadn't been in the drive. She knocked on his office door and when she didn't get a response opened it to find the room deserted. She walked back toward the stairs and noticed the door was open to the guest room at the end of the corridor. Odd since that particular room had remained closed off, awaiting renovations. Surely Ash wasn't hiding out in there. On the off chance he was, Karen headed down the hall to investigate.

She didn't find Ash in the room but she did find furniture, a stark bedroom suite made of pine with a lone dresser and a bare, queen-size mattress. Her heart took a dive when she realized Ash had done what he'd said he would do—prepared a place for himself to sleep, a place that didn't include her. But hadn't she told him that was fine?

It wasn't fine. Not in the least. She wanted him in her bed—*their* bed—and if her plan worked, maybe she would have him there tonight.

On that thought, she hurried down the stairs and practically sprinted through the living room where one worker stood on a ladder, applying molding to the ceiling.

Karen glanced up at him for only a second but it was enough to distract her from skirting the furniture moved helter-skelter about the room. Before she realized what was happening, her foot tangled in a drop cloth and she tumbled down to her knees. She rolled onto her back and a groan escaped her parted lips, more out of fear than the sharp, stinging pain in her ankle.

Closing her eyes tightly, she said a silent prayer for her unborn child as she laid a palm on her belly. At least she hadn't landed flat on her face. She didn't have any other pain aside from her ankle and hoped upon hope she hadn't done any real damage beyond a minor sprain. As she tried to sit up, a hand on her shoulder stopped her. She opened her eyes to the man who'd been on the ladder, an older gentleman with silver hair and a smile that reminded her of her father.

"Are you okay, lady?" he asked.

"I think so. I'm pregnant, so I'm a little worried."

He shook his head. "Sheesh, that's not good. Maybe I should take you to the hospital to get you checked out."

"I think you're right. I should probably go to the hospital. You'll find a number on the refrigerator beneath a magnet. It says 'Daniel and Phoebe.' If you call them, they'll come and take me."

"Are you sure? It wouldn't be a problem to drive you myself."

She didn't like the idea of getting in a car with a stranger, even one who seemed nice. But she did want to make certain everything was okay with the baby. "I appreciate your offer, but my cousin and his wife wouldn't mind taking me."

"Okay. If you're sure."

The man left for the kitchen while Karen hoped and prayed for Phoebe or Daniel to be home. Hoped that they hadn't changed their plans and left for their second honeymoon before next week. Her prayers were answered when the workman returned and reported that Phoebe was on her way.

Karen probably should call Ash on his cell phone but

more than likely he had it turned off, his usual practice while in a business meeting. She didn't want to leave a message on his voice mail saying she was en route to the hospital. It would be better if she reported to him after she was sure nothing was broken and the baby was fine. He would only worry himself sick. Still, she needed him more than ever now, needed his comfort, needed him to tell her it would all be okay. But if things didn't work out between them, she would again have to rely only on herself.

Ash tore into the house, not knowing at all what to expect. Daniel had left him a message on his voice mail stating that Karen had injured her ankle but was otherwise fine after a visit to the hospital emergency room. Ash wanted to believe that was the case. Yet he doubted Daniel would have told him if something was more seriously wrong with Karen or their child.

He strode into the living room to find Daniel seated on the sofa. "Where is she?"

Daniel rose and said, "Slow down there, Ash. She's in the bedroom with Phoebe. She's okay."

Ash clutched the paper bag in his fist, resisting the urge to tear it to shreds out of anger and frustration. "Why did she not call me?"

Daniel slipped his hands into his pockets. "You'll have to ask her, but I'm guessing she didn't want to worry you. Maybe she was afraid of your reaction. Considering you rushed in here like a raging bull, maybe she was justified."

"Of course I'm concerned. She's my wife. She's carrying my child. She's everything—" *To me.*

Daniel gave him a significant look. "It seems this little marriage arrangement between you two has taken a surprising turn." He paced in front of the sofa, occasionally glancing at Ash now and then. "Yeah, it looks as if the sheikh has finally met his match."

Ash didn't appreciate Daniel's goading though he recognized the truth in his friend's words. He had met his match in Karen. A perfect match. If only he could convince her of that.

Phoebe walked into the room carrying a tray containing a bowl and a half-full glass of milk. "Did an unexpected storm happen to come through the house? The slamming door rattled the walls."

Daniel presented a wry grin. "No storm, just the sheikh looking for his wife."

Phoebe nodded toward the corridor leading to the master suite. "She's tucked away in bed. I think she could use some company."

But would she want his company? Ash decided she was going to have it whether she wanted it or not. "Then she's doing well? The baby—"

"They're fine," Phoebe said. "It's only an ankle sprain, nothing broken, no other damage done. If fact, she's wide-awake and stir-crazy. She wanted to get out of bed and finish making dinner for you but I wouldn't let her."

Dinner? Was that to be the last meal before her departure? "I am very relieved to know she has limited injuries, and I'm very grateful to you both."

"No problem," Daniel said.

Phoebe stared toward the kitchen and halted then faced Ash again. "I can fix you a plate of food if you'd like. Karen made a very nice roast."

The last thing Ash desired was food. He needed to see about his wife. "That is not necessary. Please make yourself comfortable, or if you wish, you may return home now. I will handle the situation from here.''

Daniel's grin deepened. "I'm sure you'll handle everything fine. Just remember Karen has a bum ankle, so you're going to have to be careful while you're doing the handling."

"Daniel, behave," Phoebe scolded. "I'll just put this away, Ash, and then we'll get out of your hair."

Ash thanked the heavens for Phoebe's common sense. "Again, I'm in your debt."

Daniel offered his hand for a shake. "And believe me, I'll find a way to collect. I've been studying the markets—"

"You're incorrigible, Daniel Barone," Phoebe said with amusement as she walked into the kitchen.

"And you love me for it," Daniel called out to his wife.

"I suppose you wouldn't mind seeing yourselves out as I see to Karen." Ash normally wouldn't be such a poor host, especially in light of his friends' assistance, but he wasn't willing to wait another moment before he was at Karen's side.

"Go ahead," Daniel said. "I'm sure she's eager to see you, too."

If only that were true, Ash thought as he walked down the hallway toward the bedroom. He paused outside the door to gather his thoughts and muster his courage. Although he despised the thought of her being in pain, even if only a minor discomfort, perhaps the accident had bought him more time. She could not very well leave if she could not walk. At the moment he could probably use a miracle.

He slowly opened the door to find Karen reclining

against a pillow, and another one bolstering her ankle that had been wrapped like a turban.

When she looked up, Ash noted the surprise in her hazel eyes, perhaps even joy. Or perhaps he only wanted to see that so badly he was imagining its existence.

He set the paper bag on the dresser and approached the bed, pausing to look upon her injured ankle. "Is there much discomfort?"

"A little," she said. "I'm just thankful that I didn't do more damage. I was afraid…"

When tears welled in her eyes, Ash sat on the edge of the bed at her side. He wanted to hold her, to assure her that everything would be all right, that he would make certain of it, but he did not want to do anything that she would not welcome. He settled for taking her hand.

"I am sorry for not being here for you, Karen," he began. "I am also sorry that you felt you could not call me."

She wiped her free hand over her damp eyes. "That wasn't it. I didn't want to worry you until I knew everything was okay. That's why Daniel called you from the emergency room after the exam."

"Then everything is all right?" He needed her personal pledge, despite Daniel and Phoebe's assurances.

"Yes, everything is fine, as far as our baby is concerned." She studied their joined hands. "But everything isn't fine as far as we're concerned."

"You have decided to leave before our child's birth."

Her gaze came to rest on his, reflecting confusion. "Leave?"

"When I realized you'd left this morning without waking me, I assumed you were probably searching for a place to live."

"Ash, you assumed wrong. I went shopping. I'd

planned to have a nice dinner and, afterward, a chance for us to talk. To really talk. I have something I need to tell you.''

Ash experienced a momentary rush of relief then a good portion of concern when he considered that what she needed to tell him might not be what he wanted to hear. ''I have something that I need to say to you as well.''

Her hand tensed in his. ''Okay.''

''Perhaps you should go first,'' he said.

''No, you go first.''

''All right, I will.'' He brought her hand to his lips and kissed it softly. ''What I am about to say to you will probably be the most difficult message I have ever tried to convey, so I will ask for your patience.''

''I'm listening.''

He shifted on the bed to face her fully in an effort to gauge her reaction. ''For many years, I believed I had a satisfying existence. I had my business, my friends, my freedom, my title. But I did not have the very thing that makes one truly feel alive, until you came into my life.''

He touched her face and wiped away a tear with his thumb. ''You were everything I feared, a woman who had the means to tear away the wall I have built, unearthing emotions I have never welcomed. I saw it as a weakness, yet in you I have found a strength I never knew I possessed.''

He paused to say the words he had never thought to say again to any woman. ''You asked me once about my dreams, my wishes. You are all those things, Karen. You have made me whole again.''

Her tears came full force now, tearing at Ash's heart. ''Oh, God.''

He let go of her hand, believing he would be forced

to let her go as well. "I am sorry to cause you more pain, but this is how I feel. I respect your decision if you want to adhere to our original terms. If you still wish to leave, I will not stop you. I would rather spend my life alone than spend it with someone who is not with me of her own free will, even if I do love her with everything that I am."

She sniffed and brought his palm to rest against her cheek. "You're so wrong, Ash. I'm not having any pain, and I'm not going anywhere."

He frowned. "I do not understand."

"It's very simple, really. I've been the same as you, closing myself off out of fear of losing control of my life. But the truth is, with you I'm finally starting to feel that my life makes perfect sense. In other words, I love you, too."

She might as well have offered him the key to heaven considering the lightness in his heart. "You do?"

"Yes, and I've probably loved you since the moment I found you sitting naked in the hotel. Maybe even from that first moment you kissed me. I was too afraid to tell you. But I'm not afraid anymore."

He brushed a kiss across her lips, finding them warm and inviting. "It seems we have both been living in a house built on pride."

She wrapped her arms around his neck and pulled him closer. "Yes, we have, but I think it's time we tear that house down."

"As do I." He kissed her fully then, with the love he had fought so hard not to claim. He could not deny the fire the kiss incited within him, but he had to consider her current condition, and that he had more to offer beyond making love to her.

Pulling away, he said, "I have something for you. A special gift. Actually, three gifts."

"I don't know how you're going to top what you've already given me, a baby and a future."

"I would hope that you would allow me to try." He came to his feet and walked to the dresser to retrieve the bag he'd discarded upon entering the room.

When he returned to Karen's side, she eyed the sack with blatant curiosity. "Did you bring me a bagel? I've really been wanting a bagel."

He pulled the jar from the bag. "Olives. But I see you have changed cravings without my knowledge."

She laughed. "I still want the olives *and* the bagel."

"I will see to the bagels later." He set the jar on the nightstand and fished the key from his pocket then placed it in her hand. "And this is for you as well."

She held the key up to the light. "Did you buy another house?"

"Not a house. A building near Baronessa. I've purchased it for you."

"What would I need with a building?"

He reclaimed his seat on the bed. "You will probably need only part of the building; the remaining offices can be leased out. But I believe the bottom floor will suit your interior design establishment quite well. If it is not to your liking, then I will sell it and buy you another."

Her mouth dropped open and her eyes widened. "You've bought me my own business?"

"I have bought you the location. It will be up to you to develop it. With your permission, I would like to handle the financial aspects."

"Of course. Math is definitely not my thing. But I'm not sure I should even try this until after the baby is born. Maybe not until the baby's older."

"You will have access to many rooms. One you can prepare as an on-site nursery so you will have our child with you. If you so desire, we can hire an au pair, as long as you choose a female. I do not like the thought of my wife spending time with a houseboy.''

She pulled him into another embrace before pulling away to say, "I don't need a houseboy when I have you."

He stood again and reached deeper into his pocket to retrieve the final purchase. "I have saved the most important gift for last, to prove that you will always have me."

He handed Karen the gold band and she held it up much the same as she had the key. "Ash, I'm not sure about this one. It looks too big. Besides, I already have a ring. A beautiful ring."

"It is for me, Karen. A symbol that I am truly your husband and that this marriage is real in every sense. If that is how you wish it to be."

"That's the only way I want it to be." With another rush of tears, Karen lifted his hand and slipped the ring on his finger. She looked up at him with a love that he, too, felt soul-deep. "This means so very much to me. And you know what else I would like?"

"Anything."

She nodded toward the journal she kept at her bedside. "It took too many years for me to know my true heritage. Don't let that happen to our child. Forgive your father and ask him to be a part of our baby's life. Our lives."

So much she was asking of him, but for Karen he would put aside his past. "I will call him first thing in the morning, but I make no guarantees he will speak to me."

She pulled him back down beside her. "Maria told me recently that people change, Ash. She was right."

How well he knew. "You have most definitely changed me with your love."

Her eyes misted again. "We've changed each other, for the better. Which leads me to another bit of unfinished business."

She reached around him, opened the drawer in the nightstand and handed him a bundle of papers. "Here."

He unfolded the document, discovering it to be the original agreement they had signed prior to their wedding. "What do you wish me to do with these?"

"I want to rip them up in little pieces."

"I would like nothing better."

Yet before Ash could make even the slightest tear, Karen said, "Wait."

"You have changed your mind?"

"No." She worked her way off the bed, sliding her feet to the floor. "I want you to throw them into the ocean, and I want to watch."

"You should not be walking on your injured ankle."

She smiled. "I know that. You'll have to carry me."

"Gladly." After slipping the document into his pocket, he picked Karen up and carried her onto the porch.

When he set her on the wall's ledge, she said, "Hold on to me, Ash. The last thing I need is to take another fall."

Ash had taken his own fall into love with her, a fall he would never regret. He tightened his arms around her and softly kissed her lips. "You may rest assured that I will never let you go."

"And you may rest assured that I'm not going to let you let me go. You're stuck with me." To prove that fact, Karen took the papers from his shirt pocket and shredded them into tiny little pieces, tossing them over her shoulder the way her mother had tossed the salt when she'd spilled it from the shaker, for luck. Who needed luck in the presence of love?

After she was finished, Karen wiped her palms together then placed her hands on Ash's wide shoulders. "Now you know what else I need?"

"A bath?"

She grinned. "You're on the right track." She opened her robe and held it out like wings, letting the cold ocean breeze ride over her bare skin, her laughter floating out to sea along with all of her former fears of letting go.

"You are not playing fair," Ash said, his eyes darkened to the color of night. "My hands are not free."

Karen felt remarkably free, totally liberated. "You don't have to use your hands, you know."

"An astute observation." He rested his lips in the valley between her breasts, but before he could work his wonders on her, he lifted his head and met her gaze. "You know where this will lead. In light of your injury—"

"I feel great, so stop worrying." Karen framed his beautiful face in her palms. "Ash, I want to make love with you knowing that's what we're doing, really making love." She painted kisses over his cheek. "Besides, I'm sure a creative guy like yourself can manage it. After all, you've said there are many ways to make love. I want you to show me."

"I would be happy to show you, but I believe we best do so in our bed. As I recall, we have yet to make love there."

Karen thought a minute. "You know, you're right. In fact, we haven't made love in several places, including your office. That should be next on our list. Do you think your desk will work?"

Ash laughed then, a low, deep laugh that resounded

with joy. "I fear I may never be gainfully employed again."

"I fear you may be right."

When Ash hoisted Karen from the ledge, she wrapped her legs around his waist and her arms around his neck as he carried her inside.

Ash set Karen in the middle of the bed, removed her robe and panties and gingerly propped her leg back on the pillow. As he undressed, she looked at him with wonder, studying every detail as if seeing him for the first time. In many ways it was a first, loving him so openly. She felt so very glad that she had given herself to him, as he had given himself to her.

Once he'd removed all his clothing, he came to her and took one pillow to place underneath her knees and another beneath her hips, careful not to disturb her ailing foot. For the longest moment he simply stared into her eyes before touching his lips to her ankle then moving between her parted legs to do the same to her belly, where he paused to say, "Our child is a testament to our love."

Karen laid a hand on his dark hair. "I couldn't agree more."

He whisked his hands over her flushed body and invited her to do the same with his. They spent lingering moments only touching, caressing, learning the intimate territories as if they had all the time in the world.

After Ash sent Karen spiraling into pleasure with a sweep of his hand and again with his persuasive mouth, he slid inside her so gracefully, so tenderly that Karen wanted to cry. And she did, shedding joyful tears as she realized she would never again be alone. She had her baby and the man who had made it all possible. The man who had so effectively captured her heart.

After they lay spent in each other's arms, Karen felt completely connected to Ash, not only through their joined bodies, not only through the child they had made, but also through a love she had never imagined.

Ash laid his head against her breast and told her, "If there is anything I have failed to give you, you need only ask."

Karen took his palm and laid it against her abdomen. "You've given me this." Then she lifted his hand and placed it over his heart. "And this. What more could I need?"

He showed her his love through his perfect smile and another perfect kiss. "You will always have my love."

Karen trusted his words to be true. She finally trusted herself. And most important, she trusted him. The father of her child. Her lover and partner in life.

Her husband—in the sweetest, truest sense of the word.

*   *   *   *   *

BORN TO BE WILD
by
Anne Marie Winston

ANNE MARIE WINSTON

loves babies she can give back when they cry, animals in all shapes and sizes and just about anything that blooms. When she's not writing, she's chauffeuring children to various activities, trying *not* to eat chocolate or reading anything she can find. She will dance at the slightest provocation and weeds her gardens when she can't see the sun for the weeds any more. You can learn more about Anne Marie's novels by visiting her website at www.annemariewinston.com

To Kathleenest.
The bestest roommate ever.

Prologue

"She said *what?*" Twenty-one-year-old Reese Barone, seated in the parlor of his family home in Boston's Beacon Hill district, stared at his father in shock. "She's lying!"

"Eliza Mayhew says that she's pregnant and you are the father." Carlo Barone stood in front of the elaborate marble fireplace, hands clasped behind his back. He eyed his second-to-eldest son sternly. "Needless to say, your mother and I are very disappointed in you, Reese. Let's not make this more difficult than it already is."

"But I never—"

"Reese." His father's voice was colder than he'd ever heard it, even more so than the time Reese had been caught and disciplined for putting two baby goats in the headmaster's office on April Fools' Day. The fact that he hadn't taken into account their ten-

dency to eat everything in sight—and promptly re-
cycle it from the other end—had been a significant
problem. "There will be no discussion. You will do
the right thing and marry Miss Mayhew at the end of
the month."

"I—huh? I will not." Reese leaped to his feet,
nearly upsetting the elegant wing chair in which he'd
been sitting while he'd waited to find out what could
possibly have gotten his old man's drawers in such a
twist. "That baby isn't mine."

On the love seat facing them, his mother, Moira,
bowed her head as a sob escaped.

Carlo's face darkened with anger. "Haven't you
already done enough to damage our family name?"
he demanded. "First you get involved with that fisherman's daughter in Harwichport—"

"There's nothing wrong with Celia," Reese said
hotly, "except that she doesn't come with a pedi-
gree."

"It's not the lack of family connections," his
mother said. "I would hope you know us better than
that. It's just that… Oh, Reese, she's so young. And
she comes from a world that's very different from
yours—"

"Being of Portuguese descent doesn't make her
different."

But his mother ignored the rebuke. "How could
you ever expect to have anything in common?"

"Besides the obvious," put in his father. "Which,
might I point out, you appear to have in common with
other women, as well."

"I already told you," Reese said tightly, "I can't
be the father of Eliza's baby. I—"

"Enough!" Carlo made an angry gesture. "I will

OFFICIAL OPINION POLL

ANSWER 3 QUESTIONS AND WE'LL SEND YOU
2 FREE BOOKS AND A FREE GIFT!

0074823 ‖‖‖‖‖‖‖ ‖‖‖‖‖ ‖‖‖‖‖   FREE GIFT CLAIM # 3953

YOUR OPINION COUNTS!

Please tick TRUE or FALSE below to express your opinion about the following statements:

Q1 Do you believe in "true love"?

"TRUE LOVE HAPPENS ONLY ONCE IN A LIFETIME."
○ TRUE
○ FALSE

Q2 Do you think marriage has any value in today's world?

"YOU CAN BE TOTALLY COMMITTED TO SOMEONE WITHOUT BEING MARRIED."
○ TRUE
○ FALSE

Q3 What kind of books do you enjoy?

"A GREAT NOVEL MUST HAVE A HAPPY ENDING."
○ TRUE
○ FALSE

YES, I have scratched the area below.

Please send me the **2 FREE BOOKS** and **FREE GIFT** for which I qualify. I understand I am under no obligation to purchase any books, as explained on the back of this card.

DETACH AND POST CARD TODAY!

D4II

Mrs/Miss/Ms/Mr   Initials

BLOCK CAPITALS PLEASE

Surname

Address

Postcode

Visit us online at www.millsandboon.co.uk

The Reader Service™ — Here's how it works:

NO STAMP NEEDED!

THE READER SERVICE™
FREE BOOK OFFER
FREEPOST CN81
CROYDON
CR9 3WZ

NO STAMP
NECESSARY
IF POSTED IN
THE U.K. OR N.I.

If offer card is missing write to: The Reader Service, PO Box 676, Richmond, TW9 1WU

not tolerate lying. Miss Mayhew is the daughter of a family friend as well as a classmate of your sister's. How could you be so careless?''

"Has she had a paternity test done?'' Reese demanded. ''Maybe you'd better think about who's being careless.'' He could feel his temper slipping the tight leash he'd held, and the words spilled out. Even the pain in his father's eyes couldn't halt his tongue. ''Taking someone else's word without giving me a chance to defend myself? Fine.'' His eyes narrowed. ''I don't need this, Dad. I'm not marrying Lying Eliza and you can't make me.'' He strode toward the door to the hallway.

''Don't you dare walk away when I'm speaking to you!'' Reese had come by his temper honestly. Carlo stepped forward and reached for his son's arm, but Reese shoved him away in a red haze of anger.

''You ever put your hands on me again and I swear you'll be sorry,'' he snarled at his father. He barreled down the hall to the heavy front door, oblivious to his mother's frantic cries. As he slammed through the door and the thunderous sound of its closing echoed behind him, he swore one thing to himself: he would never set foot in the same room with his father again until he'd received an apology from the old man.

His chest was tight with pain and he blinked rapidly. No way, he told himself, *no way* was he ever going into that house again until his father apologized. He couldn't be the father of that baby—he'd never even slept with Eliza! But he hadn't been allowed the chance to explain. Hell, his father hadn't even given him the courtesy of pretending he might be innocent.

He was getting as fast and far away from Massa-

chusetts as he could on the first flight out. To hell
with finishing school. Who needed a degree from
Harvard, anyway? He was good with the stock market, had already managed to significantly increase the
million he'd inherited on his last birthday.

But...if he quit school, what would he do?

The answer came to him as easily as if the idea
had only been waiting for the question to be asked.
He'd dreamed of sailing around the world since he'd
been old enough to steer a boat.

Around the world! Oh, yeah, he was outta here.

As he jumped into his car and roared away from
his childhood home for the last time, he decided he'd
ask Celia daSilva to join him. Images of her naked
body glowing in the golden sunlight filled his head.
God, he loved her. They could even get married!

Then cold sanity kicked in. Celia wouldn't be eigh-
teen for over another month. Wouldn't his father just
love the chance to catch him with a minor! And he
knew Celia's father wasn't exactly thrilled that she
had been glued to Reese's side all summer.

Five more weeks...

He couldn't stick around that long. Anger continued to race through him. He could barely wait to get
out of town. Today. Besides, he knew Celia too well.
If he went to her now, she would try to talk him into
waiting until he was calmer, into talking with his father. And if that failed, she'd pester him to take her
along. The hell of it was, he wasn't sure he had the
willpower to resist her. Even if it landed him in jail
if they were caught.

He'd write to her. Write her and tell her what his
father had done, explain to her why he'd had to leave
so abruptly. She would understand. That was the one

thing he could count on. Celia always understood him. Yeah, he'd write. Ask her to come with him after her birthday...ask her to marry him.

His hands tightened on the wheel as he punched the accelerator of his sleek sports car against the floorboard. To hell with his old man. He didn't need anyone else as long as he had Celia.

One

Thirteen years later

"**H**ey, Celia! Guess what I heard?"

With an abstracted smile Celia Papaleo glanced up from the paperwork on permanent moorings. Thank God it was finally October. They'd reached that time of year when Harwichport residents could begin to breathe again after the tourists overran Cape Cod for the summer, flinging money and flouting rules and generally making the South Harwich harbormaster and everyone else who worked for her crazy.

"Roma." She raised her head and smiled at the petite woman in the bright red sweater who'd entered her office, sitting back in her chair. "What did you hear?"

Roma had been Celia's best friend since their elementary school days. She held a tiny girl in one arm and a toddler by the hand.

Celia rose and automatically reached for the infant, ignoring the sharp sting of pain that pierced her heart as she cuddled baby Irene close. How she'd loved holding Leo this way when he was a baby. Leo... He would have been five next week—

"Ceel?" Roma snapped her fingers, waving one hand in front of Celia's face.

Celia focused on her friend's concerned blue eyes, knowing Roma would worry. Pushing aside the grief that inevitably welled up, she made an effort to smile again.

"Sorry," she said. "I was just thinking how glad I am summer's over."

"Amen to that." Roma's voice held feeling although she still studied Celia too closely. "Adios, tourists."

"Those tourists put food on our tables," Celia felt compelled to point out.

"Yeah, but they're still a huge pain in the—"

"All right. I get your point." Celia chuckled. She gestured to Irene and little William, who was busy pushing a truck around the seat of one office chair with pudgy fingers. "So what's so important that you had to drag these two down here instead of just picking up the phone?"

"Oh!" Roma perked up. "Almost forgot. You'd better sit down," she warned darkly.

Celia's eyebrows rose. "Why?"

"Reese Barone docked over at Saquatucket Marina last night."

Reese Barone...Reese Barone...Reese Barone... The name echoed through her head, a blast from the

past she surely could have lived the rest of her life
without hearing. Her muscles tensed, her heart
skipped a beat. For a single crystalline instant, the
world froze. Then she forced herself to react.

"Wow." Her voice would be calm if it killed her.
"It's been years since he was here, hasn't it?"

Roma snorted. "You know darn well how long it's
been. He hasn't been back since he dumped you for
the pregnant deb."

"Technically, he didn't dump me for anyone. The
last I heard, he refused to marry her and took off for
good." She handed Irene back to Roma and picked
up the papers on her desk, aligning all the corners
with unnecessary care. "I doubt we'll see him here.
Saquatucket caters more to the yacht crowd than we
do."

"He might look you up."

Celia forced herself to laugh. "Roma, he probably
doesn't even remember me. We were kids."

"Kids? I think not." Roma cocked her head and
studied Celia until she blushed.

"Okay, we weren't kids. But we were really young.
My life has changed completely since those days and
I'm sure his has, too."

"Maybe." Roma didn't sound as if she believed it.
But then she shrugged. "I'm off to the grocery store.
I just have time for a quick run before I pick Blaine
up from kindergarten."

Celia nodded, although another arrow of pain shot
into her to nestle beside the first. Leo had been seven
months younger than Blaine, but because of his October birthday he would have been a year behind in
school. This would have been his last year at home
with her. *Don't go there, Celia. You're not an at-*

home mom anymore. You're not a mom, period. Or a wife. You're just the harbormaster now.

"See you." Roma corralled her younger son and blew a kiss at Celia before she swept out the door.

Celia could only be grateful that her friend hadn't perceived her pain. Leaning both elbows on her desk as she sank into her chair again, she pressed the palms of her hands hard against her eyes, refusing to shed the tears that wanted to spring free.

After two and a half years she didn't think of them as much now, Milo and Leo. Only a few times a day as opposed to a few times a minute. The agony had faded to a dull ache—except for momentary flare-ups like this one. Often, they were triggered by Roma's three children. She suspected her friend knew it, because Roma didn't bring them around as much as she once had.

But Celia refused to crawl into a hole and hide for the rest of her life, which was what she'd have to do to avoid seeing children. She loved Roma's kids and her husband, Greg. She'd lost her own family but that was no reason to cut Roma's out of her life. Still, sometimes it was hard. Just…so *hard.*

She turned her mind away from the thoughts because she couldn't stand them anymore. Lord, she couldn't believe Roma's news.

Reese. On the same small piece of land with her. She'd given up all hope of ever seeing him again years ago. But before that…before that, there had been a time when Reese Barone had been so much a part of her that she'd never even imagined she could have a life that didn't include him.

Reese. Her first love, the boy with whom she'd spent a carefree long-ago summer making love and

sailing every moment she wasn't working. Looking
back, it was easy to see that she would never have fit
into Reese Barone's world on a permanent basis. She
had been a fisherman's daughter, a motherless girl
who knew more about where the best stripers were
than she did about fashion or feminine pursuits. She'd
been seventeen to his twenty-one, a local Cape girl
who'd only ever been to Boston on a high school field
trip, inexperienced and easily won.

They couldn't have been more different. He was
the grandson of a Sicilian immigrant whose ambition
and drive had brought the Barone name both fortune
and fame. Second of eight children in a large and
loving family, Reese was born knowing how to make
money. Well-traveled, confident, he'd had no lack of
females vying for his attention. Why he'd been interested in her would always remain a mystery.

Reese. She'd heard rumors that he'd been disowned
by his family years ago. He'd gotten a girl pregnant
then refused to marry her. Had it been a girl like
Celia, she had little doubt his prominent, wealthy
family would have reacted with such ire. But the girl
supposedly was a debutante whose family was close
to the Barones, and his refusal to marry her had set
off a Barone family explosion the reverberations of
which had been heard clear up to the mid-Cape village of Harwichport where they made their summer
home.

Reese. Ridiculously, it still hurt to think of him.
Were his eyes still that beautiful shade of gray that
could turn as silver as a dime or as stormy as a rough
sea? Was his hair still long enough to blow in the
ocean breezes that filled the sails?

Don't be silly, Celia. You remember a fantasy.

Maybe her memory had embellished on eyes that were really quite ordinary. Maybe the hair had silver in it now. Maybe that lean, whipcord body had softened and filled out a little too much. Maybe—

It didn't matter. He'd sailed away without a word to her after the news of his impending fatherhood had trickled out to the Cape from Boston. She'd been left with the realization that she'd meant nothing more to him than a little convenient summer sex. The only good thing she'd had to cling to was that he hadn't gotten her pregnant.

Although…

There was a tiny, traitorous part of her that had regretted, for a very long time, that he hadn't. He wouldn't have stayed, but she'd have had a little piece of him to hold on to.

That part of her had softened when she'd married Milo and had melted completely away after she'd finally gotten pregnant and had Leo. She couldn't honestly say she'd forgotten Reese, but she hadn't entertained any more thoughts of ever seeing him again.

Well, it was probably a moot point. She briskly straightened her papers again, then reached for the phone. She had work to do.

Thirty minutes later, one of the young men who worked for her at the marina skidded to a halt just inside her office door. "Hey, Mrs. P.! You gotta check this out! There's an eighty-footer coming in. I swear it looks brand new!"

Celia rose from her desk, quickly pasting a semblance of a smile on her face as the kid babbled on about the incoming yacht. Most of the staff had worked for Milo before she'd taken over, and she hated for them to see her blue. Their spirits rose and fell right along with hers.

She went to the door eagerly, glad for the distraction. The kid was easily impressed, but if he was right, she wanted to see the yacht. The young worker said it was one of the newest models available—and one of the costliest. Extraordinary wealth was common in the area around the Cape but a brand-new yacht built to spec from any of the top makers was worth a close look. If only to drool over.

Walking to the door of the shack, she stepped out onto the pier, shading her eyes from the morning sun as she squinted southeast toward the opening of the small harbor. The sleek silhouette of a cruiser glided in and she watched as one of her staff directed its captain to a slip then waited until the boat was tied up. A man leaped from the deck of the yacht to the pier and conferred with the dock worker for a moment, and she saw the boy pointing her way.

The man came striding up the pier toward her. He was tall and rangy, with wide shoulders and a lean, easy movement to him that would make a woman look twice. His dark hair gleamed in the sunlight—

And her heart dropped into her stomach where it promptly began doing backflips. The man coming up the pier was Reese Barone.

She barely had time to recover, to gather her stunned sensibilities into some semblance of a professional attitude. Thank God Roma had warned her that he was in the area.

"Hello," she called as he drew near. "You need a temp mooring?"

"I do. I'd really like to get a slip at the dock if you have one available for short term." The voice was very deep and very masculine, shivering along her hypersensitive nerve endings like the whisper of a feather over flesh. He extended a hand. "Celia. Dare I hope that you remember me?"

"Reese." She cleared her throat as she took his hand, giving it one quick squeeze before sliding hers free and tucking it into the pocket of her windbreaker. Was it her imagination that made her feel as if her palm was tingling where their hands had met? "Welcome to South Harwich. It's been a long time." There. Nice and noncommittal.

"Thirteen years."

She couldn't look at him. "Something like that."

"Exactly like that." There was almost a thread of anger in his low tone, and it startled her into looking at him. Instantly, she was sorry. His eyes weren't nearly as ordinary as she'd hoped, but as extraordinary as she'd remembered. Thick, dark lashes framed irises of gray. At the moment they looked as dark and stormy as his voice sounded. Crackling energy seemed to radiate from him. What could *he* have to be mad about? He was the one who'd taken off without a word.

"Mrs. Papaleo?" Angie, her office assistant, stuck her head out the door. "Maintenance is on the phone."

Maintenance. She needed to take the call. She had to get the fourth piling replaced; it hadn't been the same since that boat crashed into it on the Fourth. Angie could help Reese. Twenty-two and supremely capable, Angie Dunstan had worked for the marina since before Milo had died. Angie could charm a bird from its tree—and she'd be delighted to entertain Reese. Let her deal with him.

"I have to go," she said to Reese. "Come on in the office and Angie can show you what's available."

"You're the harbormaster?" There was a definite note of skepticism in his voice.

"Yes." A small thrill of pride lifted her chin as she turned and headed back up the pier. But she couldn't ignore the sensations that tingled through her as she walked. She could almost *feel* him behind her.

Well, it didn't matter. He'd asked for temp space, which meant he'd be gone again in a few days.

"How long have you had the job?" he asked from behind her.

She didn't turn around or slow down. "Over two years."

"Somebody retire? I can't even remember who worked this marina."

She was at the door of the office by now, and she took a deep breath, turning to meet his eyes squarely. And just as it had in the old days, her stomach fluttered when those gray eyes gazed into hers. "My father-in-law was the harbormaster for years," she said quietly. "When he died, my husband got the job. Then the selectmen offered it to me after Milo passed away."

"I heard you were widowed."

She nodded. God, how she hated that word.

"I'm sorry."

She saw something move in his eyes and she looked away quickly. Compassion from Reese, of all people, would do her in. "Angie, how about putting Mr. Barone in the Margolies' slip along pier four. They won't be back until May and they gave us permission to rent it out on a temp basis." She gave a perfunctory nod of her head without meeting his eyes again. "Enjoy your stay."

Enjoy your stay.

That night, lying in the stateroom of his boat, Reese's teeth ground together at the memory of Celia's glib words. She'd blown him off as easily as she had thirteen years ago. No, he corrected himself, even more easily. Last time, she'd had her father do it.

Father. That led to thoughts of other things she'd said. Father-*in-law*. He knew, on an intellectual level, that time had passed. But he didn't feel any older. And Celia still looked much the same. It was hard to believe she'd married and buried a husband since he'd seen her last.

Had she had something going with the Papaleo guy that summer while she'd been with him? His memory of this marina was vague, since his family had always kept their crafts at Saquatucket, but he could dimly recall the wiry Greek fellow who'd kept things in order years ago. He had an even less reliable memory of the man's son, no more than another wiry figure, possibly taller than the older man.

No. If she'd cheated on him, he'd have known it. He'd been sure of Celia back in those days. She'd been his. All his.

He swore, gritting his teeth for an entirely different reason as his body reacted to the memories, and flipped onto his back.

Celia. God, she'd been so beautiful she'd taken his breath away. Today had been no different. How could that be? After thirteen years she shouldn't look so damned good. She was thirty—he knew she'd just had a birthday at the end of September.

The thought pulled him up short. Why did he still remember the birthdate of a woman he'd slept with years ago for one brief summer?

She was your fantasy.

Yes, indeed. She had been his fantasy. At an age when a young man was particularly impressionable, Celia had been lithe, warm, adoring and pliable. If he'd suggested it, she'd rarely opposed him. She truly had been every man's dream. But that was all she'd been, he assured himself. A dream.

A dream that had evaporated like the morning mist over the harbor once she'd heard the false rumor about him and that girl from Boston.

An old wave of bitterness welled up. He didn't often allow himself to think about the last words he and his father had exchanged all those years ago. To people who asked, he merely said he had no family.

And he didn't. He'd never opened nor answered the letters from his mother or his brothers and sisters, mostly because there was nothing to say. He hadn't done a damn thing wrong, and he had nothing to apologize for. Nick had been the most persistent. Reese bet he'd gotten fifteen letters from his big brother in those first five years or so. There were probably more out there floating around. He'd sailed from place to place so much there would have been no way to predict his movements or the places he might have chosen to dock.

On the other hand, he'd never received so much as a single line from his father. That was all it would have taken, too. One line. *I'm sorry.*

He exhaled heavily. Why in the hell was he thinking about that tonight? It was ancient history. He had a family of his own now, was a very different person than he'd been more than a decade ago.

The thought brought Amalie to mind and he smiled to himself. He'd never pictured himself as a father, and he certainly wouldn't recommend acquiring a child the way she'd come into his life, but he loved her dearly. If he could love a child who wasn't even biologically his so much, what would it be like to have a child of his own?

As if she'd been waiting for the chance, Celia sprang into his head again. He was more than mildly shocked when he realized that, subconsciously, he'd always pictured her in the role of his imaginary child's mother. Dammit! He was *not* going to waste any more time thinking about that faithless woman.

Throwing his legs over the side of his bunk, he yanked on a pair of ragged jeans and a sweatshirt and stomped through the rest of his living space to the stairs. On deck, he idly picked up a pair of binoculars and scanned the horizon. Nothing interesting, only one small fishing boat. A careless captain, too, he observed, running without lights.

Casually he swung the binoculars around to the shoreline. The area had been developed considerably since he'd been gone, as had the whole Cape and the rest of the Eastern seaboard. A lot of new houses, some right on the water. The only place that would still be undisturbed completely would be the Cape Cod National Seashore on the Outer Cape, but here along the Lower Cape he couldn't see that.

The quiet sound of a small, well-tuned motor reached his ears and he glanced back toward the south. The little boat he'd seen was coming in, still without lights. Then the motor cut out and he saw the flash of oars. Why would the guy kill his power before he reached the dock?

The quiet *plish* of the oars came nearer. The boat was close enough that he could now see it easily without the binoculars, then closer still, and he realized the guy intended to put in right here at the marina.

There appeared to be only one sailor aboard, and a small one at that. Probably a teenager flouting the rules, which would explain his cutting the motor early and trying to sneak in. The boy tied up his boat and caught a ladder one-handed, nimbly climbing to the dock while carrying a fishing cooler in his other hand.

Reese grasped the smooth mahogany rail of his boat and vaulted over the edge onto the dock. He walked toward the boy, intending to give him a rough education in proper night lighting, but just then the boy walked beneath one of the floodlights that illuminated the marina.

The ''boy'' was Celia daSilva. No, not daSilva. Papaleo.

''Celia!'' He didn't even stop to think. ''What the hell do you think you're doing? Of all the irresponsible, un—''

''Shh!'' He'd clearly startled her, but she recovered quickly. She ran toward him, making next to no noise in her practical dockside slip-ons. Before he could utter another syllable, she clapped one small hand over his mouth.

Reese wasn't a giant but he was a lot bigger than Celia, and the action brought her body perilously close to his. He could feel the heat of her, was enveloped in a smell so familiar it catapulted him instantly back in time to a day when he'd had the right to pull that small, lithe figure against him. His palms itched with the urge to do exactly that and he rubbed them against the sides of his jeans, trying to master the images that flooded his mind.

Her eyes were wide and dark, bled of any color in the deep shadow thrown by the angle at which she was standing. But he could see that she recognized the familiarity of their proximity almost as fast as he did.

"I can explain," she whispered, her voice a breath of sound. "Just don't make any more noise."

The words had barely left her mouth when a light snapped on aboard a nearby yacht. "Mrs. Papaleo? Is that you?"

It was a deep, slightly accented male voice. Reese felt the vibration as the man leaped onto the dock, much as he had a moment before, and walked toward them.

"Don't say *anything*," Celia warned. To his astonishment, her hand cupped his jaw, sliding along it so that her thumb almost grazed the corner of his lips. At the same time he felt her bump his hip with the cooler she still carried. He lifted his own hands automatically, curling his fingers around the handle, over hers and putting his other hand at her waist. A part of him registered the fact that the cooler felt a lot lighter than it should if it was full of fish. But a larger part of him was much more attentive to Celia's proximity, the way her soft hand felt curled under his and the way her palm cupped his jaw. Her hands were warm and he knew the slender body concealed beneath the wind shirt and jeans would be even warmer. Even softer.

She waited the barest instant until the man walking toward them couldn't help but see the intimate pose, then she slowly stepped away a pace, letting her hands slide off him as if reluctant to let him go despite the interruption.

"Hello, Mr. Tiello," she said. "It's me. This is, uh, an old friend. Reese Barone. Reese, Ernesto Tiello."

Reese stepped forward and extended his hand automatically, trying to ignore his racing pulse. What was she up to? She'd deliberately made it sound as if he were a very *good* old friend. "Nice to meet you."

"And you, sir." Tiello was a bulky fellow, probably ten years older than Reese himself, with a heavy accent that might indicate nonnative roots. The man looked from one to the other of them. "Were you out on the water?"

"Yes." Celia turned to face Tiello. Her free hand reached for and found Reese's and she intertwined their fingers. "A little night fishing. We used to do it all the time when we were young."

A gleam of amusement lit the dark eyes and Tiello smiled. "I see."

Reese felt his own lips twitch as he fought not to chuckle. Celia was going to be sorry she started this.

Another boat light along the dock snapped on. "I thought I heard your voice, Ernesto." The voice was feminine, smoky and suggestive. It instantly made a man wonder if the woman attached to it lived up to its promise.

Tiello's tanned features creased into what Reese assumed was a seductive smile. "It is, indeed, and I'm flattered that you thought of me, Claudette."

A form leaped from the deck of the yacht from which the light shone. Backlit by the brightness, the woman appeared tall and slender. Then she drew closer. She had blond hair caught in a thick braid that trailed over one shoulder so far that Reese knew if it was unbound her hair would reach her hips. Big blue eyes, a heart-shaped face and a slight cleft in her chin added even more interest to her pretty face, but the mouth changed it all. "Pretty" became "sexy as hell" at the first glimpse of those lips.

"Hello," she purred, extending her hand and favoring him with a brilliant smile that revealed small, perfect white teeth. "I'm Claudette Mason."

"Reese Barone." He repeated the ritual he'd just completed with Tiello, who was wearing a distinctly sulky look on his face.

"Did you just arrive?" Her gaze drifted over him. "I'm sure I would have noticed if you'd been here earlier."

"I docked a few hours ago." Celia's fingers had gone stiff and uncooperative in his; he glanced down at her but she was wearing an absolutely expressionless mask that would have served her well in a poker game.

"I hope you'll be here for a while. We could get to know each other." Claudette had yet to acknowledge Celia's presence, let alone the fact that he was holding her hand.

"Er, thanks," he said, "but I'll be occupied while I'm here." He dragged Celia's hand up with his to display their entwined fingers. "Celia and I haven't seen each other in a while and we have a lot to catch up on."

"Ah. I see." Claudette Mason made a moue of regret. Without even a pause, she turned back to

Tiello. "Could I interest you in a drink, Ernesto? Mr. Brevery has gone to Boston for the night."

The man's face brightened as if she'd brought him a gift. "I would be delighted," he said. He turned to Celia and Reese. "Very nice to meet you, Mr. Barone. Have a lovely evening, Mrs. Papaleo."

"Thank you. You do the same." Celia tugged discreetly at the hand he'd lowered, but he kept her fingers imprisoned in his. "Are you ready to go, Reese?"

As the other pair walked back down the dock toward the woman's yacht—the *Golden Glow,* he noted—he lifted a brow and looked down at Celia. "Sure." In a lower voice, he added, "But it might be nice if I knew where I was supposed to be going."

"You'll have to walk home with me." Celia sounded grumpy and grudging as they moved out of range of the other couple, and he felt his own surly mood creeping back over him. "I guess I owe you an explanation."

Reese nodded. "I guess." Sarcasm colored his tone as he allowed her to tow him along the dock toward the street.

"Thank you," she said curtly. "I appreciate you going along with my...my..."

"Deception?" he offered pleasantly. "Fabrication? How about lie?"

They were walking along the edge of the harbor now and as she turned onto a street away from the marina, Celia yanked her hand free. "There's a good reason." Her voice sounded defensive.

"I imagine so," he said, allowing the cutting edge in his voice to slice, "since I can't think of any reason you'd want to hold my hand after dumping me thirteen years ago.''

"*I* dumped *you?*" Celia stopped in her tracks. "Excuse me, but I seem to recall you being the one who dropped off the face of the earth." Then she started walking again, fast, and despite his superior size, he had to take large strides to catch up with her. "Why are we arguing? As you pointed out, it's ancient history. It doesn't matter anymore."

He could feel the anger slipping free of his control and he clamped down on it, gritting his teeth to prevent another retort. It made him remember gritting his teeth in a very similar manner—but for a very different reason—just a short while ago, and he pulled up a vivid mental image of himself smacking the heel of his hand against his forehead. *How stupid would I have to be,* he lectured himself, *to care about what happened when we were still practically kids?* He wasn't any more interested than she was in resurrecting their old relationship.

"No," he said softly, definitely. "It doesn't matter anymore."

They walked in awkward silence for a few hundred yards.

"Who's Mr. Brevery?" It was an abrupt change of topic but he wanted to show her how little he cared about the past.

Celia cleared her throat. "Claudette's employer. He's put up here every October for at least a half dozen years."

"And Tiello?"

Her mouth twisted. "Playboy. Too much money and too much time to waste. This is the third year he's visited us in the fall."

The same probably applied to him in her estimation. So what? He'd stopped caring what Celia thought of him long ago. "So why were you out on the water with no lights?"

She looked around and he realized she was checking to be sure no one was near. "I'd rather tell you when we're inside."

Inside. She was going to invite him into her house. Although he knew she was only doing it because she'd entangled him in whatever little scheme she was up to, he still felt a quickening interest, as if he were still a teenage boy who saw a chance to score.

She broke your heart, remember? You're not interested.

Right. That's why you came back after you stopped by Saquatucket in late August and found out she was still around.

"Here," she said. She pushed open a gate in a low picket fence and led the way up a crushed-shell path to the door of a boxy Cape Cod farmhouse-style home. The place clearly was an old Cape treasure. She paused on the stoop to unlock the door, then pushed it open and beckoned to him without meeting his eyes. "Please come in."

Formal. She was nervous. About having him around? About what he'd interrupted? He told himself it didn't matter. "Nice place," he said. When she was young, she'd lived in one of the most modest cottages on the Cape. This house probably was on the historic register.

The living room was furnished with heavy pieces in shades of creams and browns, with an irregularly shaped glass coffee table mounted atop a large piece of driftwood. Over the mantel hung a painting of the harbor as it must have looked a hundred years ago, with small fishing boats moored along the water's edge, stacks of lobster pots and nets piled haphazardly and a shell path leading to small, boxy cottages similar to the one in which he stood. There was a bowl filled with dried cranberries on the coffee table, and as he watched, she switched on additional lights.

"Thank you." She hesitated. "It was my husband's family home for four generations."

"Your husband the harbormaster."

"Yes." She sounded faintly defensive. "Would you like something to drink?"

"No." He flopped down into a comfortably over-stuffed chair without invitation. "I'd like an explanation."

Two

Celia took a deep, nervous breath, trying to calm the fluttering muscles of her stomach. What on earth had possessed her to involve Reese in this mess? She'd reacted instinctively, knowing she'd had no time to waste. And knowing Reese was safe. The one thing she did know was that he couldn't possibly be involved. That would have required him to be in the area in the last few years.

"I was looking for drug smuggling activity."

"Drug smugglers?" He sounded incredulous. The faint air of hostility she'd sensed from him disappeared as he sat up straight and stared at her.

She perched on the edge of the couch and clasped her hands together. "It's imperative that none of the clients along the dock learn about it."

"Why?"

"It's possible that someone moored here could be a part of a drug operation."

"So when I came along and blew the whistle, you decided to use me as a cover?" Reese's eyes were intent, unsmiling.

She shrugged. "I didn't know what else to do. You were shouting loud enough to wake folks on the other side of town."

The side of his mouth twitched, as if he were struggling not to smile. "Sorry." He leaned back against the rough fabric of the chair, stretched out his long legs, then looked at her skeptically. "Drug smuggling?"

She popped up off the couch, uncomfortable with his questions and annoyed at the derisive tone. "I'm not crazy," she said defensively. "You'd be amazed at the amount of illegal stuff that goes on around here."

He laughed aloud, but she had the sense that he was laughing at her rather than with her. "I've been in dozens of harbors along dozens of shorelines and, believe me, I've seen more kinds of 'illegal stuff' than you could imagine. I'm just wondering what you think you can do about it."

"Maybe nothing." She carefully looked past him, hoping her face wasn't too transparent.

"Celia." He waited until she reluctantly dragged her gaze back to mesh with his. "You could be putting yourself in serious danger. Drug runners are criminals. They wouldn't think twice about hurting you if they caught you spying on them. Leave the investigation to the law enforcement guys who get paid to do it."

She wanted to laugh, an entirely inappropriate reaction, and she bit the inside of her lip hard. If he only knew! "I'll be careful," she said.

"Careful isn't good enough." His tone was harsh. "Do you think I'm kidding about getting hurt? This isn't a game—"

"I know it's not!" Her voice overrode his. "They killed my husband and my son." *Dear God, help me.* She couldn't believe she'd blurted that out.

The words hung in the air, still stunning her after two years. She collapsed again on the couch like a balloon that had lost its helium, putting her face in her hands. An instant later she realized that Reese's weight was settling onto the cushions beside her.

"I'm sorry," he said. A large, warm hand settled on her back and rubbed gentle circles as if she were a baby in need of soothing. "I am so sorry, Celia. I didn't know."

"I didn't expect you would." She pressed the heels of her palms hard against her eyes, pushing back the tears. She wasn't a crier; tears accomplished nothing but making you feel like you needed a nap to recharge the batteries you drained bawling. "It was just local news." *Except to me.*

There was a small silence. "Tell me what happened."

She hadn't spoken of it in a long time. Not even to Roma, who she knew worried over her silence. But for some reason, she felt compelled to talk tonight. Maybe it was because she had a certain degree of familiarity with Reese due to their shared past. Maybe it was because he hadn't known her family and therefore could be less emotionally involved. Most likely it was because she knew he wouldn't be around long and it wouldn't matter.

Drawing in a deep breath, she sighed heavily and shifted back against the couch, her hands falling limp in her lap. Reese sat close, his arm now draped along the back of the couch behind her shoulders. It should have bothered her, but the numbness that had been so familiar in that first horrible year of her bereavement was with her again, and she couldn't work up the energy to mind.

"We only had been married for two years when Milo's dad passed away and Milo was asked to take over as harbormaster. He'd been raised on the pier and he knew the work already." She smiled briefly, looking into the past. "He was good at it. Everybody liked Milo."

Reese didn't speak, although she saw him nod encouragingly in her peripheral vision.

"Our son was born three years later. We named him Emilios, like his father and grandfather. Leo was his nickname. I had worked at the marina but I stayed home with him after he was born." The numbness was fading and she concentrated on breathing deeply and evenly, forming the words with care. Anything to keep from letting the words shred her heart again.

"When Leo was two, Milo mentioned to me that he thought there was something funny going on down toward Monomoy Island. One night in September he came home and told me he'd called the FBI, that he was pretty certain some kind of illegal contraband was being brought ashore."

"That was smart." Reese's voice was quiet.

"He didn't know what else to do," she said. "After he showed them where he thought the action was happening, he stayed away. The federal agents got a lot of information from him and that was it. Almost a year passed and nothing happened that we knew of. We figured they probably were proceeding cautiously, starting some kind of undercover operation. And then one day Milo took Leo with him on an errand over to Nantucket. Halfway across the sound, their boat exploded.''

Reese swore vividly. "What happened?"

She took another deep, careful breath. "At first I assumed it was an accident. Just a horrible, awful accident. And then federal agents came around one day and told me there had been an explosive device attached to the bottom of the boat. It had been detonated by someone close enough to see them go out on the water.''

She stopped speaking and there was silence in the room, broken only by the steady tick-tock of the old captain's clock Milo's father had restored. She wound it every morning when she came downstairs.

"How old was your—Leo?"

Her heart shrank from the question. She could deal with this if she just didn't think too much about it. But she couldn't talk about Leo. She just couldn't. "Two and a half. He would have started kindergarten next year." Her voice quavered. *Shut up, shut up. Stop talking.* "He was very blond, like I was as a child, and he had big velvety-brown eyes. He adored his daddy and there was nothing he loved better than going out on the…the boat w-with Milo.'' Her voice was beginning to hitch as sobs forced their way out.

She felt Reese's arms come hard around her, pulling her to his chest as the floodgates of long-suppressed grief opened. "Shh.'' His voice came dimly through the storm of agony that swept over her.

"I wish—I w-wish I'd died, too.'' She stuffed a

fist in her mouth, appalled at voicing the thought that had lived in her head since the terrible day she'd buried her husband and her baby boy.

"Shh," he said again. "I know." She felt a big hand thread through her hair, cupping her scalp and gently massaging. He'd done that years ago, she remembered, when she'd been upset with her father's reaction to him the day she'd introduced them.

Abruptly, it was all too much. Her father, her family, Reese…

She cried for a long, long time. Reese did nothing, simply held her while she soaked the front of his sweatshirt with tears. At one point he reached over to the end table and snagged a box of tissues—probably afraid she'd use his shirt to blow her nose—but he didn't let go of her and as soon as he handed her a tissue he put his arm around her again.

His hands were big and warm and comforting. His arms made her feel ridiculously secure. She hadn't allowed herself to lean on anyone in so long….

Reese tilted his head and glanced down at the sleeping woman in his arms. He'd been shaken to the core by her flat recital earlier. His problems, his *issues* with his family, seemed petty in comparison.

Not for the first time, he wondered if his parents were still living, if his siblings were all right. Some of them might be married now. For all he knew, he could be an uncle. He'd frozen them forever in his mind, but they'd moved on with their lives just as he had.

Although he really hadn't. In more than a dozen years he'd done nothing of note besides win a few silly boat races here and there. He'd made plenty of

money and given a lot of it away, but he couldn't
think of one single lasting thing of importance that
he'd leave behind if he died tomorrow. Except Amalie, and he couldn't take credit for her.

Celia must feel like that, too. Only it must be worse
knowing that she *had* had something lasting and it
was gone. A steady relationship and a child to carry
on her genes—yes, it was much worse for her. He
was sure her marriage had been good, just from the
way she uttered her husband's name, as if the mere
speaking of it could evoke warm, fond feelings of
affection. A ridiculous feeling of jealousy swept
through him. She wasn't his, hadn't been his for
years. She'd chosen another man. And yes, she'd
definitely had something lasting...until it had been
ripped away from her in one brutal moment.

Jealousy faded beneath compassion and pity. *I wish
I'd died, too.* What would it be like to lose the people
you loved most in the world? Particularly the child.
God, losing someone close to you, a friend, was bad
enough, as he well knew. And he had firsthand experience with a child who'd lost her parents. But to
have your child go before you— He shivered, thinking of his adopted six-year-old daughter, Amalie, a
bright butterfly flitting through his life, bringing ra-
diant colors to his days. It wasn't natural for any child
to die and there was no way to accept it. He couldn't
even imagine what he would do if he ever lost Ammie.

And she wasn't even his. Well, she was now,
thanks to the adoption laws of the State of Florida.
But her parents had been his best racing buddy, Kent,
and his wife, Julie. They'd died at sea before Amalie's second birthday and he'd been called on to honor

his pledge to be Amalie's godfather in a far more intimate way than any of them ever had expected.

He lifted one hand and wearily rubbed his temples. He needed to call down to the Keys where he'd made his home, to check in with Velva, his housekeeper, nanny and surrogate mother all rolled into one, to talk to Amalie. This was the first time he'd left her in the four years since her parents had died and he hadn't been sure it was a good idea. But Velva and Amalie's teacher both had urged him to take a few weeks for himself. He hadn't sailed anywhere alone since Kent and Julie had died and he'd finally let himself be talked into this vacation. He'd decided to have one last carefree fling before selling the cruiser. He was a man who had responsibilities now. No more world-cruising for him.

One carefree fling? Ha. The minute you heard Celia was still around, you made plans to come back up here and see her for yourself.

He pulled his head back farther to look at Celia. Hard to believe she was lying here in his arms, even if it was only because she needed comfort. She'd wept silently, her slender body set in tense denial as huge tears rolled down her cheeks and soaked the fabric of both their shirts, until he'd told her to stop holding it in. And then she'd finally broken. She'd let him draw her against his chest and she'd sobbed and sobbed. Awful, desolate sounds that had made his own throat ache. How the hell long had it been since she'd let herself cry? Surely the woman had friends, if not family, around. She'd lived here all her life.

But there was something almost austere about Celia now that she hadn't had when she was young. The woman she was now didn't need people—or didn't *want* to need them, he'd bet. The woman she'd been when he'd known her, a flower just in the first fresh moments of full bloom, had had no such boundaries. She'd been free with her hugs and her bright silvery laughter; her face had been open and alive, always smiling. And when she'd seen him coming, that smile had lit up the world.

As he thought of the girl he'd known, another memory floated through his head. It wasn't of the first time they'd made love. Though he could remember that, too. She'd been a virgin and it hadn't been particularly fun for her, he suspected, although she'd never told him so, and she'd made him feel like the king of the world.

No, the memory that haunted him was of an entirely different time....

"Reese! It's the middle of summer a-and it's broad daylight. There are tourists everywhere!"

He laughed, enjoying the way her eyes widened when he took her hand and pulled her down onto the deck of the catamaran, his purpose clear. It was a small boat with no cabin, but it did have a low railing around the deck. If they were careful... He'd fantasized about making love to Celia under the bright summer sun since the first time they'd been together more than two months ago.

"This little bay is fairly private, though." He slid *his hands over her bare, tanned torso, gently tugging at the strings that tied her bikini top into place until he could toss the scrap of cloth aside. "It's an unwritten law of the sea. You never approach a moored boat if you've hailed them and nobody answers."*

Her finely arched eyebrows rose. "I can think of a dozen times I've broken that rule myself."

But she wasn't really arguing with him. Her small hands ran lightly up his arms, over the swell of his biceps and onto his shoulders, and she shivered, falling silent as he flicked his thumbs over her nipples, bringing them to beautiful taut points. He'd never seen her before in bright light and her skin was so satiny, her peaks and valleys so smoothly curved, that she literally stopped his breath.

"Celia." He breathed her name as if it were a prayer, finding her mouth with easy familiarity, feeling the thrill that always shot through him at her instant response.

"I love you." Her words were a whisper of sound, barely audible as he nibbled his way along her jaw, then slid his mouth down the tender column of her neck, pressing kisses to the delicate arch of her collarbone. He trailed his tongue along her skin, catching the faint scent that wasn't perfume but merely the essence of her.

"You're so beautiful." His palms cupped the sweet weight of her breasts and he drew back just far enough to feast his eyes on the soft, feminine flesh he'd uncovered. Her nipples were a glowing coppery color, begging him to taste them, and he leaned down again, touching her with his tongue, lightly at first, then tugging her fully into his mouth to suckle one tender tip until she arched against him, twisting and crying out.

Smiling against her skin, he released one tight nubbin and blew on it. Celia's eyes flew open. "Reese…" Her hands had been clutching his shoulders. Dragging them down over his chest, she indulged in a little teasing of her own, running her fingers through the dark mat of hair that spread across his breastbone and arrowed downward. She touched his flat nipples, rubbing small circles, making his breath come faster as the sensation triggered an even more intense need within him.

As she trailed one finger down along the ribbon of hair to his navel and beyond, he stripped out of his bathing suit one-handed and kicked it away without leaving her. The mere act of freeing himself from the restrictions of clothing turned him on even more as he felt the warm air move over him, the sun hot on his back. All that lay between them now was one tiny piece of fabric. He stroked her ribs, her hips, her belly, moving slowly down her body, savoring her. He loved the feel of every smooth inch. His finger skimmed the delicate dip of her navel and farther, over her hipbone and down to where the elastic of her bathing suit bottom impeded his exploration.

With slow, deliberate motions, he slipped a finger beneath the elastic and ran it back and forth, then delved a bit deeper until his long fingers combed through the dense mat of curls between her legs. She was dewed and slippery, and she arched beneath him, one long silken leg curving up over his hip and pulling him hard against her. They both made small sounds of delight as their bodies reacted to the sweet pressure.

Gently, reluctantly, he slid away from her long enough to hook his fingers in the fabric and pull it down and off. Celia watched him, her breath rushing in and out, but as the sun poured over her gloriously naked body, she made a motion to cover herself with her hands. "This makes me feel…exposed."

He chuckled, lowering himself to her, taking her wrists and pulling them up beside her shoulders as he covered her. He shifted, snuggling himself firmly into the cleft of her thighs, groaning a little at the exquisite pressure that resulted from sandwiching himself between them. "Is this better?"

She smiled up at him, her lips quivering slightly. "Yes. But what if someone—"

He covered her mouth with his own again, using his tongue to draw a response from her until she was fully engaged in the kiss. When he released her wrists she clasped his shoulders, clinging to him, pressing her bare flesh against his chest and making him growl with approval. He worked one hand between their bodies, bypassing his straining flesh in favor of the soft fleece that hid her feminine secrets. Slowly, slowly, he inched one finger down, until he felt the pouting bump beneath his finger. Equally slowly, he pressed and circled gently, ignoring his body's urgent demands until she was writhing and frantic beneath him.

"Reese," she begged him, tearing her mouth from his. "Reese…"

"What, baby?" He used the moment to push his hand farther between her thighs, loving the slick, moist heat and the fact that he'd been the one to make her respond that way. "Do you want me?"

She nodded, reaching one small hand down to encircle him. He groaned as an involuntary surge of excitement threatened his self-control. She'd only recently gotten brave enough to touch him but she was a fast learner and the mere thought of what she could do to him— Under the circumstances, he thought, it might not be such a good idea. As she traced one finger across the sensitive tip, he reared back, re-moving himself from her grasp. He set his hands on her inner thighs, pressing them apart and looking at the secret treasure they yielded.

Celia reached for him, her modesty all but forgotten. "Hurry…"

He was dragged from his reverie by Celia's hand, which he held loosely in his, slowly rising to tuck her hair away from her face. It was only quick thinking that kept him from pulling her hand down to palm the hard ridge pushing at the front of his pants. Her eyelids fluttered as she stretched and he caught his breath, further aroused by both the memory and the soft slide of her body against his. Then her eyes opened and she blinked at him. "Reese." She didn't sound surprised, only cordial and a bit wary. "What time is it?"

He glanced at the old clock that had faithfully announced the hour as well as the half all night long. "Nearly six. Sleep well?"

"Nearly six?" She tried to shove herself upright. "Oh, no! You were here all night."

"Yeah." He held her easily in place though he was careful not to settle her too snugly into his lap. There was no way she could miss the evidence that would betray his thoughts if she lay against him any more closely. "Relax," he said, stroking her back. "All we did was sleep. Literally."

"Yes, but—"

"And you *did* make sure those folks down on the pier knew that I was coming home with you, remember? This will just make your story more convincing."

She stopped pushing against him, but her body felt stiff. It made him realize just how much he'd liked having her draped bonelessly over him in slumber. They'd never slept together all night way back when…and he was reminded of his daydream before she woke.

Without giving himself time to think, he asked, "Do you remember the first time we did it on the boat? We fell asleep afterward and my butt got sunburned."

"Reese!" A startled half laugh burst out of her and she sat up again, pushing herself away from him as he reluctantly let her go. "What brought that on?"

He shrugged, wishing he'd kept his mouth shut. "I was thinking about that summer." He didn't need to clarify. "So do you?"

"Do I what?"

"Remember."

She was avoiding his eyes. "Yes," she said quietly. "I remember."

"That was the first time we ever made love on a boat." He was gratified to see that she was breathing fast, her breasts rising and falling rapidly beneath her soft T-shirt. Oh, yeah. She remembered.

"I don't want to talk about this." She shot off the couch and stood over him, rubbing her arms briskly as if she were cold and her velvety-brown eyes held a determined look. "Are you leaving?"

She wanted to get rid of him. His pleasure in teasing her died instantly and he narrowed his eyes. "Aren't you going to offer me breakfast?"

"I have to grab a shower and get down to the pier. We have a couple of charters going out early this morning."

He decided he should get a gold star for not suggesting that they shower together. "All right," he said. "You go shower and I'll make breakfast. You have to eat or you'll feel bad."

Celia stood for a moment and he could almost see the argument going on in her head. If she let him in her kitchen while she showered, that would be a little more intimacy than she wanted. No, a lot more. But she'd been raised to be polite, and tossing him out without breakfast after he'd gone along with her story last night wouldn't set well with her conscience.

Finally she said, "All right. Thank you," in a tone so grudging that he nearly laughed aloud before she turned and walked out of the room without another word.

Reese got up and walked toward her kitchen, stopping at a little bathroom he found beneath the stairs on the way. The kitchen was shadowed in the first rays of dawn coming from a skylight that added a contemporary cachet to the old house. It was a charming combination of modern practicality and Cape Cod history, with Nantucket baskets and copper pots, a bowl of polished sea glass and shells. Two elegant seascapes graced the walls, and she'd laid handwoven rugs and placemats, while a stunning wreath of cranberry and local greens hung above the old fireplace that now boasted a gas inset. His little village girl had done well for herself with her marriage.

Another image of Celia from all those years ago, standing on the dock waiting for him, flashed through his head as he started her coffeepot. God, how he'd loved her. Only a very young man could be that deeply, head-over-heels infatuated with a woman.

He'd never felt anything remotely like it since, never expected to again. That kind of feeling couldn't last.

Could it?

Of course not. He didn't harbor any feelings for Celia anymore, and surely he would if that wild, exuberant, bone-deep infatuation had really been love.

Sure. That's why you came flying over to this marina when the guys at Saquatucket told you she was harbormaster here now.

Simple curiosity. He'd wanted to see how she'd aged. At first he'd almost been disappointed to find that she looked nearly as youthful as she had the last time he'd seen her. He would always carry that image in his mind, because at the time, he hadn't realized they'd never be together again. She'd been waving wildly from the dock as he'd taken the cat back to his family's summer house, her slender body still warm from his caresses, lips swollen and eyes languorous as her hair streamed back from her face.

She still looked youthful, and initially he'd thought how little she'd changed. But as he'd drawn closer, changes had indeed been evident. She was slightly fuller in the breast and hip than she'd once been, a becoming difference. But the once-mobile lips were compressed, reluctant to curve into a smile, and her beautiful, soft, doe eyes were shadowed with secrets he couldn't decipher. The girl had become a woman—an extraordinarily lovely woman—but her coming of age clearly hadn't been smooth.

Upon the heels of the mild disappointment had been relief…and, if he was brutally truthful, an unkind pleasure that life hadn't been all roses and moonlight for her.

And then she'd told him about her family and any

lingering self-righteousness had fled in the face of the horror and sympathy her story evoked. He'd reached for her without thinking and it had felt so right when she'd come into his arms. So right that he'd been sorely tempted to jump her bones the next morning, like a total cad. Which he wasn't.

Okay, you might have been noble this morning, but you wouldn't say no to another close encounter, pal.

No. No, he wouldn't. In fact, he could easily imagine staying the night with Celia—or having her snuggled in his queen berth aboard the yacht—every night while he was moored here in Harwichport.

He thought about her as he surveyed the contents of the refrigerator, withdrew two cinnamon buns and put them in the microwave. He should be grateful to her for showing him that what they'd shared hadn't been real, even though it had hurt like hell at the time. She'd been the one who had made him realize that there was no such thing as real love. But he still *liked* her, just as a friend. And there was still an undeniable attraction between them....

He had three weeks' vacation left, if he didn't give in to the ridiculous urge to rush back to his daughter. Who, he reminded himself wryly, hadn't seemed in the least perturbed at the idea of her adoptive father going on an extended trip. That was a good thing, he knew from talking with the counselor he'd consulted periodically since Kent and Julie had died. Ammie felt as secure and comfortable as any other well-adjusted kid with only one parent.

So that, at least, wasn't something he had to worry about. It felt good—no, great—not to be worrying about Amalie. That was probably why Velva had

kicked him out. She'd known he was far more appre-
hensive about a separation than his child would be.

So the bottom line was, his daughter would do fine
without him for a few more weeks. Which meant he
had plenty of time. He'd originally intended to stop
briefly on the Cape, just to see how it had changed
in the years since he'd been gone.

At least, that was what he'd told himself. But now,
standing in Celia's kitchen in the light of early morning, having held her in his arms throughout the night,
he had to face the truth. He'd come back to find her.

He'd never imagined she might be single, or perhaps he hadn't allowed himself to hope so, anyway.
But she was. And so was he, and perhaps it was inevitable that they'd be drawn together again. After all,
they shared a past no one else could ever take from
them. She still felt comfortable with him at some elemental level she had yet to acknowledge or she
never would have fallen asleep in his arms last night.

As he searched for napkins, mugs and plates, he
thought about how revealing her actions had been.
And he thought about how he'd felt as he'd held her
in his arms again. It was difficult to admit he'd never
gotten her out of his system. And he suspected that
he had never been completely out of hers.

The telephone rang, interrupting his mental spec-
ulation. His eyebrows rose as he glanced at the clock.
Damn early for a casual caller. He hoped nothing was
wrong. It rang a second time, then a third. He couldn't
hear the shower running anymore but he didn't hear
Celia running for the phone, either. Did she have an
answering machine? After the fifth ring, he decided
she might not. With a mental shrug, he reached for

the phone. She wanted people to think they were having a fling anyway, didn't she?

"Hello?"

There was dead silence on the other end of the line. Then, "I beg your pardon. I believe I have a wrong number." It was a quavery yet regal female voice, definitely a bit long in the tooth.

"Are you trying to reach Celia Papaleo?" He'd had time to practice the sound of it on the short trip from one marina to the other yesterday after he'd learned she was still around, but married.

"Why, yes," the caller was saying. "I am looking for Mrs. Papaleo. Is this her residence?"

"Yes, ma'am, it is. May I take a message?"

"Yes, you may. Might I ask to whom I am speaking?" If this old dame wasn't an English teacher in her day, he'd eat his shorts.

"This is Reese Barone, ma'am." The courtesy came naturally; he'd been drilled in it as a child and even suffered through etiquette classes where he and his brothers had been forced to dance with obnoxious little girls and to practice manners.

"Well, Mr. Barone, my name is Hilda Manguard and I am the chairwoman of the Harwich Historical Society. I would like you to pass along the following message to Mrs. Papaleo. Ask her to return my call and confirm that she will bring over the wreaths that she's making for our annual Autumn House Tour. Please tell her that I apologize for calling so early but I've been trying to contact her without success all week." And the old lady rattled off her number while Reese scrambled to find a pencil.

Just as he set the telephone back in the cradle, he heard a sound. He turned to find Celia standing in the doorway glaring at him. She wore jeans and a T-shirt beneath a V-necked fleece sweater designed to ward off the early morning chill. Her hair was slicked back from her face and already appeared to be half dry— which might explain why she hadn't heard the phone ring.

"Hey," he said, as if she weren't looking like she'd enjoy skinning him. "You have a message."

"What are you doing answering my phone?" she demanded.

"You didn't," he said. "And your machine didn't kick on."

"I don't have one." She practically snarled the words as she stalked toward him and snatched up the piece of paper on which he'd written the message. "Great. Now everybody on the Cape will know you were at my house at six in the morning."

"Was she an English teacher?"

Celia looked at him blankly. "Who?"

"Mrs. Manguard. She sounded like an English teacher."

"Miss. And yes, she was a long time ago. Then she became the principal of one of the elementary schools until she retired about twenty years ago." She pointed to one of the two places he'd set at the table. "Sit. Eat. And then you're leaving."

He nodded, figuring he'd pressed his luck far enough. "All right."

As she slipped into the seat across from him, he said, "So where are these wreaths you're making for the historical society?"

"Oh, no!" She mimed smacking her palm against her forehead, then snatched up the note she'd laid on the table and hastily scanned it. "I forgot all about those wreaths. Why did I say I'd do that?'' she asked herself.

"I take it this project isn't quite finished?''

"It isn't even *started*. I agreed to donate ten wreaths. They hang them in the homes on their annual house tour and sell chances on some of them. At the conclusion of the tour, the winners are drawn.'' She wiped cinnamon glaze from her fingertips. "And they want them on Saturday.''

"Today is Thursday.''

"I know that.'' From the tone of her voice, his helpfulness wasn't appreciated.

"Are they cranberry wreaths like the one in your living room?''

"Some are. Others are made of marsh grasses and decorated with shells. Ack! And I'm out of marsh grass. Sometime before this evening I've got to get my hands on more.'' She sighed. "This is *not* going to be a good day.''

"And that includes the way it started?'' he asked wryly.

Her troubled gaze met his across the table. "Reese, I do appreciate you letting me cry all over you last night. And I can't deny that your willingness to play along with my charade helped cover up my little trip out on the sound. So...thank you.'' She stood and stacked both their empty plates, carrying them to the sink. "It's been nice seeing you again.''

He stood, as well. "It's good to see you, too.''

Busying herself at the sink, she spoke with her back to him. "I have to get down to the marina. You can let yourself out when you're ready to leave. Just lock the door behind you.''

"May I see you again?''

ANNE MARIE WINSTON 53

She turned to face him and there was a remote
quality in her sad eyes that told him the answer before
she opened her mouth. "No," she said. "That
wouldn't be a good idea." She laid the dish towel out
to dry and walked to the door, then turned back to
him one more time. "Thank you."

He stood in the kitchen as she let herself out and
walked down the crushed-shell path. It might not be
a good idea in her mind, but as far as he was concerned, it was a great one. She wasn't indifferent to
him, he was positive. There was nothing specific he
could put his finger on, just a quickening feeling in
his gut and the way her eyes danced around, never
quite meeting his. She'd been exceedingly careful not
to touch him after she'd woken up sprawled all over
him, too.

As he locked her door and walked down the path
after cleaning up her kitchen, Reese was whistling.
He had a kayak to rent.

Three

It was midafternoon and Celia was heartily sick of paperwork. Soon she'd be wishing for something to keep her busy during the long winter days when there were far fewer customers, but right now the big fish were running. Which meant that she was up to her ears in equipment rentals, slip requests, repairs, guided fishing expeditions and whale watches, not to mention novice fishermen who expected to land a fifteen-foot shark on a lightweight line off the end of the pier.

She picked up her mug of tea and took a big gulp, grimacing at the cold beverage. Heavy footsteps outside the shack alerted her that someone was about to enter.

"Hey, there." Reese stood in the doorway, grinning at her.

She set down her mug so hard, tea sloshed perilously close to the rim. "Hello."

"Did you forget about the sea oats?"

She sighed as the morning's telephone call returned. "It was marsh grass. Although some sea oats would be nice, too. And no, I didn't forget. Well, not exactly." Then she raised her eyebrows, wondering what possible interest he could have in sea oats. "Why?"

"I rented a kayak. If you'd like to take a break, we could go now."

"We?" She made the tone deliberately dubious.

But Reese only grinned wider, his dimples carving deep grooves in both cheeks. "I thought you might enjoy some company."

"No, thanks." She shrugged. "I'm used to going alone."

"Being used to it and enjoying it are two different things. Besides, it would go faster if you had help."

She was growing annoyed. He wouldn't take a reasonably polite refusal, so she supposed she was off the hook if she got rude. "Reese, I thought I made it clear this morning that I didn't want to reestablish a...friendship with you. It's been thirteen years—"

"And one month and five days."

She stopped, dumbfounded. "You're making that up."

"Nope. Last time I ever saw you was on August the twenty-seventh. It's the second of October." His face grew sober. "I guess I can't blame you for not wanting to renew our friendship. I just thought..." He stopped. "Never mind." He turned away from the door.

"You thought what?" The words were impulsive.

She couldn't believe he knew to the day when he'd
left. As much as she'd thought of him over the years,
she hadn't even known that. She'd been so miserable
when he'd left her behind that her memories of that
time had simply blurred.

He paused, his back to her, and his shoulders rose
and fell. "I've been away from home for a long time.
I cut my ties when I left, family, friends, everything.
It just was...really, really *nice* to be with someone
who shared my past."

There was a heavy moment of silence in the wake
of the words, and her heart filled with pity. The very
fact that he knew to the day how long it had been
since he'd left had far more to do with the estrange-
ment from his family than it did her, she was sure.
She was on her feet and across the small office before
she even realized what she was doing. "I'm sorry,
Reese. I guess I'm too touchy." She put one hand on
his forearm. "I know how it feels to be alone."

He wore a short-sleeved T-shirt with a yacht man-
ufacturer's logo on it and, beneath her fingers, his skin
felt hot, rough with whorls of heavy masculine hair,
the tendons and muscles tough and hard and tense.
The sensations made her acutely aware of how tall
and powerful he was, how feminine and needy he
made her feel. She knew it was stupid to spend any
more time in his company. He could upset the carefully balanced emotions she'd worked so hard to manage in the past two years and leave.

And leave. That was exactly right. And then he'd
leave. If she could remember that, and treat this as a
temporary visit from an old friend who wouldn't be
staying long, surely she could manage it.

Reese hadn't moved. Finally he nodded his head

her way. "I'm sorry if I've made you uncomfortable." He turned and looked her in the eye, his gaze
warm and full of unmistakable affection. From the
memories they shared? "It was good to see you again,
Celia. Really good." Briefly he lifted his free hand
and clasped it over hers where it still rested on his
arm. Then he put his hand out and opened the door,
stepping away from her.

"No! Reese, wait. I'd like to go kayaking with
you." She followed him through the door. "In fact,
I'd appreciate the company. I spend too much of my
time alone."

He froze in midstride, then slowly turned back to
her, eyes cautious. "Sure?"

She took a deep breath, then met his eyes and nodded. "I'm sure." She indicated her office. "Just let
me get this stuff organized and tell Angie I'm leaving."

Twenty minutes later they'd donned jackets against
the light breeze and soon were stroking through the
water in smooth unison. She set the pace while Reese
sat behind her and it gave her a funny feeling to see
the flash of his paddle synchronized perfectly with
hers. It was ridiculous to interpret the action as intimacy, and yet that was exactly how it felt. She was
left awkward and tongue-tied.

"It's still a lot like I remember." Reese's voice
startled her as they paddled out of the harbor and
around a corner of the Lower Cape shoreline.

"In the off season, it is," she agreed, relieved by
the ordinariness of the topic. "But in the summer, the
crowds are horrific. Seems like there are twice as
many tourists as there were when I was a kid."

"It's that way in Florida, too."

''Florida?''

''That's where I live now.''

''Ah.'' She couldn't prevent a small burst of laughter.

''What's so funny?''

She shrugged. ''I guess I assumed you were still a drifter, sailing from one place to another.''

He laughed, too. ''Thirteen years would be a long time to drift.''

''I guess it would, but that's always how I thought of you. Sailing around the world, seeing new places just like you always said you wanted to.''

''You thought of me?''

She could have hit herself over the head with her paddle. ''You know, just in passing.''

''I thought of you,'' he said softly.

She didn't know what to say. Finally she said, ''I suppose it's only natural that each of us has wondered about the other from time to time.''

Now Reese was the one who was silent.

They paddled along, skirting the broken coastline and the many little inlets along it. Seagulls checked them out to see if there was any chance of scrounging a meal, and they passed a tidal flat where two young girls in overalls squelched in the mud, raking half-heartedly for quahogs.

''I did it, you know.'' He broke the quiet.

''Did what?''

''Sailed around the world.''

''I never doubted it.'' That was the truth. ''Tell me about it.'' Even she could hear the wistful quality in her voice. She'd always said she wanted to leave the Cape and see the world. There'd been a time when she'd assumed she'd be doing it with him.

"I headed south and down through the Caribbean. Stopped for a week here, a few days there. My favorite island was St. John in the Virgins. Extraordinary scenery and at that time still mostly undeveloped. Then I came north on the west side of the Florida coast, went across the Gulf, down around South America and up the other side to the Pacific—"

"That must have taken a while."

"I wasn't in any rush."

Translation: he'd had nowhere to be, nobody to whom he'd needed to report. "Were you alone?"

"Yeah. I had a small cruiser that I could handle myself. But I met a guy in Hawaii who started crewing for me and we headed across the Pacific." The timbre of Reese's voice reflected fondness. "He stayed with me the rest of the trip. Remind me to tell you sometime about the hurricane we weathered."

"My God, Reese!" Her heart shot into her throat, despite the fact that he was sitting right behind her, alive and well. "What possessed you? You could have been killed."

"Don't think that didn't occur to us about two hundred times," he said dryly. "Let's just say that I have no desire to repeat the experience."

"I should think not." Then she gestured toward the shore. "Let's head into that thicket. I gather grass there a lot. It's got a good variety of stuff."

"Isn't it protected?"

"I've got a permit," she said smugly. "Local economy, and all that."

"All right." Reese dug his paddle into the water and turned the kayak efficiently. "The lady's wish is mine to grant."

As they moved into the shallower waters and followed a stream that wound among the shrubby bushes and long-stemmed marsh plants, Celia lifted her face to the autumn sun and said, "I love this time of year. And it's so peaceful out here. I can't remember the last time I did this."

"When you gathered grasses for wreaths?" Reese suggested.

She shook her head. "I paid one of the neighbor kids to come get them for me last time. Too busy."

"You spend a lot of time at the marina?"

She nodded, shifting so that she could look at him. "It's a full-time job."

"Did you work there when your husband was harbormaster?"

It was touchy ground and she could tell from the regretful look on his face that he recognized it the minute he'd said it. "I didn't work."

"You were a full-time mother."

It didn't hurt quite as intensely as she expected and she actually felt her face relax into a soft smile as an image of Leo's little head bent intently over his building blocks flitted through her mind. "Yes."

"Why did you take over after your husband passed away?"

She shrugged. "I knew how to do it. Before we were married I worked for his father. That's how we met. And after we were married, I still helped out sometimes until Leo was born." She paused. It was the first time she could remember that she'd been able to speak of her son without falling apart. "I didn't go to college so my options were pretty limited."

"Wasn't there life insurance?"

The question startled her. "Wha— Oh, yes." Then she realized he thought she needed the money. "Actually, Milo left me in good financial shape,'' she told him. ''I just didn't want to sit around the house all day.''

''Too lonely.'' Unspoken between them was the knowledge that her husband hadn't been all that was lost.

''Yes.'' She was glad her voice was steady. She concentrated on using the sickle she'd brought along to cut wide swaths of some of the prettier stands of grass. Autumn was a good time to gather it. While she used more supple, still-green flora in wreaths, she also dried bunches of grasses for the standing arrangements she donated to several local charity efforts throughout the year.

After a few moments the quiet work began to soothe her. Reese seemed to anticipate her every move because he maneuvered the kayak around so carefully that she was rarely out of reach of the plants she was seeking. He was right—it did go much faster with his help.

''Look.'' His low whisper caught her attention. ''What is that?''

She scanned the direction he was pointing, finally finding the speckled bird neatly camouflaged among the greens, grays and browns of the marsh grasses. ''It's a duck. A gadwall, to be exact. Aren't they pretty?''

''Very. Different from most of the ducks I'm familiar with. Isn't it a little late to be hanging around here?''

''The ducks don't migrate,'' she told him. ''Most of the local varieties stay here all winter long. It's when they find their mates.'' Good grief. Could she have said anything more awkward?

But Reese didn't leap onto her unintended innuendo as she'd feared. "I never spent a winter out here. Our place was strictly a summer residence."

"It's open now."

Reese's gaze shot to hers. "It is?"

She shrugged, not wanting him to think she kept tabs on members of his family. "I heard in town that one of your brothers was going to be there for a week or so with his family."

"Which brother?" His lips twisted in a smile that was more bittersweet than amused. "I didn't even know any of them had gotten married."

"I believe it was Nicholas." She knew exactly who it was.

"Nick's married?" He was completely still, and she could see the regret in his face. "He wrote to me after I left. I got letters from him for a couple of years."

"You lost touch?"

"I never got *back* in touch," he corrected her.

She was shocked. "At all?"

He shook his head.

He'd mentioned cutting ties, but… "Are you telling me you haven't had *any* contact with anyone in your family since you left?"

He nodded again, his expression unreadable. "Right."

Impulsively she said, "Why don't you give your brother a call? I'm sure your family has missed you as much as you've missed them."

His face was set. "I'll think about it."

Sure he would. "Please," she said, "consider it, Reese. You'll be sorry for the rest of your life if you don't take the chance while you still can."

"I said I'd think about it," he said irritably. Then he made an effort to smile. "Sorry. Coming back here has me thinking about all kinds of things I haven't let myself think of in years."

The silence hummed with unspoken words and she turned back to her task, supremely uncomfortable again. She knew exactly what he meant.

They didn't address anything of consequence for the rest of the trip and returned to the marina shortly before six. She ran home and brought her car down to the marina to load the grasses into the trunk while Reese waited. A part of her wanted to dismiss him and to get far, far away from Reese Barone before she did something stupid, but an equally insistent part of her lobbied for more contact.

"Would it go faster if I helped?" he asked as they brought the newly harvested materials into the workroom she'd converted in the adjacent shed. "I've never made wreaths before but I'm game to try."

She had to smile at the image of the rugged outdoorsman working at the delicate craft. As she smiled she said, "I don't know if you'll want to once you see what it takes, but at the least, I should feed you to thank you for your help."

His gaze caught and held hers and she found that she couldn't take a deep breath for the butterfly wings that crowded into her stomach. "That would be nice."

As they turned and walked toward the kitchen door, he caught her hand in his, threading his fingers through hers. Neither of them spoke. When they reached the door, he let her hand slide free as naturally as if they held hands every day.

But as she assembled a salad and started defrosting

some spaghetti sauce she'd made a few weeks earlier, she realized she was trembling. What was she going to do about Reese Barone?

In the end she did nothing. After the meal he helped with cleanup before they returned to the shed. She showed him how much wire she needed to fasten the wreaths together and he cut it while she worked the grapevine into sizable wreaths that she then began to decorate with a variety of materials.

When she'd finished the raffia bow on the last wreath, she turned to him with a relieved smile. "Thank you for taking me to the marsh today. It was fun."

"How long has it been since you let yourself do something just for fun?" His eyes were serious.

Her hands stilled on the extra grapevine she was coiling. "I don't know. A while."

"How long is a while?"

She concentrated, but she honestly couldn't come up with an answer. She gestured helplessly. "I can't remember."

"That's what I thought."

"But today was lovely."

"It was," he agreed, "but it wasn't solely dedicated to the pursuit of fun. You need to give yourself permission to relax and enjoy life again, Celia."

Instantly she felt her eyes fill with tears. Oh, damn. "Maybe I don't want to. I feel guilty, Reese. Can you understand that?"

"Not like you can. But I know what you mean." He laid down the wire cutters he'd been about to put away and came around the table. When he reached out and took her by the elbows, she let him pull her against him but she kept her head down, stubbornly gazing at the buttons on his knit shirt. "My best friend, Kent—the guy I mentioned earlier—and his wife were killed in an accident at sea a few years ago. Every once in a while I feel absolutely awful for living and laughing and just being happy when they no longer can."

"Oh, Reese, I'm so sorry." She put her arms around his broad back and hugged him closer. "Life hasn't been terrific for either one of us, has it?"

"No." He brushed a stray tendril of hair back from her face with a gentle hand. "But it's getting better again." His gaze locked with hers and for one long, intense moment, his eyes remained unguarded. In them she saw regret, longing, tenderness, desire…and she tore her gaze away, unable to sustain the intimate exchange.

"Celia." The word was a rough whisper of sound. One long finger, calloused from hours of sailing, slipped beneath her chin and lifted it. His dark head came down, blotting out the light, and she closed her eyes automatically as his lips slid onto hers.

Her whole body leaped in delighted response as his mouth settled firmly over hers, molding and shaping. *Yes!* it shouted. Without giving herself time to think about the foolishness of kissing Reese Barone, she sank against him with a soft hum of pleasure, her hands sliding up to the back of his neck and stroking through his thick, warm hair.

Reese's arms tightened. His mouth grew demanding, and she parted her lips to allow him inside as one large hand slid down her back to press her body against his. He was hard and hot and utterly male, making her feel feminine and fragile and surprisingly vulnerable, though it wasn't an unpleasant sensation.

She hadn't been held by a man since Milo died. Dear heaven, she'd forgotten how good it could be.

It was never this good with anyone but Reese.

"Spend the day with me tomorrow." It was a command.

She hung in his arms, clutching his heavy biceps, unable to process the words.

"Say yes," he said, and his voice was urgent.

"Yes," she repeated obediently.

"Good!" He claimed her mouth again before she could take back the word, then quickly released her and stepped away. "I would stay longer, but I'm not sure I'd be able to make myself leave," he said frankly, "and you're not ready for anything more."

And before her befuddled brain could formulate a response, he sketched her a quick salute and headed out the door. "I'll be here at ten."

The phone rang as Celia was getting ready to meet Reese in the morning.

It was Roma, and she was bubbling over with questions. "I called you yesterday afternoon but Angie said you'd gone out on the water with Reese Barone."

"Yes." She knew Roma would have a fit if she didn't explain, and she couldn't resist teasing her a little.

"And…?"

"He helped me gather some stuff for my wreaths."

"And…?"

"The weather was beautiful."

"Celia!"

She chuckled. "Did anyone ever tell you you're nosy?"

"Yes. What happened?" It was hard to insult someone who freely acknowledged her failings.

"Nothing happened." *At least, not while we were out on the water.*

"Why'd he come back?"

"I don't know. His family does have a home here, remember?"

"That didn't seem to matter to him before." A pause. "Is he still the same as you remember?"

"More or less. It's been...nice to talk to him again."

"Oh, come on, Ceel. I bet it's been more than 'nice.' Angie says he's still a total hottie."

"He's not bad."

"So...do you still have feelings for him?"

"That was thirteen years ago, Roma. I married another man, remember?"

"So you do." Roma cut right through any attempt to distract her.

Celia sighed. "I have wonderful memories of my first love. Seeing Reese brings back a lot of those memories. But it doesn't mean anything more than that."

"Right." Roma's voice was dry.

"It doesn't!" She was getting a little annoyed and it showed in her voice.

"Sorry." But Roma didn't sound sorry. "But I've known you long enough to know when you're fibbing. What if Reese came back to find you after all these years? Would you still be interested?"

"He didn't, so it's a moot point. But no, of course not. I moved on and I imagine he did, too."

"Maybe." Roma didn't sound convinced. "But I

still think it's odd that he'd show up here out of the blue. Angie says he's alone and he's not wearing a wedding ring.''

She was going to have to talk to Angie about encouraging these fantasies of Roma's. ''I didn't check.'' That much was true. It had never occurred to her that Reese might be married.

''Well, if he's not, then there's no reason you two couldn't get back together.''

''I am not interested in getting married again.''

''Who said anything about getting married?'' Her best friend's voice was relentlessly cheerful and supremely innocent. ''A steamy fling might be a good thing for you. And who better to scratch your itch than a guy you already know you're compatible with in that way?''

''Are you nuts?'' Celia demanded. ''I do *not* need any itches scratched.''

''All right.'' Roma sighed gustily. ''Just trying to help.'' Her voice grew gentle. ''It's okay to go on living, honey.''

''I know.'' She was abruptly perilously close to tears. ''But jumping into bed with an old flame just because it might be fun isn't my style.'' She glanced at the clock above the sink in her kitchen. ''I have to go. I'll talk to you next week.'' No way was she telling Roma she'd kissed Reese last night, or that she was spending time with him today. She already knew she should have her head examined.

After ending the conversation, she dressed quickly and went down to the marina. If she was going to take time off, she needed to check in at the office to make sure everyone had their instructions for the day.

* * *

An hour later Reese stuck his head into her office. "Hey."

"Hey." She looked up from her computer and smiled. Then the smiled faded as she remembered the way they'd parted last night, and a ridiculous shyness spread through her.

Reese stepped inside and closed the door behind him. As he started across the office, he held her gaze and her heart leaped into her throat. She rose from her chair. "What's wrong?"

"Nothing." His voice was husky, his eyes serious. "I figured that if we don't get this out of the way first, we'll both be wondering about it all day."

"What?"

"This." His hand curled around the back of her neck and tugged her toward him as his head came down. He kissed her sweetly, lingering over her mouth and finally drawing back with a bemused smile. "I used to try to convince myself that it really hadn't been that great between us, that you were so unforgettable only because we'd split up while things were still fantastic." His brushed his lips over hers one more time. "I was wrong."

She didn't know what to say. It seemed disloyal to admit how often she'd thought of him. She could barely admit that to herself. But she couldn't resist lifting her hand and briefly cradling his lean cheek in her palm. He closed his eyes and tilted his head into her hand.

And then the door opened.

They leaped apart like two teenagers caught parking by a cop.

"Oops!" Angie's voice was merry. "Sorry, boss.

I just need the invoice for that bluefish charter to-day.''

''Not a problem.'' Celia was proud that her voice was steady. She turned back to her desk, found the piece of paper, then handed it over to Angie. ''So you have everything under control?''

''No problem.'' Angie smiled at Reese. ''Get her out of here. She never takes a break.''

Four

To Celia's surprise, Reese asked if she'd like to go to the arts festival over on Nantucket. When she agreed, he led her down to his slip and they boarded the *Amalie*.

She couldn't help wondering about the unusual name. Who was Amalie? Had she been a woman important to Reese in the thirteen years he'd been away?

She wasn't about to betray how unsettled she felt at the thought. It was ridiculous—and totally naive— to expect that he hadn't had some serious relationships. Her stomach did a funny little dance. He even could have been married. Reese, married to someone else. True, she'd married someone else, but... She could hardly acknowledge the rush of wicked jealousy she felt at the mere idea of Reese and another woman.

Was it possible that he felt the same way, thinking

of Milo? If he did, he certainly hid it well. Even the
night she'd told him about her family, he'd been nothing but kind and sympathetic. He'd shown absolutely
no trace of the foaming-at-the-mouth fury she could
feel if she allowed herself to think about it much
more.

And she suddenly felt very deflated. Of course he
hadn't been jealous. Reese had moved on years ago.
He'd proven it when he'd left her behind.

"Celia?" Reese took her hand. "Watch your
step." He stopped her just before she would have
tripped over someone's deep-sea fishing equipment
spread out all over the dock as they cleaned the decks.

Summoning a smile she said, "Thanks." She
couldn't meet his eyes, though, and she was thankful
for the bright sunlight that had demanded she wear
her sunglasses.

Before casting off for Nantucket, Reese gave her a
quick tour of his boat, a design less than a year old
with every conceivable amenity. The interior was
warm, rich mahogany with lighter accents. There was
a large-screen television, a computer and a navigation
system with all the bells and whistles, and three state-
rooms, one of which contained an enormous bed covered in a gorgeous ivory comforter.

She went topside fast, not caring if Reese thought
she was running away. She was. Being in a room with
Reese Barone and a big bed was a bad, bad idea.

They made the short trip across the sound to the
old whaling town. Walking away from the wharf, Celia felt as if every resident on the Cape was there,
staring at the Widow Papaleo and her new companion. It was all in her head, she was sure, because
locals rarely attended these things. They were strictly

for the tourists and had supplanted the sea as the mainstay of the whole Cape's economy, but still, there was no denying she felt odd. Intellectually she knew what it was. People expected certain things of those who were grieving. And even though it had been more than two years, she was afraid they would be critical if they saw her with another man. Why wouldn't they? She was critical of herself!

She wondered if she would harbor the same guilty-pleasure kind of feeling if her companion was a new acquaintance, someone with whom she hadn't shared such a complicated—and intimate—past. Maybe that was it. She felt as if everyone walking by knew exactly what she and Reese had been up to on all those boating expeditions years ago.

But Reese didn't appear to entertain any of the same concerns. He took her to a lobster bar for lunch and they dined on a rooftop deck beneath a sun umbrella. It might be October, but the whole year had been unseasonably warm and dry and it was still pleasant during the day. After lunch they wandered the terraced cobblestone streets and eventually headed down to Old North Wharf where they perused the work of the many local artists who immortalized Nantucket's charm.

"I like this guy's work," Reese said, stopping before one easel. "The view of the town from the harbor is a nice perspective."

Celia chuckled. "Guess you didn't see the painting hanging above the sideboard in my dining room. It was done by him."

But Reese wasn't listening anymore. His attention was riveted on the window of a small pub that fronted the street.

Celia followed his gaze, trying to discern what had distracted him. All she saw were families and couples enjoying late-afternoon cocktails and snacks. One couple, in particular, looked as if they were enjoying each other a lot more than their drinks, and she winced as the man dragged the woman close and devoured her mouth in a sloppy display of far-too-public lust.

When she glanced back at Reese, his expression mirrored her own.

She couldn't help smiling. "Don't care for PDAs?"

"PDAs?" He was still watching the couple.

"Teen slang for Public Display of Affection. Hiring so many kids keeps me up on high-school-speak."

"Mmm."

"Reese? Is something wrong?" He was still focused on the couple.

"That man," he said, "is my cousin Derrick."

"Your cousin!" She was torn between happiness for him that he might get to talk with a family member and dismay that the man appeared so oblivious to appropriate public behavior. "Maybe he's had a bit too much to drink. He seems a little…unaware of his surroundings."

"I doubt it." Reese's voice was surprisingly cool. "Derrick will do just about anything for attention."

"He's certainly getting it now." Around the couple, people were casting covert, scandalized glances as hands strayed and mouths wandered. One couple got up, took their young children firmly by the hand and left a nearby table with a scathing comment. Reese's cousin looked after them and Celia was slightly shocked when he laughed. He had to be close to Reese's age and yet he was acting like a hormone-driven teenage boy.

Reese was shaking his head. "Derrick's point of view has always been a little off kilter."

"Off kilter? Like how, exactly?"

Reese shrugged. "He had what I can only call a mean streak. We all learned not to tell him about things that mattered to us or he'd ruin them and laugh about it. In fact," he said as he looked again at the couple, "I could almost swear that woman with him is Racine Madison. She was his brother's girlfriend all through high school. I can see Derrick wanting her just because she was Daniel's once upon a time."

"She's not Racine Madison anymore," Celia informed him. "Her last name is Harrow now, and she's married to the junior senator from New York."

Reese's eyebrows rose and he whistled. "Derrick hasn't changed, then. He's just graduated from coveting other guys' girlfriends to having affairs with other men's wives." His face wore an expression of resignation. "Amazing. I'm gone all these years and I come home to find at least one thing completely unchanged."

"What do you mean?"

"Derrick has a twin, Daniel, who's the nicest guy you'll ever meet. He's also good-looking, smart, popular and excellent at sports. Derrick, I think, spent most of his childhood feeling like he ran a poor second. He was always trying to get attention any way he could. The older he got, the more obnoxious he got." He shook his head. "His brother and his sisters are great people, so it can't have been his upbringing. He certainly wasn't lacking for money, he's decent-looking enough, and he's got more smarts than most of the rest of us put together. And yet he spent our growing-up years looking for ways to cause trouble."

"Some people are just like that," she said. "There may not be a reason, except for one that didn't really exist outside his own imagination."

Reese nodded and she saw a touch of sadness in his eyes. "I think he never believed that anyone could accept him for who he was."

"Would you like to go speak to him?" After all, this was a member of Reese's family whom he hadn't seen in years, albeit not his favorite one.

"No," he said decisively. "This sounds harsh, but Derrick is probably the one person I *haven't* missed. Today is our day. Come on." He reached for her hand and threaded her fingers through his, tugging her along the wharf in the opposite direction.

Celia followed automatically, awash in the sensations and feelings produced by the simple clasp of their hands. He'd held her hand just like this years ago. In fact, they'd rarely walked anywhere that he hadn't been touching her in some small way. It had made her feel safe and secure, half of a whole. It was only now that she realized how incomplete her life had been after he left. No wonder she'd walked around in a fog. He'd been her anchor, her strength, her reason to get up in the morning.

And then he'd left. For a while she'd been too depressed to care about anything. But gradually she'd realized that life would go on and, if she was going to survive, that she'd better depend on herself rather than soak up some man's reflected strength.

And she had. Even when she'd married Milo, she'd never let him mean as much to her as Reese once had. Tears stung her eyes as a whole new barrage of guilt assaulted her. She hadn't been as good a wife as she knew she could have been, because she'd been so determined to protect her heart that she'd never let Milo beyond a certain point. Telling herself that he'd never known anything was wrong was little consolation.

She tugged at the grip of Reese's hand, trying to slide her fingers free. But Reese only tightened his grip. "What's the matter?"

"I don't want the whole Cape buzzing about me holding a strange man's hand," she said. "Could you please let go?"

But he ignored her. "Don't you like it?"

Well. She couldn't say no, because she *did*, far too much. But she couldn't say yes or he'd be smug for the rest of the day. Besides, admitting it would give him far too much power over her. "That's beside the point."

"So you do like it. Good. So do I." He lifted their joined hands and brushed a kiss across her knuckles. "I never let myself think about how much I missed you until I saw you again."

She closed her eyes against the serious intensity of his. It just didn't seem fair, somehow, that he could desert her for so long, and yet the moment he showed up, her body and her emotions were more than ready to take a flying leap back into the middle of a relationship with him. This was only the third day since he'd returned, and already she felt as if they were a couple again.

He still had her hand enclosed in his, and she suspected that arguing with him about it would only be a waste of time. Reese had an instinct for distracting her and he made her arguments seem silly and inconsequential. She might as well save her energy.

Besides, if she were completely honest, she was enjoying every second of the day.

Better not enjoy it too much. He'll leave again and you'll fall flat on your face just like the last time. It was good to remind herself of that. No matter how much she enjoyed his attention and his caresses, he'd be leaving. So whatever she did with him, she had to keep in mind that it was just a temporary thing.

After another hour of strolling the small whaling community, they worked their way to the top of the town, then decided to head back to his boat, docked at Straight Wharf. In a small ice-cream shop on the way, they found Baronessa gelati, the Italian ice cream Reese's grandfather had established in Boston, famous nationwide now.

"Have you kept track of the family business at all?" Celia asked as they sat on a graceful wood-and-iron bench along Upper Main Street, eating their gelati. The day was cooling but still lovely, the reds and yellows of the autumn foliage enhancing the rosy bricks of so many of the historic buildings.

"No. It was never something that interested me much to start with. My mother used to say I was born to be the wild one." His smile was tinged with sadness. "I guess she was right. My older brother, Nick, was the one who liked the whole business angle. We all figured he'd become Mr. Baronessa someday, and he did."

"Yes." She knew that Nicholas Barone was the CEO of the family company now. "But have you heard anything about the fire or the problems the company has had?"

Reese's gaze sharpened. "What fire?"

"Several months ago, in the spring, there was a fire at the manufacturing plant. One of the family members was injured—"

"Who?" His concern was evident.

She shrugged helplessly. "I'm sorry, I can't remember the name. It was a woman."

"Colleen? Gina, Rita, Maria—"

"No. Do you have a sister named Amy, or Annie?" *Amalie.* Maybe that was where the boat's name came from. "I think it was something like that."

"Emily?"

"That was it." Her heart sank. Not Amalie, but Emily.

"She's not my sister, she's my cousin. Derrick, the guy we saw today, is her brother. Was she badly hurt?"

"I don't think so. But the last I heard, the investigators were calling it 'suspicious in origin.'"

"Meaning arson."

"Yes."

"Arson," he repeated. "Who would want to burn down our plant?"

She wondered if he even realized he still thought of himself as a member of the Barone family. "I can't imagine. Does Baronessa have rivals?"

He snorted. "Every company has rivals. But there's a big difference between competition and burning down a rival's business."

"What about someone who's angry at someone in your family? Some kind of grudge, maybe."

His eyebrows rose, and his eyes were focused on a distant past as he answered her. "Our family has had a sort of feud going on for years now with another

Sicilian family who owns a restaurant called Antonio's. But that feud involved my grandfather, and I can hardly imagine it carrying over into our generation. Besides, it's impossible to imagine the Contis sanctioning arson.''

They finished their gelati in silence, then walked back to Reese's boat and headed home to the Cape.

As they skimmed across the choppy sound to the marina, she thought, *What a perfect day.* It was too darn bad that Reese was still the most impossibly attractive man she'd ever known. And that he still could light her fire with no more than a look from those silvery eyes she'd always loved so much. It would be all too easy to get used to being with Reese again, and that would be a terrible mistake.

Because she knew from bitter experience that he couldn't be trusted to stay.

When they docked at the marina he could sense that she was eager to be gone. He vaulted over the rail onto the dock before she could scurry off and said, ''Let's get some shrimp for dinner.''

Celia hesitated. ''Reese,'' she said in a strained voice, ''today was very nice. But I don't think—''

''I do.'' He took her hand and started to pull her along the dock before she could refuse him. ''We both have to eat. We might as well eat together.''

''I can't. I already have plans,'' she said, and her voice was sincere. ''I'm sorry. If I'd known you were going to be in town, I'd have postponed.''

Until you were gone. She didn't say it aloud but he suspected she was thinking it.

Well, he had news for her. If she thought he was

going to disappear from her life again, she was dead
wrong.

Whoa! Say what?

He took a deep breath. All right. He might as well
admit it. He was falling for Celia all over again and
he had no intention of leaving this time. At least, not
unless she came along.

"Reese? Come back." She was waving a hand in
front of his face. "I really am sorry. But there's something I have to do."

"It's all right," he said. "It's not as if we're on a
tight schedule." She got a funny look on her face,
but before she could pursue his statement, he threaded
her fingers through his. "Give me a kiss to keep me
going until tomorrow."

Her eyes widened. "Are you crazy? I'm the boss.
I'd never live it down if anyone saw us."

He made an exaggerated crestfallen face.

She chuckled. Then, gazing into his eyes, both
hands still entwined with his, she pursed her lips and
sent him a single, long-distance kiss across the space
between them. She was smiling slightly, and it was
the craziest thing— Despite the fact that she hadn't
moved one inch closer, the moment felt more intimate
somehow, than if he'd taken her in his arms. Her eyes
were tender with unspoken words and they simply
stood for what seemed like a long, long time, holding
the eye contact.

He nearly asked her what she was thinking, but
words would have marred the moment. Finally he offered her a crooked smile. "I guess that was an ac-
ceptable compromise."

Her eyes sparkled. "Good."

"This time." He lifted one hand and pressed a final

kiss to her knuckles as he had earlier in the day. "See you tomorrow."

"See you." She hesitated a moment, then turned with resolute steps and made her way back to the harbormaster's shack.

He had a solitary dinner of fried clams in his tiny mess that evening. Ordinarily he might have gone looking for a little bar where the locals traded fish and tourist tales, but if he couldn't be with Celia, he didn't want to be with anyone.

Yikes. Thoughtfully, he rolled the single can of beer he'd had with dinner back and forth in his palms. Seemed like every time he allowed himself to think, his brain came up with another idea he hadn't consciously let himself consider.

But it was true. He *didn't* want to be with anyone other than Celia. In the thirteen years they'd been apart, he'd met a lot of women, known some of them intimately. Once he'd even let a girlfriend move in briefly, just long enough to realize it was a colossal mistake. He'd never preferred spending any time outside the bedroom with a woman to hanging with his buddies, and he'd certainly never felt that he couldn't live without one.

Until now.

After he cleaned up his dinner, he watched the evening news. By then it was almost dark and he took a second beer, grabbed a sweatshirt and headed topside to sit in a deck chair, prop his feet on the rail and look at the stars. It was peaceful. Most of the other yachts weren't occupied and he practically had the dock to himself.

So what was he going to do about Celia?

"Hey, Reese! How you doing?" A feminine voice broke the silence.

Damn. He really didn't feel like being social this evening. The voice belonged to Claudette Mason, the woman he'd met the night he'd caught Celia sneaking around. He'd seen Claudette a few times since then, working around her employer's boat or walking to and from the market, but he'd made it a point to be brief. The woman was as unsubtle as they came and clearly on the prowl.

"Hey, Claudette. I'm great." He purposely didn't ask her how she was in return. Maybe she'd get the hint.

"Hello, Mr. Barone. I'm Neil Brevery." It was a smooth, unfamiliar masculine voice. "We haven't met but Claudette has mentioned you."

Ah, hell. He rose to his feet and crossed the deck to the side, where he stepped onto the pier and extended his hand. "My pleasure, Neil. Call me Reese."

The man standing before him was easily twenty years older than the curvaceous Claudette, at least half a foot shorter than he was, slight and almost comical in baggy Bermuda shorts and a brightly patterned tropical shirt. Reese wondered exactly what Claudette's job description was; it was difficult to imagine that Brevery had hired her solely for her skills with a boat. "Are you one of the Boston Barones?"

"Actually, I live in Florida." He'd repeated the words many times in response to that very query and found that they usually discouraged further prying. "Just up here visiting an old friend. And you?"

"I have several homes around the world. Strictly in warm locations." Brevery gave a dry chuckle. "I like to visit the northern regions but I could never live here when it gets cold.'' Then he gestured toward his own boat, docked a number of slips away. ''Ernesto Tiello's coming over for a game of poker. Would you care to join us?''

''Oh, yes, please do.'' Claudette was all but purring. So much for the hope that she'd tone down the vamp act in front of her employer.

He really didn't want to spend the evening gambling, which he loathed. And he wanted to spend it even less with a bunch of strangers. ''I'm sorry,'' he said, lying through his teeth unapologetically, ''but I've got plans in just a little while. Perhaps some other time.''

''Most definitely.''

''Yes. We'll be here for at least another two weeks.'' Claudette struck a pose that thrust her considerable assets into prominent view.

''We may,'' Brevery corrected her. ''Then again, I may take a notion to head for another port.'' There was an edge to his voice. ''Come, Claudette. Let's not keep Ernesto waiting.''

''Yes, sir.'' Claudette's eyes lowered. He got the distinct impression she'd received a reprimand, though he couldn't imagine why.

Brevery extended his hand again. ''Nice meeting you, Reese. We'll have to try to set up a card game for another night.''

''Nice meeting you, also.'' *I'll be busy every night I'm here.* He had to stifle the urge to speak the words aloud as Brevery moved on, Claudette sauntering along in his wake.

Damn. Now what was he going to do? He was quite sure there would be some surreptitious checking going on to see when and if he left his yacht. So much for his quiet, relaxing evening. Served him right for lying in the first place. But he wasn't sorry. No way did he want to spend the evening fending off nosy neighbors' questions and a pushy female's advances. He vaulted back onto the deck and picked up his empty beer can, taking it into the galley and crushing it in the recycler. There was no help for it. He was going to have to go *somewhere*.

What the hell. He'd go sit on Celia's porch. Surely she wouldn't mind. And it wasn't as if she'd be home. He'd just stay an hour or so and then come back. By then, he could make excuses about an early night.

With the decision made, he slipped into his dock-side shoes and locked the cabin, then left the pier and hiked through the little town of Harwichport. Many of the tourist places were dark, but the residents' homes had light spilling from windows and he caught the occasional glimpse of a family moving around inside.

Families. If he'd waited for Celia, or if he'd returned when she was older, would they have had a chance? Could they have had children of their own by now, and a home filled with the same cozy scenes as those he passed? He loved Amalie dearly, but he was thirty-four years old and just beginning to realize how much he'd like to have children of his own someday.

He tried to picture his own kids, but all he could come up with was a troop of dark-haired children much like the ones in family snapshots of his siblings and himself when they were small. A few of them had gotten coppery highlights from their mother's brilliant locks, but for the most part they were dark-

haired, wiry kids with wide, gap-toothed smiles and
deep tans from their Harwichport summers. Yeah,
he'd like to have a few of those.

With Celia. Another revelation. But one he realized
he'd subconsciously imagined for years.

He wondered what her son had looked like. There
were no pictures on her walls, no photographs lovingly framed and displayed, of either her son or her
husband. It was as if she wanted to forget that that
period of her life ever existed.

Having glimpsed the anguish she carried in her
heart the night she'd broken down and cried herself
to sleep in his arms, he felt his throat tighten. He
could understand how difficult it would be to live
with that loss, much less be reminded of it on a daily
basis every time she saw their faces. And who was
he to talk? He'd suffered far less and yet there were
no pictures of his family around anywhere, either.

Reaching her house, he let himself in through the
little garden gate and mounted the single step to the
low porch. He took a seat in one of the old captain's
chairs she kept beneath a trellis of roses that probably
provided welcome shade in the summer. It was quiet
and as peaceful as the night had been earlier. There'd
already been the first frost so no crickets or night
insects stirred the silence. He slouched back in the
chair and exhaled a deep, contented breath, feeling
vaguely silly. Celia wasn't even home and yet he was
comforted just by being near her things, sitting in a
spot he imagined she sat in frequently through the
summer. He closed his eyes, tilted his head back. This
was nice.

Then a soft, scraping sound caught his attention.
Someone was opening Celia's front door from the in-

side. Instantly he was on his feet. Outrage and adrenaline rushed through him. Celia had been through enough in her life; he had no intention of allowing a burglar to destroy the secure little nest she'd made for herself. His muscles tensed as he prepared to launch himself across the porch to take down the black-clad intruder.

And a second later he realized that the "burglar" was Celia.

"What the hell are you doing?" he growled, unaccountably furious at her.

She jumped and squealed in the way only females could do. But she recovered fast. "What do you mean, what am I doing? What are *you* doing hiding on my front porch?"

"I wasn't hiding," he said stiffly. "I thought you weren't home and the marina was too lively, so I came up here to sit on the porch and enjoy the night." He looked more closely at her clothing, noting the black turtleneck sweater, jeans and sneakers and the black watch cap that covered her head, and a suspicion took root. "Exactly what kind of meeting are you going to at…eight-twenty in the evening?"

"That," she said precisely, "is none of your business."

"It is if you're up to what I think you're up to," he said.

Even in the dark he could see her eyes widen with outrage. "I have a date." Her voice was haughty. "And you're making me late."

"Oh, don't mind me." He walked to her side. "I think I'll just tag along and meet this date."

"You will not!"

"Because there is no date, is there?" He took her

arm and shook her lightly. "You're going out on the water to do your amateur spy thing again, aren't you?"

"Yes." Her voice was defiant. "And don't think for a minute you're going to stop me. I'm not a big fan of caveman behavior."

"I wasn't planning to stop you," he said, forcing a mild tone into his voice, although he longed to tie her up and keep her safe. Caveman, indeed. "But I am coming with you."

"Reese...no." She sounded horrified. "What if something happens?"

"I'm going to do my best to see that it doesn't," he assured her. Then, touched by the anxiety he heard in her voice, he smoothed an errant lock of hair back beneath the edge of the cap. "Celia, how do you think I'd feel if something happened to *you* while you were out there alone?" He felt heat creep up his neck. The last thing he wanted to do was to sound pathetic or needy.

"I—I don't know," she muttered, dropping her head. "You left me alone before."

He wanted to shake her. "Yes, I did. Biggest mistake I ever made."

Her head shot up and she stared fully at him for the first time. "What?"

"I'm never leaving you again," he said tightly. What the hell, he'd already opened the lid. He might as well spill the rest.

The words froze in the chilly autumn air. Celia's eyes were wide and dark in the dim light, and her mouth was a round *O* of surprise.

"Well, hell," he finally said. "I guess this isn't the best way to lead into this conversation."

"I guess not." But the antagonism was gone and her tone sounded almost amused. "Are you serious about coming with me?"

He sighed. "If you're serious about going. But I still think it's a lousy idea. You could get hurt if the wrong people realize what you're doing. I can't believe the Feds would ask a civilian to do such a risky thing."

Celia was silent, her gaze dropping away from his again.

"You little…deceiver," he said through his teeth. "You haven't been asked to do this at all, have you?"

"They did ask me to report any suspicious behavior," she said. "How can I report it unless I see it?"

Reese sighed. "All right. If you insist on going, then I'm coming with you. But this is the last time you do anything like this if I have to tie you to your bed every night."

Her gaze flicked to his and then away again and he knew he'd stepped over the invisible line she had drawn between them.

"Sorry," he said. "I don't know why but all I seem to be able to think of when I'm around you is beds."

As he'd hoped, his wry tone lightened the tense moment and she laughed. "Soon we're going to have to start a list of all the things you can't talk about."

He snorted, turning to lead the way down the steps. "It might be easier to list the topics that *aren't* off-limits."

"I'm sorry." She stopped and he turned around. She raised her hands to his chest and the feel of her small, warm palms burned a hole straight through his clothes to brand his skin.

He shivered, wanting nothing more than to drag her onto one of the chairs in the deep shadow of the porch and shove aside clothing until he could sheathe himself deep within her.

"I don't mean to be so difficult," she whispered.

"I know." He took her wrists and pressed a kiss to the fragile inner side of each, ignoring his arousal in favor of the sweet moment. "You just can't help it."

She chuckled, and he was ridiculously pleased when she didn't immediately move away. "Something like that."

Five

But she wasn't laughing three hours later. They'd untied a kayak that she'd moored at a small pier down the street from the marina and slipped out of the harbor, hugging the marshes here and there along the shoreline. They'd seen nothing; no boats, no lights, no suspicious silhouettes of darkened boats, no unusual activity. Nothing. Finally, just before midnight, he talked her into giving up the vigil.

"What makes you think that this drug activity is based at Harwichport?" They were motionless in a stand of scrub and marsh grass, and he spoke close to her ear in a low voice.

"It may not be here. They could be working out of Wychmere, Saquatucket or Allen. But I can't figure out why Milo would have been a target if they weren't worried about him seeing something at our marina."

He nodded, and she knew she had a point. Her husband wouldn't have posed a threat if the drug trafficking had been centered elsewhere. "It could have been simply a revenge thing," he said.

"I've thought about that, too. But it doesn't make sense. Usually revenge is done with a public purpose in mind, to teach someone else a lesson. Unless it's extremely personal, which I doubt this was. Milo never offended anyone in his whole life. Besides, no one else knew Milo had spoken to the FBI."

"That you're aware of."

She was silent for a moment. "True."

They didn't speak again until they got back to the dock and tethered the boat. Walking up the street to her house, he said, "Celia, you don't know who else might be involved in this. You could wind up the same way your husband and son did if the wrong person suspects you're still digging around."

"I know." She stopped on the small porch. "And until recently I didn't even care. But now…" She shook her head, not caring if he saw the tears on her cheeks. "Dammit, Reese, why did you come back here?"

He stepped forward and gathered her into his arms, laying his cheek against her hair, and she savored the moment as she slipped her arms around his waist and clung. "Because," he said, "I couldn't stay away any longer."

Dropping his head, he sought her mouth. The kiss he gave her was tender, rife with deep feeling, healing lonely aches inside her that she'd known since her family had died. Celia clung to him, needing to be cuddled and coddled, needing the warmth of his hard body surrounding and protecting her. It had been so long since she'd felt safe that she'd forgotten how good it was, and she reveled in his gentle touch.

But it wasn't long before his mouth hardened, became more demanding, his tongue plunging into her moist depths in search of her response. And respond she did. She went limp against him, letting his arms support her, letting him pull her so closely against him that he made a deep growling sound in the back of his throat as their bodies fit together.

He bent her backward over one arm, his free hand slipping beneath her black sweater to caress the silky skin at her waist. His fingers were rough and determined, and she shivered helplessly when his hand slid upward, stroking and exploring her torso. His fingers glided over her ribs until he could cup her breast in his palm, his thumb rubbing ceaselessly over her sensitive nipple, and she shivered in his embrace, her arms coming up to clasp his dark head. Each small stroke sent wild arrows of arousal down to center between her legs, and she writhed against him.

He dragged her back to the swing, deep in the shadows, and settled her across his lap without ever breaking the demanding, tongue-tangling kiss they shared. Celia twisted as he tugged up her sweater to bare her breasts in the shadowed darkness, and when he bent his head and took one nipple into the hot cavern of his mouth, she stifled the sound she made against his shoulder.

"Don't hold back." He plucked at the other taut nipple and she squirmed, pressing her legs tightly together to alleviate the throbbing ache centered there. "Don't hold back," he said again. His free hand left her breast and smoothed down her body, gently probing at her navel, spanning her small waist. She felt a slight tug as he freed the fastening of her pants, and then his warm hand was in her panties, splayed across her abdomen, the tips of his fingers brushing back and forth over the tiny curls he found.

Celia's arms clenched around his neck. Her whole body felt supersensitized, her breath coming in shallow gulps. Had it always been this...*intense* with Reese?

Yes. Always.

His mouth suckled harder at her breast and suddenly she felt a shocking nip of strong teeth as he closed them over the sensitive peak. She gasped and he gentled his mouth immediately while at the same instant he slid his middle finger over her feminine mound and deep into the wiry curls. She gasped again and he lifted his head from her breast and claimed her mouth in another intimate kiss, echoed by the finger between her legs probing gently but insistently at her tight folds. "Spread your legs," he urged. She obeyed. Her whole body tightened when she felt him slide one finger deep into her, and her back arched involuntarily as her body clenched around him, pushing him even deeper.

"Celia," he gasped. "I forgot how good you feel." He rotated his finger slightly, grinding the palm of his hand against the throbbing button of need at the top of her opening, and she cried out, dazed by the intense sensations. The sound of her own voice was startling in the deep shadow of the night porch, and for the first time, she fully realized that they were outside, on her front porch, within hearing—and possibly within sight—of anyone who happened by.

"Wait." She struggled in his arms, gripping his wrist tightly. She had no chance of moving his hand from its intimate nest unless he chose to do so, a fact that she was keenly aware of with the vulnerable knowledge only another woman could understand. Reese stilled his hand, although he didn't withdraw.

"It's all right, baby. It's all right."

"No," she said. "It's not." She swallowed painfully, so aroused by the feel of his hand between her legs that she nearly forgot why she'd protested. "I—I'm not ready for this, Reese."

In the darkness she saw the white flash of his teeth. One finger moved, drawing a whimper of need from her. "I beg to differ. And—" he shoved his hips forward against her hip so that she could feel the rock-hard bulge of his arousal "—I sure as hell am."

"No," she whispered again. "I—I want to but…I'm just not ready."

He stilled, and she realized he understood that she meant it. Finally he heaved a sigh. "Okay. Okay, I can wait. I don't want to rush you into anything." Slowly, he withdrew his hand and she closed her eyes tightly as her body jerked involuntarily at the glide of flesh on flesh. His finger left a cool path of moisture behind and even in the dark, she blushed. Then he spoke again. "Can you tell me why? I mean, I've already stayed the night, technically, so if you're worried about your reputation—"

"It's not that. I just…have to think. A few days ago we hadn't seen each other in thirteen years and now here we are, ready to…"

"Yeah. Ready to." There was wry humor in his voice. He carefully refastened her pants and tugged her sweater down into place, then lifted her and set her beside him on the swing, cuddling her in the crook of his elbow. "Where do you see us going with this, Celia?"

She was silent. "That's not a fair question," she said. "I've barely gotten used to the idea that you're back again."

"It hasn't been any longer for me," he pointed out, "and I'm used to it." He took her face between his palms and gently stroked her lips with his thumbs. "I'm willing to leave the past in the past. Are you?"

She hesitated and his hands dropped away. "Or are you still punishing me for taking off all those years ago?" His voice was rough, frustrated, impatient. "I'm not looking for an affair for a few weeks while I'm in town, so if that's all this is going to be to you, tell me now."

"What *are* you looking for?" She swallowed painfully. "I'm not the same girl you used to know, Reese. I don't have a lot to offer anymore."

"You have everything I want." His voice was low, soothing.

"Not if you're looking for a wife and a family," she said bluntly, too agitated to soften the words. "I don't want children. Ever. I just…I couldn't handle that." She stopped, aware that her voice was rising toward hysteria.

He was silent, and her heart felt as if someone had attached lead weights to it. This was it. Now he would leave. She'd told him how she felt so that he wouldn't expect more than she could give…but she couldn't prevent herself from praying that he didn't walk away.

She caught his wrist and rose with him when he would have moved away from her. She knew she could never be what he wanted. It was wrong of her to encourage him, to give him hope and yet...

"Reese?"

He hesitated, but he didn't pull away from her. Finally he turned and touched her cheek with his free hand, then linked his fingers through hers. "I want you, Celia. Just you." He bent and kissed her swiftly, then walked down the path to her gate. "See you tomorrow."

In the morning the first thing she thought of was Reese. Why had she turned him away last night? Was it self-preservation? Or was he right? Was she punishing him?

She worried at the notion the whole way to the marina, but when she entered the office, Angie's expression erased all thoughts of personal matters from her head. "What's wrong?" she asked.

"Hurricane." Angie indicated the small television they kept atop a file cabinet. "The one they thought was going to move northeast off the coast? Well, it's coming in for a visit."

"Oh, no." Her mind raced. "How long do we have till it gets here?"

Angie shrugged. "Maybe the rest of the day. It tore up the Carolina coast and is headed straight for us." She laid a stack of papers on Celia's desk. "Did you have a boat out last night? I found life preservers hanging on the doorknob this morning."

Celia stiffened. "Yes. Reese and I went night fishing." Duh. Hadn't she used that very same excuse on the night she'd run into Reese?

Angie laughed. "Sure, boss. Night fishing." She was grinning as she walked away.

Celia studied the weather pattern as the meteorologist on the screen droned on. The brunt of the hurricane had missed the southern coastline. But Cape Cod stuck out too far. If it continued due north, they were going to get slammed. She'd seen Hurricane Bob do the same thing more than a decade ago, and that hadn't been nearly as powerful a storm as this one was currently.

Quickly she gathered the rest of the staff and began issuing orders. All equipment needed to be put away, including any watercraft small enough to be removed from the water. Bigger ones should be moored on long lines or moved to small harbors with marshes or sand beaches where they could be grounded without causing the damage that would result if they were tossed by waves into large piles of ruined boats at the pier. Anything that could blow away, even heavy deck furniture, should be stored. Flags and banners down, cancel all charters, close the marina. Get out the plywood and start covering all the windows, tape any that don't get boarded up.

Many of the yachts were already gone, others were battening down and their owners were taking rooms in town. Lodging was easy to come by, since the autumn tourists were fleeing, clogging Route 6 up to the Sagamore Bridge where they headed west away from the water or north toward Boston.

Angie helped her remove the important files and compact discs, and take apart the computer. Then they took the whole mess over and set it up at her house, which would be far safer than the office. Her headquarters was commonly known as ''the shack'' despite its sturdy appearance. It would be exposed to the waves and storm surge and could easily fall apart if the pier should go.

While she was at home, she double-checked the small generator that would keep her freezer and refrigerator going when the power went down as it inevitably would, pulled oil lanterns from storage and filled them, and brought in armloads of firewood. She filled the bathtub and several extra buckets with water, just in case, and checked the batteries in her flashlights.

Then she headed back to the shack to help finish boarding up before she sent everyone home. Reese's boat still sat in its slip, and she allowed herself to wonder where he was and what he would do during the storm. Part of her wanted to invite him to spend the time with her; the other part told her she was crazy, that she was heading for heartbreak.

"Celia." Ernesto Tiello lumbered up the pier toward her, a sleeveless men's undershirt stretched a little too tightly over his bulky body. He was heavily muscled rather than fat, and he reminded her of nothing so much as a Mafia-type don on one of her favorite television shows. She wondered momentarily whether he kept a weight room aboard his boat. The thought made her shake her head. Rich people.

"Hello, Ernesto. Staying with us through the storm?"

He nodded, his dark eyes grim. "Yes. But I have another question. Have you seen Claudette Mason this morning?"

She shook her head. "No. Did Brevery leave?"

Ernesto shook his head. "No. He has decided to stay, as well."

"I imagine Claudette's probably helping him."

"No." His accent was thicker than ever. "Neil has not seen her this morning. He thinks she may simply have quit. But I am concerned. She would have told me if she were planning to leave."

"I'm sure she's around," Celia soothed. "Why don't you check with the rest of my staff? One of them might know where she got to."

"Thank you. I shall. And you will let me know if you should find her?"

"Of course." She shook her head as Tiello moved along the pier to where some of her staff were working. The poor man was wild about Claudette, but Celia was sure Claudette didn't return the feeling. Maybe she had simply taken off.

Still, she'd seemed quite content acting as a hostess or whatever it was she did for Neil Brevery while she flirted with everything in pants. There didn't seem to be a physical relationship between Claudette and her employer, although Celia had noticed the woman jumped to attention when the small man spoke. The rest of the time, she acted like a cat in heat.

Now, Celia, be nice. Just because she's drooled over Reese a few times is no reason to show your own claws.

"Hey, woman, why are you scowling?"

She jumped, startled out of her thoughts. Reese stood right in front of her. If he only knew! She smiled, then said, "Never mind. Have you seen Claudette Mason?"

Reese grimaced. "No, thank God."

She couldn't prevent the chuckle. "Been ducking her advances?"

"Been running like a gazelle," he countered. "There's someone else I'd rather advanced on me."

"Oh?" She cast him a flirtatious glance, then caught herself. Lord, she was as bad as Claudette.

"Are you going to invite me to weather the storm with you?" He stepped a pace closer and his eyes grew heavy with sensual intent.

"I hadn't thought about it," she lied. "Can't find a room in town?"

He shook his head. "No. It's terrible. Everything's booked solid. Even the emergency shelter at the high school is full. One guy offered me his stable, but I'm too big to sleep in a manger, so…"

She was laughing. "Con artist. I suppose you can come over. Let me finish getting everything stowed here and we'll go." She indicated the television. "From the look of things, this storm is moving a lot faster than they expected. We're not going to have hours to sit around and wait for it."

And they didn't.

He arrived home with her around four, bringing a duffel bag of clothing with him. She felt a little funny marching through the streets with a man carrying what amounted to a suitcase, but she told herself that with the storm coming, everyone would be too busy to wonder about it.

At her house, he nailed the gate shut, took down the porch swing and put away the chairs in her shed, then helped her in the kitchen as she made several dishes that could be eaten cold over the next few days.

The wind had already picked up by seven, and they checked the forecast as a meteorologist pointed out the eye of the enormous storm system moving straight toward them.

They snuggled on the sofa watching the Weather

Channel, which had devoted itself almost exclusively
to coverage of the storm. She'd felt both exhilarated
and awkward when he'd first put his arm around her,
but when he'd made no further moves she relaxed.
Now she leaned into his big, warm body with pleasure. He didn't appear to be angry about last night,
and for the first time she allowed herself to wonder,
just for a moment, whether they had any chance at a
future together. Then he spoke and she abandoned her
thoughts with relief.

"This could be bad. I guess you've been through
your share of wicked storms."

Celia nodded, trying to ignore the erotic sensation
of his breath feathering her ear. "A few. But a lot of
times, the hype is worse than the actual event. And
most of the worst ones were nor'easters. We don't get
slammed by hurricanes as often as the southern states
do. How about you? Were you living in Florida when
Andrew came through?"

Reese shook his head. "No. And my home isn't
anywhere close to where the worst of the damage was
done. But hurricanes can be killers. I learned that the
hard way."

"What do you mean?"

A shadow passed over his features. "Nobody ever
thinks bad things can happen to *them*. I told you about
my friends Kent and Julie, but I didn't tell you how
they died. They took their boat down to the Bahamas
for a couple of days. They had a baby at home and
hadn't had much time together, and Kent wasn't too
worried that there was a hurricane coming. He was a
good sailor. He figured if he kept an eye on the fore-
casts and got out in time, they'd be heading north-

west, away from a storm so they'd beat it to the mainland.''

Celia felt a clutch in her stomach as he continued, his face grim and stony.

"But the storm changed course and caught them. I was in radio contact with them for five hours and then...nothing.''

"Oh, Reese." She turned in his arms and circled his shoulders. "I'm so sorry."

"The coast guard never found them, although a few pieces of their boat did eventually wash up." He dropped his head to rest against hers.

Poor Reese. He'd lost his family—through circumstances she still didn't entirely understand—then he'd found a friend—and lost him, too. She didn't speak, sensing that words would be superfluous. The comfort he needed from her superceded oral communication. So she simply pulled him more closely to her and rubbed small circles over his back.

"Celia?"

"Yes?" She pressed a kiss to his jaw.

"There's something else I'd like to tell you about Kent and Julie—" But his voice was interrupted by a loud banging at the back door. They both jolted.

"Who in the world is that?" It had already begun to rain and the wind had picked up significantly, although she doubted the winds were gale force. Wrenching open the door, she held it tightly to prevent the wind from ripping it out of her hands. "Roma!" Her friend was drenched, her fine black hair plastered to her head despite the raincoat hood she had over it. "What's wrong?"

"Greg fell off the ladder." Her friend's voice

caught. "I hate to impose, but do you have time to help me finish the windows?"

"Of course!" She turned to call to Reese but he was standing right behind her.

"We'll both come," he said. "Have you taken him to the medical center?"

"My father did. Mom's keeping the kids."

"How bad do you think he is?" Celia was already reaching for her raincoat on a hook in the mudroom.

"He's going to need stitches, I think." She made a gesture toward her eye. "He cut his eyebrow open pretty deep."

Celia winced. "Bet he'll have a shiner."

They covered the block and a half to the Lewises' home in short order, and despite the increase in wind and rain, they were able to help Roma nail plywood over her larger windows and put asterisk-shaped crosses of gray electrical tape over the remaining ones.

Just as they were finishing, Roma's father and Greg returned. Rather than stitches, the cut in his eyebrow was covered by a shiny clear coat of something that resembled nail polish. Roma's father explained that it was a special skin sealant—a type of superglue for humans—that wouldn't leave as much of a scar as stitches might.

"I made clam chowder," Roma told them in a half shout over the rising roar of the wind. "Come on in and have some. The least I can do is feed you after working you like that in the middle of this storm."

"Oh, that's all right—"

"Thanks. We'd love to." Reese cut in right over Celia's attempt to wriggle out of the offer.

"Great." Roma turned and headed for the door.

"We'll hang your coats by the woodstove so at least they'll dry a little before you go out again."

As they followed her into the house, Celia cast Reese a dark glance. "Why did you do that?"

"I thought it would be nice to get to know your friends," he told her quietly. "Unless there's some reason you'd prefer I didn't."

"No," she said. "It's not that…"

"Then what?"

But Roma's voice saved her from a reply. "Come on, you two. It's getting nastier out there by the minute!"

They weren't in the house ten minutes when he realized why Celia had been reluctant to stay for dinner. He'd thought—feared—that perhaps she didn't want anyone to see them together. But it wasn't him at all.

Greg and Roma Lewis had three small children. The oldest couldn't have been more than six, and they plainly adored Celia. An older woman he assumed was Roma's mother was feeding a baby girl when they walked in, and the infant squawked and reached for Celia with a wide grin that displayed four teeth and an astonishing amount of drool.

"I know, I know," the woman said, her voice amused. "Gramma can't compete with Aunt Celia. Here." She handed the spoon to Celia. "Would you like to finish the job?"

"I'd love to." Celia took a seat and began feeding the baby, and Reese watched in fascination as she coaxed the little mouth open by repeating a ditty about a choo-choo train entering a tunnel, complete with the *whoo-whoo* of a whistle. This was a side of her he'd never seen and for the first time he could finally envision her as a mother.

Roma introduced him to her parents and her husband, Greg, who shook his hand before wincing and settling into a rocking chair with an ice pack pressed against his head. "Thanks for helping Roma finish up," he said. "I don't know how the hell that happened. One minute I was on the ladder, the next I was eating dirt."

The smaller of the two boys wandered over and surveyed his father with a puckered brow. "Daddy have a boo-boo?"

Greg nodded. "A big boo-boo. But I bet it would feel a lot better if someone kissed it."

"Me, me!" the little boy demanded. His father carefully leaned forward and the child gingerly delivered a loud, smacking kiss near the wound above his eye.

"Ah," said Greg. "It feels better already. Thank you, William."

The little boy nodded with satisfaction and moved away again.

Reese felt a surprising tightness in his chest. He could barely remember Amalie at that age; Kent and Julie had died mere months before and he had still been trying to adjust to the role of father. Without a lot of success, he added mentally. The little girl had been withdrawn and silent for months after her parents died. It had been more than a year before the two of them had begun to really adjust to their new family status.

He glanced at Celia without quite realizing that he wanted to share the touching moment with her, but she wasn't looking at him. Instead she was watching little William as he toddled off with a toy in his hand. There was such naked pain on her face that he nearly reached for her before he caught himself. Checking Roma, he caught her watching, as well, and when her gaze flashed his, he saw that Celia's friend was fighting tears.

It was then that he realized why Celia had tried to decline Roma's invitation. It hadn't been reluctance to have him get to know her friends. He'd been ridiculously self-centered in coming to that conclusion. She simply hadn't wanted to open the door and admit the pain and loss she lived with every day. He mentally kicked himself around the room. How could he not have realized the impact that a small child—much less a houseful of them—would have on her? And hadn't she told him her son would have started kindergarten this fall? Roma's oldest child looked to be about that age. Talk about rubbing salt in a wound.

He took deep breaths, feeling extraordinarily agitated. He couldn't stand the thought of her suffering like that. Without thinking, he sprang to his feet. "Listen," he commanded.

Everyone in the room except for the smallest child fell silent and turned expectantly to him. Avoiding Celia's gaze, he spoke to Roma. "That wind is getting stronger by the minute. We'd better take a rain check on that dinner invitation, Roma, if you don't mind. I'm afraid we're asking for trouble if we stay much longer."

"You're welcome to weather the storm here with us," Greg offered.

"No," Roma said. "Celia feels just like I do. If something's going to happen to my house, I want to be there to straighten it out right away." She had looked away but then glanced back at Reese as she spoke, and he saw approval in her eyes. She knew exactly what he was doing.

"Reese is right," Celia added. She handed the baby's spoon back to Roma's mother and stood, leaning forward to press a kiss to the little one's forehead. "We'd better go while we still can."

The baby's little face screwed up and she immediately started to fuss.

"Well, at least let me send some chowder along with you," Roma said above the din. She quickly ladled soup into a large jar, screwed the lid on tight and wrapped it in a dishtowel. "That should keep it from burning you," she said as Reese put it in the pocket of the capacious oilcloth raincoat Celia had given him before they'd set out.

"Thanks," Celia told her.

"Thank *you*," Roma said. "I'd never have gotten everything done in time by myself." She stretched up and planted a light kiss on Reese's cheek as Celia moved off to say her goodbyes to the rest of the family. "Thank you," she said quietly. "I opened my mouth before I thought."

"Yeah, but you did it for the right reasons." They grinned at each other.

"Get her home safely."

"Don't worry." Reese smiled down at Celia's best friend, absurdly pleased at her apparent acceptance of his return to Celia's life. As Celia came to stand beside him again, his gaze caught and held hers for a long moment. "She's not going to get away from me."

A few moments later they stepped out into the storm again.

"Yikes," said Celia. "You were right about the wind getting worse."

Reese took her hand, bending his head against the stinging pellets of rain hurled at them by the blast of the wind. "Did you think I was kidding?"

"No," she said, "but I did think you might be exaggerating as a way to get me out of there faster." She squeezed his hand. "Thank you."

"You're welcome." The wind was making it difficult to converse without shouting. "You can thank me again once we're home."

That startled a laugh from her and they fought their way the short distance back to Celia's sturdy house.

They hung their dripping slickers in her mudroom and hustled into the warmth of her kitchen. Reese set the clam chowder on the butcher-block counter and they worked together to assemble a small meal, which they carried in and set on the low glass-topped driftwood table in front of her large fireplace made of water-smoothed stone.

"We'll have to let the fire burn down soon," she said as they lingered over coffee afterward, "because the wind will start driving the smoke back into the house."

Reese surveyed her, nestled into a mound of pillows with a cranberry-colored woven blanket draped across her lap. "That's all right," he said. "There are other ways to keep warm."

"Reese…"

"Celia…" he teased. He rose, holding her gaze, and he saw her swallow visibly. "Let's clean up these dishes."

Her eyes widened. She chuckled then, tossing a balled-up napkin at him as she rose and began to stack their plates. "You like keeping me off balance," she accused as she brushed past him into the kitchen.

He followed her with a second load. "That's because I live in hope that you'll fall into my arms."

Celia set down the dishes and moved aside so he could do the same. "Reese," she said, her voice troubled, "we just had this discussion. You've been here less than a week. I know I invited you to stay here during the storm, but…we barely know each other."

He made a rough sound of denial and moved forward, capturing her waist in his hands. "That's not true and you know it. We knew each other about as well as any two people on the planet thirteen years ago and I don't think either of us has changed that much." He took her hand and lifted it, pressing her palm flat over his chest. "You still make my heart beat faster," he said. "And I still want you as much as I ever did."

Her face softened and he felt some of the tension leave her body. "You always know exactly what to say, don't you?"

"Only to you." His voice sounded rough and rusty even to his own ears. Slowly he gathered her closer until there was no space between their bodies. "I have missed you so damn much," he said.

"I missed you, too." She brought her hands up to cradle his face as he dropped his head and sought her mouth. Her response to his kiss was everything he'd imagined during the many fantasies he'd had in which they met again. But there was one difference—he'd lost the desire to hurt her as she'd hurt him.

He pressed the tip of a finger to her lips, accepting the instant current of electric attraction that arced between them when he touched her. Then he walked her backward across the room, deliberately letting his body bump hers with each step.

She stopped when she came up against the wall, and her hands flattened on his chest. ''What are you doing?''

He ignored the question as he slipped one arm around her and pulled her against him, sliding the other up to cradle her jaw. ''I've never been able to forget you.''

Her eyes closed. ''I know the feeling.'' Her voice was rueful. Then her palms slid slowly from his chest up to his shoulders, and she leaned into him, laying her head in the curve of his neck.

Euphoria rushed through him as her breath feathered a warm kiss of arousal down his spine. The memory of the kiss they'd shared last night had simmered in the back of his mind all day, of the way she'd softened and let herself relax against him. It was the same thing she'd always done years ago, as if the moment he touched her she became his and his alone. It was an intense turn-on and he wondered if she had any idea how it made him feel when she made that soft sound of acquiescence. Her body aligned with his perfectly when she stood on her toes, and when he'd had her lying open and trusting on his lap, it had been all he could do to restrain himself from yanking open his own pants, stripping hers off and fitting himself into the soft, wet warmth of her spread legs.

Tonight he wasn't going to walk away without finishing this.

Six

Reese threaded one hand into her hair and tugged her head up from his neck, nuzzling along her jaw to her mouth. As his lips slid onto hers, she opened her mouth eagerly, and with that welcome, his tenuous control fell away.

He ran his hands down her back and pulled her hard against him, feeling the full weight of her breasts press into his chest. She'd had beautiful breasts thirteen years ago and he was fairly sure they were even more lovely now. They'd certainly felt fine last night, though it had been too dark for the thorough inspection he longed to make. As she wrapped her arms around his neck and wriggled herself closer, he tugged up the short T-shirt she wore and laid his hand against the smooth, warm flesh of her midriff.

She didn't protest or draw away and he realized that since last night she'd come to some kind of peace, some decision about letting him back into her life. Encouraged and incredibly aroused, he let the shirt ride up over his wrist and forearm and he slid his hand steadily higher until his fingers touched the lacy edge of her bra. The underside of her breast rested on his knuckles and he raised his hand and brushed back and forth over the tip of her breast beneath the fabric.

Celia moaned. She drew back and he knew a crushing disappointment, until she yanked the T-shirt over her head and threw it on the floor. Her eyes met his and her gaze was clear and steady as she stood before him in a black bra that did next to nothing to conceal breasts that were fuller and even more lovely than he remembered. When her hands drifted to the bottom of his own T-shirt, he was galvanized into action and he tore it over his head and let it drop even as his hands reached around her to unclasp her bra.

Her eyelids flickered as the fabric came away. He hooked his fingertips beneath the straps and pulled it down and off so that her breasts fell free and unfettered, swaying gently with each gulp of breath she took. Her nipples were a dusky copper, large and dark, and he groaned, bringing both hands up to fill his palms with the silky globes.

He'd been missing her for so many years and until this moment he hadn't allowed himself to truly think about what it was he'd missed. She was looking down at his hands and she lifted her own, covering his palms and pressing them hard against her flesh. "Touch me," she whispered.

He *was* touching her, but it wasn't enough and he knew exactly what she meant. Releasing her breasts, he put his arms around her and drew her against him,

skin to skin, and they both murmured at the intense
pleasure in the contact. He bent his head and sought
her mouth, and the passionate kiss they exchanged
sent fiery streamers of desire streaking through his
body, demanding more, more, more.

He lifted her into his arms without breaking the kiss
and carried her to the wide sofa in front of the old
stone fireplace. On the rug, he stood her on her feet
again. He wanted her naked, wanted to touch every
gently curving inch, wanted to explore her secrets, to
wallow in the familiar and to discern the changes the
years had wrought. He unsnapped her pants and
tugged them down, slipping his thumbs into the black
cotton bikini briefs she wore and taking them off in
the same motion. They pooled around her ankles and
he took a moment to slip her feet out of her shoes
and socks, then sat back on his heels and looked up
the length of her.

Her face grew pink. She made an involuntary gesture as if to cover herself and he chuckled, catching
her wrists and holding them at her sides. "Don't. I
want to see you." He leaned forward and pressed a
kiss to the soft curve of her belly, just above the dark
tangle of curls. "How can you still be so beautiful?"

She laughed, although the sound was strained. "I
have stretch marks." But her hands gently sifted
through his hair, scratching lightly over his scalp and
sending shivers of arousal through him. "You've got
on too many clothes."

He rose. "That can be fixed." He pulled her hands
toward him and set them at the buckle of his belt.
"Help me."

She looked down, concentrating on the task, and
he sucked in a harsh breath at the feel of her fingers

against his stomach. Slowly she opened the belt and pulled it wide, then undid the front button of his khaki pants. He was so hard and ready that his clothing was uncomfortable, and when her small fingers gently slid down the tab of his zipper, he had to steel himself against the surge of pressure that threatened his control.

Quickly he reached down and captured her hands, forcing a smile when she looked up at him inquiringly. "Not a good idea right now," he informed her. "I'll take it from here."

She smiled, and he dispensed with the pants and briefs in one smooth motion before straightening and holding out his hand to her. Celia's eyes were wide and shadowed as she looked first at his body, then at the hand he extended. But finally she smiled at him as she linked her fingers through his, and he felt a tension evaporate that he hadn't even fully recognized. As a wave of relief rolled through him, he pulled her against him.

Her body was long and sleek and beautifully muscled from the active work that was a part of her normal routine. She felt so familiar that his throat tightened with an unexpected surge of emotion and he closed his eyes before she could see his reaction. How had he managed to live without her all these years? Not just her body, although as her soft belly cradled his hard, aching flesh between them, he thanked God for it, but the way she smiled at him from beneath her eyelashes, her sly sense of humor, the way she threw herself wholeheartedly into anything she did.

Her hands ran over the solid muscles of his arms and back and she couldn't help but compare his body

with the one she'd known so long ago. There was
nothing left of the boy in him now. Even his shoulders seemed broader. This was a man beneath her
searching fingers—a heavily muscled, hairy-chested,
undeniably aroused man.

He gathered her against him, palming her head in
one large hand and holding her against his shoulder
while he kissed her deeply, repeatedly, teasing her
with his tongue while his free hand slid from her
shoulder to her breast, catching the taut nipple between two fingers. Gently he pinched and rolled until
she could barely stand, her whole body trembling
with the need that shot down to pool between her
legs, and she clutched at his arms. "Please," she said.
"Now."

"What's your rush?" He laughed, a low, growling
sound, as he trailed his lips along the line of her throat
and down the slope of her breast, and she cried out
as his mouth took her in, suckling strongly. Her back
arched and his hand stroked a path down her torso,
spreading wide over her ribs, dipping lightly into the
well of her navel, then brushing with the lightest of
feather touches over the curls between her legs. She
pushed her hips forward, wordlessly begging him, and
suddenly she felt the sharp shock of one long finger
sliding down, testing, tracing, gradually opening her
as he'd done the night before, and she moaned, pressing her face against his shoulder. Her body trembled
in the grip of sensual pleasure; her breath came in
short pants.

Then she felt his finger again, slick and moist,
seeking and pressing against the very heart of her,
and her whole body jerked. She lifted her head from
his shoulder and looked down, exulting in the contrast

of his darkly tanned skin lying against her lighter flesh in that private part, loving the way he cupped her so carefully, aroused by the sight of his hand covering the dark curls there. She moved her hips against his finger and he immediately took up a rhythm, rubbing and circling the locus of her desire as she writhed against him.

Pleasure built swiftly, inexorably carrying her higher and higher. The world shrank as her whole being focused on the big hand controlling her, inciting her response. She sank her teeth into his shoulder, muffling the sounds she made as her hips shifted into a faster, primitive beat that could have only one conclusion.

Suddenly he thrust his hand forward, grinding his palm hard against her as one finger sank deeply into her and she screamed, throwing her head back as her whole body convulsed, reacting to the intense pleasure of the invasion.

"That's it," he muttered against her throat. "That's what I want." He touched her deeply, intimately, until she was a boneless heap of throbbing female moaning softly in his arms.

Finally she opened her eyes. Reese was staring down at her, his eyes brilliant slits of desire. He still cradled her body, his hand still nestled between her thighs. A fine tremor of tension shivered through his body and she drowsily lifted her arms, encircling his neck, lying her head against his shoulder. He bent and lifted her, laying her full length on the rug and coming down beside her.

Somehow the horizontal position seemed even more intimate than what had come before, although she knew that was just plain silly. He lay propped beside her, one leg bent and lying half over hers, and she could feel the very real need that surged through him pulsing at her thigh.

Celia swallowed. Milo had been thin and wiry, slim and slight...all over. The hard shaft pressing against her hip couldn't be called slight in any sense of the word. She'd forgotten, or more likely, if she was truthful, hadn't allowed herself to remember Reese's solid build and how small and feminine she'd always felt in his arms. He shifted, bringing his full weight over her, supporting himself on his forearms, and she felt the first stirrings of panic. She was remembering, too, how uncomfortable their early lovemaking had been until they'd both learned to give her time to adjust to him.

"Reese, wait."

"I've waited long enough." His gaze was fierce and intense, burning with desire as he tore open a condom and quickly rolled it into place, but even then he recognized her unease and sought to allay it. His features softened slightly and he gave her a crooked smile as he pulled her into his arms again. "You're ready, baby. Trust me."

And she did. He moved forward, guiding himself to her, and she sucked in a sharp breath as she felt the blunt, probing force steadily invading her most private place.

"Slowly," she breathed into his ear. "It's been a long time."

He tensed against her, buttocks tight beneath her stroking palms. "And you're just a little thing."

She relaxed, realizing that he understood and remembered the source of her hesitation. "I'm not sure that I'm the one who's unusually sized."

He gave a snort of laughter and she felt him push another small increment deeper. It didn't hurt, and she opened her legs wider, inviting him in as he said, "As I recall, once we got the hang of it, you didn't seem to mind."

"I didn't." She was intoxicated with the sexual innuendo, overwhelmed now with memories, and she playfully reached down between them, curling her hand around him. "I won't." She stroked him lightly and he shuddered.

"Whoa." His voice sounded choked. "I'm trying to make this last, woman."

"Why?" She didn't stop. "We can start all over again as soon as we like."

"There's a thought." With that, he reached down and took her hand away. Holding her gaze, he pushed himself steadily forward, forward, forward, until Celia was gasping and he was lodged deeply within her. He stopped and looked down at her, and her heart turned over at the tenderness in his gaze. "I was afraid I might never get to do this again," he said in a low tone.

Then he twined his fingers with hers, supporting himself on his elbows and holding her hands to the rug.

And he began to move.

How could I have forgotten this?

Celia fought tears, overcome by the wonder of the feelings that flared, new and familiar at the same time, as he established a strong, steady rhythm, advancing and retreating, building another small fire inside her that quickly threatened to explode as his rhythm disintegrated into a frantic maelstrom of movement. He pounded into her, their slick, wet bodies making a satisfying slap with each surge, his breathing hoarse gasps in her ear, his heart thundering against hers.

She could feel herself gathering into a taut knot of need, writhing beneath him as she wrapped her legs around his waist. He touched every part of her with each stroke and as the pace increased, she began to moan again, then to cry out until finally she reached her peak a second time and her body bucked wildly in his arms. Her release triggered his, and with a rough groan of pleasure, Reese finally shuddered and arched against her, his strength shoving her hard against the rug until he slowly relaxed, slumping over her heavily.

After a long moment, he heaved himself onto his elbows again, then dropped his head and sought her lips for a gentle kiss. "No wonder I couldn't forget you," he said. "This was meant to be."

Then he rolled to one side and gathered her into his arms, her back to his front, spoon fashion.

She was lying there, trying to decide how to respond to his statement, when she realized that he was fast asleep.

She lay there for a while, listening to the wind howl around the cottage, feeling safe and secure and happier than she'd been in a long, long time.

This was meant to be.

Was he right? Could it be that easy?

He whistled all the way back down to the marina the next morning. Even the sight of the mess the hurricane had left couldn't dampen his mood. At the last minute the full brunt of the storm had moved off to the east, out to sea, and though the Cape had taken a beating, there didn't appear to be widespread destruction, just a whole lot of annoying junk to clean up.

He'd promised to help Celia with marina repairs—

Celia. He could almost feel his chest swell like a cartoon character guzzling spinach. She made him feel as if he were ten times the man he'd been before he'd found her again.

And he'd better quit mooning around and get busy or he'd never get anything done.

The first thing he did after getting to his boat and finding everything still undamaged was to call Velva and Amalie to let them know that he was all right. The sound of his daughter's cheery little voice lifted his spirits even higher. He missed her like crazy but he wasn't really worried anymore. The kid sounded happy and busy and much too well-adjusted to make herself sick missing him. He couldn't wait to introduce her to Celia.

After the phone call ended, he showered and changed, then went topside for a closer look around the harbor. He was just about to head for the harbormaster's shack to see if Celia had arrived yet when a shocked cry and a rising murmur of distressed voices had him turning in the opposite direction.

Debris littered the coastline. Down the shore a short way, a knot of people in small boats gathered around a stand of grass. He hopped a ride with a guy in a canoe and they headed over to see what was wrong.

As they neared the site, the other man yelled, "What's the matter?"

"There's a body here," said a woman who sounded as though she was one step away from losing it altogether. "I came along here to retrieve some stuff that got away and there she was."

"Guess she got caught in the storm and washed into the water," said another man, shaking his head. "Young, too. Anybody know her?"

Reese gazed down on the battered body wedged into the marsh grass. The woman's long blond hair floated eerily around her head. Her limbs were tangled in a fishing skein that had gotten caught on a dead tree stump and held the body in place when the storm surge receded. The body was facedown, features hidden, clad in a torn bathing suit top and ragged cutoff jeans.

As he studied her, he realized the man who'd just spoken had missed one critical detail. The woman might have gotten caught in the storm all right, but that wasn't what had caused her death. A neat bullet hole in the barely visible right temple probably had been responsible for it.

Just then, a strong wave lapped against the grass and the body did a graceful roll. The hair streamed back in the undertow, exposing a ghostly pale face. Reese swore.

The body in the fishing net was Claudette Mason.

Celia felt numb with disbelief. Claudette was dead. And she hadn't died in a storm-related accident. She'd been murdered in cold blood. Whoever had done it clearly hadn't expected her body to be found. The fishing skein had been wrapped around her too neatly to have been accidental, and it was torn in places that suggested that it had been weighted. Investigators theorized that the force of the hurricane had torn the body from the weights and left it tangled in the marsh.

Celia sat quietly in a corner of her office as two FBI agents questioned members of her staff. Angie was answering a query at the moment, telling the two men that she had seen Claudette walking around Neil Brevery's yacht the morning before the storm, but that they hadn't spoken.

"I can't believe it," Angie said, a lone tear streaking down her cheek. "Murders just don't *happen* here." Then, as if realizing what she'd said, her eyes darted to Celia in silent apology.

"We believe Miss Mason may have been involved in a drug transaction," said the taller, older agent. "As you know, Harwichport was the focal point for drug activity several years ago and the DEA has acquired recent evidence that suggests it hasn't ceased."

"What evidence?" Did they know things they hadn't told her? Celia understood, on an intellectual basis, that the FBI couldn't go around blabbing their information to civilians, but her interest was far from casual and they knew how she felt. She hadn't had any idea they were still actively investigating in the area.

"Sorry, Mrs. Papaleo, we can't discuss an ongoing investigation." The younger agent sounded sincere. He and his partner had spoken with her a number of times after Milo's boat exploded, so she was familiar with them. "We'll let you know personally if there's any new information released."

That evening Reese walked her home and they made dinner together while they discussed the bizarre turn the day had taken. Celia seemed jittery and upset and he imagined that Claudette Mason's shocking death had stirred up a great many memories she'd prefer to have left at rest. He could only be thankful she hadn't been with him when the body was discovered.

They sat down afterward to watch the news and he wondered if she would let him stay tonight. He put his arm around her and she turned to him, smiling and snuggling into his side in a motion so natural it felt as if she'd done it for years.

Stretching up, she put her mouth against his jaw, and he could feel her hot breath feather over his neck as she said, "Would you like to stay tonight?"

He grinned, tilting his head and catching her mouth beneath his. "Would you believe I was just plotting a way to do exactly that?"

Her lips curved as she shifted in his arms, her hands sliding up over his shoulders. "I'd believe it."

Much later, they lay together in her bed. Moonlight silvered a patch across the quilt over them.

In the darkness he felt melancholy steal over him. They could have been married for years by now, with children of their own. If he hadn't left. If she had gotten in touch. "We've lost so much time," he said quietly.

She hesitated, her palm creeping up to lie over his heart. "Yes."

"When did you first hear the rumors?"

As he'd expected, she knew what he meant. "About a week after you left. People started saying…that you'd gotten a girl pregnant." Her voice shook.

"Yeah." He still couldn't prevent the hurt that had sliced at him that day from echoing in his voice. "The worst thing was, my father didn't even consider that maybe I hadn't done it. He *assumed* I was the father of that baby. Do you know he actually thought he could force me to marry her?" He shook his head. "We had the mother and father of all fights. I swore I was never setting foot in that house again until he apologized. But now...now I realize I was as unfair as he was. I didn't just shun Dad. I left my entire family."

He sighed. "Being back here with you, realizing this is the life I should have had, makes me miss them so damn much. It doesn't seem nearly as important to me anymore to hang on to all that anger. What do you think? Should I extend the olive branch and forget about the apology?"

Celia's body stiffened again, surprising him. He hadn't thought the question was that big a deal. He tried to hold her but she struggled until he let her go. Pushing herself out of his arms, she sat up and turned slightly to face him. "Reese, I owe you an apology." She took a deep breath. "When I heard about the other woman's pregnancy, I was shattered. And when you left without even getting in touch, I was so hurt. I..."

Her voice began to recede as incredulity crept in. *She hadn't believed in him.* All these years, that had been the one equation he'd never figured. Never considered.

"You believed it. You believed it, didn't you?" The ugly truth was beginning to register and his voice was harsh. He surged out of bed, yanked on his shorts and plunged one hand recklessly through his hair, leaving short spikes sticking out at wild, stiff angles. "All these years you thought I was the kind of guy who would tell you he loved you at the same time he was screwing around with somebody else."

"Well, what was I supposed to think?" she shouted.

She clapped a hand to her mouth, clearly appalled at her loss of control. Then her defiant gaze dropped and she pulled the sheet up, concealing her body from him as if she were no longer comfortable with the intimacy they'd shared.

"Reese, I was a very naive seventeen-year-old. You tell me you're going back to Boston to start school but that you'll be coming back the following weekend. The next thing I know, everyone's buzzing about you getting some girl pregnant and having a big fight with your father—and I never hear another word!"

"The letters weren't good enough, I guess," he said sarcastically. "You didn't waste any time writing me off."

"Letters?" Her head came up and her face was a study in troubled disbelief. She shook her head. "I never received any letters from you."

He went still. Hurt continued to slice through him, and he fought the urge to hurl words at her in return. But there had been a note of truth in her tone that he couldn't ignore. "Celia, I sent you three letters. If you never received them, then…someone kept them from you."

She stared at him, silent and clearly shocked, and he could see in her eyes the dawning of a terrible truth. "Oh my God," she whispered. She shook her head blindly. "My father wouldn't have— Daddy would never— Oh, God!" She buried her face in her hands. "He worried about me that summer," she said in a muffled tone. "He was a good man, despite the drinking. But if he thought…he might have…" She raised her face and Reese saw in her expression a sad resignation. "My father kept them from me. What did the letters say?"

He shrugged, still cut to the quick at the way she'd condemned him without a second thought, just like his own family. What was the use in getting into this now? "Nothing important."

Celia went still, studying his face. "Please, Reese," she said quietly. "What was in those letters?"

"An explanation." He turned away abruptly, walking to the window and placing his hands on the windowsill, leaning forward until his head nearly touched the glass. "My first impulse was to run to you. But even before I picked up the phone, I realized my father would like nothing better. If he'd been able to catch me in a compromising position with an underage girl, he could have used the threat of statutory rape charges to force me to do what he wanted."

Celia's eyes went wide. "Surely your father wouldn't have done that."

His mouth twisted. "Looking back, probably not. But I wasn't exactly thinking clearly. So I took off, left the States. That's when I wrote the first letter, telling you I'd be back the day of your eighteenth birthday."

She made a stifled sound, bringing her fisted hand to her lips.

"In the second letter, I told you about starting my trip around the world. I hadn't heard from you yet, so I wrote again and asked you if you'd marry me. But I never got an answer."

Celia fought to hold back the tears. Dear God. She'd thought she was nothing more than summer entertainment to him. How could she have been so wrong? "Oh, Reese, if only I'd known. I'm so sorry."

"Forget about it." He still faced the window but she didn't need to see his face to know she'd unknowingly hurt him. "It was for the best. I got to see the world. I made buckets of money and I did whatever I damn well pleased for more than a dozen years. If I'd tied myself to you, I might still be stuck here."

She flinched as the cold words slapped her. But behind them, she heard the pain. He'd been rejected by his family, and then he'd thought she'd done the same thing. When he'd realized how easily she'd accepted his guilt, it must have compounded the betrayal he must have felt. She'd give anything if she could turn the clock back and fix it.

Getting out of bed, she went to him, slipping her arms around his waist and pressing herself against him, heedless of her nudity. "I'm sorry," she said, pressing a kiss to the center of his strong back and speaking against the warm flesh. "I should have believed in you. I have no excuse for it, and I'll regret it until the day I die."

He stiffened noticeably beneath her touch and she clutched at him more tightly, prepared for rejection. But she wasn't prepared when he said, "Look! Look out there and tell me what you see."

He grasped her wrist and pulled her around in front of him, placing his hands on her shoulders as she looked out the window across the darkened water, visible from her second story. Her eyes were already acclimated to the dark and it was only a moment before she saw what he had. "It's some kind of small yacht, running without lights, I think.'' She whirled and ran from the room, rummaging in the closet for her binoculars, which she quickly opened and handed to Reese.

"It is,'' he said. "Definitely. And it looks very much like it just came out of your harbor.''

She sucked in a breath of outrage. "I'm calling the FBI first thing in the morning.''

Reese put a cautionary hand on her arm. "Celia, we need to make sure no one finds out we saw this. Claudette's murder most likely proves they're still here. These people apparently don't consider either of us a danger or we'd be dead by now, too.'' His thumbs caressed her forearms lightly. "I know it goes against the grain, but you need to be careful about stirring this particular hornet's nest. They've already proven they can be lethal.''

"We can't let them keep using my harbor,'' she said hotly.

"Celia,'' he said patiently, "I'm not telling you to ignore it. I'm just saying we need to be careful.'' He set down the binoculars and put his hands at her waist, drawing her to him. "I won't take chances with your life.''

"What happened to 'it was for the best'?'' She kept her tone light, trying to let him know she understood the hurt that drove him to lash out.

Reese grimaced. "I was mad, okay? Even after all these years, it still hurt to think that you didn't trust me. But knowing you never got my letters...I guess if I'd been in your shoes I might have thought the same thing.'' His fingers tightened on her waist. "I don't know if we can sort out everything that's behind us, and I don't know if I care.'' He snuggled her closer. "What I do care about is us, right now. And I'm not going to throw that away. We've already missed too many days we should have shared."

When he bent his head again, she met his mouth with urgent desire, needing to show him that she cared, too. Unlike Reese, who seemed to have it all figured out, she wasn't sure where this was going or how it would end. But Reese had made her *feel* for the first time since Leo and Milo had died, and she wasn't giving that up without a fight.

Seven

"It's so horrible," Angie said as they restored the office equipment to its proper place the next afternoon.

Celia nodded. "I know. Poor Claudette."

"And it's scary, too. There could be a murderer right here on this pier."

"There could be."

"Do you think there is?"

"I don't really have any idea." She put an arm around Angie's shoulders briefly. "But I want you to try not to worry so much about it. The FBI is doing everything possible to catch these people."

"That's what we all said the last time," Angie said baldly.

Celia flinched and Angie's expression immediately switched to regret.

"I'm sorry," she said. "This just has me so on edge."

"We're all on edge. The only thing to do is keep on with our normal routine and let the professionals do their job. And speaking of which—" she flipped the schedule on the desk around so that she could read it "—did you have any small craft out last night?"

Angie hesitated, apparently thinking. "No. Everything was returned by six. Why?"

Celia shrugged. "I just wondered." She made a show of checking the list. "So today we have two all-day charters and three small group rentals?"

"Yes." Angie leaned in to check, but then she straightened. "I almost forgot. A guy just docked a few minutes ago. He asked for Reese, but there was nobody aboard the *Amalie*. I came in to see if you knew where he was."

"He walked down to the video store," Celia said. "Who's the guy?"

"Don't know, but if I had to guess, I'd bet he was a Barone. He looks a little like Reese, and his boat is the *Baronessa*."

Reese's brother. Celia leaped to her feet and headed for the door. She'd forgotten that Nicholas Barone had been on the Cape. The Barones rarely used her little marina, preferring Saquatucket, which was closer to the family compound. She was willing to bet Nick Barone turning up at Harwichport wasn't a coincidence.

As she hurried down the pier, Ernesto Tiello was walking toward her. He moved slowly, like a very old man, and she suddenly remembered the way he'd followed Claudette Mason around like an eager puppy. Her heart squeezed with pity.

"Mr. Tiello," she said as he drew nearer. "I'm so sorry about what's happened to Claudette. I know you two were close."

Tiello's face was drawn and haggard, and deep in his eyes she saw a flare of pain at her words. "Yes," he said, dropping his gaze to the ground. "We had become good friends. Her death has been...most difficult."

Impulsively she reached out a hand and squeezed his shoulder. "Is there anything I can do?"

He shook his head without looking at her. "There is nothing to be done. Except, perhaps, allow the authorities to do their job and catch whoever did this."

She nodded, agreeing. "I hope they're successful." Looking past Ernesto's portly frame, she noticed that a tall man with dark hair and shoulders as broad as Reese's was coming her way. "Please excuse me," she said to the distraught man. "If there's any way I can help you, please don't hesitate to ask."

"Thank you." Ernesto Tiello moved on past her and she walked along the dock toward the stranger who was rapidly approaching.

She extended a hand as she came to a halt in front of him. "I'm Celia Papaleo, the harbormaster. I understand you're looking for Reese."

"Celia." His eyes were full of knowledge as he clasped her hand in a firm grip. "Nick Barone." He paused and studied her for a moment. "The same Celia who used to date my brother?"

She nodded. "The same."

"And how about now?"

"Excuse me?"

"Are you dating him now?"

She hesitated, wondering how to answer him. Dating? Not exactly. But…

"Never mind. That was rude." He grinned and her heart skipped a beat; that smile was a close relative to the one Reese employed when he was teasing her. "Do you happen to know where he is?"

"He walked down to the video store. Would you like to come into my office to wait for him?" She turned and gestured toward the shack and they walked up the pier, but before she could show him inside, a familiar figure came striding toward them.

"Reese!" she called, wanting to give him time to…

To what? Compose himself? Brace himself? Get himself under control? "Your brother stopped by."

Just for a moment, she detected a slight hesitation in his smooth gait. But he recovered quickly and came toward them, his face blank and unreadable. He extended his hand. "Nick. It's been a long time."

There was a frozen moment and then Nick Barone grabbed his brother's hand and hauled him into a hard embrace. "You damned idiot," he said. "Your quarrel's with Dad, not with me." He pounded Reese's back. "God, I've missed you."

Celia turned away to hide the tears she couldn't suppress. She knew how much Reese missed his family; this unconditional love was exactly what he'd needed.

Behind her, Reese said, "I've missed you, too." His voice sounded thick.

"So why in hell didn't you answer my letters?"

She turned back, alarmed at the frustration and strain in Nick Barone's voice. If he thought she was going to stand by and let him hurt Reese even further, he could think again.

Reese shrugged, stepping back a pace. "I don't know."

She could sense him backing off mentally, as well, and before either of the brothers could do something stupid, she said, "Nick, would you like to join us for dinner tonight? That will give you plenty of time to catch up."

Two sets of eyes turned her way. One was a piercing blue while the other was a steely silver, but two nearly identical gazes pinned her like a butterfly to a mat. She could almost see each of them thinking.

Finally, Nick said, "Thank you. I'd like that...if my brother doesn't mind."

Reese cleared his throat. "Of course I don't mind. Let's make it seven o'clock since Celia will be here most of the afternoon."

Reese heard her feet on the porch an instant before the back door opened.

"Hi," she said when she saw him standing in her kitchen. Then she sniffed. "What is that? Smells great."

"Stuffed baked chicken breasts in wine sauce. And a spinach salad." He handed her a glass of the Fume Blanc he'd picked up on his way over to start dinner. "But I forgot dessert. Shall I run back out to the store?"

"No." She set down her bag and left her shoes by the door. "I have a pumpkin loaf in the freezer that can be cut and served after a five-minute defrost. That'll do, won't it?"

Reese set down the cutlery with which he'd been

about to set the table. He walked toward her and took
her hands, tugging her against him for a sweet kiss.
She opened her mouth beneath his so willingly that
he felt an immediate rise of desire, and more. God,
he loved the way she responded to him. He'd dreamed
of this for thirteen years, and now that she was finally
his again, he could hardly believe it.

Slipping his arms around her, he said, "Pumpkin
loaf sounds great. And now we have all kinds of extra
time since we don't have to worry about dessert." He
lowered his head and kissed her again, hungrily drinking in her response, stroking her soft, lithe curves pos-
sessively. "Wonder what we could do to fill the
hours."

Laughter gurgled up out of her throat. "Gee, I
don't know." She slid one hand down his body, her
small palm covering the hard evidence of arousal that
pushed at the front of his pants, and smiled when he
shuddered. "We'll think of something."

As he carried her up the stairs, she wound her fingers into his hair and cradled his scalp. "I was afraid
you might be mad at me."

"For what?"

"For inviting your brother to dinner."

"Oh." He shrugged. "At first I was a little annoyed, but then I realized I really wanted to have
dinner with him, so I couldn't be mad, could I?" He
dropped his head and kissed her. "Thank you."

She responded to him with all the sweetness he
remembered from their loving years ago, her body
rising to meet his. As he stroked and petted her, she
writhed beneath him with complete abandon, stoking

the fires of passion until she flared into a wild conflagration that seared his senses and consumed him, as well.

An hour later they were lying side by side on her bed. Reese had his arm around her, her bare body aligned with his, and he lazily stroked her back with his free hand. She snuggled closer, loving the cuddling, the closeness. Loving him.

She felt the final, small knot of denial loosen and drift away from the close guards she'd put on her heart. She loved Reese Barone. Had she ever stopped loving him?

No. She'd buried it, said goodbye to her girlish dreams of a life with Reese after he'd left. But the feeling had never died. Now he was back and there was no way to deny it. She loved him, had always loved him. *Would* always love him, until the day she stopped breathing.

A rush of emotion swept through her and she turned her head so that she could press a kiss to the hard pad of muscle over his heart. *I love you.*

Reese's arm tightened around her. "I don't remember you being so noisy years ago." His words interrupted her moment of introspection. He grinned as she balled a fist and delivered a punch to his shoulder. "Not that I'm complaining."

"I was young and inhibited."

"Not too inhibited to make love on a catamaran in the middle of the day." His free hand tipped up her chin and he gave her a deep, stirring kiss. "It's one of my favorite memories."

"Mine, too."

"So you didn't totally forget me." His tone wasn't

smug and satisfied, as she'd expected, but rather diffident.

"Did you really think I could ever forget you?" She shook her head slightly. "You were my whole world that summer."

"And you were mine." He paused. "I, uh, have to tell you something."

She twisted a curl of the hair on his chest around her finger and glanced up at him, alerted by an odd note in his voice. "Oh?"

"I was here briefly at the end of August. I found out you were still around and that's why I came back."

She propped herself up on his chest, her heart aching strangely as his words arranged themselves into meaning in her head. "You came back...to find me?"

He grinned at her, but it wavered around the edges. "Yeah."

"Did you know I was...single?"

He nodded. "Somebody over at Saquatucket mentioned you'd been widowed." He ran his hands lightly up her back. "I just had to know if you really were as special as I remembered."

"It's hard to live up to an idealized thirteen-year-old memory," she said, striving for a light tone.

"Celia." He twisted, lying her flat on the pillow and leaning over her on one elbow, his eyes intense and serious. "You haven't lived up to it."

Shock left her speechless. She supposed she should feel pain, but she didn't—yet.

Then he said, "You've exceeded it. To be honest, I came back hoping, I think, to get you out of my system so I could get on with the rest of my life. Instead—" he paused, stroking a finger along her cheek "—I'm having a hard time imagining what it would be like without you now."

Her throat closed up as her eyes began to sting. Why was it that she couldn't simply enjoy his sweet words? While part of her reveled in knowing that he wanted her as badly as she wanted him, a wary corner of her heart backpedaled. She hadn't planned on caring for anyone ever again, hadn't planned on letting anyone get so close that she'd be devastated if they were torn from her. She might love him, but she realized suddenly that she hadn't allowed herself to consider thoughts of a future with him. The whole notion was so frightening that she simply couldn't face it.

Did she love him? Yes, yes, *yes!* But loving someone was no guarantee of anything, except heartbreak. Conflicting feelings raged within her. *Hide,* said one voice. *Protect your heart.*

Another urged her to tell Reese how she felt. True, he hadn't said the words, but neither had she. And hadn't he just practically admitted that he still cared? His words skirted the edge of a marriage proposal, didn't they?

And with that thought, panic rose. No. No, no, no, she couldn't do it again. Dear God, what would happen if she lost Reese? She'd thought her life was over when Milo and Leo, her precious baby boy, had died. But if Reese died... The mere thought chilled every cell in her body. She couldn't do this. *She couldn't.*

She turned her head to one side, hating the weak tears that seeped from beneath her eyelids. "Reese, I—I don't know. It's not that—"

She felt him freeze against her. "Baby, the last thing I want to do is make you unhappy." He stroked her hair. "One day at a time, remember? If that's what you want, that's what we'll do."

Clearly, it wasn't necessarily what he wanted or needed, but he'd give her space. Thinking of the future was one giant step beyond where she could tread right now.

But how long would Reese tolerate her reticence? How patient could he be? A chill traced icy fingers up her spine. He'd left once before, when she'd never even imagined he would. Now she knew better.

What if he left again?

Nick arrived promptly at seven with a bottle of wine for his hostess, which they opened equally promptly. Celia had prepared a tray with crackers, apples and cheese, and Nick joined Reese in the living room while she returned to the kitchen. Reese watched her leave the room, knowing she was being thoughtful, giving him time for a private reunion, but wishing she were by his side anyway.

Pouring the wine into deep-bowled crystal glasses that Celia had retrieved from a cupboard and hastily washed, Reese handed Nick a glass of Merlot. Nick held the glass by the stem, swirling it competently and eyeing the color before inhaling its bouquet. The last time they'd seen each other, they'd barely been legal, and as Reese recalled, their drink of choice was dark Mexican beer. The contrast served to remind him again of the distance he'd maintained through the years. Once again regret nipped at him.

God, it was good to see Nick. They were only a year apart in age and had been inseparable companions during their childhood, along with the next brother down the line, Joe, who was only a year younger than Reese.

"So, how are you?" He tried not to stare, drinking in the familiar yet different features, measuring the subtle changes adulthood had brought to Nick.

"Good, good. Married."

"Married," Reese repeated. "Celia said she thought you were. Any kids?"

"One. A daughter."

Reese shook his head, again unable to process the changes in his brother. "Not possible."

Nick grinned wickedly, and for an instant their old closeness returned. "Quite possible. Want me to explain it to you?"

Reese returned the smile. "No, thanks. I think I've got it." He hesitated, feeling awkward again. "How'd you find me?"

"Daniel."

Daniel. Reese's cousin, Derrick's twin brother, though the two were as different as two men could be. Reese was genuinely puzzled. "How did Daniel know I was here?" As in here at Celia's.

Nick must have read his mind. "He didn't. He was at the Cape house in August on his honeymoon and when he came home, he told me he was pretty sure he'd caught a glimpse of you." Nick's face tightened. "I thought about it and thought about it and finally decided to come see if he was right."

Reese was astounded by the coincidence. "I was only here for two days that time. Then I went home again—Florida is home, by the way—and arranged for a longer vacation."

"To see Celia."

"To look up Celia," he corrected Nick. "I heard she might be single."

"And obviously, she is. Waited for you all these years, huh?"

Reese realized Nick must not know that Celia was a widow, but he decided not to get into all that for the moment.

"Not exactly," Reese said dryly. He looked straight at Nick. "I was planning to get in touch while I was here. You beat me to it."

"Right." There was the faintest note of derision in his brother's tone.

"I saw Derrick last week, over on Nantucket, and it made me realize how much I wanted to see the rest of you." There was no point in telling Nick everything he'd seen.

"He didn't mention that." Nick looked disgusted. "He's even more of a royal screwup than he was when you were home. I swear he enjoys stirring up trouble."

"I didn't talk to him." Reese spread his hands when Nick's eyebrows rose. "It wasn't a good time and I didn't have a lot to say."

"He'd have probably bent your ear about how badly he's being treated right now," said Nick.

"Meaning?"

"How much have you kept up with what's happening at Baronessa?" Nick stood and began roaming the room, examining Celia's knickknacks and pictures, but Reese got the impression he wasn't really seeing them.

"Not much." Reese stood, too, watching his older brother prowl. "Celia told me someone started a fire. Why would anyone want to burn down the plant?"

"I wish I knew." Nick looked frustrated. "That wasn't the first incident but it's by far the most serious. Someone has a grudge, and I think it's personal."

"The Conti family?" Funny how the word "grudge" immediately brought their grandfather's old rival to mind.

"We don't have any proof of that. But last week the Contis hired a private investigator," Nick said.

"What for?"

His brother shook his head. "Don't know. And believe me, we'd like to. Claudia's been unofficially appointed to try to find out why. And that's got Derrick's boxers in a knot. He thinks he should be in on the investigation of the investigator."

Reese had to smile.

"But you know how abrasive he can be. That hasn't changed in thirteen years. He's the last person I want messing around the Contis, and I finally had to tell him straight out to stay clear of it."

"Bet that went over big."

"Yeah, like mud in a milkshake."

"Celia heard that Emily was hurt in the fire. Is she all right?"

Nick hesitated. "Yes and no. Physically, she's recovered. She wasn't burned, but she had a head injury from falling debris."

Reese winced. "How bad?"

"She's recovered, as I said, but she's experienced some significant memory loss. It's possible that she saw whoever set that fire but she can't remember. Hell, it's possible whoever set that fire intended her to die in there."

"God." He was shaken by the thought.

"The only good thing to come out of it is that the

firefighter who carried Em out of there is her fiancé now.''

Her fiancé? He chuckled despite himself, shaking his head. Although he knew it was foolish, it was hard to rid himself of the thirteen-year-old images of his family. ''When I left home, she was eleven. How can she possibly be engaged?''

But Nick didn't return the laughter. ''We're all grown now. You've been away a long time, Reese.''

He sobered quickly in the face of his brother's unspoken censure. ''I know how long it's been.''

''Why didn't you stay in touch? Answer my letters?''

''I don't know.'' He looked at the ground. ''I was just so pissed…and hurt, more than anything.'' Funny how he could finally admit that. ''I wasn't mad at any of you guys except the old man, but I couldn't…I couldn't see any of you. I had to get away, fast. And once I was gone, time sort of got away from me.''

There was hurt, deep hurt, in Nick's gaze, and such reproach that he had to look away again. ''It sure did.''

There was a heavy silence. He knew it was his fault they'd been out of touch for so long. Early on, several of his siblings had tried to communicate—but he'd been such a jerk. And now they'd lost more than a decade of precious memories that they could never replace. It was only since Kent had died that he could fully appreciate how important shared memories could be. ''So tell me about the rest of the gang.''

''Mom and Dad are well. They miss you, too,'' Nick said. He ignored the slight stiffening Reese couldn't prevent and smoothly moved on. ''Let's see. I'll just go down the line so I don't forget anyone.

Joe was married and widowed young. It was a terrible thing, but he's married again to a great woman. Colleen became a nun—''

''A nun?'' On second thought, he wasn't completely surprised.

''But she left her order a couple years ago and recently got married. Guess who she married?''

Reese raised an eyebrow.

''Gavin O'Sullivan!''

''O'Sullivan! You're kidding.'' Nick's best friend from childhood had been one of Reese's best buds, as well.

''Nope.'' Nick ticked off their siblings on his fingers. ''Alex is married and a father, Gina's married. Rita's a nurse now and she's married to a doctor.''

''And Maria?'' He couldn't imagine his youngest sisters all grown up and married.

Nick hesitated. ''Maria's...missing.''

Missing? ''What the hell does that mean?''

''She went away last month. She left a note so we wouldn't worry, but nobody knows where she is.''

''Do you think she's okay?''

Nick spread his hands. ''I hope so. If she isn't back by the date she promised, I'm calling out the National Guard.''

''So how about the cousins?''

''Cousins!'' The worry fell away from Nick's face and he actually laughed. ''Derrick, Daniel and Em I already mentioned. And Claudia...Claudia is a force of nature. Still single, totally gorgeous and as bullheaded as ever. But here's a shocker. We have a new cousin!''

Reese was confused. ''One of them has a child?''

"Not yet. The new cousin is Uncle Luke's daughter."

He was positively staggered by the news. Their father's twin brother had been abducted from the hospital when they were just two days old, and despite massive efforts by the police, no trace of Luke had ever surfaced. Reese's memories of his grandmother were of a sweet, gentle Italian matriarch with an aura of sorrow that never completely left her eyes. "You guys found Uncle Luke?"

"Not exactly." Nick's face fell. "Turns out he's already passed away. But his daughter, Karen, figured out who she was when some pictures of a family reunion in July made the papers. She got in touch, and now we've got another family member. Several, actually, since she's married with a baby on the way."

"Whoa. Can't wait to meet her."

"Does that mean you're considering coming home?"

Damn. Nick always had been a persistent cuss. "I've thought about visiting," he said cautiously.

"So will you come for a visit? Bring Celia, too, if you guys are serious." When Reese didn't immediately acquiesce, Nick said, "You could stay with us if you don't want to stay at the house."

"I'll think about it." But first he needed to find out what—if any—direction this dance he and Celia were doing was going. *Were* they serious, as Nick put it? He hoped so. Because he'd like nothing better than to have her with him, to introduce her to his family. Preferably as his wife. "I'll think about it," he said again, "and get in touch."

"Reese," Nick said softly, "Dad's sorry about that fight. He's been sorry since the day you left. Mom hardly spoke to him for at least a year. She wanted to hire people to find you but he wouldn't let her. He said if you didn't want to ever see him again he couldn't blame you and that if you wanted to come home, you would.''

Reese stared at his older brother. A bitter wash of regret tasted sour in his throat. ''If he'd ever uttered one word of apology, I'd have been home like a shot,'' he said stiffly. ''But I wasn't coming back so I could be falsely accused and screamed at again.''

''You wouldn't have been,'' Nick informed him. ''Eliza Mayhew confessed that she'd lied about the baby's father. He was some guy from her university. I don't think Dad will ever forgive himself for not trusting you.'' He swallowed. ''Deep down, I believe he thinks he shouldn't ever be forgiven. Living without you is his punishment.'' His mouth twisted. ''Only thing is, it's punished all the rest of us, as well.'' He gave Reese an affectionate punch in the shoulder. ''Jerk.''

''Hey, you two.'' Celia's slim frame was silhouetted in the light streaming into the room from the kitchen. ''The meal's about ready.''

The evening had been surprisingly enjoyable, Reese thought, cuddling her closer in her bed that night. He'd expected more tension. Suppressed anger. There'd been the occasional awkward moment, but all in all, it had been damned good to see his brother again.

Nick had mellowed, somehow. He'd always been intense and driven, but tonight he'd been different. Maybe marriage was responsible. Reese was looking forward to meeting his new wife.

Celia stirred in his arms. "How are you?" Her voice was soft, tentative.

"Good." He kissed her temple. "Seeing Nick was terrific."

"I'm glad. I worried all day that I'd pushed you into something you weren't ready for."

"I didn't think I was," he said reflectively. "Maybe I needed a little nudge in the right direction."

They were silent again. His hand swept up and down her back, stroking the silky skin in a gently abstracted manner as he thought about what he'd just said. Maybe he wasn't the only one who needed a little nudge, he thought.

He cleared his throat. "I haven't really told you, but I'd like to hear about Leo if you ever want to talk about him. I'd like to know about your pregnancy, his birth, what kind of stuff he liked. Anything you'd like to share."

Celia's body went rigid in his arms. "You said his name." Her voice sounded wounded. "Do you know how long it's been since I've heard anyone say his name? Everyone thinks they're helping if they don't remind me, I guess." A sob broke loose and he felt the warmth of tears dampen his skin beneath her cheek. "But it's like he and Milo never existed sometimes."

He pulled her closer, each tear that touched him feeling like a live ember. "They still exist, baby. They'll always live in your memories." He took a deep breath. "Any time you want to talk about them, I'll listen."

She went still in his arms. "That," she finally said, "is an extraordinarily kind offer."

He smiled and kissed the top of her head. "Yeah, considering I'm eaten alive with jealousy when I let myself think that it should have been me you shared those years with, that I should have been your son's father."

Celia's body had gone stiff in his arms again. Well, tough. He was tired of her resisting him. "This is how it should have been all those years ago. We should have gotten married, made a home of our own and started a family." He took her arms and shook her lightly. "I still want those things," he said, tipping up her chin with a relentless hand until she met his eyes.

But she dropped her gaze, closing herself away from him, shielding her thoughts. Quietly she said, "But will you still want me if children aren't a part of the equation?"

Now it was his turn to pause. He should tell her now that he already had a child. But…she'd made it pretty damn clear that she didn't want more children, and he found he couldn't force himself to speak. He needed more time. Time to let her get used to the idea of *them* again, time to cement the bonds of love with the meeting of flesh as well as emotions. She'd loved him once, and he was beginning to be pretty sure she still did.

"I want you any way I can get you," he said in a rough voice. He rolled over, pushing her back against the pillows as he settled himself snugly against her. She made a small, soft noise of approval in her throat and he knew exactly how she felt. They had been made for each other. Making love to her was like finding his own personal miracle.

He stroked the tears from her face with his thumbs.

"Any way at all," he affirmed as he sought her mouth and his hands began to slide over her silky skin.

Sensitive now to her desire not to create scandal, he left in the soft almost-morning light that pearled the sky above the ocean to the east. They kissed on the stoop and he felt like a teenager again.

"Will I see you later?" He still held her loosely against him.

She nodded. "You can join us at the marina if you like. We still have a lot of storm cleanup to take care of."

"Work? Me?" He grinned, and she smiled as he'd intended her to. He drew her to him for one final, lingering kiss. "All right. I suppose I could manage that if I had some incentive."

"Ah," she said against his lips, "have I got an incentive program for you. Why don't you plan on coming over for dinner and we'll discuss it?"

"I have a better idea," he said, running his palms up and down the long, smooth line of her back. "Let's have dinner aboard the yacht tonight. We could sail up the coast and back afterward and enjoy an evening on the water."

She laid her head against his shoulder and he enjoyed the feel of her snuggled against him. "That sounds lovely. Let's do it."

Eight

He visited a local bakery where he'd discovered an incredibly good corn bread made by the proprietor, then bought lobster and shrimp from a fresh fish shack on the waterfront. A salad and one of Celia's apple cobblers would be all they would need.

Except each other, he thought, his blood heating as he thought of the night to come. Then he shook his head, laughing at himself. He was as bad as he'd been during the summer he'd spent with Celia, unable to get enough of her. No matter how many times he made love to her, it seemed all he did was think about the next time he could get her into his bed.

It wasn't just the physical fulfillment, although he had no complaints in that department. No, it wasn't just their lovemaking, but the closeness he craved, both physical and emotional. He'd been without her for so long that he doubted he would ever get enough of simply holding her next to him, feeling her heart's steady beat as her blood coursed through the fragile blue veins at her wrists, her temples and just under the petal-soft skin of her breasts. It delighted him when they finished each other's sentences, when they laughed at the same thing at the same moment, when a mere glance from her could calm and reassure him.

How amazing was it that after thirteen years he'd come back at the right time and found her? If he were inclined to believe in fate, he might think their getting together again had been inevitable. Only this time, the ending was going to be different. He was going to make sure of it.

Suddenly the little detail that he'd kept from her—his daughter—reared up and smacked him full in the face. Panic clutched at his chest.

He had to tell her tonight. He had to. He never should have kept it from her for so long, never should have let things get so serious between them until she knew. Now there could be no easy way to introduce the topic. He could hear himself now.

Oh, by the way, did I mention I have a daughter?

…This boat? Oh, I thought I told you. It's named after my daughter, Amalie.

…Celia, I don't know how to tell you this, but I have a daughter. What? The reason I didn't tell you before? Well, I was sure you'd drop me like a hot potato.

And she just might. There was no excuse for not telling her that he had a child to raise—except that he was a complete and total coward. And he'd been terrified he might lose her. It had seemed smart to get their new relationship off to a solid start before springing the notion of a child on her.

It had seemed smart because he'd been too chicken to let himself think about what might happen and he'd been doing his damnedest to portray an ostrich, hoping that if he stuck his head in the sand, the problem would go away.

Well, no more delays. No more procrastinating.

He had to tell her *tonight*. Because he'd made up his mind to ask her to marry him. He knew how she felt about having children; she'd made no secret of it. And he'd seen her pain with his own eyes. Was it fair to ask her to consider another child?

No. He'd cut off his arm before he'd put her in a position to have her life shattered as it had been once. But it wasn't as if he was asking her to have another baby. A small, sharp pain pinched his heart but he forced himself to ignore it. In an ideal world he would love nothing more than to make Celia his wife and to spend the next few years making babies of their own.

But he'd seen what losing her son had done to her. And he'd rather have Celia with no children than live without her ever again. Raising Amalie was different, he told himself stoutly. Ammie wasn't her biological child.

Oh, he knew that taking on a ready-made family wouldn't be easy for Celia. But once she got used to the idea, they would be happy. She could move to Florida, or he and Am could move up here if she didn't want to leave the Cape.

He took a deep breath. His hands were clammy as he set the small galley table and put a bottle of Riesling on ice. There was a knot, an unpleasant burning sensation lodged dead center in his chest, and he wondered briefly if he'd given himself an ulcer worrying about her reaction to his announcement.

"Knock, knock."

It was her voice, calling from the pier, and he jolted, almost dropping the wineglasses he'd gotten out. "I'm below," he called.

He heard her footsteps as she crossed the deck and a moment later she was descending the stairs to the interior of the boat.

"Welcome," he said, leaning in to kiss her, lingering over the greeting until she tore her mouth away and laughed.

"I need to breathe!"

She was even more beautiful tonight than usual, her tanned skin glowing against the warmth of a pale aqua twinset that made her eyes look enormous and mysterious.

He took the basket she carried, sniffing appreciatively as the mouth-watering scent of apple cobbler permeated the air. "Wow. Can we eat this first?"

"No way." She eyed the wineglasses as he set the basket on the counter behind him. "We're going to do things in order."

Could there be a better opening? He hadn't really considered *when* he was going to tell her about Amalie, but sooner was definitely better, especially where his rolling stomach was concerned.

"Uh, Celia, why don't we sit down over here?" He heard the strain in his tone and imagined she could, too.

Her eyebrows rose. "This sound serious. Shall we have some of that wine first?"

"Sure." He slipped out his pocketknife and slit the foil, then deftly used the attached corkscrew to pull out the stopper. She held up two glasses and he filled them about halfway, then set the bottle back in the ice bucket. Taking her hand, he led her over to the couch in the entertainment area and seated her, then lowered himself beside her.

"Now what?" she asked, and he realized he'd been sitting there silently. Duh.

"I, uh, want to talk to you about something important."

"So I gather." Her eyes sparkled. "Feel free to start anytime."

He took a deep breath. Held it. Exhaled explosively. "This isn't easy to say."

Her eyes grew wary. "You're leaving." Before he could react to the assumption, she stood abruptly, setting her wineglass down with a sharp clink on the coffee table. She walked rapidly around the table and turned to face him, her mouth a determined line. Then she took a deep breath of her own. "I knew you'd go sooner or later. It's just that…" She tried to smile but her lips quivered and she pressed them tightly together for a moment. "I was getting kind of used to having you around."

His heart felt as though someone had slammed into it with a bulldozer and ground it into the dirt. He stood, walking around the table to her side and taking her elbows in his palms. "That wasn't what I wanted to say. I don't want to leave you." He swallowed. "I want to marry you."

Her mouth fell open and her eyes widened as she lifted her head and found his gaze. "You…what?"

She sounded so completely dumbfounded that he found himself feeling defensive. "I want to marry you," he repeated. "I wanted to marry you thirteen years ago and now that we've finally found each other again, I want that more than ever."

She didn't speak, only ducked her head as she stood there twisting her fingers together.

"Celia," he said to the top of her head, feeling desperate. "What are you thinking?" He lightly ran his hands up and down her arms from shoulder to elbow, as if that small contact could divine her mental state.

She smiled a little then and her eyes shone with the beginnings of tears as she met his gaze again. "We've been apart longer than we were together. Are you sure this is what you want?"

"I came looking for you, didn't I?" He took her in his arms, tenderness sweeping through him. "I love you. We were both too young the first time, or we never would have let anything separate us. But it did, and much as I regret it, I can't change that, can't get back all those wasted years. All I can do now is look forward."

"Oh, Reese," she said, "I love you, too." She laid her head on his shoulder. "Yes, I'll marry you."

Euphoria, relief, exultation swept through him like a flash flood and he suddenly felt like a superhero. He tilted her face up to his and covered her lips, kissing her with hot, deep possession and need, telling her without words what her acceptance meant to him.

But as he reluctantly ended the kiss and lifted his head, he realized what he'd just done. And more importantly, what he *hadn't* done. Cold dread slipped in, erasing the high of a moment before. But she'd just told him she still loved him. *She loved him!* Suddenly the prospect of explaining his child to her didn't seem nearly as daunting as it had a few moments before.

"Come sit down." He tugged her back to the

couch, cuddling her against his chest. "I'm getting ahead of myself."

"Where do you want to live?" she asked. "Here or Florida? Or somewhere else altogether? I wouldn't mind moving."

He cleared his throat. "I still have something to tell you before we start discussing that." When she stopped and looked at him expectantly, he marshaled his courage and cradled both her hands again, running his thumbs gently over her knuckles. "It won't just be the two of us," he told her. "I have a daughter."

Her eyes were wide, trusting, happiness shining from them with a love so strong he felt humbled. Then, as his words penetrated, the light went out.

In the merest instant, in the tiny space between one second and the next, something in her closed down so completely he could practically hear a metal door clanging shut. Her smile faded slowly until all that was left of it was a wounded expression that would haunt him until the day he died.

"You...have a child?" It was a whisper.

He nodded, holding on to her hands when she would have pulled them free. "Her name is Amalie and she's six years old. She's adopted," he said, the words falling all over each other as he tried to make her see. "I was her guardian. Her parents were the friends I told you died in the hurricane, remember? I didn't have a choice, Celia. I—"

She yanked her hands from his grip and stood, bolting around the table again. Her face was white and her eyes burned with pain. She tried to speak, choked on it and shook her head fiercely, then spoke again in a tone that was barely audible. "I told you how I felt. Right from the beginning, you knew I didn't want more children…. I told you,'' she repeated, her voice breaking. "I can't—"

"Can't or won't?'' he demanded, fear making his voice harsh as he saw refusal on her face. "I'd like to have a child of our own someday, but I was prepared to forget about that. Amalie is—"

"I can't go through that again,'' she broke in. "Do you know how much it's taken for me to deal with loving you and knowing I could lose you, too?"

"You can't spend the rest of your life in a cave just because something bad might happen. What about all the wonderful times you're missing?"

"Something bad *might* happen.'' Tears began to roll down her cheeks and there was a torment in her eyes that made him feel as if someone were striking *him* with a whip, so sharp was the pain that radiated from her. "You don't know what it's like to lose someone you love."

"Yes. I do.'' He was pleading now, begging for his life. For *their* lives. "Not a child, and not in the same way you've experienced loss, but I lost thirteen years with all the people I loved most in the world."

But he might as well not have spoken.

"No,'' she said, backing away from him.

"Celia—'' He read her intentions in her eyes and stood, and that motion was enough.

"I can't!'' she said brokenly as she wheeled and bolted for the hatch. "It's not fair of you to ask me to do that."

As the sound of her ragged breathing faded, it was briefly echoed by her footfalls as she ran across the deck and up the pier.

"Celia, wait!"

But in a moment the sound of her footfalls disappeared altogether, leaving a dark, empty void into which he could feel the rest of his life sliding mercilessly. Alone…alone…alone…

''Dammit!'' In a fit of rage he snatched up one of the half-full wineglasses and heaved it at the cabin wall, where it smashed with a shocking sound, spraying glass and golden liquid everywhere.

He was suddenly furious. Not only with her, but with himself. What had made him think that biology would play any role in how much Celia loved a child? She had one of the biggest hearts of anyone he'd ever met, and he realized that if she let Amalie behind those walls she'd worked so hard to erect, she would love her with every fiber of her being, as much as she would any child born of her body.

He slumped into one of the captain's chairs, his head in his hands. Despair spread steadily, invading every cell.

Oh, God, he hurt. He physically ached. He'd lost her once and forevermore had felt as if something inside him had died. And it wasn't until he'd returned and found her that his world had once again made sense.

Without her, it would never be right again. Without her… How could he start again without her?

Defeat weighed him down, sucked him under. There was no point in being here one more second, he realized. His life was what it was, and he couldn't change the way Celia felt simply because it was what he wanted.

He might as well go back to Florida. Tonight. Regardless of the emptiness that threatened to swallow him, he had a child to raise.

* * *

I can't do it. I can't do it. I can't do it.

The sentence became a litany of self-justification.

I can't do it. I can't do it. I can't do it.

"Well, I *can't!*" she said aloud as she rushed up the rise toward her cozy little house. Her mind was frozen, the only coherent thought was the denial that played over and over. She'd survived once before, when her world had been shattered, and she couldn't do it again.

He had a child. *A child!* How could he have kept a secret of that magnitude from her? Shock and fear began to recede, and anger slipped into the empty spaces. A child.

Granted, it wasn't his. And in some ridiculous way it was important to her that he hadn't fathered a child. Which, she conceded, was extremely hypocritical of her. She'd married and started a family of her own. She'd done her best to forget all about Reese Barone, and she'd been succeeding.

But he hadn't forgotten her. He'd come looking.

She knew she never would have done the same. She might have thought of him with regretful longing from time to time for the rest of her life, but she never would have had the courage to go looking for him, in hopes that after thirteen years there might still be something between them.

And you'd have missed the chance for love. You don't deserve him anyway.

That stung. Her heart thudded dully within her chest, and she put a hand over it. How much should one person be asked to handle in one lifetime? What if she married Reese and grew to love his daughter and then something happened to the child?

But you told Reese you'd marry him. What if something happened to him?

The thought was so awful she stopped walking altogether. Something could happen to Reese. No one knew it better than she. And yet, she'd said yes to his marriage proposal without giving her fears a single thought.

It was a shock to realize that sometime over the past week, the fear that had dogged her life since the day she'd gotten the news about her husband and son had receded. Yes, she still worried, but it wasn't a crippling emotion anymore. She'd been fully prepared to say yes to a life with Reese, knowing full well that there were no guarantees.

So why would it be any different with a child?

It just *was,* though she had to think about why that was so. Leo had died so young. Her biggest source of sorrow and regret was for all that he'd missed. He'd never even really had a chance to experience life before his had been taken. And she hated that, hated thinking about all the things he should have had time to try and hadn't, all because she'd let him go out on the boat with Milo that day.

And that led to the real crux of the matter. It had been her fault. *Her fault.* She was his mommy; he looked to her to protect him from anything bad, and she'd failed him.

The thought of being the anchor in another child's life terrified her. She just wasn't up to the task. She'd already failed once.

Confronting her deepest insecurity was a blinding source of light in the dark corner of her heart where she'd been nursing her fear and anger and sorrow.

I did my best, she reminded herself. *I did my best. It was not my fault.*

She repeated the words aloud—and suddenly, though she'd said the same things to herself before, this time she felt them sink into her consciousness, settle into the truths that defined her life. *I had no way of knowing there could be any danger that day.*

And she hadn't. She'd had no mystical premonition, no uneasy feeling. No way to know.

It wasn't my fault.

A ten-ton weight lifted from her shoulders. No, off her spirit. Her husband's and son's deaths had been a terrible accident, one for which she couldn't have prepared, couldn't have been responsible. And it was long past time to forgive herself, to absolve herself of blame and to let go.

Suddenly she knew without a doubt that if she hid herself away from love and life and a second chance, she'd regret it for the rest of her days. *Second? Try third.* She'd been so very lucky. Reese had been the first to teach her what love was. What she'd shared with Milo wasn't the earth-shattering, heart-swelling emotion she'd known with Reese, but it had been love. Sweet, steady and utterly comfortable. But Milo was gone and Reese had come back.

After thirteen long years he'd come back. And she'd been incredibly fortunate that the bone-deep feelings they'd known in their youth had been far, far more than raging hormones. They'd been in love and still were. A true, solid love built on that early foundation.

And she would have to be an utter fool to throw that away.

Without another thought, she turned back to the marina.

It took her about ten minutes, undoubtedly the longest of her life, to walk back. As she walked, she worked out the wording of her apology to Reese.

But when she began to walk down the pier, she got the shock of her life. The *Amalie* wasn't in her slip. Her chest grew tight, her throat felt as if someone had grabbed her and was squeezing her windpipe shut.

Where had he gone? He couldn't have left so quickly, could he?

Of course he could have. *He didn't think there was anything here to stay for, remember?*

She swallowed painfully, desolation sweeping through her. She was the one who'd rejected him. What if he never forgave her?

You're doing it again. And it had to stop. She'd spent the last few terrible years beating herself over the head and she was not going to do it anymore.

This time she wasn't going to give up. Reese loved her. He loved her enough to seek her out and to overcome her resistance. He'd made her see how extraordinary their feelings for each other were.

Now it was her turn. He'd come north to find her. She could go south and do the same thing. She had an apology to make and she intended to do it even if she had to catch a flight to Florida to deliver it. Whether or not he forgave her was beside the point. Well, okay, no it wasn't. But she had no control over that. All she could do was attempt to soothe the hurt she'd inflicted with her self-centered attitude and pray that his heart really was as big as she thought it was.

Automatically she scanned the water as she thought about what to do next. If he had left, had already gotten out onto the open ocean and up to cruising speed, she had no hope of catching up with him. The *Amalie* was one of the newest yachts on the market, with an engine to match her sleek lines.

Just as she was about to turn and walk back home again, a movement on the water caught her eye. It looked like a yacht. It looked like Reese's! She nearly cried out with happiness until she realized that what she was seeing was the stern as the boat headed away from the marina.

Then another light winked on, some distance beyond the *Amalie*. The boat appeared to be all black, barely visible against the dark sea.

And she knew, with a sickening certainty that she didn't even question, that on that boat were the people responsible for her family's deaths.

"Reese!" She screamed it even though he couldn't hear her as she ran for the shack and grabbed the keys to the nearest launch.

As she raced out the pier, a man loomed beside her, heavy footsteps pounding. "Celia," he said. "Where are you going?"

It was Ernesto Tiello, and she was briefly amazed that a man of his bulk and seeming sloth could run at all. "Reese is out there," she tossed over her shoulder, "and there's another boat that I'm certain are the drug runners everyone's been talking about are in."

They had reached the launch. "Wait," said Tiello. "I've already called for law enforcement."

"You saw them, too?"

He nodded. "We should stay here and let them handle it."

"And take a chance on those murderers getting away?" She shook her head. "No."

His face darkened. "Then take me with you."

"No," she said again as her fingers worked at the lines. "It could be dangerous."

But he was already leaping aboard the aft deck, and when he held out his palm, she saw a badge in it. "FBI," he said. "I've been after these guys since before they killed your husband and your little boy." He paused. "Claudette Mason was an agent."

Astonished, she gaped at him for a moment, then rallied, knowing there was no time to lose. "Come on. I don't want them to hurt Reese."

Tiello pulled a heavy black handgun from the back of his waistband. "Let's go."

She ran below for her binoculars, then returned to the deck and put them to her eyes and focused.

The black boat was turning and she saw a man briefly illuminated in the light that had just snapped on. He had his arms up to his shoulders—and with a shocking sense of horror and futility she knew what it was he held although she'd never seen one before in her life.

She was looking at a rocket launcher. And it was being aimed straight at Reese's boat.

Reese was madder than he'd been in years. Madder, even, than he'd been at himself thirty minutes before when he'd handled things so badly that Celia had run from the boat.

He'd pulled anchor and headed southeast away from Harwichport and the wreck he'd made of his chance for a future with her. But he'd hardly cleared the marina pier before he noticed a barely visible silhouette against the night sea just ahead of him. No running lights. He narrowed his eyes, realizing that whatever was out there was a decent-size yacht. His pulse kicked up a notch as he realized he might have inadvertently stumbled onto Claudette Mason's killers and he made an instant decision.

A moment later he had the Coast Guard emergency response on the line. If he was mistaken, the worst that could happen was that he embarrassed himself and had to apologize to some innocent person. If he wasn't, it was just possible that the men Celia had been hunting so diligently were less than a mile away from him.

Celia. God, it hurt even to think her name. He shook himself, refusing to allow himself to linger on the ugly scene they'd just played out.

He got out his binoculars while he talked to the dispatcher, but there was little to be seen even with the strong magnification. The boat was dark in color all over and if there was anyone about, he couldn't see them.

Then, as nicely as if he'd asked, a light came on. Three people, clearly visible with the binoculars, stood on deck. One was a large man whom he'd never seen before. The other two... His stomach flipped over and shock rushed through him, making his scalp tingle. There was a man as well as a woman standing on deck with the large man. The second man was trim and small and neat. Neil Brevery. One of the people to whom Celia rented a slip.

Claudette had worked for Brevery; how coincidental was that? His suspicions grew as he continued to survey the boat. And then he trained his binoculars on Brevery's companion and the breath went out of his lungs.

Rage kindled and began to build. The third person

on the deck of the other boat was Celia's assistant, Angie. God, had she been working with a killer?

Grimly he went below and unlocked the rifle he kept in a safe place in his stateroom. The Coast Guard had said they had gotten one call and were on their way, but he was taking no chances. The other boat wasn't going anywhere.

Moving back on deck, he gunned his engine and pushed the yacht up to speed, heading directly for the other yacht, the rifle under his arm, barrel down. He grabbed the binoculars again for a closer view.

Brevery and Angie looked as if they were arguing. They both were at the rail, peering in his direction as the boat steadily turned around.

Could it be true? Could that harmless-looking young woman be responsible for Claudette's murder? For the deaths of Celia's family?

It was hard to fathom. Maybe he'd leaped way off base in search of an answer, but he'd rather be wrong than let them get away.

Swinging the binoculars to starboard, he focused on the third man. The guy was large, unfamiliar, but the thing he lifted to his shoulder, which looked like a length of plumbing pipe from this distance, raised the hair on the back of Reese's neck.

As the man aimed the weapon—and he knew that was exactly what it was—straight at the *Amalie,* survival instincts took over and Reese dove over the rail as far as he could from the boat.

Nine

"Noooooo!"

Celia screamed as she saw a flash and watched a trail of fire fly straight at Reese's boat. A second later she took a deep gasp of relief as the rocket sailed over the boat and splashed harmlessly into the sea.

But then, as her uncomprehending gaze swung back to the dark boat, a second shot flared. It hung in the air, speeding straight for Reese's yacht, and she screamed again, helplessly, as the *Amalie* blew apart in a roiling cloud of smoke and flame.

Ernesto Tiello cursed vividly, standing beside her at the wheel. Then he pointed at the sky. "Look," he shouted.

A helicopter had appeared, winging low over the water, and from the same direction Celia could see the powerful searchlights of three launches speeding toward the black boat, which was attempting to turn and put on speed. Her heart was a leaden weight in her chest and she registered the drama distantly, but her attention was fixed on the dusky blotch of smoke that still marked the site of the explosion. She kept a steady course for the spot where Reese's boat had gone down, although the chase was moving off in another direction.

Please, please, please. Please let him be there.

As they approached, bits of debris began to appear, shattered lengths of timber, rags, buckets and empty life preservers, a deck chair half-submerged. Despair swamped her.

Dear Lord, please. Not again.

But hope waned as they circled the area. There was no sign of a body. No sizable pieces of debris bigger than a four-foot length of wood. The second assault must have been a direct hit, she realized, sinking the yacht within moments. By the time the worst of the obscuring smoke had cleared, the *Amalie* was no more.

Panic fluttered behind her breastbone and she beat it back fiercely as she continued to scan the water. Reese was still alive. He had to be. *He had to be.*

A boat approached, a white Coast Guard launch, and she listened with half an ear as Ernesto talked with them. The other boat had been apprehended, the three people aboard taken into custody. She turned briefly when she heard that Mr. Brevery was the brains of the business, and that Angie Dunstan had been his eyes and ears locally.

She was stunned. "Angie...?" and the two men nodded.

Blindly she turned back around to the sea. Angie. Celia still thought of her as a girl even though she knew Angie was twenty-two now. Milo had hired the young woman fresh out of high school. She'd been pleasant, efficient—and probably responsible for his death, Celia realized suddenly.

Then a movement on the water caught her eye.

Hope surged.

"Reese!" It was a hoarse scream and both Tiello and the men aboard the Coast Guard cutter whipped around to stare at her. She barely noticed, already gunning the engine as she marked the feeble lift of a hand in the far-off swells.

"Hang on, Reese," she called again and again as they neared him. Ernesto had climbed over the ladder and lowered his bulky body into the sea; she maneuvered the launch as close as she dared, while Tiello dragged Reese aboard the boat.

He had a deep gash across his forehead and one arm hung at an odd angle as they lay him down and covered him with blankets. Tiello got on the radio, requesting air transport to a medical facility, while Celia took the thermal blankets the Coast Guard had tossed aboard and tenderly tucked them around Reese. Hypothermia was a real danger in the cold autumn waters of the North Atlantic and the relief she'd felt dissipated quickly as she took in the pallor of his face and his blue lips.

"Shh," she said when he moved restlessly. "Don't try to talk. We're going to get you to a hospital."

He lifted his good hand and indicated the sea, and she realized he wanted to know what had happened. "They sank your boat," she began, but he shook his head.

"I know," he said. "Wh-wh...where...?"

"They're in custody." She smiled down at him.

"Coming after you was their downfall. It gave the Coast Guard and the FBI time to get to them."

"An-An-An—"

She nodded, her smile fading. "Angie. I know." She shook her head, wondering at the amorality that had allowed the young woman to work side by side with the widow and mother of the innocent people she'd had a hand in killing.

Reese's hand lifted, stroked down her cheekbone, and she focused on him again. "You're freezing. We've got to get you to a hospital."

"T-talk." It was a demand, and she smiled, letting the love she felt for him shine in her eyes as she dropped her head and brushed a kiss over his chilly lips.

"We'll talk later. Everything's going to be fine."

Everything's going to be fine.

He clung to the words, and to the memory of her kiss, while he was airlifted to the nearest hospital and his injuries were treated.

His left arm was fractured, he needed stitches to close gashes on his forehead and his back, and he felt bruised all over, as if he'd been beaten with a giant pipe over every inch of his body. They told him he had a concussion, which might explain the fuzzy vision and the way his mind kept losing track of what he'd been thinking about.

Everything's going to be fine.

What had she meant? Had it simply been reassurance for an injured man? Surely she wouldn't have kissed him if that were the case. And what had she been doing out on the water anyway?

"Mr. Barone?" The emergency room doctor came

in. "I'd like to admit you overnight for observation. Given your—"

"No," said Reese.

"Yes." The voice was feminine, familiar, and his heart began to beat faster. When he turned his head to look, Celia stood in the doorway. Actually, to his concussed eyes, there appeared to be two of her standing there. "He'll stay," she told the doctor.

"Only if you stay with me," he told her.

She smiled and he felt something tight and fearful inside his chest ease for the first time since she'd rushed off his boat. "You've got a deal," she said.

They took him to a private room on an upper floor. Celia walked beside the gurney on which he lay and held his hand, and he allowed himself the smallest glimmer of hope.

"I called Nick."

"Why?" He was a little startled. It never would have occurred to him to contact his brother.

"It's going to make the papers, Reese," she said patiently. "You wouldn't want your family to find out from a newspaper article that you were almost killed."

He was silent for a minute. "You're right. Thank you." Then a thought struck him. "If I give you the number, would you...would you call down to Florida for me?"

"Yes." Her voice sounded noncommittal, and renewed fear dampened his budding hope.

Once he was settled and all the hospital personnel had come and gone, there was silence in the small room. Celia sat in a reclining chair beside the bed. She'd pulled it around so she could face him, and her hand was clasped in his atop the sheet.

"Reese," she said.

"Hmm?" His head hurt. Everything hurt. Even his eyes hurt when he moved them to look at her. And he was afraid, frankly. Afraid to talk, in case he was wrong and she didn't still—

"I love you."

Suddenly the aches and pains of a moment before seemed far less debilitating. "I love you, too. Wanna come up here and show me?"

She laughed. "Not a chance, buddy."

There was another silence and he was sorry he'd been flippant. This was too important for stupid jokes. He couldn't stand it. "Celia—"

"Shh. We'll talk later." She lifted his hand and brushed a kiss across the knuckles, then looked him dead in the eye. "I'm not going anywhere ever again."

He'd slept at last, waking only when the nurses checked his pupils periodically, and coming to when the breakfast tray arrived in the morning.

Celia had stayed through the night, leaving only to run to her home and bring him a set of clean clothes. It was a good thing he'd left a few at her house, she thought, remembering his beautiful boat sadly. Then she shook herself. The boat could be replaced. Reese couldn't, and she was so very thankful he was safe.

When she returned, he'd already eaten and bathed and was scanning the morning paper, awkwardly turning the outsize pages with his good hand. The other was in a temporary cast, which would be replaced when the swelling subsided, and he wore it in a sling across his chest.

"Hi," he said softly as she entered the room.

"Hi." She knew it was ridiculous to be nervous, but she had to stop herself from twisting her fingers together.

"Come sit down." Reese patted the edge of the bed.

Carefully she went to him and seated herself at his side. "How do you feel this morning?"

He smiled. "Like one of those cartoon animals that gets mashed flat by a boulder or a truck."

She had to laugh, but the memory of the *Amalie* disintegrating into a shocking ball of flame superceded the amusement, and, to her dismay, she suddenly found herself fighting tears.

"Hey." Reese put his arm around her and gently pulled her against her shoulder, stroking her back. "It's okay."

"I thought you were dead." She kept her face pressed into his neck and curled against his side, careful not to jostle the damaged arm between them.

"Shh." She felt him kiss her temple. "I thought I was dead, too, when I saw that rocket launcher aimed my way. It seemed to take forever before the thing actually blew up my boat."

"He fired two," she recalled. "The first one missed."

"That explains it. I dove over the side and swam away from the boat as fast as I could. The missed shot probably saved my life." He shook his head slightly. "Even so, the blast rolled me through the water like a damned doll. I don't remember what happened after that."

"You must have been hit by debris. You've got a couple of nasty cuts in addition to that arm."

"I know." She felt him smile and his voice was

rueful. "I remembered when I started moving around this morning. Man, did they ever sting." He pulled her slightly away from him and looked down into her eyes. "Can we talk now?"

She nodded. "I'm sorry, Reese. I've spent the past couple of years trying to protect myself from getting hurt ever again. After I left last night, I realized that life makes no guarantees. I'd already let you back into my heart, and if anything happens to you—" Her voice wavered.

"Celia—"

She held up her hand. "Let me get this out." She took a deep breath. "I would be honored to marry you and be a mother to Amalie. If you still want me," she added in a small voice.

"If I still want you?" His voice was hushed. "Woman, I've wanted you forever. I love you, Celia." He touched his lips to hers. "I was wrong not to tell you I had a kid right up front. But I knew how much it would hurt you, and I—I was afraid. Afraid you might not give me a second chance if you knew I came with a sidekick."

She laid her head on his shoulder and sighed. "Your instincts probably were right. I might not have."

Reese turned his head and sought her lips again, capturing her in a sweet, hot exchange that left her breathless. "As soon as that doctor checks me over, I'm getting out of here and we're going to get married."

She smiled. "I don't think we can just go get married today."

"We can if we fly to Vegas." His voice sounded utterly serious, and her heart turned over.

"You've got me there. But—" She shook her head. "I'm not letting you go anywhere until the doctor gives you the go-ahead."

He had already opened his mouth to respond when the door swished open. "All right, Doc," he said. "It's about time..." His voice trailed away.

Celia had turned and tried to put some space between them, but Reese held her in place as an older man and woman walked into the room. She was afraid to hurt him by pushing against his chest, so she let him keep her there at his side.

The man wasn't as tall as Reese but she knew in a heartbeat who he was. Reese's father still had thick dark hair, though silver shone at his temples, and she had a sudden vivid image of what Reese would look like in thirty years.

The woman with him was gorgeous, her figure stunning, her hair a vibrant red. There were a few threads of silver in it, as well, or Celia never would have believed that this woman could be old enough to be Reese's mother.

Mrs. Barone had tears in her eyes. "Reese," she said, coming to the side of the bed. "Nick called us. I know we might not be welcome but...we wanted to see for ourselves that you're all right." She put out a hand, then tugged it back and held it against her waist. To Celia, it appeared that she desperately wanted to hug Reese, but was unsure of her reception.

"Thank you for coming. As you can see, I'm a little banged up but essentially okay." Reese's voice was neutral. A part of her wanted to kick him, but she recognized the insecurity hiding beneath his calm surface. He was afraid to be rejected again.

"Reese." His father cleared his throat, his eyes

steady as they rested on his son's. "I owe you an apology for leaping to the wrong conclusion all those years ago. I'm sorry I left it so long. When you didn't come home… I thought that you no longer wanted to be in contact with us and I couldn't blame you."

Reese was silent for a moment. The tension in the room was so thick, Celia understood for the first time what people meant when they said they could cut it with a knife. She had a ridiculous urge to get the small pocketknife from her purse and try it.

Finally, Reese said, "Thank you. I apologize, too, for losing my temper and staying away so long." He turned then and took her hand. "Mother, Dad, this is Celia Papaleo." Although there wasn't exactly a note of challenge in his voice, she recognized that he was using her as a test.

Mrs. Barone immediately offered an outstretched hand to Celia across the bed. "It's so nice to meet you at last, Celia. Please call us Carlo and Moira." She gave the younger woman a warm, genuine smile. "Reese spoke of you often when he was younger. I know you're very special to him."

"As are you." Celia went with instinct and leaned forward, embracing Moira Barone in a warm hug. "Thank you."

"It is truly a pleasure, Celia," Carlo Barone said. He came around the end of the bed to where she sat and kissed her formally on each cheek in a courtly manner.

She nodded, smiling at him as he stepped back.

"Celia has just agreed to marry me." The announcement fell into the momentary silence.

His mother made a small sound of delight. "Congratulations!"

"Welcome to the family," Carlo said to Celia. "Everyone is anxious to see Reese again. They'll all be thrilled to hear this news."

"Have you set a date?" asked Moira.

"Um, no," Celia said. "We're very newly engaged."

"She just said yes before you walked in the door," Reese said, grinning.

"So that's what we interrupted," Carlo said to his wife. "See, I told you we should have knocked!"

"We're not planning on a long engagement." Reese dragged the conversation back to the earlier topic. "In fact, if I have my way, we'll be husband and wife right away." He paused, giving his parents a conspiratorial grin. "How would you like to fly to Vegas and witness our wedding?"

"We'd love to," his mother answered.

"He means today," Celia informed them. She turned to Reese. "You really need to rest—"

"I really need to marry you. Today." He caught her hand and pressed a kiss to her knuckles. "We've waited too long as it is."

Carlo Barone was laughing. "You might as well stop arguing, Celia. Nobody wins an argument with a Barone man."

"Ha." Moira winked at Celia. "You just let him keep on thinking that for the next fifty years and you'll do just fine together."

Reese tugged on her hand, pulling her down to the edge of the bed. When she acceded, he immediately drew her to him for a kiss, and as she thought of how close she'd come to losing him, she sank against him with a quiet sigh. He'd told her he was born to be wild, but she'd had enough wild to last her a lifetime already.

A lifetime. She kissed him back fervently, forgetting all about their audience. She knew better than most how fragile happiness could be. If he wanted to get married today, she'd do it.

And then she wanted to meet his daughter—*their* daughter—and start living the rest of their lives together.

* * * * *

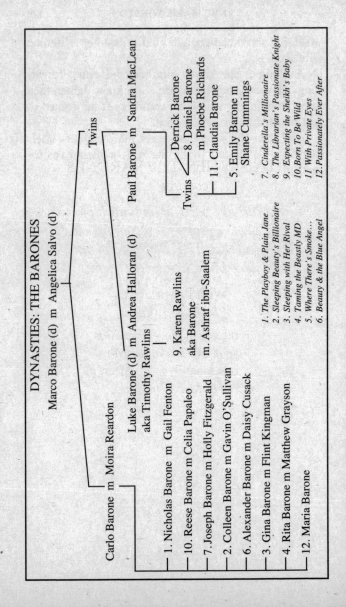

DYNASTIES: THE BARONES

Marco Barone (d) m Angelica Salvo (d)

Carlo Barone (d) m Moira Reardon

Luke Barone (d) m Andrea Halloran (d)
aka Timothy Rawlins

Twins

Paul Barone m Sandra MacLean

9. Karen Rawlins
aka Barone
m. Ashraf ibn-Saalem

Derrick Barone
8. Daniel Barone
m Phoebe Richards

Twins

11. Claudia Barone

5. Emily Barone m
Shane Cummings

1. Nicholas Barone m Gail Fenton
10. Reese Barone m Celia Papaleo
7. Joseph Barone m Holly Fitzgerald
2. Colleen Barone m Gavin O'Sullivan
6. Alexander Barone m Daisy Cusack
3. Gina Barone m Flint Kingman
4. Rita Barone m Matthew Grayson
12. Maria Barone

1. The Playboy & Plain Jane
2. Sleeping Beauty's Billionaire
3. Sleeping with Her Rival
4. Taming the Beastly MD
5. Where There's Smoke...
6. Beauty & the Blue Angel

7. Cinderella's Millionaire
8. The Librarian's Passionate Knight
9. Expecting the Sheikh's Baby
10. Born To Be Wild
11 With Private Eyes
12. Passionately Ever After

DYNASTIES: THE BARONES
continues…

*Turn the page for a bonus look
at what's in store for you in the next
DYNASTIES: THE BARONES book—
only from Silhouette Desire!*

With Private Eyes
by Eileen Wilks

*is on sale in November 2004
in a 2-in-1 volume with*
Passionately Ever After
by Metsy Hingle.

With Private Eyes

by

Eileen Wilks

Uncle Miles had always told him his sense of humor would get him hung one of these days, Ethan reflected. Maybe today was the day.

"I'd like to start as soon as possible." The blonde sitting on the other side of his desk gave him a bright smile. "This is going to make a terrific article."

Maybe it was his curiosity that would get him in trouble this time. As much as it tickled his sense of the absurd for Claudia Barone to present herself in his office posing as a reporter, he wouldn't have let her run through her spiel if he hadn't wanted to know what she was up to. "I haven't agreed yet," he pointed out.

"Oh, well." She said that tolerantly and crossed her legs, sliding one long, silky thigh over the other. "How can I persuade you?"

Then again, those legs might be the real culprit.

The moment she'd appeared in his doorway in her lipstick-red suit he'd wanted to get her into the visitor's chair in front of his desk. He'd wanted to find out how much that one-inch-too-short hiked up.

They were world-class legs, he thought regretfully. And she knew it. She'd crossed and uncrossed them four times since she sat down. "I don't imagine you can."

Not a whit discouraged, she launched into a repetition of her asinine story, her hands flying enthusiastically. It was an intriguing contrast, he thought. Her posture was very proper—shoulders squared, spine straight—and she certainly didn't raise her voice. But her gestures were as loud as the color of her suit.

Even on ten minutes' acquaintance, he could tell Claudia Barone was crammed with contradictions. She looked like the prototype for a tall, cool sip of blond elegance. She was pale and slim—*too skinny,* he told himself—with blue eyes and classic features marred by a nose too assertive for its setting. Her honey-colored hair was pulled back in a kind of roll at the back, very sleek and polished. Her suit was conservative, too, if you ignored where the hemline hit.

And the color. Which was echoed in the siren-red gloss she'd sleeked over a cute little rosebud mouth.

Her story might be crazy, but her voice was worth listening to, even if it did tug at memories he'd prefer stayed safely buried...

* * * * *

Your opinion is important to us!

Please take a few moments to share your thoughts with us about Mills & Boon® and Silhouette® books. Your comments will ensure that we continue to deliver books you love to read.

To thank you for your input, everyone who replies will be entered into a prize draw to win a year's supply of their favourite series books*.

1. There are several different series under the Mills & Boon and Silhouette brands. Please tick the box that most accurately represents your reading habit for each series.

Series	Currently Read (have read within last three months)	Used to Read (but do not read currently)	Do Not Read
Mills & Boon			
Modern Romance™	❑	❑	❑
Sensual Romance™	❑	❑	❑
Blaze™	❑	❑	❑
Tender Romance™	❑	❑	❑
Medical Romance™	❑	❑	❑
Historical Romance™	❑	❑	❑
Silhouette			
Special Edition™	❑	❑	❑
Superromance™	❑	❑	❑
Desire™	❑	❑	❑
Sensation™	❑	❑	❑
Intrigue™	❑	❑	❑

2. Where did you buy this book?

From a supermarket ❑   Through our Reader Service™ ❑
From a bookshop ❑   If so please give us your Club Subscription no.
On the Internet ❑

Other _____   _____ / _____

3. Please indicate by number which were the 3 most important factors that made you buy this book. (1 = most important).

The picture on the cover	___	I enjoy this series ___
The author	___	The price ___
The title	___	I borrowed/was given this book ___
The description on the back cover	___	Part of a mini-series ___

Other _____

4. How many Mills & Boon and /or Silhouette books do you buy at one time?

I buy ___ books at one time ❑
I rarely buy a book (less than once a year) ❑

5. How often do you shop for any Mills & Boon and/or Silhouette books?

One or more times a month ❑   A few times per year ❑
Once every 2-3 months ❑   Never ❑

6. How long have you been reading Mills & Boon® and/or Silhouette®?
_____ years

7. What other types of book do you enjoy reading?

Family sagas eg. Maeve Binchy ❑
Classics eg. Jane Austen ❑
Historical sagas eg. Josephine Cox ❑
Crime/Thrillers eg. John Grisham ❑
Romance eg. Danielle Steel ❑
Science Fiction/Fantasy eg. JRR Tolkien ❑
Contemporary Women's fiction eg. Marian Keyes ❑

8. Do you agree with the following statements about Silhouette? Please tick the appropriate boxes.

	Strongly agree	Tend to agree	Neither agree nor disagree	Tend to disagree	Strongly disagree
Silhouette offers great value for money.	❑	❑	❑	❑	❑
With Silhouette I can always find the right type of story to suit my mood.	❑	❑	❑	❑	❑
I read Silhouette books because they offer me an entertaining escape from everyday life.	❑	❑	❑	❑	❑
Silhouette stories have improved or stayed the same standard over the time I have been reading them.	❑	❑	❑	❑	❑

9. Which age bracket do you belong to? Your answers will remain confidential.

❑ 16-24   ❑ 25-34   ❑ 35-49   ❑ 50-64   ❑ 65+

THANK YOU for taking the time to tell us what you think! If you would like to be entered into the **FREE prize draw** to win a year's supply of your favourite series books, please enter your name and address below.

Name: _____
Address: _____
_____
Post Code: _____ Tel: _____

Please send your completed questionnaire to the address below:

READER SURVEY, PO Box 676, Richmond, Surrey, TW9 1WU.

SILHOUETTE®

Desire 2 in 1

are proud to introduce

DYNASTIES:
THE BARONES

Meet the wealthy Barones—caught in a web of danger, deceit and…desire!

Twelve exciting stories in six 2-in-1 volumes:

0104/SH/LC78

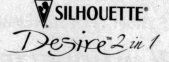

♥ SILHOUETTE®

Desire 2 in 1

AVAILABLE FROM 17TH SEPTEMBER 2004

MAN IN CONTROL Diana Palmer

Texan Lovers

Since Agent Alexander Cobb had rejected Jodie Clayburn eight years ago they'd been sworn enemies. But now they were working together on a drug-smuggling case and Alexander was finding Jodie hard to resist.

THORN'S CHALLENGE Brenda Jackson

Thorn Westmoreland had wanted a commitment-free affair with Tara Matthews. But he soon found himself striving to win her love. Would she give her heart to this tough tycoon?

❦

SHAMELESS Ann Major

The Country Club

With loan sharks on her trail, Celeste Cavanaugh turned to ex-marine Phillip Westin for help. He was the only man she'd ever loved but she'd broken his heart. Now he wanted her back in return for his help...

DESPERADO DAD Linda Conrad

When Randi Cullen offered refuge to Manuel Sanchez she didn't expect him to be an undercover agent hunting a ruthless killer! She agreed to marriage in order to protect his cover—but then found herself falling in love with him...

❦

BILLIONAIRE BOSS Meagan McKinney

Montana

Kirsten Meadows's boss Seth Morgan was sophisticated, rich, sensual and completely off-limits. But one look at Kirsten and this playboy tycoon knew he wanted to be more than just her boss!

IN BED WITH BEAUTY Katherine Garbera

King of Hearts

Sarah Malcolm needed security in her love life. So why couldn't she keep away from Harris Davidson? He was certainly wealthy, powerful and sexy but he'd also made it clear he had no room in his life for a woman...

AVAILABLE FROM 17TH SEPTEMBER 2004

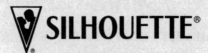

SILHOUETTE®

Sensation™

Passionate and thrilling romantic adventures

DOWNRIGHT DANGEROUS Beverly Barton
RISKING IT ALL Beverly Bird
WEDDING AT WHITE SANDS Catherine Mann
IRRESISTIBLE FORCES Candace Irvin
THE PERFECT TARGET Jenna Mills
TRUST NO ONE Barbara Phinney

Special Edition™

Life, love and family

FOUND IN LOST VALLEY Laurie Paige
MAN IN THE MIST Annette Broadrick
THE FERTILITY FACTOR Jennifer Mikels
THE RANCHER'S DAUGHTER Jodi O'Donnell
THE MISSING MAITLAND Stella Bagwell
HARD CHOICES Allison Leigh

Superromance™

*Enjoy the drama, explore the emotions,
experience the relationship*

THE HEALER Jean Brashear
A HUSBAND OF HER OWN Brenda Novak
PRACTICE MAKES PERFECT Kathryn Shay
THE REPLACEMENT Anne Marie Duquette

Intrigue™

Breathtaking romantic suspense

A WARRIOR'S MISSION Rita Herron
THE FIRSTBORN Dani Sinclair
UNDER HIS PROTECTION Amy J Fetzer
SARAH'S SECRETS Lisa Childs

0904/51b

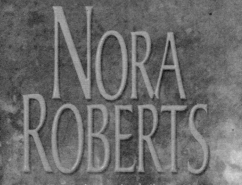

THE TRUEBLOOD
Dynasty

Isabella Trueblood made history reuniting people torn apart by war and an epidemic. Now, generations later, Lily and Dylan Garrett carry on her work with their agency, Finders Keepers.

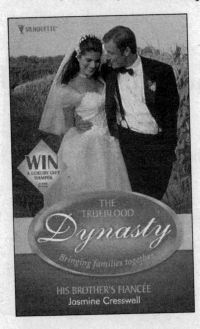

Book Two available from 17th September

Available at most branches of WH Smith, Tesco, ASDA, Martins, Borders, Eason, Sainsbury's and all good paperback bookshops.

SILHOUETTE SPOTLIGHT

Two bestselling novels in one volume
by favourite authors, back by
popular demand!

The Millionaire Affair

Mystery Man *by Diana Palmer*
Mandy Meets a Millionaire *by Tracy Sinclair*

Handsome, powerful and wealthy.
These sexy millionaire men had
everything except true
love – until now!

Available from 17th September 2004

0904/064

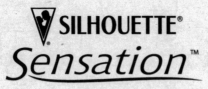

SILHOUETTE®
Sensation™

presents…

Cherokee Corners

by Carla Cassidy

Where one family fights crime with
honour—and passion!

Last Seen…
(May 2004)

Dead Certain
(August 2004)

Trace Evidence
(November 2004)

0504/SH/LC85

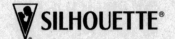

SILHOUETTE®

SPECIAL EDITION™

proudly presents

a brand-new series from

CHRISTINE RIMMER

The King's Daughters

Three royal-born, California-bred sisters are about to rediscover their roots—and find love— at home.

THE RELUCTANT PRINCESS

July 2004

PRINCE AND FUTURE...DAD?

August 2004

THE MARRIAGE MEDALLION

September 2004

is proud to introduce

DYNASTIES: THE DANFORTHS

*Meet the Danforths—a family of prominence...
tested by scandal, sustained by passion!*

Coming Soon!
Twelve thrilling stories in six 2-in-1 volumes:

0105/SH/LC96

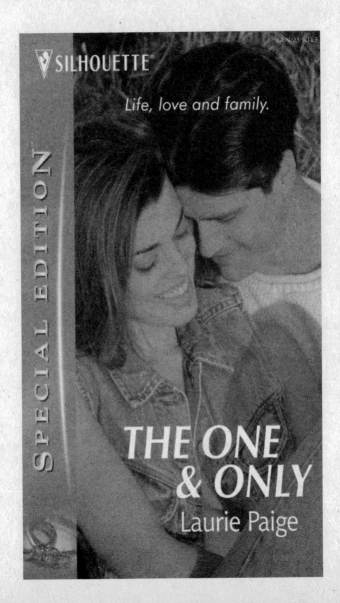

Life, love and family.

GEN 23/KTL5

THE ONE & ONLY

Laurie Paige

GEN/18/RTL5

▼ SILHOUETTE

*Passionate and thrilling
romantic adventures*

Sensation™

NIGHT
WATCH

Suzanne Brockmann

FREE!

2 Books
and a surprise gift!

We would like to take this opportunity to thank you for reading this Silhouette® book by offering you the chance to take TWO more specially selected titles from the Desire™ series absolutely FREE! We're also making this offer to introduce you to the benefits of the Reader Service™—

- ★ FREE home delivery
- ★ FREE gifts and competitions
- ★ FREE monthly Newsletter
- ★ Exclusive Reader Service offers
- ★ Books available before they're in the shops

Accepting these FREE books and gift places you under no obligation to buy, you may cancel at any time, even after receiving your free shipment. Simply complete your details below and return the entire page to the address below. You don't even need a stamp!

YES! Please send me 2 free Desire books and a surprise gift. I understand that unless you hear from me, I will receive 3 superb new titles every month for just £4.99 each, postage and packing free. I am under no obligation to purchase any books and may cancel my subscription at any time. The free books and gift will be mine to keep in any case.

D4ZEF

Ms/Mrs/Miss/Mr ....Initials...................................
BLOCK CAPITALS PLEASE

Surname...

Address...

....Postcode ....

Send this whole page to:
UK: FREEPOST CN81, Croydon, CR9 3WZ·

Offer valid in UK only and is not available to current Reader service subscribers to this series. Overseas and Eire please write for details. We reserve the right to refuse an application and applicants must be aged 18 years or over. Only one application per household. Terms and prices subject to change without notice. Offer expires 31st December 2004. As a result of this application, you may receive offers from Harlequin Mills & Boon and other carefully selected companies. If you would prefer not to share in this opportunity please write to The Data Manager, PO Box 676, Richmond, TW9 1WU.

Silhouette™ is a registered trademark owned and used under licence.
Desire™ is being used as a trademark. The Reader Service™ is being used as a trademark.